SHOT TO HELL

ALSO BY TODD E. CREASON

NON-FICTION

Famous American Freemasons: Volume I

Famous American Freemasons: Volume II

A Freemason Said That?
Great Quotes of Famous Freemasons

FICTION: TWIN RIVERS SERIES

One Last Shot

A Shot After Midnight

Shot To Hell

SHOT TO HELL

A TWIN RIVERS NOVEL

TODD E. CREASON

Moon & Son
Publishing Co.

SHOT TO HELL
A Moon & Son Book

Published by Moon & Son Publishing Co.
Fithian, Illinois

Cover design by Anna Barnes Media

ISBN 978-0-9831156-2-5

PRINTED IN THE UNITED STATES OF AMERICA

For my father, Don Creason,
who gave me my greatest skill—humor.
Every time you laugh reading this, he's the reason why.

"Truths and roses have thorns about them."

—*H. G. Bohn*

"The habits we acquire are little worth;
The nature that was ours before our birth
Will master us, while yet we live on earth."

—UNKNOWN, *Hitopadesa* (c. 1200)

Chapter 1

"It won't be long before I have to find a new waitress," April Jenkins said as she placed a cup of coffee in front of Deputy Ben Walker, who was leaning over the coffee counter to examine the engagement ring on Nichole Larsen's finger.

"I wouldn't hang the help wanted sign quite yet," Nichole said, knowing that April was happy for her but also sad in a way.

For more than forty years, Harv and April had run the small restaurant in Twin Rivers, but both were in their late sixties now. Harv had been having health issues related to his excessive weight and diabetes, and forty years of being on her feet had taken a toll on April's knees. Everyone knew that since they had no children of their own, the plan was to sell the restaurant to Nichole, who'd worked for them on and off for over ten years. But one popped question had changed the succession plan overnight.

The news of Nichole's engagement had spread like wildfire through the small town of Twin Rivers, thanks to the local grapevine. By dinner time, Harv's Diner was full of customers who'd come to congratulate her and see the ring.

"That's a nice diamond," Ben remarked as he sat down on a stool at the counter and picked up his coffee cup. "Congratulations, Nichole."

"Thank you," she said.

"You two want to stop fussing over that rock and sling a little hash," Harv bellowed through the order window. "There's three orders up here waiting to go out."

"Oh, Harv, you big bully," April shot back, "don't you remember what it's like to be in love?"

"Not lately," Harv muttered as he wiped his hands on his kitchen whites.

"Buy me a ring like that, and I'll be more than happy to refresh your memory," April said as the diner erupted into laughter.

Chuckling to himself, Ben swiveled on his stool and glanced around the busy diner. He was a fit, handsome, ex-Army man in his mid-thirties, who looked as if he should be on a recruiting poster. After spending eight years in Iraq and Afghanistan, he'd resigned his commission and gone into law enforcement.

Ben hadn't really looked around at who was in the diner when he'd walked in since April had descended on him the moment the bell jangled and had led him right up to the counter to look at the ring. Now he noticed a stunning woman with kinky blonde hair and deep-green eyes waving at him from a booth. He waved back, picked up his coffee, and walked over to join her.

"Hello, Adam," he said, touching the little boy's blonde head as he maneuvered around the high chair at the end of the booth and scooted in across from her.

Recognizing Ben, Adam gave a delighted squeal that cut well above the noisy din of the diner.

"Doesn't Nichole's ring make you want to buy one for Amber?" Tori said with a sly smile.

Amber worked as dispatcher and receptionist at the Twin Rivers Police Department. She and Ben had dated secretly for a year before they'd begun being seen together.

"Don't start with me, Tori. We've been dating for only . . ." He paused, trying to remember.

"Nearly two years," Tori finished.

"I know how long we've been dating," Ben said quickly.

The look on Tori's face said she didn't believe that for a minute.

In the nearly two years Ben had been Chief Billings' deputy, he'd gotten to be good friends with the Garveys. Tori's husband, Levi, was a best-selling novelist. They lived in an old Victorian house that his family had owned for generations. It sat on six acres just outside the edge of town. When Levi Garvey returned to Twin Rivers after a twenty-some years absence, he and Tori Buchanan had reunited. Then together, they'd uncovered the fact that two of their classmates were serial killers—Police Chief Doug Malone and Deputy Alan Haig. That had made national news. Then just over a year ago, Levi and Tori had stumbled into another dark secret from the past—the fact that Chief Clifford Craig, who had come out of retirement to take over for Doug Malone, was actually the missing bank robber in the 1971 bank heist of the Calloway First National Bank.

The Garveys had been very hard on law enforcement in Twin Rivers, but the new chief, Ray Billings, recently retired from the Savannah Police Department, was an old friend of Levi's. He had quickly proven to be just what the town needed after two dirty police chiefs had been uncovered. Fortunately, things had been quiet ever since. As everyone in town always said, "Nothing ever happens in Twin Rivers."

Ben hadn't seen much of Tori since Levi had gone on a book-signing trip.

"When does Levi get back?" Ben asked, changing the subject.

"Tomorrow," Tori said. "He's been gone two weeks. Part of writing books is promoting them, but he truly dislikes book tours. He says they're shameless self-promotion."

"Yeah, I bet he hates all that attention and long lines of people waiting to buy his books and get his autograph," Ben said sarcastically.

"And those horrible interviews where he has to talk about himself and his novels ad nauseam," she added, winking at him. "He just hates that!"

They both burst out laughing. Levi might grumble about his celebrity, but he really loved the attention.

"I'm sure you'll be happy when he's back home," Ben remarked.

Tori nodded. "I've missed him, but it's been kind of nice having only one child to take care of."

Ben laughed. Then when the bell over the door jangled, he looked at who'd come in.

"Oh, great," Ben said coldly as he recognized the man.

Tori looked also. The man in the doorway was tall and sickly thin with long graying hair and a scruffy goatee. His checks were sunken, and there were dark circles under his eyes, which scanned the diner before they fell on the person he was obviously looking for. Quickly, he walked to a table in the back and joined a man who was dining alone.

"Is that Jay Snider?" Tori said in a low voice.

Ben nodded. "I don't think I've ever seen him in here before, but it can't be a good thing. Trouble follows him everywhere."

Glancing over her shoulder at the table where he sat, Tori asked, "Who's he with?"

Ben shrugged. "I have no idea. I don't think I've ever seen him before."

Suddenly, April was standing beside their booth. "I need you to do something for me, Ben."

At that moment, a loud bang caused the diner to go quiet. Everyone looked towards the men in the back. Jay had slammed his fist onto the table. Now he was shaking his finger in the face of the man he'd just joined. Seeming quite unconcerned about the threatening gestures, the man was regarding Jay with a bored expression on his face.

"I want Jay out of here, Ben," April said. "We threw him out years ago, and he was barred from coming back. He's seriously nuts."

"Oh, I know," Ben said as he climbed out of the booth. "I know all about Jay Snider."

Ben walked to the back of the restaurant and stood over the table where the two men were sitting. Jay's finger was still wagging inches from the other man's face, which continued to indicate that he could've cared less.

"You're not going to pull this crap on me, old man," Jay hissed through clenched teeth—his face a mask of rage. "I know things about you. I can take you down on a whim. Don't you ever forget that."

"Excuse me," Ben said, looking down at them. "Jay, you need to leave."

"I'll leave when I'm ready, Deputy Dawg. I'm not bothering any-one."

"Actually, you are," Ben said calmly. "You see all the people looking back here? You're causing a scene. And the owners tell me you aren't sup-posed to be here to begin with. They've asked that I escort you off the prem-ises right now."

"I'll leave when I'm damned good and ready," Jay snapped back.

"I'm not giving you that choice," Ben said firmly. "You can leave on your own or with me. But if you leave with me, you're going to be my guest for the night—if you know what I mean."

"I'll notify you when I'm ready to leave," Jay said, glaring up at him. "Why don't you go finish your pie or something. I've got business with this man. It won't take long."

"Okay, we'll do this the hard way," Ben said, taking a step back from the table. "Stand up, and put your hands behind your back."

Slowly, Jay rose and faced him. "I'm not the kind of man you want to tangle with, Deputy Fife."

"Yeah, that's what you're always telling me, and yet I always do. I sure get tired of arresting you. Last chance. Do you really want to go to jail tonight? Or would you rather just go home—maybe have a nice cold beer and watch some television?"

Jay glanced at the determined look on Ben's face. "Okay, fine. You win. I don't want to go to jail tonight."

Jay took a step towards the door. Then he spun suddenly, throwing a fist towards Ben, but Ben, who'd dealt with Jay before, was ready for it. In fact, he fully expected the attack. Jay Snider never did anything the easy way. Ben easily deflected the blow, caught Jay's wrist, and twisted his arm behind his back. Jay grunted loudly as Ben threw him hard, chest down, across the top of an empty table and kicked his feet apart.

As he snapped on the cuffs and emptied Jay's pockets, Ben said, "Why do you always have to do everything the hard way? You make things difficult every time."

Jay cackled wildly. "That's the way God made me. But I damned near got you this time."

"No, you didn't." Ben sighed as he pulled Jay up from the top of the table and started him towards the door. "It's good that you believe in God. At least you'll have somebody to talk to in your jail cell tonight."

As they approached the door, Jay started to drag his feet. Then he broadcast loudly to the patrons of the diner, "I had a lovely time this evening. We'll have to do this again soon. Sorry about my friend Deputy Dawg. He's always creating a scene, so I can't take him anywhere! He's got anger issues. It's overcompensation for a small—"

"That's enough, Jay!" Ben growled as he pulled him up and walked him on his tippy toes the rest of the way to the door.

Harv Jenkins, who was holding the door open for them, was having a tough time keeping a straight face. "Overcompensation," he said with a chuckle.

Ben shot him a look which withered that smirk instantly.

Chapter 2

Ray Billings pushed away from the dining room table and rocked his chair back on two legs. His massive athletic form caused the chair to creak loudly as he tossed his napkin onto the table and rolled up the corners of his handlebar mustache with his fingertips. Even in his late fifties, he was in great shape and cut an impressive form in his khaki police uniform.

"That was terrific, Bernice. You've outdone yourself."

"It was spaghetti," she said flatly.

She stood up from her end of the table, took his plate and hers, and, without a word, walked into the kitchen. He looked down at his German shepherd, Bo, then glanced at the door to the kitchen. He took a piece of bread out of the basket on the table and tossed it to him. Bo greedily snapped it out of the air.

Suddenly, Bernice was standing in the doorway. At fifty, she was still a beautiful woman with a remarkably trim figure that curved in all the right places, auburn hair that framed her high cheekbones, and gold-flecked amber eyes.

"Must you feed that dog at the table?"

She collected a few more things from the table and walked back into the kitchen. Ray watched her go. She was wearing those tight jeans—the ones that drove him nuts.

Ray tossed Bo another piece of bread, then rubbed his ears as he chewed it. It didn't matter anymore. He knew things weren't working. He'd become an expert at trying not to see the problems, but they couldn't be any more obvious.

When he'd retired from the Savannah Police Department and moved to Twin Rivers to take the job as police chief, he'd done so for two reasons. He wasn't ready to retire at age fifty-five, but he was being pushed towards the door by his new captain. This job was a chance to keep working—a chance at a new life and a change of scenery. The other reason was that he had a good friend in Twin Rivers—Levi Garvey.

He'd given up on love after his fourth divorce. But Bernice, his first wife—she was different. She was the only one he'd remained friends with after the divorce. She was the only one he regretted letting get away because he still loved her. When she showed up in Twin Rivers, he thought it was perfect—a second career and a second shot at a relationship he'd let slip away when he was too young to realize what he was losing.

And for a while, being with Bernice was all he'd hoped it would be. The passion was still there after twenty-five years and the friendship as well. But after a few months, he'd begun to realize that she'd changed—or maybe he had. She was more concerned about her happiness than his. It wasn't long before it became obvious that she hated everything about his new life. She'd come back into his world only to drag him back into hers. There'd been little passion or romance in the last couple of months—he shouldn't have been surprised. He'd slowly begun to remember that even twenty-five years ago she'd used her amazing body to get whatever she wanted from him. When he was a much younger man, that tactic had worked very well for her. But he was older now, and it wasn't as effective as it once had been. Even so, he wasn't completely immune to her manipulation.

It frustrated her that she couldn't control him now as she once had, so they fought often. And her mood this evening signaled that soon the battle would start all over again. I might as well kick it off, he thought as he walked to the kitchen door.

Ray had bought this beautiful house in Twin Rivers from the former chief of police—Clifford Craig. Of course, it wasn't until later that he and the Garveys had discovered Craig was the missing bank robber in a forty-year-old heist that had left a police officer dead. Despite the house's connection to a calculating killer, masquerading in a police uniform, and the recent deaths he'd caused, Ray loved his house—and he'd truly wanted to live there with Bernice.

Ray's pulse raced as he stood in the doorway, watching Bernice lean over to load the dishwasher. She knew he found her skin-tight jeans irresistible, and on this occasion, she'd pulled out all the stops with the addition of a low-cut blouse which was unbuttoned clear to the top of her bra. She wanted something. Ray hated to admit it to himself, but her tight jeans-cleavage strategy was working.

Do I really want to fight tonight, he thought as his eyes wandered over her curves.

"I haven't been paying enough attention to you lately," Ray said.

She glanced up at him momentarily, saying nothing.

"Ben's working this weekend. Maybe we can get away and do something together."

"Maybe there's a flea market somewhere," she said coldly. "Or we can see a seventy-year-old movie at the Comet Theatre. Or go to a tractor pull. Or sit on a pontoon boat on Olton Lake all day and fish. Or all your friends can come over for the third time this week, and we can play pool and drink beer in your little social club in the basement. Or if we're real lucky, maybe some Masonic Lodge somewhere is having a fish fry, and we can stay after and help fold up tables and chairs and wash dishes. The possibilities are limitless here in the Midwest!"

Ray's face tightened at her sarcastic tone, and his anger rose.

"Why are you here, Bernice?"

"I thought we still had something," she said.

"Do you still think that?"

"I think it's obvious we do," she said, smiling, as she walked over and wrapped her arms around his neck.

Looking into her eyes, his anger drained. His mind started thinking about better ways to spend the remainder of the evening. But a voice screamed in the back of his head. Find out what she wants, it said.

"But you aren't happy. What will it take to make you happy?" Ray said.

"I want to go home," she said simply. "To our home in Georgia."

See, I told you so, the voice in the back of his head said mockingly. Twin Rivers was at the root of all their battles.

"We've had this conversation before. This is my home now," Ray said. "I like it here, and there's nothing for me in Savannah anymore."

"There's nothing for me in Twin Rivers," she snapped back.

"You've made that choice, Bernice."

"What's that supposed to mean?"

"You know what it means," Ray said, reaching over to button up her blouse to the neck—a gesture which sparked anger in her eyes. "You've made no effort to make friends here. In fact, you've gone out of your way to make my friends feel uncomfortable. I think you do that on purpose."

"Now why would I do that?"

"Because you think if I don't have friends here, I'll be more likely to pack up and move back to Georgia with you. But Bernice, as much as I still love you, it's not enough. I've never made friends easily, but I've made more here in the last couple of years than I did in the first fifty years of my life. I have a job that I enjoy doing a great deal, and for the first time, I feel like I belong somewhere. The folks in this town have gone out of their way to make me feel like one of them. They'd do the same thing for you—if you'd let them."

"They don't like me," she said.

"No, you don't like them, and they realize that," Ray said. "Let me be clear about this. I'm not leaving Twin Rivers, so you can either get used to the idea of living here with me for the rest of your life, or you can pack up and go. I'd like you to stay, but if you do, it isn't going to be like this."

"So you really don't care if I'm happy or not," Bernice spat back.

"I care as much about your happiness as you do about mine," Ray answered. "I'm not fighting with you tonight, Bernice. I'd love to roll around in bed with you for a few hours this evening, but I refuse to pay for sex. To be perfectly honest, your rates are way too high."

"You son of a—" she hissed as she drew her hand back to slap him.

He grabbed her wrist.

"I'm tired, and I'm not in the mood to deal with this drama." Turning, he called to his dog, "Come on, Bo."

Bo trotted into the kitchen, his nails clicking on the tile floor.

"Where are you going?"

"Out."

"When will you be—"

"We're not married, Bernice," he said curtly. "I'm well over fifty now, and I don't need your permission to come and go. This is my house, and I'll do as I damned well please. Don't forget that you are a guest here."

Chapter 3

Ray heard the newspaper smack the front door as he poured himself a cup of coffee. Setting it on the kitchen island, he walked down the narrow hallway to the front door, opened it, and reached down to scoop the paper up off the mat. He stood in the doorway for a moment, taking in the expansive front lawn. It was a beautiful February morning. The American flag flapped gently in the wind from the bracket on the front porch post where it was put out each morning and brought in every night without exception winter, spring, summer, and fall.

He walked back to the kitchen, picked up his coffee, and settled into the breakfast nook with the bacon and eggs he'd just made. The morning sunlight poured in through the south windows, bathing the nook and the kitchen in golden morning light. As he scanned the front page of the newspaper, he was suddenly aware of being watched. He glanced at the two German shepherds—father and son—sitting beside him, staring up with rapt attention.

"You two beggars," he said with a chuckle as he took a piece of bacon off his plate, broke it in two, and held half up.

"Say please, Rosco."

After Rosco barked once, Ray tossed him the bacon, which he snapped out of the air.

"Say please, Bo."

Bo barked once and was rewarded the same way.

As Ray was finishing his eggs, Rosco's ears went up. He turned and quickly bolted down the hallway towards the front door, his tail wagging. Ray strained to hear what the dog had heard, but it was quiet in the house. Nearly a minute later, he heard the sound of a motor he knew well, followed by the sound only an old truck door makes when it is slammed closed. Rosco was whining and barking at the door, his tail banging on the wood floor in the foyer. When the door opened, Ray heard the familiar voice greet the dog and then the footsteps up the hall toward the kitchen.

"Honey, I'm home!" the voice called as the man walked into the kitchen.

"I sure missed you, Sweetie-pie," Ray said with a broad grin on his face.

Levi Garvey's deep-blue eyes stared at him from under the brim of his Panama hat. Then he glanced around the kitchen. The last thing he expected to find seated at his kitchen table was Ray Billings this early in the morning. Levi took off his hat, tossed it onto the kitchen island, and ran his fingers through his rapidly graying blonde hair.

"What have you been up to with my wife since I've been gone?" he asked with a grin.

"I didn't want you to find out this way," Ray said. "Tori and I didn't think you'd be home until tomorrow."

"Yeah, yeah," Levi said as he walked around the island, took a mug down from the cabinet next to the sink, and poured himself a cup of coffee. "Where are Tori and Adam?"

"Adam had a checkup scheduled this morning in Calloway with Dr. Jackson," Ray said.

"Ah," Levi said as he slid into the breakfast nook and snatched the newspaper out of Ray's hand.

"You want some eggs? I'll make you some."

Tapping his chest with his fist, Levi said, "I'm good. I bought a delightful breakfast burrito at a gas station in Kankakee."

Rosco put his paws up on the edge of Levi's chair and licked his face. Levi smiled at him.

"How's that burrito working out for you?"

Levi belched and tapped his chest with his fist again. "Not that well," he admitted.

"How was the trip?"

"Exhausting," Levi said. "I hate book tours. But there were a few things that were certainly memorable. I had lunch with Arnold Schwartzenegger. Actually, he seemed like a really nice guy."

"No kidding?" Ray said. He knew Levi Garvey was a huge cinema fan.

"I'm serious. It was a strange sensation to be sitting across the table from the Terminator," Levi said. "He's not exactly in that kind of shape anymore since he's like sixty-five now, and it certainly shows. My life has its surreal moments—I almost had to pinch myself."

Ray knew what Levi meant. Since Ray had been in Twin Rivers, he'd gone head to head with the notorious Chicago crime boss Tony O'Malley and his Four Horsemen and survived, and he'd had a few beers on the front porch of the Garvey house with none other than Clint Eastwood, who'd directed the most recent movie based on one of Levi's bestselling novels.

"What did Arnold want?"

"Not like I have any control over it, but the studio mentioned he might want a part in the next movie. I think he wants to play Chief Ray Billings."

"He wants to play me? Now that would be something."

"You mean the Southern lawman with the thick Austrian accent?" Ray laughed.

"Anyway, I told the studio he was way too young to play you."

"Oh, you can kiss my ass," Ray said.

Levi laughed. Ray noticed, not for the first time, that Levi's laugh was starting to sound an awful lot like his Uncle Ed's mule laugh.

"It was a good trip," Levi said, "but when I got back and climbed into Old Blue and turned the key, I discovered the battery was dead as a hammer. I'd gotten to the airport early in the morning, just after the sun came up, and I left my headlights on. Sadly, there's no little bell that goes off in a '60 Ford pickup when you open your door and your lights are still on."

"Nope, the technology just didn't exist back in Old Blue's day," Ray said with a grin.

"Fortunately, they're used to dead batteries in the parking lot at the airport. I got a jump and was on my way in a few minutes. Anyway, as I said, it was a good trip, but I'm sure glad it's over."

There was a long pause as Levi looked at Ray with his deep-blue eyes. There was a question lingering between them.

"I slept in Ed's old room in the basement last night," Ray said.

Levi nodded and sipped at his coffee, but he said nothing. Ray had stayed with them when he'd first come to Twin Rivers. He'd spent the first night in the guest room upstairs, but then he'd found out that Ed Garvey had had a bedroom and bathroom in the basement of the house. Of course, Ed hadn't lived in the house for years, but the bedroom was still there. Ray had quickly moved to the more private quarters in the basement. An outside entrance allowed him to come and go as he pleased without disturbing Tori and Levi.

In the last few weeks, Ray had stayed in the basement several times. He had a key to the house for emergencies. There were few people Levi trusted more. Ray would come late and leave before anyone got up. He obviously didn't want them to know, so they'd said nothing. Tori had figured it out first when she'd seen a couple of Red Stripe beer bottles in the trash can outside. There was only one man in Twin Rivers who drank Jamaican lager.

This was the first time Ray had been obvious about his overnight stays. It was the first time he'd come up from the basement and made himself breakfast.

"It's not going well, Levi," Ray said.

"I thought as much. Not the first night you've spent down there recently, is it?"

Ray shook his head. "I figured you knew."

"We did. You're always welcome."

"I know. I didn't mean to sneak around about it, but what's going on with Bernice is embarrassing—the way she treats my friends and the folks in Twin Rivers. I just don't know what to do yet. I'll figure it out."

"Anything we can do?"

"Nope. It will either work itself out, or it won't."

"You think it will?"

Ray shrugged. "It might, but it seems unlikely at this point."

There was a long silence between them.

"I miss anything while I was gone?" Levi asked.

"Nope," Ray replied. Then suddenly, he snapped his fingers. "Oh, there was one thing. Rosco took another little excursion. Tori had Ben and me beating hedgerows and searching cemeteries for him. I don't know where the hell that damned dog goes, but it isn't cemeteries or hedgerows. He was gone about a day and a half before he got sprayed by a skunk and came home."

Levi looked down at his dog. Rosco whined, and his ears went flat.

"Again with the skunks, Rosco? What's that, about six times now in two years?"

"Tori said it was seven times, and she wasn't at all happy about it. Rosco spent a week not being allowed outside unless he was on a chain. He wasn't very happy about that."

"Sounds like nobody was very happy then."

Ray smiled. "And Nichole Larsen and Chuck Franklin are engaged. Wedding is being planned for next June."

"Well, that's nice."

"One day you'll have to tell me how a man like Representative Chuck Franklin managed to fall in love with a diner waitress like Nichole Larsen," Ray remarked.

"It's not that complicated," Levi said. "Nichole volunteered to work on his election campaign. She's cute, and he noticed. After he won the election, they stopped seeing each other every day. I think he suddenly realized how much he missed her. Next thing you know, Chuck Franklin is coming home from Springfield a lot more often."

"Love conquers all," Ray remarked.

"It wasn't without some difficulty," Levi remarked. "The Franklins are very wealthy. Chuck's father, Charles Sr., inherited a fortune and then probably tripled it himself on Wall Street. He's some kind of venture capitalist or something. I don't really understand financial stuff like that."

"Basically, he has more money than God," Ray said. "I've heard that phrase a few times recently about the Franklins."

"About everyone knows that Charles wasn't happy with his son's choice of a Twin Rivers waitress, even though she's pretty and younger than Chuck," Levi said. "Charles is an arrogant jerk basically. Chuck's mother died when he was little, so Charles has controlled Chuck's life from the beginning. He pushed him as a quarterback—the Comets actually won the state championship in 1985. Then he got him into politics. The rumor is he'll run for the

U. S. House or maybe even the Senate soon. He'll have a really good chance winning either. But you have to give Chuck credit. He stuck by his decision to date Nichole. Even though his father has run his life for decades, apparently Chuck decided he wasn't going to let him control his love life."

"Wonder what his choice would be if his dad cut off the money?" Ray remarked.

"You are so cynical."

"No, I'm a realist," Ray said with a smile. "Nichole would be out, right?"

Levi shrugged. "I hate to say it, but you're probably right. Money is, and always has been, very important to the Franklins."

"Well, it's a good thing Chuck didn't have to make that choice," Ray said.

Levi laughed. "Anything else go on around here while I was gone?"

"You know nothing ever happens in Twin Rivers," Ray said, winking at him.

Levi smiled and sipped his coffee. Like hell it doesn't, he thought.

Glancing at the kitchen clock, Ray said, "I guess I'd better be getting to work. We have one locked up—Jay Snider. I need to go set him loose."

"Jay Snider? Again?"

"Yeah, he caused a scene at Harv's last night. Took a swing at Ben. He's quite a piece of work."

"He's bat-shit crazy," Levi said.

"I know," Ray said.

He carried his breakfast dishes to the sink and loaded them into the dishwasher. Then he picked up his flat-brimmed trooper hat off the counter and headed to the kitchen door.

"I'll catch up with you later," Levi said. "Maybe some pool tonight in the basement."

"I'll see you at lunch," Ray said. "Tori said, if I saw you, to tell you they'd be back for lunch at Harv's as usual."

"Hey," Levi said, stopping him in the doorway. "You forgetting something?"

"Oh, yeah," Ray said. "Come on, Bo."

Chapter 4

Deputy Ben Walker put the cruiser in park and looked around. He was on one of the River County gravel roads that wound through the woods near the Calloway River. He'd seen a few nice homes a few miles earlier on the blacktop, but he hadn't seen anything since the road had turned to gravel. According the directions Amber had given him, the house should be right where he was parked, but he saw nothing there.

He was on a call from a woman who'd phoned the police department to report a missing person. Apparently, the woman didn't drive, so he was going out to see her.

"Amber, there's no house here," he said.

His girlfriend pretty much ran the Twin Rivers Police Department. She was the receptionist, dispatcher, accountant, and computer whiz. The department wasn't exactly high tech, but Amber had sure been working on that deficiency. Unfortunately, neither Ben nor Ray was particularly computer savvy, but slowly, they were learning to use the new tools and to see a few of the advantages.

"Hang on," her voice said over the speaker. "Let me see where you are."

He could hear her fingers tapping on the keyboard.

"Are you on a road?" she said.

"No, I'm hovering over a field in the Twin Rivers Police Department helicopter," he said, his voice dripping in sarcasm.

"Well, would you please set her down because I can't track you in the air," she shot back brightly.

"I'm down," Ben said as he listened to her fingers tapping away.

"Can we go back to the first question then?" Amber asked. "Are you on a road? It looks like you're in the middle of a wooded area with no roads."

"Well, it's not much of a road, just one lane gravel. Let me guess. This road doesn't exist on your map."

"No, wait. I've got you now. I switched views to satellite, and I can see the road. You should be able to see the house. It's about a hundred yards from where you're parked."

"Amber, there's not a house here. I've been doing this long enough to actually know what houses look like."

She ignored his tone. "Are you facing east or west?"

"I've been winding down this road for a couple of miles, so I'm not sure."

"Ben, I loaded a compass on your phone. Use it."

"You're asking me to use a compass in this day and age?"

"Yes, I can see your location, but since you aren't moving, I can't tell which way you're facing. And by the way, you're using a compass on a state-of-the-art smart phone while I monitor your position on a computer 5.3 miles away in real time. Weren't you an Eagle Scout? You should be able to figure out how to use a compass. If you'd rather, you can always get out of the car and check to see which side of the trees the moss is growing on."

Muttering, Ben pulled the phone out of his pocket and opened the compass.

"I'm facing west."

"Was that so hard? Now drive until I tell you to stop," Amber said.

Ben put the car into gear and slowly moved forward.

"In about another fifty yards or so, you should see a house on your right. That's where you're going."

Ben sighed and accelerated. "I'm telling you, there's not a damned thing—" He cut off suddenly. "Well, I'll be damned."

"You see it, don't you?" Amber said. He could hear the I-told-you-so tone in her voice.

"I see a lane on the right. That must be it," he said as he turned into it.

The narrow lane was surrounded by thick woods. About fifty yards in, the woods opened up. An old run-down house sat close to the lane, which continued on through the woods. Ben pulled into a muddy driveway beside the porch.

"I got it," he said as he came to a stop.

"You're welcome," Amber said cheerfully.

Ben pushed the phone icon button on his steering wheel like Amber had shown him. When he heard the electronic beep, he said in a slow, clear voice, "Hang up on Amber."

A bright female computer voice sounded from his car speakers. "I'm sorry. I don't understand the command. Did you want to send a text message to Amber?"

"No, I don't want to send her a text message. I want to hang up the phone!" Ben growled as he realized that he was arguing with his car.

He could hear Amber laughing over the same speakers. "The command is 'end call.'"

Ben pushed the button again. "End call," he said.

Amber's laughter ended abruptly.

Feeling satisfied, Ben climbed out of the car and looked around.

The house appeared to be abandoned. The porch was sagging, and the siding hadn't seen paint in decades. Weeds surrounding the house were three feet tall. There was a small garage at the end of the driveway beside the house. The roof had collapsed.

When Ben walked towards the front door, he was somewhat surprised to see the flicker of a television screen through one of the windows. Stepping back off the porch, he noticed a satellite dish bolted to the roof. Returning to the door, he knocked. Rubbing his hands together—it was a brisk morning—he waited for a few moments, but he didn't hear anyone moving inside. All he could hear were faint sounds coming from the television. He walked over to the window and looked in. There was nobody in that room, but a cigarette was burning in an ashtray and a cup of coffee steamed on a side table beside a dilapidated couch. He went to the door and knocked again, louder.

"It's Deputy Ben Walker from the Twin Rivers Police Department," he shouted. "You called us. I'm here about your missing person."

He waited for what seemed like a long time. He was about ready to leave when he heard somebody moving on the other side of the door.

"Ma'am, I think you called," Ben said through the door, "about a missing person?"

A weak female voice said, "Let me see your I.D."

Standing in front of the peep hole, he pointed to the badge on his shirt. "I'm wearing it."

After a moment, the lock clunked, and the door opened a couple of inches. There was a chain across the opening. A red-rimmed eye peered at him from the darkness inside.

"You called us—about a missing person," Ben repeated.

"I did?" the voice said as she stepped closer to the crack in the door.

She appeared to be an elderly woman. Her face was a roadmap of deep lines.

"Is somebody missing, ma'am?" Ben asked, wondering now if perhaps he was at the wrong house.

"My husband is missing," the woman said finally.

"How long has he been missing?"

"He was supposed to be here this morning with . . ." She paused as the one eye Ben could see scanned him up and down. Then she added, "Groceries. He was to bring me groceries."

"So he went shopping and never came home?"

"He doesn't live here," she said. "We're separated."

"Why don't you open the door, ma'am. I'll take a report," he said. "Do I smell some coffee?"

Her eye narrowed. "I don't know if I should."

"I'm here to help you. I'm not going to talk to you through a crack in the door."

She looked at him suspiciously for a long moment. Then after the door closed, he heard her working the chain. When the door swung open, he stepped into the entrance. It wasn't much warmer in the house than it'd been on the porch.

"I have some coffee in the kitchen," she said.

She headed down a hallway towards the back of the house. Ben followed her.

The house was as run down on the inside as it was on the outside. There was no carpet. The floors were bare wood worn smooth. Both paint and wallpaper were peeling, and the ceilings were stained with water that had leaked through the failing shingles.

Nobody should be living in this house, Ben thought as he stepped into the kitchen.

The window over the sink had been boarded over on the outside with plywood. A single bare bulb hung from the center of the ceiling. The woman poured coffee into a filthy, chipped mug and handed it to him with a shaking hand. Then she sat down at a small kitchen table.

It was the first chance Ben had to get a good look at her. She wasn't as old as he'd first thought. In fact, he put her in her early sixties. He was reminded of an expression his father used to use to describe someone who'd aged badly—rode hard and put away wet. She was wearing a tattered pink robe. He couldn't tell if her hair, which hadn't been washed in a long time, was gray or blonde. The distinctive odor in the house indicated what was going on here—she was a crack addict and, judging from her appearance, a very heavy user at that.

"So your husband is missing," Ben said.

She glanced up at him, seemingly lost for a moment. He wasn't sure she remembered who he was.

"He didn't bring the groceries," she said finally.

"He doesn't live here," Ben said, repeating what she'd said earlier.

"Oh, no," she said. "Not for years. But he takes care of me."

Ben glanced around the kitchen. A calendar on the wall was ten years old.

"How long have you lived here?"

She was quiet for a long moment. Just when he thought she wasn't going to answer or had drifted off from the conversation, she said, "Four or five years, I think."

Ben looked down at the murky cup of coffee in his hand. "You got any cream? Maybe some sweetener?"

"What?" she said, looking at him confused.

"That's okay. I'll get it."

He opened the refrigerator, which was full of food, and pulled out a gallon of milk. It was fresh, but it wouldn't have mattered if it were sour since he had no intention of drinking the coffee. He poured a little milk into his cup. Then under the pretense of looking for sweetener, he opened a few cabinets. They were also full of food—soup, canned goods, pasta, mac and cheese, canned tuna. Ben knew exactly what the woman was running low on—and it wasn't food.

"So your husband hasn't been missing very long?"

She startled as if she'd forgotten he was there.

"He was supposed to bring groceries this morning. I'm out of groceries."

He walked over to the phone hanging on the kitchen wall.

"Have you tried to call him?"

"I don't have a phone."

Picking up the receiver, he held it to his ear. It was dead. He should have known since it was covered in dust.

"What's your name?"

She looked at him blankly.

"You have a name," he said, smiling gently.

She nodded but said nothing. Then she frowned

Her silence sickened him. This woman hadn't used her name in a long, long time. Names are important only when people interact, Ben thought.

Finally, her face relaxed. "My name is Selena," she said. Then the frown returned briefly before she added, "Long. I'm Selena Long."

A chill ran through him. That name rang a bell. Suddenly, he knew something was very wrong here.

"What's your husband's name?"

She hesitated as if trying to decide if she should tell him. Then she said, "It's Peter, but most people call him Pete."

Ben had heard that name for the first time just the evening before. Peter Long was the man whom Jay Snider had threatened at Harv's. Ben, like most lawmen, didn't believe in coincidences.

"How long have you been married?"

She smiled just a bit, revealing yellowed teeth. "He's fifteen years older than me. I married him when I was only sixteen back in 1985."

Ben's face fell. He looked at her closely as he quickly did the math. My God, he thought, could she be only forty-five years old? He'd figured her to be at least fifteen years older. Maybe her drug addled brain had it wrong, but it was likely she was right.

"We're going to find Pete for you, Selena," Ben said.

"Thank you! I don't have any groceries."

"Yes, I know. I'm going to my car to call this into the police station so they can start looking for him. Then I'll come back. I'll have some questions you'll need to answer for the report."

* * *

"Amber, you need to call Ray right now," Ben said. "He needs to get out here. And send the paramedics—she's in need of medical attention."

"Okay, hold on," Amber said as she left him on hold while she made the calls.

Ben could see Selena's pale face in the window. There was something about her that seemed familiar. He'd think of it later.

"They're on their way," Amber said suddenly. "What's going on, Ben?"

"I think she's been a prisoner out here for a long time—at least ten years. This house should be condemned. She's drug addicted, and her husband was supposed to bring the drugs she needs, but he didn't show up. She's going to be in crisis very soon. We need to find that husband and find out what's been going on. His name is Peter Long."

"Does she have a phone number for him?"

"I didn't ask her. She doesn't have a phone," Ben said.

There was a long pause on the other end.

"Amber? You still there?"

"Ben, if she doesn't have a phone, then how did she call us?"

Suddenly, Ben felt like the dumbest man on earth. "Well, maybe I ought to go find out."

"Call if you need me," Amber said.

Ben climbed out of his car. He'd taken a few steps towards the house when he heard a loud bang coming from the woods further up the lane—the distinctive bang of somebody slamming a truck tailgate closed. He walked to the end of the driveway and looked up the lane, but he couldn't see very far because it travelled up a steep hill. Momentarily, he thought about waiting for Ray but decided instead to check the noise out himself. Perhaps he'd already located the missing husband, Peter Long.

Ben walked about fifty yards up the narrow lane to the top of the hill. From there, he could see an old 1970s large red metal machine shed—the kind commonly used to store farm equipment, such as tractors, combines, and cultivators. It looked as if the shed hadn't been used in years. The large white sliding doors were streaked with rust. But the narrow lane was rutted with fresh wheel tracks. Somebody had been up and down that old lane with great regularity.

Ben didn't see any vehicles, but he knew what he'd heard. The lane swung to the right around the machine shed. There was most likely another set of double sliding doors on the other side. The vehicle he'd heard was probably parked on the back side of the shed. Ben ducked into the woods as he approached, just in case somebody was watching. As he neared the shed, he crouched to get a better look. There was a steel entry door on the end, which appeared to be open a crack.

Deciding to risk a quick look, Ben walked from the edge of the woods across the open area to the door. He paused to look around. Though the door was open a little bit, he neither saw nor heard anybody. Perhaps the truck had left. Perhaps the lane continued on through the woods to another way out.

When Ben started to push the door open, he noticed two things that should've stopped him. One, there were lights on inside—lights shining brightly through the crack in the door. Two, there was no knob on the heavy steel security door. The only way to open that door, Ben figured, was to punch in a code on a keypad that was probably inside the metal box on the right.

Now Ben was sure somebody was inside. A padlock lay on top of the metal box that covered the panel beneath. Carefully, he opened the cover to check out the security panel. What he saw inside wasn't at all what he expected. It was a security panel, without a doubt, but not some 1970s burglar alarm that might be found on an old shed to protect combines and planters and ATV's from thieves. This state-of-the-art security panel was something out of a James Bond movie—a high-tech biometric thumb scanner. If a thumbprint matched an authorized person, the door opened. If it didn't, an alarm would probably sound.

But Ben didn't need to worry about that because the door was already open. He hesitated, knowing he should wait for Ray, but then curiosity overrode his common sense. Pushing the door a bit wider, he stepped into the machine shed—and gasped. Sitting on tables made of 2x4s and chicken wire were rows and rows and rows of marijuana plants, growing under bright fluorescent lights.

"Holy crap," Ben said out loud.

Instantly, he realized just how far a voice can echo inside the interior of a huge machine shed. A surprised face suddenly popped up over the top of a table about seventy feet down one of the rows. The look on the man's face was one of utter surprise—a look that mirrored the one on Ben's face. Just as quickly as the face appeared, it vanished. Seconds later, the man appeared in an aisle, a gun in his hand.

Ben barely had a chance to dive down before three rounds hit the steel door where his head had been seconds before. As quickly as the man had popped up, he was gone again. Ben was sitting on the ground, leaning against the door, trying to come up with a plan. Slowly, he rose from the floor and peeked over the top of a nearby plant. Another head at the far end of the building popped up.

Crap, he thought. There are two of them.

Ben slid down the door to the ground again. Then he finally pulled his Glock, chiding himself for not having it drawn when he'd entered the building. As he sat there, considering his options, he suddenly realized just how vulnerable he was. The danger wasn't just from over the tops of the tables. It was from below as well.

Quickly, he rose to his feet, took a couple steps, and lunged towards the top of the first row of tables closest to him. Another burst of gunfire smashed into the steel door where his legs had been seconds before. The perp had shot at him from under the tables, just as Ben had realized the danger.

Ben knew he was in real trouble. He wasn't safe exposed on top of the tables, and he certainly was no safer below them on the ground. Both perps knew exactly where he was, so there was no sense in hiding anymore. He reached for his radio, realizing with sickening clarity that Amber might be the last person to hear his voice.

"Shots fired. Officer in distress. Requesting immediate back-up."

"Ben?" Amber said in his earpiece.

Ben was on his feet. There was only one way out of the situation he was in, and it wasn't on the floor or back through the door. Instead, he bolted down the tops of the flimsy tables towards the spot where he'd last seen the closest perp. As he leaped across the aisle between one row of tables and the next, he saw the second perp turn tail and run through a crack between the sliding doors.

One down and one to go, Ben thought. If there are only two.

It was all adrenaline as he leaped across another aisle and almost fell as the planters on top of the table nearly tripped him. With his every step, the poorly made tables wobbled and groaned under his weight, threatening to collapse. As he ran closer to the last known position of the man who'd shot at him, he thought there were only three more aisles to jump over before he was on top of the guy.

But he was wrong. When he leaped across another aisle and landed heavily on the next table, he heard a sharp crack as the legs began to fail. At the same time, the gunman rose just six feet away—his gun leveled at Ben. Ben pushed off from the edge and leaped towards the man. It was an act of pure desperation.

Then every detail of the action played out in slow motion—the muzzle flash from the gun, the searing pain under his arm, the crashing of their bodies into a table as shards of orange pottery, leafy plants, and flimsy 2x4 tables covered in chicken wire exploded around them. When they hit the ground, Ben wrestled his way on top. Then with his elbow, he gave the perp a savage blow to the chin—a blow so hard Ben was sure he'd killed him.

Shakily, Ben rose and stood over the lifeless body of the man who'd first tried to take his head off and then seconds later his legs. As he stared down, Ben noticed blood dripping onto the man's dirty flannel shirt—blood flowing freely down his arm and off his fingertips.

That should hurt, he thought.

But it didn't.

It will, he thought.

Then he heard a motor start. He bolted towards the gap between the large sliding doors. Outside, a red Dodge Ram was peeling out, throwing mud in all directions. From ten feet away, Ben leveled his Glock with shaking hands and fired multiple rounds at the two back tires. He hit one and missed the other. He fired again, taking out the other tire just as the Glock clicked empty. The back of the truck sank down on the two flat tires. As the driver revved the motor, the metal rims shredded the rubber tires in the soft muddy lane.

Ben struggled to load another clip, but with only one good arm, he didn't have time. The driver's door opened. The second perp stepped out, reached inside his jacket, and pulled a gun out of his shoulder holster. Ben's heart pounded as his world was going fuzzy at the edges.

Suddenly, a large form stepped around the side the machine shed close to the stalled truck. Ben heard the sound a fist makes when it solidly connects with a jaw. The man spun around, bounced off the side of the truck, and fell to the ground.

Ray reached down, picked up the gun, and tossed it away. Then grinning and shaking his head, he put a knee in the man's back. Ben fell to his knees. Ray glanced at him as he snapped one of the cuffs securely around the perp's wrist. The edges of Ben's vision were very gray now, and Ray's voice was distorted—like a record played at the wrong speed—but Ben heard the words, "You dumbass." Then, before he toppled over, Ben saw the color drain out of Ray's face.

"Oh, my God! You're hit."

Seconds later, Ray yelled into his radio, "Officer down, officer down, officer down!"

As Ben slipped into unconsciousness, he heard Ray's voice again. "Ben? Ben? I'm sorry. I didn't know you were wounded. I was only kidding. Ben? Ben?"

Chapter 5

Ray was sitting on the hood of his cruiser, watching the paramedics carefully load Ben Walker onto the gurney. He had to give Amber credit—the River County Police and Illinois State Police had arrived right behind him. They were swarming the scene. He couldn't remember the last time he'd felt more shaken. He was fearing the worst about Ben.

When Ray heard some angry shouts behind him, he looked towards the lane. A white tow truck was weaving its way up the lane around a half dozen county and state police cars, and the driver was being less than polite in telling them to "get the hell out of the way." His dog was being just as rude, barking at everyone from the passenger window. The tow truck pulled in next to Ray's cruiser, and Ed Garvey climbed out slowly.

"What the hell happened, Ray?"

Ed's face was tight, and the blue eyes of the old Marine sniper were filled with worry. In the last couple of years, Ray and Ed Garvey had become close friends—almost as close as Ray and Ed's nephew, Levi.

"Ben's been shot. I don't know how badly yet, but I think it's bad," Ray said, his throat tight and dry.

"What did Ben stumble into?"

"Hundred and hundreds of marijuana plants. That machine shed is bursting with them."

"A greenhouse operation," Ed said with a whistle. "That must be worth a fortune in a shed that large."

"Millions, I'd imagine," Ray said.

When one of the paramedics ran towards them, Ray stood suddenly and said, "Don't candy coat it. How bad, Duane?"

"The bullet raked his ribs under his left armpit, and he lost some blood," Duane said as he caught his breath. "It left an ugly wound, but it's not life threatening. Ben's in excellent shape, so he should recover. Even so, he'll be feeling this misadventure for some time, and he'll have a scar to re-member it by. We're taking him in now."

"I thought when he passed out that he was dying," Ray said, wiping a tear from the corner of his eye. His relief was obvious.

"He was all pumped up on adrenaline, and he's still a little shocky," Duane said. "Wounds like his are horribly painful. It's all muscle and gristle along the ribs."

"Is he awake?" Ray asked.

"Yeah, but he's groggy. We gave him a pain killer."

"And you're sure he's going to be okay?"

"He's going to be fine," Duane said.

Ray headed towards the ambulance with Ed following. When they got to the rear, Ben glanced up at them from the gurney inside.

Ray restrained his urge to smile. "I'll repeat what I said earlier. You dumbass, what the hell is wrong with you?"

Ben smiled weakly. "Oh, thank God. I'm going to live. I was convinced Duane was just telling me what I wanted to hear."

Ed's laughter rang out over the scene.

"Oh, you're going to live," Ray said. "And when you get on your feet, I'm going to kick your ass. What in the hell were you thinking?"

"I wasn't," Ben said. "I'm in trouble, huh?"

"We'll talk about your stunning lack of judgment later," Ray said.

"Dumbass," Ed repeated with a smirk on his face.

Ray shot him a look, and the smirk vanished.

"That guy inside the shed? Did I kill him?" Ben asked, a pained expression in his eyes.

Ed and Ray glanced over at the State Police who were just bringing the man out of the machine shed in handcuffs.

"Let me check," Ed said.

"Hey, pothead!" he yelled towards the man in handcuffs. "How are you feeling?"

The cuffed man lunged towards Ed and yelled, "Screw you, old man!"

Ed looked down at Ben with feigned seriousness on his face. "It may be touch and go for a while, but I think he'll survive to stand trial."

Ben chuckled, then winced. "Don't make me laugh, Ed. It hurts."

"Now the guy that I clouted," Ray said proudly, "he's already on his way to the hospital with a fractured jaw."

Ben sighed.

"By the way," Ray said, "I spoke to the State Police captain. They're giving you credit for the arrests—a nice gesture on their part. That will look good on your record."

Ben smiled faintly.

Ed scratched his head as he watched the two officers lead the man in cuffs towards the cop car. "I don't see even one bruise on that guy. Do you see any marks on him, Ray?"

"No, I don't see any either," Ray admitted.

"I hit him so hard, I was sure I'd killed him," Ben said.

Ray and Ed restrained grins.

"Maybe he just passed out in fear," Ray said.

"Or maybe he did what people are supposed to do when bears attack them," Ed suggested.

"Yeah, he played dead to prevent being mauled by a dangerous animal," Ray said with a snicker.

"Or maybe Ben learned some ninja fighting skills in the Army," Ed said. "Like the 'touch of death.' Those ninjas can touch you in a certain way and never leave a mark. Then like a week later, you keel over dead."

Ben held up his hand in a claw. "Come here, Ed. I'll show it to you."

"That's enough," Duane said, stepping in front of them. "This brave officer has been shot in the line of duty. Can you at least give him a break until he's been treated by a doctor?"

"We'll see you at the hospital," Ray said.

"Call Amber, would you, Ray?" Ben said.

Ray nodded.

"You might want to put him in restraints, Duane," Ed said. "He's a very dangerous man. And he's got his claw out. You heard that veiled threat against my person, didn't you?"

"Yeah, yeah," Duane said as he closed the ambulance doors.

Chapter 6

It had already been a long day when Ray Billings pulled back into Twin Rivers in his cruiser, and it wasn't yet three o'clock.

He'd gone to St. Anne's Hospital in Calloway to see if Ben was all right, and he was. He didn't require surgery, but after cleaning the wound, the emergency room doctor had stitched him up with a couple dozen stitches. Ben would be off the job for some time.

When Ray had arrived at the hospital, Amber was there—surprisingly calm about the whole thing. The Garveys were there, too. And for the first time in anyone's recollection, Harv and April had closed the diner so they were there, along with half the town. The waiting room was full, and people were standing in the halls, waiting for word of Ben's condition. Finally, Amber told Dr. Jackson that he should go down to the waiting room and tell everyone, family or not, what Ben's condition was. When he did, everyone applauded. Then slowly, the crowd thinned out.

Only in a small town, Ray thought as he smiled.

Ray had managed a few minutes alone with just Ben and Amber. Ben had been able to fill Ray in on everything that had happened at Selena Long's house and at what they had dubbed the "pot shed." Ray was trying to decide if Selena's problem and the marijuana operation were connected in some way. He tended to believe they were not, and he hoped the investigators would come to that conclusion as well. Then the State Police, or possibly the DEA, would investigate the pot shed. That would leave him to figure out what was going on with Selena Long, Pete Long, and Jay Snider.

When Ray turned onto Main Street, he saw that it was mostly deserted since the diner was still closed. There were only a couple of cars parked on the whole block. Ray swung into his space in front of the Twin Rivers Police Department and climbed out. A Lincoln Town Car he didn't recognize was parked in the space next to his.

In the office, Claire was sitting at the front desk. She'd worked part-time at the police department for nearly thirty years, but she struggled with some of Amber's new technology.

"Afternoon, Chief," she said, handing him a pile of phone messages.

Ray had to admit that he preferred Claire's written phone messages to the emails and text messages Amber sent him—he was kind of old school about a lot of things.

"Anything going on?" he asked as he thumbed through the messages.

"Ann Childers called twice to complain that the neighbor boys were setting off fireworks in the alley behind her house again."

Ray sighed. "How long ago?"

"I took care of it," Claire said.

Ray looked at her with a raised eyebrow.

"I figured it was those rotten McAllister boys," she said. "The oldest one is on my grandson's soccer team, so I called my grandson to get his cell number."

Ray suppressed a grin. "And you said what?"

"That if I heard any more fireworks coming from over that way, I'd send the chief over, and you were in a rotten mood today, and I wouldn't want to be them when you showed up."

"And?"

"All's quiet on the western front."

"You're a treasure, Claire."

Ray smiled as she beamed broadly.

Then, becoming all business again, she said, "You've got a guy in your office. I told him to wait because I knew you'd want to talk to him."

"Who?"

"Peter Long."

"Interesting," Ray said, rubbing his chin.

"I thought so, too," Claire remarked.

Ray walked into his office, took off his flat-brimmed trooper hat, and hung it on the coat stand behind the door. Then he turned to greet the man.

"Mr. Long," he said, extending his hand. "I'm Chief Ray Billings."

The man rose and gave Ray's hand a firm shake.

"It's nice to meet you, Chief," he said. "I thought you might want to talk to me."

"I do," Ray said, motioning to the chair.

Ray settled behind his desk and studied the short, round man sitting before him. He was meticulously dressed in a fashionable suit and silk tie. His gray hair was neatly trimmed and his nails manicured. He wore several large gold rings and an expensive gold watch. He had a pencil thin mustache just above his lip. Ray put him in his late fifties to early sixties. Everything about him indicated gentlemanly manners and financial success.

"I suppose you want to know about Selena," Pete said, shifting uncomfortably.

"I reckon that's why you're here," Ray said, leaning back in his chair and rolling up the corners of his mustache in his fingertips. "Might like you to talk a little bit about Jay Snider, too, if you don't mind."

"You're not from around here," Pete said, regarding him carefully.

Ray chuckled. He got that a lot. His Georgia accent was noticeable enough, but he also seemed to speak more slowly than people in the Midwest, and his manner was more relaxed.

"Georgia?" Pete asked.

Ray nodded. "Savannah."

A touch of smugness crossed Pete's face after he was able to place the accent so precisely. They looked at each other for a long moment. Then Pete shifted uneasily again. Ray could tell he'd rather be anywhere else on earth than sitting in that chair.

"Tell me about Selena," he said. "This has all happened so fast I haven't really had time to mull it over much, but it's a damned odd situation if you don't mind me saying so."

"It is without a doubt," Pete said. "And I'm sure you think I'm some kind of villain in this, but I'm not."

"I'll save any judgments until after I hear the story," Ray said.

"I met Selena more than twenty-five years ago. I was in my early thirties, and she was in her early twenties—or so I thought. She was one of the most stunningly beautiful women I'd ever seen. We fell in love, but then I found out she wasn't in her twenties—she'd lied. She was only sixteen. With the permission of her parents, I married her, and we were happy for nearly fifteen years."

"Children?" Ray asked.

Pete shook his head.

"So what happened?"

"I had become rather successful, and my business took me away a lot. I really hadn't been paying enough attention to her as I built my empire. She got bored living so much of the time by herself. There were other men." Pete paused, then cleared his throat and added, "And I'm sure you know by now that she'd developed other problems as well."

Ray nodded.

"I don't know how many rehabs I sent her to during the last five years we were living together, but without success. I took her credit cards and her access to other money, hoping to curb her cocaine habit. When I cut her funds off, she found a cheaper and much more deadly form of the drug to use. She'd sometimes disappear for weeks at a time and then suddenly reappear looking like death itself. I just couldn't take it anymore."

"Crack cocaine," Ray said. "But you never divorced her?"

"If I'd divorced her, she'd be dead right now," Pete said. "The court would've most likely given her alimony and half of my estate which I'd built during the time we were married. With those resources, she'd have overdosed in a couple of months—or less."

He swallowed hard as his eyes clouded.

"One time when she disappeared, I suddenly realized that I might know where she was. Her mother had passed away, and her family home was empty. I was right. What I saw there—" His voice cracked. He took a deep breath before finishing. "I knew it was bad, but I had no idea how bad it had become or the things she'd do to get what she needed."

"I think I know," Ray said, interrupting.

He'd seen it himself. He knew what drug addicted women sometimes did.

"So we separated, and she never left her family home. She has no source of income, but I certainly didn't want her going back to what she was obviously willing to do to get her drugs. So for the last fifteen years or so, I've kept her fridge full, paid her taxes and utilities, and given her a very small weekly income."

Ray nodded. "You've been her enabler."

"I still love her," he said flatly. "I tried everything to get back the beautiful young woman I'd married, but she was gone, and I just couldn't let her kill herself. And she would have."

Ray felt a hot stab in his chest. He could understand that. People you love sometimes change, and it's often something you just don't want to see or admit. But you can't go back. You have to learn to accept the way things are in the present.

"So tell me about this encounter you had with Jay Snider," Ray said.

"I haven't seen Selena in more than five years," Pete said. "The last time . . . well, she'd destroyed herself. I just didn't want to see her again. It was too difficult. I arranged for Jay to take her groceries out each week and deliver the cash—a very small amount, just enough to get her by. It seems to keep her drug habit in check."

"Jay Snider is probably her drug connection?" Ray asked.

"Most likely. I have nothing to do with that or how she spends that money," Pete said, his face flashing in momentary anger.

"But you knew, of course," Ray said. "If you didn't, you'd write her a check each month. You didn't because you knew that with that much cash she'd probably go on a binge and overdose."

"Of course, I knew she was using that money to buy drugs, but at least she wasn't using her body—or worse."

"And what was Jay's problem?"

"I met him back in the 80s. We were good friends at one time, but he's mentally ill. He's gotten worse over time. I knew he lived near Selena in a small house above the Calloway River. Jay Snider is crazy, but, believe it or not, he's very dependable. If he tells you he's going to do something, you can rest assured that he'll do it."

"But . . ." Ray said.

"But he wanted to borrow some money for a new business he was starting. It was a sizable chunk of change, and he wouldn't be very specific about this new venture, so I politely declined. I suspected it might be illegal, and I didn't want to get involved. He got really angry and threatened me. When I talked to him on the phone a few days ago, I told him he was really pushing his limits with me. Then I told him I was about to find somebody else to take care of Selena, and he went berserk. So I drove over from Olton Lake to talk to him. When he wasn't home, I went to Harv's for a bite to eat, and he found me. He threatened me again—threatened to expose my dirty little secret."

"By dirty little secret he meant Selena."

Pete nodded. "As a businessman, it would be rather embarrassing to have that come out. I was going to give him the money he wanted—not as a loan but as a gift. I was going to tell him that, but your young deputy interrupted our discussion and arrested him. That's the whole story. It's ugly. It's embarrassing. Even my association with Jay Snider isn't something I'd want known, but it is what it is."

Ray sat for a moment, thinking. Then he leaned forward and put his elbows on the desk. As the seconds ticked away, Pete Long tapped his foot nervously.

"There's another part of this story we haven't discussed yet," Ray said.

Pete looked at him blankly.

"A little further up that lane Selena lives on, we found what is probably a multi-million dollar marijuana operation in a large machine shed."

"I don't know anything about that," Pete said, his eyes wide.

"Seems like a hell of a coincidence," Ray said. "I'm not going to find out you own that land?"

"Of course not!" Pete spat, his gentlemanly manners quickly forgotten. "I don't own any land in that area. As I said, I don't even own Selena's house. I have no idea who owns the land adjacent to hers, and Selena owns less than a quarter of an acre where the house and garage are."

Ray believed him. He'd been a cop for a long time. It was hard to fake some things. If Pete had been expecting that question, he would've been more prepared for it.

"What do you do for a living, Pete?" Ray asked.

Although sweat had popped out across Pete's forehead during the last couple of minutes, the question seemed to relax him a little. He leaned back in his chair. Then he pulled a handkerchief out of his pocket and gently dabbed the sweat from his forehead and upper lip.

"Primarily, I'm a club owner. I own about a dozen nightclubs and bars in the state. I started out small with only one rundown club, and I built from there. I've bought properties, mostly commercial space, and I lease those. I also own two rather unremarkable music recording studios, one in

Nashville and the other in St. Louis, along with a video production company. We do mostly television advertising spots, but we've done a few larger productions."

"Anything I'd know?" Ray asked.

Pete seemed to sit a little taller in his chair. "A few years ago, my video studio was approached by a famous historian who'd written a book about the attempt to steal Abraham Lincoln's body from his crypt in Springfield. With the help of the historian, I produced a documentary based on his book. You might've seen that on the History Channel a couple of years ago."

Ray smiled. He had seen it.

"I'd like to thank you for coming in," Ray said, rising. "I know this was uncomfortable for you."

Pete reached over and shook his hand. He started towards the door, then turned.

"Selena?"

"She was taken to St. Anne's Hospital," Ray said. "I haven't heard what her condition is."

Pete looked at him for a long moment. Then he walked out of the police station.

Ray watched Pete through the slats in the blinds as he climbed into his car. Pete sat for a long time in the driver's seat with his face in his hands before starting the car and backing out of the parking space.

I do believe him, Ray thought.

"Chief?"

Ray was so lost in his own thoughts that he jumped.

"Sorry, Chief. I didn't mean to startle you."

"What is it, Claire?"

"Jeff Dunwoody, the CSI, just called. He's at Selena Long's house. He's found something he thinks you might want to see."

Ray walked over to the hat stand to retrieve his hat.

Chapter 7

Before Ray had gotten up the steps of the dilapidated house, he'd been stopped by Captain Perkins of the Illinois State Police. They'd been talking for several minutes. Ray was well over six feet tall, and Captain Perkins seemed to be a couple of inches taller than that. Ray found him painfully devoid of humor and strictly by the book.

"We haven't found any evidence connecting these two cases," the captain said as he finished his summary of their findings. "I think Deputy Walker stumbled into the drug operation while on an unrelated call, so that's how we're going to handle them—as two separate cases."

Ray listened, looking down at his feet while trying to scrape mud off his boots on the edge of the porch.

"So the DEA is going to handle the investigation of the pot shed?" Ray asked.

The term "pot shed" caused the captain to wince slightly.

"We don't think the *marijuana operation* is a local matter," Perkins said. "It's too well organized. There's probably a larger organization behind it."

"I assume they'll let me know if there's any assistance I can provide," Ray said.

"Of course. And I assume you can handle the other matter."

"We will," Ray said. "Thank you, Captain. Please tell your boys I appreciate your quick response to this emergency."

"It's our job," he said, turning quickly and walking away.

Ray suppressed a smile. It was a huge relief to know that the drug investigation was being taken over by people better equipped to handle it. Ray walked into the old house where Jeff was waiting in the living room.

"You found something," Ray said.

"It's a sad scene, but I found something in the bedroom that piqued my interest. I thought you'd like to see it."

They walked together down a narrow hall into a dingy, dimly-lit bedroom barely larger than the bed that was in it.

"In the closet over here," Jeff said, pointing to an open door.

There were hardly any clothes inside. Instead, a large bookcase full of old VHS tapes took up most of the space.

"So she likes movies," Ray said, somewhat irritated.

That fact hardly seemed to warrant a trip out to the old place.

"She doesn't own a VCR," Jeff said. "Have a little closer look."

Ray pulled one of the VHS boxes off a middle shelf. As soon as he looked at the cover, his eyes widened. On the front of the box were two naked blondes, and on the back was a collection of movie scenes depicting all varieties of lewd sexual activities.

"Porn?" Ray said, looking at Jeff.

"Every single one of them," Jeff replied.

Ray was baffled. "There must be a hundred movies here. And they aren't new either."

"There are eighty-eight movies, and VHS went out the window in the late 90s," Jeff said. "I've looked through them. The earliest one was produced in 1984 and the most recent in 1993. They seem to be in order by release date—oldest on the top shelves and newest on the bottom."

Ray replaced the tape he held and took another. It was similar—with beautiful naked women on the front and hardcore pornographic movie scenes on the back.

"What do you make of it?" Ray asked.

"I have no idea," Jeff said. "It just kind of surprised me. It was the last thing I expected to find. I thought maybe you should have a look."

Ray reached for a tape on the bottom shelf, one of the more recent in the collection.

"Wait a minute," he said, rolling up the corners of his mustache.

He pulled the first video tape he'd looked at off the shelf and looked at it again.

"Check this out, Jeff."

Ray pointed to the hand of a porn actress on each tape. There was a small red heart tattoo on the webbing between her thumb and first finger.

"It's just a tattoo," Jeff said.

Ray pulled four tapes at random from the shelves.

"There," he said, stabbing a finger at what he knew he'd find. "And there and there and there."

Looking closely at each box, Jeff said, "That's the same tattoo."

"It's the same woman," Ray said."

For several minutes, they pulled tapes, discovering the heart tattoo again and again.

"The actors and actresses are listed on the back. There's one name in common on all of these so far," Jeff said, pointing at the name.

The light suddenly dawned on Ray. He pulled one last box. On the front cover was that name again and the tattoo. The actress was in a starring role in this production instead of a supporting role. Ray read the words on the front of the box, "*Hot Housewives* starring Selena Fine."

"Unbelievable," Jeff said.

"This isn't some perverts porn collection, Jeff. This is Selena Fine's scrapbook—or as we know her, Selena Long."

"I saw her before they took her away in the ambulance. She certainly didn't look like that," Jeff said, pointing at the buxom blonde on the cover.

Ray was suddenly very angry with Peter Long, who'd played him like a pro. Ray had noted another commonality in the collection of porn—they were all made by the same studio. Video production studio, my ass, he thought. He was starting to understand Selena's drug addiction a little better now. She'd likely been exploited by an older man she trusted, perhaps even loved. Ray figured that he now knew what Pete Long's "dirty little secret" really was.

"You mind if I take these?" he said, holding up a couple of the boxes.

"According to the DEA, the house isn't part of their crime scene anymore. We've been released, so unless you tell me differently, I see a tragedy here but not a crime. The video tapes aren't evidence. They're the personal property of Selena Long."

"I'll bring them back," Ray said. "You boys lock up the house and leave the premises ASAP. As you pointed out, this isn't a crime scene, and we have no business here—yet."

Chapter 8

For over an hour, Ray had been watching him. He'd driven to Olton Lake with every intention of confronting Pete Long. Ray was furious that he'd been so easily fooled, especially when he'd learned what the truth of the matter really was. But, once there, he was wise enough not to approach Pete in his present state of mind. And so Ray sat—watching.

He'd found the residence easily enough. The enormous house towered above the top of a bluff at the end of the lake. On the side that faced the lake, it was all glass with a huge multi-tiered deck. It was lit up like a beacon. A wooden staircase, which wound down the front of the bluff from the deck to the lake below, was illuminated by lights every ten feet or so. A long boat pier, also well illuminated, stuck out into the lake with two large boats moored to it. One of the boats looked like a party barge—a two-level pontoon boat that could easily accommodate a dozen or so revelers. The other was a sleek, powerful motorboat.

As the sun began to drop, Pete Long walked through a glass door to the edge of the wooden deck. He leaned on the railing with a drink in one hand and a cigar in the other.

Ray felt his pulse rise as his temper flared. I felt sorry for that son of a bitch, he thought. I thought he was a victim of love, and I find out he's most likely the cause of that young woman's plight.

After the sun set, Pete Long snubbed out his cigar and walked across the deck to the glass doors. When he reached them, he turned and looked towards where Ray was parked. Although Ray knew he couldn't see him in the waning light, it was likely that Pete Long had known he was there the entire time.

He wants me to know that he saw me, Ray thought. He was expecting me. Don't worry, Pete. We'll talk again real soon when I'm not quite so ticked off and you're not so well prepared.

Ray started the car, did a u-turn, and headed back to Twin Rivers. He didn't feel like going home. He'd yet to finish the last fight with Bernice, but he had no interest in finishing it right then.

When he reached Twin Rivers, he drove slowly up Main Street, taking in the sights. The Comet Theatre was fully ablaze in purple and white neon lights, and the street was packed with cars. A double feature, a part of a popular ongoing Hitchcock movie festival, was showing. The old art deco theater had been meticulously restored some years ago by Tori Buchanan, now Tori Garvey. It was the first restoration project she'd taken on as a hobby back when she was president of the First National Bank of Calloway. She was good with her hands, and she loved the work. After she married Levi, she decided to do restoration for a living.

As he pulled into a spot in front of the police station, he glanced up at the three-story facade of the building. The police department was actually the first floor tenant of the Twin Rivers Masonic Lodge. That hundred-year-old building, another of Tori's projects, had been in the midst of its restoration process when he was hired as the chief of police two years earlier. Levi Garvey was the Worshipful Master of the Lodge then, followed by Ed Garvey last year, and a few months ago, when the Lodge held its election, the Brethren had elected Ray Worshipful Master. When Ray noticed all the lights on upstairs and the small round blue meeting globe illuminated, he realized he'd missed the meeting. Even so, he knew there were enough Past Masters in attendance to find one to open and close and conduct the meeting.

Inside the police station, Amber was sitting at her desk, reading a paperback.

"All quiet?" he asked.

"Not a peep," she replied, glancing up at him with her dark brown eyes. She was in her mid-twenties, pretty, with small features and a perfect nose that turned up at the end. She was just over five feet tall and just slightly more than a hundred pounds. But she was feisty. She ran the office without question, even though everyone who worked in the office towered over her, including her boyfriend, Ben.

"You going to be here for a while?" she asked.

"Yeah," Ray said.

"Mind if I run across to Harv's and get a cheeseburger? I'm famished."

"Go ahead. I'll listen for the phone."

"Thanks," she said, grabbing her jacket off the back of her chair. "I won't be gone long."

"How's Ben?"

"He's fine," Amber said. "He may go home tomorrow."

"Only one day in the hospital?"

"The injury wasn't that serious. He just needs time to heal, and he'll probably need some physical therapy. We'll find out all about that later in the week. We have an appointment."

After Amber left, Ray walked into his office and flipped on the light. He tossed his hat onto the coat rack in the corner and crossed to the filing cabinets that lined one wall of the office. He was rummaging around in the bottom drawers when he heard the outside door open.

"You missed a good meeting tonight, Worshipful," Levi Garvey said as he strode in with Ed Garvey behind him. They were both dressed for the meeting in a tie and a jacket.

"I was following up a lead at Olton Lake," Ray said.

"That Selena Long deal," Ed said, loosening his tie. The news had spread all over town.

Ray nodded as he found what he was looking for. "Ah, there it is. I knew I'd seen it in here somewhere." Pulling a dusty bottle of Wild Turkey out of the back of one of the file drawers, he asked, "You want a drink?"

Ed glanced anxiously at Levi, who said tightly, "You know who that probably belonged to."

"It undoubtedly belonged to Chief Doug Malone," Ray said as he retrieved three coffee mugs from beside the coffee maker and set them on the desk. He sat on the edge of the desk as he twisted off the cap. "But he's dead, so I don't think he'll mind. And I need a drink."

"Don't pour me one," Levi said.

Ignoring him, Ray poured three drinks.

"You're going to want a drink after you hear what I've got to say," he said, setting the bottle down and handing one mug to Levi and the other one to Ed.

He took his own and sat down in his desk chair. After exchanging glances, Ed and Levi took chairs opposite Ray.

"What's going on, Chief?" Ed asked, taking a tentative sip of the bourbon.

Ed had killed the man who'd owned that bottle, Chief Doug Malone—the same man who'd very nearly killed Levi, first by putting a nine millimeter slug in his shoulder and then by trying to drown him in the mine shaft at Kingery Pond.

Levi left his mug on the desk, untouched.

"The DEA is going to investigate the pot shed, but we found something at Selena's house I need to follow up on," Ray said. "Selena Long was once known as Selena Fine."

Levi's eyes lit up with recognition.

"You know the name?" Ray asked.

Levi nodded reluctantly. "She was a very well-known porn star back in the late 80s. I won't deny I was familiar with her work when I was in college. I actually saw her once. A bunch of us drove to this strip club in Peoria where they were featuring several popular porn stars at the time. She was amazing. I sure didn't know she was from Twin Rivers."

"I'm pretty sure her husband, Pete Long, produced all the movies she starred in," Ray said. "And I'll bet that club you visited back then was one of the ones he owns."

Ed leaned forward. "Are you suggesting that Pete Long got his wife into the business?"

"That's exactly what I think," Ray said. "It fits. That's bad enough, but there's something else. I didn't know any of this when Pete came in here earlier today and told me a huge fairy tale about falling in a love with a beautiful young girl. I swallowed his story hook, line, and sinker. Needless to say, he left a lot out. Earlier today, Jeff found a collection of porn movies at Selena's house—all the movies she'd been in and all produced by the same porn studio."

"Pete Long's studio," Levi said.

Ray nodded. "But if you can believe it, there's an even uglier side to this story. Selena told Ben when he went out there this morning that she married Pete Long back in '85 when she was only sixteen. Pete told me the same thing. She was sixteen, and he was in his early thirties at the time."

"That's a little old for a girl that age," Ed remarked.

"Well, get this," Ray said. "The first movie she was in was made in 1984."

"She would've been only fifteen years old," Levi said as he sat forward in his chair.

Ray looked at him darkly over the top of his coffee mug. "He's kept her out in the woods and high as a kite for at least ten years. But I don't think her being underage when he started putting her in porn films is the reason why. Maybe he didn't even know at the time. If that got out, it might still hurt him, but I think Jay Snider was trying to blackmail him. That's what the fight at Harv's was about yesterday. I certainly don't believe Pete Long's version of the story. He's a gifted liar."

"You think there's more to it," Ed said.

"My gut tells me there could be a lot more to it," Ray said. "I think Jay Snider holds the key to what Pete Long is trying to hide, and I can't trust myself with Pete Long."

"Why not?" Levi said, focusing in on him with his deep-blue eyes.

"I don't deal well with liars," he snapped. "And I have a particular distaste for men who exploit young women for financial gain. I dealt with scum like that in Savannah. I saw things during my thirty years on the force that would turn your stomach. I'm afraid that when I talk to him again, I might beat his ass just on principle."

Levi and Ed glanced at each other. Ray had never said anything like that before.

"I've got to find out what he's hiding. If you'd seen that house and the conditions Selena has been living in . . ." Ray's voice trailed off.

"Are you going somewhere with this?" Ed said.

Ray reached into his top desk drawer, pulled out two heavy bundles, and thumped them down on his desk without saying a word.

"Do you know what you're asking?" Ed said, leaning forward to look at what Ray had laid on the desk.

Levi's face had gone pale. He reached for the coffee mug and belted down the bourbon in one swallow.

"You can't be serious," Levi said.

"I'm serious," Ray said as he twisted the cap off the dusty bottle and poured three more drinks. "Now let's talk this thing all the way through."

Chapter 9

Tori was stretched out on the couch, watching television in the den, when Levi walked in behind her. The only light in the room was from the television screen and a small lamp on the end table. Rosco, who was snoring on the area rug in front of the television, never moved.

"The meeting ran a little long tonight," she remarked, glancing at the clock. It was nearly midnight.

"You want a beer?" he asked.

"Sure," Tori said. "Adam went out like a light tonight. I sure hope he sleeps a little later in the morning than he has been."

She prattled on as Levi walked up the short hallway into the kitchen and grabbed two beers from the top shelf of the refrigerator.

When he returned, she said, "Anything interesting go on tonight?"

"You could say that," Levi said.

He twisted the cap off Tori's beer and handed it to her over the back of the couch. She still hadn't looked at him.

"You sound a little off tonight. Did something happen? Is everything okay, Levi?"

Levi walked towards his favorite wingback chair. As he sat down, he seemed to squeak. When Tori glanced at him, she sprayed beer all over the couch she was lying on. There was a glint of humor in his eyes as her eyes ran over the khaki shirt, the gold badge, and the black leather gun belt he wore. Tori wiped beer off her chin with the back of her hand and sat up slowly. Levi settled back into the chair, causing his leather gun belt to squeak again.

"Is this some kind of a joke, Levi?" Tori said, her eyes wide

He shook his head. "You can just call me Deputy Garvey, Ma'am."

Tori didn't smile.

He'd wondered how she was going to react. Either she'd be really angry, or, more typically, she'd take it in stride. Her initial reaction, however, could be an indication that this wasn't going to go well. He was waiting for the anger.

It took Tori a moment to take it all in, but she knew exactly how this had come about. Ray Billings was down a deputy, and he wouldn't have asked if he hadn't needed the help. She wasn't happy to see Levi in uniform, but she knew her husband had skills that Ray really needed right now.

"How does it feel to be a cop again after what—fifteen years?" she finally said.

"More like eighteen," Levi said, relieved that there was no anger in her voice. "And it's only temporary."

Right out of college, Levi had served ten years as an Illinois State Trooper—long before he'd written and published his first novel. Levi had talked about those years only once that she could recall—one terrible Fourth of July night when they were sitting on a cold concrete floor in the Twin Rivers jail.

"Ray wouldn't have asked you if he didn't need you," Tori said.

"I'm not the only new deputy in Twin Rivers," Levi said with a chuckle as he sipped his beer.

"Oh?"

"Twin Rivers has two duly sworn-in Deputy Garveys now."

"Ed?" she said.

"Ed's going to keep the town buttoned down while I help Ray investigate this Selena Long case. Ray thinks there's a lot more to it."

"Ed Garvey driving around in a police cruiser," Tori said with a laugh.

"He's already made it perfectly clear he's not chasing any teenagers at his age," Levi remarked.

"You know, he's perfect in that role," Tori said. "He knows everyone in town, he's well-liked, and even at his age, there aren't many who don't know better than to get on his bad side."

Tori smiled at Levi wickedly.

"What?" Levi asked.

"Are you concerned your skills are a little rusty after eighteen years?"

"Like what skills?"

"Oh, I don't know." Pointing at his belt, Tori smiled seductively. "Are those handcuffs?"

Levi grinned as he stood up. He walked over to the door of the den, slid the pocket door closed, and locked it.

Then, looking at Tori, he said, "Do you know why I pulled you over, Ma'am?"

"Why no, I don't," she replied innocently.

"I'm going to need you to step out of the car."

"I should resist, right?" Tori said, a gleam shining in her deep-green eyes.

"Oh, definitely," Levi said with a laugh.

Chapter 10

"You want a donut, Ray?" Levi said, holding one up from the passenger seat of the cruiser. It was the third time he'd asked.

"No, I don't want a donut, Levi," Ray said brusquely.

They were parked in front of Hillbilly Bob's Convenience Store, getting ready to head to Olton Lake. Ray wasn't in a talking mood, and Levi, who was, hadn't shut up since they'd left the police station. Levi shrugged. He took a bite out of the donut—his third—then brushed powdered sugar off the front of his uniform shirt.

"I've got plenty of them," Levi remarked with his mouth full. "I bought a dozen. I thought cops liked donuts."

Ray gave him a sidelong glance. "You're pushing it, Levi."

"Sorry," Levi said, trying not to grin. "You're a little moody today. Arthritis acting up?"

"The first rule of being a Twin Rivers deputy is not to piss off the chief of police."

"I'll try to remember that."

"It's a little late," Ray said.

"Oh," Levi said, his good cheer suddenly evaporating. "You're talking about earlier."

"Earlier?" Ray said. "You mean when you called me at 2 a.m. to ask me where we keep the spare handcuff keys?"

"Well, I realized suddenly I didn't have one," Levi said, his face flushing a bit.

"And why did you need a replacement right then? At 2 a.m.?"

"Always be prepared?"

Ray glanced at him. Levi was suddenly fascinated with the cars driving by the gas station on the slab.

"You going to shut up now, or should I keep asking questions?" Ray said.

Levi didn't reply.

"That's what I thought," Ray said as he started the car. "You're lucky Tori didn't beat the hell out of you once her hands were free."

Levi's head snapped towards him. He started to say something, but then he decided against it.

"You don't have to potty or anything, do you?" Ray asked.

"Oh, shut up," Levi said.

"If you're good, we'll stop and get you a Happy Meal on the way home."

Levi glared at him. Ray had successfully turned things around on him.

"Kind of getting the idea what it's like going on a road trip with you?" Ray said with a chuckle.

Levi didn't say anything.

"Good," Ray said as he pulled out onto the narrow two-lane highway that led to Olton.

They'd driven about a mile up the winding road when Levi glanced at Ray and started to say something. Then he stopped himself.

"What? You're dying to say something."

"I'm being serious now," Levi said, looking at him intently. "Are you sure about this plan?"

"What do you mean?"

"I know you're anxious to confront Pete Long because he lied to you, and you're convinced there is more going on here."

"There is."

"Let me throw this out there," Levi said. "You don't have much to go on besides your gut instinct, right?"

"He obviously lied to me, and I intend to find out why," Ray said sharply.

"You're kind of pissed off that you fell for his story."

"You have a better idea?" he asked, his jaw tight.

Ray knew that Levi could sometimes be a clown, but he was also a damned good investigator. He'd solved two murder cases in Twin Rivers since he'd moved back. Levi was going somewhere with this, and Ray would be foolish not to listen to him.

"I have an alternative idea," Levi said. "I don't know if it's better or not."

"Spit it out then. What are you thinking?"

"I think we should prepare ourselves for the interview," Levi said. "Pete Long is obviously a gifted liar if he managed to fool you. That's not an easy thing to do. But other than suspicions, we've really got nothing to go on and no way of knowing if what he's going to tell us is the truth or not."

Ray pulled the car off the side of the road, then turned to face Levi.

"Okay, you've got my attention."

"There are two people we haven't talked to yet. Both could shed a lot more light on this," Levi said, tossing the remainder of the third donut back into the sack. "We talk to them first to find out what they're willing to tell us. The information we get from them might give us a lot more questions to ask Pete Long and make it a lot harder for him to lie to us."

Ray thought for a moment, then sighed. He was anxious to have another little talk with Pete Long, but Levi had made an excellent point.

"You're talking about Selena Long and Jay Snider," Ray said as he absent-mindedly turned up the corners of his handlebar mustache.

"Selena is still in the hospital as far as I know," Levi said. "You could interview her this morning. And I'm pretty sure I can find Jay Snider's house out by the river. I have a pretty good idea where it is."

"I don't think you should talk to him alone. We should talk to him together."

"He's not going to talk to two of us—he probably won't talk to you at all," Levi said. "But I think he'll talk to me."

"Why?"

"Because he may remember me. When I was a kid, he used to hang out at the Beer Chaser. I'd be up there with Uncle Ed while Grandma Lucille was running errands, and sometimes we'd interact. The last time I saw him, we played the Pac-Man game, and when I was just a little kid, he taught me a few pool tips. Uncle Ed told me once that Jay was one of the best pool players he'd ever played."

Ray's eyebrows went up. He'd played a thousand games of pool in his basement with Levi and Ed. Levi was an average player, and they were fairly evenly matched. But Ray had never managed to beat Ed—had come close only once. He couldn't imagine Ed conceding there was somebody at least as good as he was.

"But was he crazy back then?" Ray asked.

"He was always a little . . ." Levi searched for the right word. "Strange? Maybe touched in the head?" Levi shrugged. "He always has been, but I'm not too concerned about Jay Snider, and I'm not exactly going alone." He touched his sidearm. "I've got Mr. Webley with me."

Ray hesitated. Then he popped the car into gear and did a u-turn back towards Twin Rivers.

"You're not mad, are you?" Levi asked, looking at Ray's tight mouth.

Ray shook his head. "No. You're absolutely right. I was letting my ego get in the way of the investigation. When I talk to Pete Long next time, I want to be ready for him. I'll drop you off at the police department and head over to question Selena. You go find Jay Snider. Call me if you have any problems."

"Agreed."

Chapter 11

It took Levi an hour to find the house on one of the many winding lanes along the Calloway River. He'd actually driven by it twice before he saw it since only the top of the roof could be seen. The little house hugged the edge of the hillside, and a small yard flatten out in front of it before the ground gave way to a cliff that fell down towards the Calloway River. As Levi drove down the impossibly steep driveway towards the garage well below him, he had concerns about his brakes. If they went out as he descended that hill, the cruiser would overshoot the end of the driveway and plunge off the edge of the cliff to the river below.

Levi pulled to a careful stop beside Jay's Jeep in front of the garage door. After climbing out of the cruiser, he looked back up the hill and tried to imagine it with a layer of winter snow on it. Trying to climb that hill on a good day would be no small task. Getting down it when it was covered in snow and ice would be potentially deadly. He walked to the edge of the cliff at the end of the driveway. The river frothed around jagged boulders far below.

Turning around, he examined the house, which wasn't what he'd expected. Knowing Jay Snider's reputation, he'd expected a dilapidated shack looking much like the way Ray had described Selena's house, which was not more than a mile away. But Jay's small house was meticulously maintained. With a coat of dark brown paint, it resembled a forest ranger station. The lawn was neatly landscaped, and planters on each side of the sidewalk contained the remains of last fall's mums. There were ricks of firewood neatly stacked along the side of the garage and fresh gravel on the driveway. Sunlight filtered through the bare branches of the trees that canopied Jay's property, dappling the ground with gold.

As Levi walked towards the house, he admired the view. From his house at the top of the bluff, Jay had a stunning view of the river for nearly a mile in either direction. Levi could actually see himself living in a beautiful, peaceful place like this.

At the front door, Levi smiled when he read the hand-lettered sign hanging there. "Knock loud. Trespassers routinely shot."

Levi laughed at Jay's humor. It didn't say "trespassers will be shot." Obviously, dealing with trespassers was something that happened all the time—*routinely*.

Levi banged on the door. There was no answer. He banged again, loudly, as the sign suggested. He waited. No reply.

Unless Jay had more than one vehicle, he must be around somewhere. His Jeep was in the driveway. Levi walked to the garage, which was perched near the edge of the drop-off, and peeked in the windows of the entry door. What he saw surprised him. The inside was bathed in natural light. There were two large skylights in the garage roof, and the far wall of the garage had been fitted out in floor-to-ceiling windows, offering a stunning view of the river and the far banks. It looked like a workshop of some kind with an old-fashioned woodstove in the corner.

Levi banged on the door of the garage. When he didn't hear a reply, he tried the knob. The door was unlocked. Opening it, he stepped inside.

"Jay?" he called as he glanced around.

Nobody was there, but an easel in front of the wall of windows caught his eye. It was covered in a cloth, but curiosity got the better of him. When he pulled back the cloth, he stepped back and smiled broadly. Jay paints, Levi thought, and extremely well.

Levi was staring at the painting when a shadow from the doorway fell across him. He started to turn but froze when he heard the unmistakable sound of a double-barrel shotgun being snapped closed.

"What do you want, Ben?" the angry voice behind him said.

Slowly, Levi raised his hands.

Chapter 12

"Selena?" Ray said gently.

She didn't stir. Ray pulled one of the chairs in the hospital room up next to the bed. He wasn't going to wake her. He'd wait.

She had oxygen tubes under her nose, and there were a number of meds being given to her through IVs. The doctor said her condition was stable for the moment, but she had a rocky road in front of her. He couldn't elaborate, he said. Ray figured he was referring to the problems she'd have as the medical team weaned her off the drugs she'd been taking most likely for decades.

Ray could hardly believe Selena was in her forties. Her skin was sallow, her cheeks sunken, her hair streaked with dingy gray. Her lips were dry and cracked, and she had sores at both corners of her mouth. Her body was painfully thin—her breasts barely raising the white sheet that covered her. Ray struggled to see any resemblance between this woman and the beautiful woman on the front of the movie boxes he'd found. In fact, he still wasn't sure she was that beautiful woman.

What if I've got this wrong, he thought as he watched her shallow breathing and her twitching face, uneasy in sleep. As he stared at the tubes and the monitors attached to her broken body, his curiosity got the better of him. He knew how he could find out if this person was actually Selena Fine.

One of her hands was visible, but the other was beneath the sheet. After thinking for several minutes, he finally decided to dare a peek. Slowly, he raised the sheet, just enough to see her hand.

Her eyes snapped open. Ray jumped back.

"What do you want?" she snapped, regarding him with her dark-blue eyes.

Ray said nothing.

"Who are you, and what are you doing in my room?" she said with the deep, raspy voice of a heavy smoker.

"I'm Ray Billings," he stuttered. "I'm the chief of police in Twin Rivers. I wanted to ask you some questions if I could—about your husband."

"I've got nothing to say to you," Selena said, glaring at him.

"I'm just trying to figure out what's going on," Ray said.

"Nothing is going on," she said.

"I found your husband," Ray said.

Selena said nothing. She closed her eyes, obviously ignoring him. When the door behind Ray opened, Selena opened her eyes. Then she smiled briefly.

"Hello, Selena," Ben Walker said, looking at her without acknowledging Ray's presence.

He was wearing a hospital robe. His color was off, and he had dark circles under his eyes. Ray thought he looked too weak to be out of bed.

"Thought I'd come by and see how you're doing," he said as he very carefully sat down in the chair on the other side of the bed, wincing as he did so.

Selena looked at him for a long moment. "You look familiar."

"You don't remember me?" Ben asked. "I was the officer who came to your house when you called about your missing husband."

Recognition registered in her eyes.

"You want some water?" he asked as he reached for the pitcher on her table and poured water into a cup.

She nodded. Ben leaned forward with the cup so she could sip the water through a straw. As she drank, she brought her other hand out from under the sheet to hold the cup with both. There was a small faded heart tattoo between her thumb and first finger.

Ray's face fell. He'd hoped it wasn't there.

"Better?" Ben asked.

She nodded as he took the cup and placed it on her bed tray.

"You let me know if you want some more," he said gently.

"Is Jay okay?" she asked Ben. "He always shows up with my groceries."

Ray leaned back in his chair and nodded at Ben. It looked like Ben would be doing the job Ray had come to do.

"He's fine," Ben said, "but I thought your husband was missing. You were a little confused, I think."

Selena looked at him. "Confused? That's a nice way of putting it."

"Jay was in jail," Ben said. "That's why he was late. I'd arrested him the evening before. Actually, I arrested him because he was in an argument with your husband, Pete. He's been released. He wasn't charged with anything very serious."

"Oh, good."

"Would you answer a question for me, Selena?"

Selena shrugged.

"When I asked if you had a phone, you said no, but you called us. How did you call us?"

Selena frowned as she thought about the question. Then she shook her head.

"We were in your kitchen, having coffee. I asked you about your phone. The one on the wall was dead."

"Oh," Selena said, her eyes lighting up. "I remember now. I don't have a house phone—haven't had for years. But I have a cell phone Jay gave me. It's got only a few numbers in it. Don't think I ever used it before. Almost forgot I had it until he didn't show up. He had it on a charger on top of the television—in case of an emergency."

Ray cleared his throat and looked at Ben intently. Ben figured that he knew what Ray wanted to know.

"When was the last time you saw your husband?" Ben asked.

"I know where you're going with this," Selena said. "I'm not answering any questions about Pete."

"Selena," Ray said gently. "I know about your past. And I know Pete played a big part in taking you down that path when you were too young to know any better."

"You think I'm a victim, huh?" Selena said, looking at Ray sharply. Her blue eyes flashed angrily. "You don't think I knew what I was doing?"

"I didn't say that—" Ray started to say.

"I knew what I was doing. And the drugs are my doing, not Pete's. Pete hates drugs and drug users. But he has a huge heart, and he still loves me. He opened a lot of doors for me, and I managed to slam most of them closed. Most men would've tossed me to the curb but not Pete. I've got nothing bad to say about Pete."

"Maybe there was another reason besides love," Ray suggested. "Maybe he takes care of you for another reason—something you saw or know about him."

"You can leave now," Selena snapped.

"We're just trying to help you, Selena," Ben said softly. "You could do so much more with your life."

Selena laughed—a mirthless sound—then fell into a fit of coughing.

"What's so funny?" Ben asked.

"Talk to my doctor," Selena said. "We had a long talk this morning. I've missed my chance. We're into the final countdown. I'm dying."

Both men looked away. Ray studied his hands while Ben stared through the windows.

"He said I have weeks, not months," Selena continued. "I'm not that upset, to tell you the truth. I lost interest in living a long, long time ago." She closed her eyes. "Now please, I want to be alone."

"Let's go, Ray," Ben said gently as he stood, but Ray sat stubbornly in his chair.

"I'm not done asking questions," Ray said. "I want to know more about your husband."

"Get out!" Selena said.

"Ray," Ben said from the doorway.

Ray sat for a long moment. Then rising suddenly, he flashed an angry look at Ben and pushed past him. He stormed down the hall towards the elevator without saying another word.

Chapter 13

"I'm not Ben Walker," Levi said, his hands over his head.

He could see Jay's shadow on the floor beside him—and the shadow of the shotgun pointed at his back.

"Then who are you, cop, and what are you doing in my studio?" Jay said angrily. "I haven't done anything wrong. You have no right to be here."

"I'm Levi Garvey," he replied. "Do you remember me, Jay?"

"Levi?" he said to himself. "Levi Garvey?"

"Yes!"

"Well, turn around," Jay said.

"Put down the shotgun."

"It's down."

"No, it's not," Levi said, pointing down. "I can see your shadow on the floor."

There was a moment of silence. Then, to Levi's relief, he saw the shadow of the barrel move to the ceiling. Levi turned around tentatively. It took a moment before Jay smiled in recognition.

"You are Levi Garvey. Why are you dressed up like a cop?"

"I *am* a cop! What in the hell is wrong with you, Jay?" Levi said, looking him over for the first time in more than thirty years.

Even after all those years, Jay didn't look that much different. Levi would've recognized him immediately. The brown hair he remembered was now gray, and there were deep lines around the eyes. But even at what—sixty?—he was the same man Levi remembered.

"It's not loaded," Jay said, glancing at the shotgun that was now pointed at the ceiling.

He pulled the trigger. It clicked dry.

"Give me that," Levi snapped as he snatched the shotgun out of Jay's hand.

Levi quickly examined it, then placed it on a bench along the wall with a clunk.

"Scared the shit out of you, didn't I?" Jay cackled. "I thought you were Ben. I wouldn't have hurt him either. Just wanted to scare the crap out of him."

"I think that would've worked," Levi said, trying not to smile and failing. "It's been a few years. How have you been, Jay?"

"They say I'm crazy," Jay said. "But that's the way God made me."

Levi pointed at the easel and said, "I like this. I didn't know you painted."

The painting depicted Main Street in Twin Rivers as it had appeared in the mid-70s if you were standing under the Comet Theatre marquee looking up the street towards Harv's Grill. The top edge of the painting showed the under side of the marquee. The main focus of the painting was the street beyond it. The detail was remarkable. The painting was so perfect it looked almost like a photograph, and it matched Levi's own memory of what the street had looked like when he was a boy.

"Did you use an old photo to paint this?" Levi asked. "I think that old Ford pickup in front of Harv's was Uncle Ed's."

Jay smiled softly as he rubbed the side of his head. "It was. If you look closely, it's his license plate number on the bumper."

"I don't remember what his plate number was back then," Levi said, "but I remember that truck very well."

"He probably doesn't remember his plate number either, but I do," Jay said.

"Where's the photo?" Levi said, looking around the easel.

Jay tapped the side of his head. "There's no photo. It's in here."

"What do you mean?" Levi said.

"Last time I saw you was about 1981," Jay said. "You were thirteen years old, playing the brand new Pac-Man game at the Beer Chaser. You were wearing a new pair of red Nike tennis shoes with a white swoosh and a black *Star Wars: Empire Strikes Back* t-shirt. Your pants were a little short because you'd grown over that summer, and you had on a leather belt with an acorn pattern stamped into it. Oh, and you also had an oversized leather wallet on a chain and a *Dukes of Hazzard* belt buckle."

Levi's face fell. He had no idea if what Jay had described was correct or not, but he figured it was since it sure sounded like his wardrobe when he'd first entered high school.

"I don't understand, Jay."

Jay tapped his head again. "It's either a gift or a curse. I have a photographic memory. I could paint you the last time I saw you at the Beer Chaser perfectly, right down to your haircut and the green plastic digital watch on your wrist. Not only you but the wall you were standing in front of, the pictures on that wall, the pattern of the tile on the floor including the cigarette burns in it, and the fact your left shoe was untied. You had band aids on three knuckles—probably from working on that old Ford pickup you and Ed were restoring at the time. That's kind of what I do now. I paint things I remember exactly as they were."

Levi looked at the painting again. "It's beautiful."

Jay shrugged. "For me, it's not really art although a few think it is. It's like I'm writing something down I've memorized. But I like painting."

"So you never forget anything?"

Jay laughed. "That's not completely correct. I don't forget anything I've seen, but I can't remember conversations very well. I don't remember how movies I've seen end, but I never forget a single detail about a scene. I have trouble with real time—I don't seem to have a concept of time like most people do. But I don't have trouble remembering the exactly date I saw that scene in the painting on that easel because I saw a calendar that day. It was June 5th, 1975. I've never forgotten anything from about first grade on. And I not only remember it. I can also paint it in detail. But it comes at a price."

"What's that?"

"Perhaps it's schizophrenia. Or maybe dementia," Jay said off-handedly. "I'm not so crazy I don't know I'm crazy. I don't know exactly what kind of crazy I am, but it's getting worse, I think. My head is too full of details, and maybe I'm running out of storage space. You know what I mean?"

"I think so," Levi said.

"That's why I live out here, and I don't go to town much. I like to stay where the pictures don't change very much from day to day. I don't own a calendar. And I certainly don't own a television any more or read books—that takes up a lot of storage space. If you asked me to paint page 223 of Stephen King's novel *The Stand* that I read twenty years ago, I could literally paint every word on that page. Other than once a week to buy groceries in Olton, I stay here. And I don't go into Twin Rivers very often because every time I do, I wind up getting arrested because I make people uncomfortable, and I can't seem to behave myself anymore."

"People think you're on drugs," Levi said.

"Maybe the problem is I'm not on drugs," Jay remarked, rubbing the side of his head as if he were getting a headache. "I've never used drugs, Levi. Not once in my life. And I don't drink anymore either. It's hard enough living with this without altering my state of mind."

"Can I ask you a few questions, Jay?"

"Make it fast," Jay said, rubbing his head again. "I'm getting one of my headaches. Too many new pictures the last couple of days."

"You were arrested the other night after arguing with Pete Long," Levi said. "We know about Selena. What were you fighting with Pete about?"

"Pete's a scumbag in a fancy suit. I've been seeing after Selena for . . . well, it's that time thing again. I'm no good with time. Maybe ten or fifteen years?" Jay stopped to think for a minute. "It was August 11th, 1997, when I started looking after her. I wrote a check that day at the grocery store—I could paint it for you if you like. Anyway, I take her groceries and cash every Wednesday. Then I go by Pete's house. I rarely see him. I have a remote for his garage door, and he leaves two envelopes on a workbench. One is cash for Selena, and the other is cash for me to pay for the services I provide and the groceries. Then I drop her groceries off and make sure she's okay. That's the arrangement."

"Where does she get her drugs?" Levi asked.

Jay sighed. "It's not me. I'd never provide her drugs. Early on, she asked me to do just that, and I refused. But I've seen a red Dodge Ram around a few times. There's a big machine shed up the lane from her. You might want to have a look at that. I'd be willing to bet that not long after I leave, there's another visitor that pays a call on Wednesdays."

Levi nodded. "What were you and Pete fighting about?"

"Couple of things," Jay said. "Selena's house is a disaster. I thought Pete should either fix it up or find someplace better for her to live. I've done what I can. I've fixed her old furnace a few times, and I boarded over the broken window in the kitchen that a branch smashed during a storm last year. But the roof leaks badly, the plumbing is a mess, and one of these days, that old wiring is going to short out and burn that house down with her in it. Last week, I waited for him at Olton Lake. When he showed up at his house finally, I talked to him. He wasn't very open to my suggestion. He told me to mind my own business. We argued, and he told me to leave."

"I heard different," Levi said. "I heard the argument was about money—a loan."

"That was months ago," Jay said, shaking his head as he thought about it. "Actually, that was nearly two years ago, on October 5th. I've got a cousin who lives in Peoria. She comes to see me about once a year. She thinks my art is amazing. She wanted to open a gallery that would feature my work and work of other Illinois artists. She's an artist herself—photography. I'm not exactly wealthy, so I talked to Pete about financing it. He said no. It wasn't a loan for me as much as it was a chance for her to start a business. I was pissed about it at the time, but that was a long time ago."

"How do you make a living?" Levi asked.

"My parents were fairly well off," Jay said. "Mom left me this house when she passed in 1980. It was our summer escape when I was a kid. My parents owned some farm ground, and I live on the cash rent. It's enough income to keep the bills paid and a little extra for a new vehicle when I need one and improvements to the house and my studio. I live pretty cheap."

"How do you know Pete?"

"I met him back in the late 70s when he was just beginning. I worked as a bouncer at his strip club in Peoria before my head was so full. That's where I met Selena later."

"So you know about the porn?"

"Sure," Jay said. "Like I said, Pete is a scumbag. Those girls in his clubs have been lining his pockets for years. There are the clubs. There are the side businesses—"

"Like prostitution?"

Jay shrugged. It wasn't a denial.

"Then there's the porn," Levi said.

"That's where the real money is. Pete's made a fortune."

"Did you know Selena was only fifteen when she was in her first porn movie?"

"Not at the time," Jay said. "Nobody knew that until later. Why do you think Pete married her?"

"What do you mean?"

"You can't testify against your husband," Jay said, smiling tightly. "Like I said, a real scumbag. He never loved Selena. She probably still doesn't know that. He married her at the time to protect himself, and he never divorced her because he's a greedy bastard."

"So that's why he's taken care of her all these years?"

Jay shook his head. "That's part of it. But unlike most of his starlets, she lived with him for probably fifteen years. I'll bet there's a lot she saw. I think that's what makes Peter Long nervous."

"You know what I don't understand?" Levi said. "Let's say he stayed married to her and has taken care of her because he's greedy. Or maybe it was something she'd seen or knows about him. Why not kill her? It would be easy—right? Just send her an envelope with a couple thousand dollars in it."

"That's a nasty thing to say," Jay said sharply.

"It's true. She might not overdose the first time. He might have to do it a couple of times, but eventually, that's what would happen, right?"

Jay nodded. "That's right—she's an addict. She'll use as much as she can get her hands on."

"So why wouldn't he do that?"

Jay thought for a moment. "Pete's a scumbag, but I can't see him ever doing that. He's taken miserable care of her, but he's a scoundrel with scruples. I just don't think that's a line he'd ever cross."

"You said maybe he took care of her because of the things she might know about him or the things she'd seen when they were together. Like what?"

"It would be a bad idea for me to tell you what I think, and it would be a bad idea for you to go poking into Pete Long's business."

"Why?" Levi pressed.

Jay rubbed the side of his head and closed his eyes. "Let's just say there are a lot of ways to make money in flesh. There are strip clubs and the prostitution that goes along with them. Then there are the porn movies. He made a lot of money in the 80s when porn came out of the closet and became mainstream. And there are lots of ways to make money in the porn industry that don't involve selling movies. Pete Long is an expert in maximizing his profits."

"I'm not following," Levi said.

"Let me give you a little advice. Don't screw with Peter Long. You'll open a can of worms you'll wish you hadn't. Believe me. Pete can be very dangerous, and he's got certain associates—"

"Like the mob?"

Jay cackled at that. "Sure, you don't do business in clubs and prostitution without having to deal with the mob on at least some level, but that's not exactly who I'm talking about."

Levi was growing frustrated. Jay had begun to evade his questions.

"Did you know what was going on at that machine shed up the lane from Selena's house?"

Jay thought for a minute. "I suspected there was something illegal going on there."

"What did you think it was?" Levi pressed.

"I'm guessing there's a big-time meth lab in operation," Jay said flatly. "Am I right?"

"You're damned close," Levi admitted. "Was Pete Long involved?"

"No," Jay said firmly. "Pete didn't dabble in the drug trade in any way, other than getting women he wanted to exploit addicted."

"Did he get Selena addicted?"

Jay laughed. "Of course, he did. You know that as well as I do. That's why you're here. That's how that business works, unfortunately. Exploitation of young drug addicted girls is the mortar and brick of the porn industry. And that's why I got out of Pete Long's employment long ago. I didn't want to see it anymore.

"Look, Levi, I'm not feeling well. These headaches come on fast— usually take me down for a couple of days or more. This is a bad one coming. Anything else?"

"I think you're lying to me," Levi said.

"About what?"

"You know more than you're saying," Levi said, walking over to the painting on the easel and looking at it again.

"You're exactly right," Jay said, "but I haven't lied to you."

"Even so, you haven't explained why you went to Harv's Grill to confront Pete Long. There's more there."

"There is, but please, Levi, leave it alone."

"I just can't get over the coincidence," Levi said, pushing his trooper hat back from his forehead with one finger. "I bought some donuts at Harv's this morning. The town is buzzing as you can imagine."

"Sure," Jay said with a smile.

"It's been twenty years since Harv and April kicked you out of the diner, and they haven't seen you there since. Then all of a sudden, you show up out of the blue and confront a man almost nobody in town knows. Do you know how rare it is that a stranger eats dinner at Harv's?"

"Probably not as rare now as it was before Twin Rivers had a celebrated author as a resident."

Levi disregarded the remark. "You were angry with Pete about something, and you haven't told me the truth about it. But you knew where he'd be. What was he really doing in Twin Rivers?"

"You've no idea what you're getting into," Jay warned. "If you dig into this too far, a lot of people are going to get hurt. I've given you the only hint I'm going to."

Levi looked at him blankly. He didn't remember being given a hint.

"You didn't give me a hint."

"Oh, yes, I did," Jay shot back. "I said more than I should've."

"Remind me," Levi said.

Jay shook his head.

"Remind me, and I'll walk out of that door. The next time you see me, I'll be here to buy one of your paintings."

"You pick the one you want. There's no charge," Jay said, waving his hand towards the canvases leaning against the far wall of the studio. "I don't sell paintings. I just paint them."

"Please, Jay," Levi implored.

"Okay. Like I said before, there are a lot of ways to make money in porn besides selling porn movies," Jay repeated.

"That's not much of a hint," Levi said.

"That's all I've got for you," Jay said. "I know you're not going to give up on this, but I sure wish you would. When you learn the truth, you won't be able to undo the damage, and you'll regret it. You're going to hurt people that don't deserve to be hurt again."

Levi nodded. He thought he understood what Jay was saying. He picked up the shotgun from the workbench and tossed it to Jay. Levi walked past him, as promised, and headed towards the cruiser.

As Levi turned the cruiser around in front of the garage, minding closely the edge of the cliff, he saw Jay watching him from the yard. It seemed to Levi like there was something he wanted to say.

Levi rolled the window down. "Something else?"

"Just a comment," Jay said.

"Say it," Levi said impatiently.

Jay walked to the window and leaned on the cruiser.

"Alan Haig used to wear a hat just like that flat-brimmed trooper hat you're wearing and Ben wears and Chief Billings wears," Jay remarked. "I don't know how many times Alan arrested me and Chief Doug Malone and before that Chief Craig. I think you killed Alan Haig in your living room, didn't you?"

Levi nodded. It was something he tried not to think about since he'd written the whole ugly story in *The Devil Within*.

"Maybe it's time the Twin Rivers Police Department bought new uniforms. There are mostly bad pictures I have of those uniforms," Jay said, tapping the side of his head. "And I'll bet I'm not alone in that feeling. I'll bet the German police don't wear Gestapo uniforms today."

Jay had made a good point.

"I may be back," Levi said. "There's a picture that I'm sure is in your head that I'd like you to paint for me one day."

"I bet I know which one," Jay said as he stepped back from the car. "I'll see you, Levi Garvey."

"You're not crazy, Jay," Levi said suddenly.

Jay cackled. "You caught me on a good day. You might change your opinion about that the next time you see me away from my little retreat here. I do tend to be a little more nuts when I venture from this familiar place and am buffeted by so many new pictures."

Levi nodded as he put the cruiser into gear and looked at the steep hill he had to climb up from Jay's house to the road above. He swallowed hard. It looked like an impossible climb. He knew Old Blue could never make it up that driveway.

"Just take a run at it, and try to keep the same speed going up," Jay called. "Don't let your tires spin, or you're done."

Levi revved the engine and took off on the short runway of flat ground before the steep hill started. When he started up the hill, the angle seemed impossible. As he climbed, gravity started slowing the car, so he gave it a little more gas, taking Jay's advice about maintaining his speed on the ascent. He was nearly at the top when he gunned the gas a little too heavily. His tires spun—he heard loose gravel pinging against the underside of the car. Sweat popped out on his forehead as the car slowed almost to a stop, but the momentum took him the last few yards onto the main road.

He stopped and wiped the sweat off his face with his arm. Then he climbed out of the car and looked down the narrow driveway. There were two deep ruts where his tires had spun. Jay was below, waving at him.

"Not bad, Garvey," he shouted.

"Next time, I'm walking down," Levi shouted back.

"Most people do, or they take the other driveway," he said, pointing to the other side of the property. "That's the one I use!"

Levi hadn't noticed that the driveway continued past the garage. From where he was standing above, he could see a nice flat driveway that led out to the main road. Jay's mailbox was at the end of that one.

"Thanks for pointing that out to me," Levi shouted down, the sarcastic tone very clear.

All he heard was Jay laughing as he walked towards his house.

No, he's not crazy, Levi thought. With a grin, he climbed back into the cruiser.

Chapter 14

When Levi walked into the police station, Amber looked up at him. It was clear that something was wrong. She nodded towards Ray's office. The door was closed, and the blinds on the window shut.

At the door, Levi paused, glancing back at Amber. She nodded again.

Levi opened the door. It was dark in the office, except for the green-shaded lamp on his desk. Ray had drawn the blinds on the windows to the street as well. His feet were up on his desk. He was leaning back in his chair with a coffee mug in his hand. The level of liquor in Doug Malone's bottle of Wild Turkey was well below where it had been the night before.

Levi closed the door behind him, sat down across from Ray, and put his feet up on the desk.

"You want something?" Ray said angrily.

"Nope," Levi replied.

Ray took his feet down from the desk and poured more Wild Turkey into his coffee mug. His eyes never left Levi.

"Something you want to say?" Ray said, putting his feet back up on the desk.

"Nope."

"You talked to Ben Walker, didn't you?"

"No, I haven't. You mad at me for some reason?"

Ray sighed and took a sip from his coffee mug. He shook his head.

"You want to tell me what's going on with you?"

"No, I don't."

"Okay," Levi said as he stood up. "If you need me, I'll be across the street getting a cheeseburger at Harv's. I thought you might like to go with me, but it's pretty obvious you're drinking your lunch."

When Levi opened the office door, Ray said, "Wait."

Levi hesitated.

"Close the door," Ray said.

Levi closed it, sat back down, and waited for Ray to say something. He'd known Ray for nearly fifteen years. They'd been best friends for all of them. He knew Ray wasn't a talker.

"Did you want something?" Levi said after the silence got long.

Ray glanced up at him but said nothing.

"Was there something you wanted to say?" Levi said as he tried not to smile.

It seemed like the questions were now reversed from when he'd first walked in.

Ray set the mug down on the desk and pushed it away. Sighing, he leaned on his elbows on the desk and rubbed the back of his neck.

"Something has got to you about this deal with Selena, but I'm not seeing any crime here. The only crime is that pot shed, and the DEA is working that case," Levi remarked. "What are we doing exactly?"

"We're going to bust Pete Long," Ray said.

"For what exactly?" Levi asked. "From what I can tell, he hasn't done anything we can bust him for. I'm sure he's done something at one time or another, but our evidence so far is that he took care of his wife who has a huge drug problem. Maybe he did something to get her hooked, maybe he helped her get drugs, but right now, the call to Selena's house was nothing more than a medical call."

"And Selena's not going to talk," Ray said.

Taking off his flat-brimmed trooper hat, Levi said, "So we've got less than nothing."

Ray rubbed his head. "Guys like Pete Long shouldn't be walking the streets."

"I agree. He's a parasite, but it's perfectly legal to be a scumbag. Selena was underage when she went into porn. That much we know, but what's the statute of limitations on that? And is it possible that Pete Long really didn't know? That's what Jay Snider told me."

"There's something else going on," Ray said. "Pete Long in town, Jay Snider fighting with him. My gut is telling me there is something there."

"It's like you're trying to pick a fight," Levi said.

"Maybe I am."

"I'm getting a little worried about you. I've known you a long time, and you've never acted like this before."

Ray glanced up at him. Neither spoke for a while.

"I have a lot going on at home," Ray said, breaking the silence. "Maybe that's why I've been divorced so many times. I just can't deal with drama. I wish she'd go. It's making me nuts."

"If it's not working, it's not working," Levi said. "I'm an expert at trying to get women to move out of my house. Surely you remember that. You want some help?"

"I'll work it out," Ray said, pushing the coffee mug away.

"Let us know if there's anything we can do," Levi remarked.

"Just don't change your locks. I might be needing that basement room a lot more coming up."

Levi laughed.

Chapter 15

Nurse Juli Adkins was thirty minutes away from coming off a particularly difficult double shift at St. Anne's Hospital. She was sitting at the nurses' station, filling out paperwork when Heather Graham returned from checking on patients.

"Everything quiet?" she asked as Heather sat in the chair beside her.

"Thankfully, yes."

Heather had pulled a double shift, too. They were both scheduled off for the next two days.

"You doing anything fun on your days off, Juli?"

"I'm going to sleep. I might sleep two full days. What a week!"

They both glanced up as the elevator bell chimed. An elderly man climbed off with two bouquets of flowers in his arms. He sauntered up to the counter slowly, checking the cards stuck in amongst the flowers. Neither nurse recognized this delivery man.

"I've got flowers for Selena Long, room 312," he said in a soft voice, "and for Ben Walker in 330."

"Just leave them," Heather said. "I'll take them down later."

"You two looked wiped out," he commented as he set the bouquets on the counter.

"We're both about half an hour away from being off a double shift," Juli said with a smile.

"I can take them down," he said. "That's what I usually do. I don't mind."

"Go ahead," Heather said. "My feet are dead."

He smiled, picked up the flowers, and headed up the hallway.

"I'm thinking we went into the wrong line of work," Heather remarked, picking up a conversation they had often.

"Don't start again," Juli said, raising a finger. "I'm too tired to argue with you."

"You'd better get used to double shifts, no raises, fewer doctors, and fewer insured patients," Heather said. "Look at Dr. Jackson. He's going to retire one day soon, and who replaces him? I mean, seriously, how is the hospital going to pay us when the insurance companies are gone? Medicaid is two years behind reimbursing the hospital, and Medicare doesn't even cover the cost of treatment."

"What do you want me to say?" Juli asked.

"That you voted wrong," she said.

"Maybe."

Juli sighed because the truth was she was already seeing glimpses of the future.

"Ha!" Heather laughed as she clapped her hands. It was the first time she'd goaded Juli into admitting it. "I'm getting out, Juli. I'm giving my notice next week. I'm going back to school. I need to get into something that has a future."

"Really?" Juli said, looking at her young co-worker in surprise.

It was getting harder and harder to find RN's, especially good ones like Heather. But she couldn't blame her. If she were Heather's age and had less time in, she'd do the same thing.

Suddenly, a shrill alarm went off. Juli snapped to attention and checked the monitor. Code Blue.

Heather was already on her feet, racing up the hallway, as Juli picked up the phone and hit the intercom button.

"Code Blue, Code Blue," she said. "Room 312. All emergency personnel, please respond."

The hallway was suddenly filled with people as the crash cart rolled up the hallway. Juli rushed to join them. Dr. Jackson stepped out of the doctors' lounge and stopped her.

"Who's in 312?" he asked.

"Selena Long," Juli said as they dashed up the hallway together.

"I was just in there ten minutes ago," Dr. Jackson said. "She was sleeping comfortably."

Nobody noticed the old man who was walking in the opposite direction. He'd been pressed against the wall as the emergency response team rushed the cart past him towards room 312.

Dr. Jackson stopped in the doorway to room 312. The crash cart was in the way, blocking his entrance.

"Get this thing out of the way," he shouted angrily.

"She's dead," one of the interns said.

"What do you mean she's dead?" he snapped. "We haven't even tried any resuscitation."

"No need," the intern replied as he pushed the crash cart back into the hallway.

Once they were clear of the doorway, Dr. Jackson rushed into the hospital room. Suddenly, he understood. Selena Long had been shot in the forehead at close range with a small caliber handgun. The entry wound looked like a smudge of raspberry jam on her forehead, but the pillow under her head was stained bright red with her blood. Another pillow was lying on her chest with a black burn mark on it. A bouquet of bright yellow daisies sat nearby on her tray table.

"Lock down the hospital," Dr. Jackson snapped.

Juli turned and ran down the hallway towards the nurses' station. As she reached for the phone, the elevator chimed. She glanced up just in time to see the elevator doors open. The old man, holding only one bouquet, stepped inside. Then turning, he looked at Juli, smiled sweetly, and gave her a little salute as the doors closed slowly.

Instantly, she knew. She grabbed the phone to call security.

"Lock the building down!" she shouted into the phone. "Don't let anybody leave the building! Stop the old man coming down in the west elevator. He's wearing a dark plaid shirt and a red baseball cap."

Suddenly, another alarm went off—Room 330.

"Ben Walker," she gasped. It was too much of a coincidence.

Her voice boomed across the intercom. "Code Blue, Code Blue. Room 330!"

As she ran up the hallway, Dr. Jackson stepped out of room 312. "What now?"

"Ben Walker," Juli said as she brushed past him. "I have a bad feeling about this."

Chapter 16

Ray and Levi were still talking in the office when the door banged open. Amber was standing in the doorway. Her face was drawn tight, and her eyes were wide.

"What is it?" Levi said.

"They just called and . . ." she said.

Shaking visibly, she was having a hard time spitting it out.

"Take a breath, Amber," Ray snapped, rising from his desk. "What's wrong?"

His sharp tone helped her find her voice.

"Selena Long is dead," Amber said.

Ray sighed. He hadn't yet had a chance to tell Levi that Selena wasn't long for this world.

"When did she die?" Ray asked.

"No," Amber said emphatically. "You've got it wrong. She didn't die on her own. She was murdered in her hospital room."

Levi was suddenly on his feet. "When?"

"About twenty minutes ago," Amber said. "Sheriff Harby just called. They locked down the hospital. They believe she was murdered by an old man delivering flowers. The sheriff wants you over there right now, Chief."

"Did they catch the old man?" Levi asked.

Amber shook her head. "He went down on the elevator, and they were waiting for him on the first floor. But, when the door opened, the elevator was empty."

"Classic diversion," Ray said.

Ray and Levi exchanged glances. They were both thinking the same thing.

"It was a hit," Ray said.

"And a very well-planned one," Levi said.

"And we both know who planned it," Ray growled.

Levi nodded. "You may get a chance at Peter Long after all."

"Let's be smart about this," Ray said, putting on his hat. "As I suspected, there's a lot more going on here than we know. Let's keep our eyes open. Let's work the case this time instead of letting the case work us."

Ray didn't need to say it. The memory of their last case, tracking down a bank robber, was still fresh in Levi's mind. They'd blundered through that one, missing obvious clues and failing to see that the bank robber was right there in their midst the entire time. And Chief Craig, the missing bank robber from the forty-year-old crime, had done a fine job misdirecting them. Those mistakes had very nearly cost them all their lives. They wouldn't make those same mistakes again this time.

"Looks like we've stumbled into another murder case," Levi said.

"We have an advantage this time," Ray said. "We've got a suspect."

"I think I'd better drive," Levi said.

Ray nodded. "Probably a good idea."

"And Amber?" Levi said.

"Yeah?" she said, looking at him with her dark-brown eyes.

"Pour out the rest of that bottle after we leave," he said.

Amber glanced at Ray, who nodded in agreement.

After they left, Amber screwed the cap back on the bottle. As she started out of the chief's office, she noticed his coffee mug, which still had a couple of fingers of bourbon in it. Glancing at the door, she picked up the mug and sniffed it. Then glancing at the door again to make sure Levi and the chief were gone, she quickly gulped the drink which burned all the way down, turning her face red and stealing her breath.

"Wow," she croaked as tears filled her eyes.

Half coughing, half choking, she pounded her chest with her fist as the fire in her throat subsided and the heat in her stomach bloomed. Then she picked up the bottle, left the chief's office, and walked to the small sink beside the microwave, where she poured the bourbon down the drain—hoping the smell wouldn't linger for long.

Chapter 17

"Here's what I don't get," Sheriff William "Billy Bob" Harby said as they sat down in an empty waiting room on the third floor of St. Anne's Hospital.

Short, round, and balding, he looked more like an accountant than the sheriff of River County. His uniform seemed to fit too tightly around his fat neck. He was constantly pulling at his collar and adjusting his tie as if he weren't used to wearing one. He wore dark-framed glasses, but, more often than not, they were hanging out of the corner of his mouth, the ear pieces well chewed.

"Why go to the effort of murdering someone who has only a few weeks to live?" Harby asked for probably the tenth time since Ray and Levi had arrived.

Dr. Jackson sat down at a small table usually reserved for the volunteer who answered the phone. He sipped at a cup of coffee. His hair was snow white and clipped short. He wore a pair of wire-rimmed glasses on the end of his nose. He'd practiced medicine in Calloway, his hometown, since 1975 when he was fresh out of medical school. He knew all the men in the room well—and had put stitches in most of them at one time or another. That list of patients included Chief Ray Billings. The doctor had stitched his hand after an accident with a locksmith's lock smasher and his head after a fall down the stairs. Then there was Levi Garvey. He couldn't remember all the stitches, broken bones, sprains, and bruises he'd tended to over the years—not to mention the nine-millimeter slug he'd taken out of Levi's shoulder a few years ago.

"Dr. Jackson, you haven't said much," Ray said. "You have anything to add to this discussion?"

"I don't think Selena had even a few weeks left. Decades of drug addiction, chain smoking, and poor nutrition—the cancer would've taken her in a few weeks, but I think she would've died even before that."

Levi glanced at him. "What do you mean?"

"Withdrawal. I've seen it too many times. She wouldn't have survived the physical withdrawal from her drug addiction. Her vitals were all over the charts. Her body was worn out. So why someone would murder a person so near death—I have no clue."

Ben Walker's head appeared in the doorway.

"You might as well come on in," Dr. Jackson snapped. "You about gave me a stroke today."

"Sorry," Ben said as he entered, holding the flimsy robe tightly closed over his hospital gown. "Can I go home tomorrow?"

"No," Dr. Jackson said bluntly. "You were shot yesterday morning, and until you listen to my orders, you'll remain under my care. And you being in here against my instructions just bought you another twenty-four hours."

Ray chuckled.

"You were no better a patient, Ray," Dr. Jackson said.

"I never made you mad," Ray said.

Dr. Jackson shook his head and rubbed his brow. He was tired. It'd been a long day.

"I thought Dr. Jackson was unflappable. What did you do to him, Ben?" Levi asked.

Ben glanced at Dr. Jackson. "Well, I heard the Code Blue go over the intercom and recognized the room number, so I got up to check it out. There was a loud commotion in the hall. I heard Juli shout something about the killer getting away."

"Ben was wearing a monitor," Dr. Jackson mumbled. "One of those little fingertip clamps that monitors a patient's pulse. He took it off again, about the fourth time today, and set off an alarm at the nurses' station. Again."

"A second Code Blue," Ben said. "I'm sorry, Dr. Jackson."

"So help me, I sure hope I'm retired by the time the next generation of Garveys and Walkers comes along. I just don't have the strength anymore." He sighed.

Levi and Ben grinned at each other.

"So what do we know so far?" Ray said to Sheriff Harby.

Harby pulled his notebook out of his pocket and thumbed through the pages. Ray was glad to see the notebook, instead of a smartphone, for a change.

"An old man comes up the elevator with two bouquets of flowers right at the end of the shift," he recited. "That may mean something. He may've known when the shift ended."

Dr. Jackson chimed in. "Nurses or volunteers most often take flowers to the rooms, but it's not that unusual for the delivery man to take them if they're busy."

"Especially at the end of a shift while they're waiting for their relief to arrive," Ray said.

Dr. Jackson nodded. "It takes a little time once the relief shows up to pass off all the information about the patients, especially the new ones that the relief shift doesn't know anything about. Usually, only one nurse goes off shift at a time so there's some overlap, but Juli and Heather were both going off shift at the same time after working doubles."

"It's unlikely our hit man could've known that," Ray remarked.

Harby agreed. "The security camera picked him up, checking in downstairs. Then he rode the elevator up and talked to Heather and Juli. He offered to deliver both bouquets—one for Selena Long and one for Ben Walker. Then he went to Selena's room. There are no cameras in the rooms obviously. He killed Selena and left one bouquet in her room."

"So we'll have some fingerprints," Ben remarked.

"Unlikely," Harby said. "He was wearing gloves in the video. It's a cold day."

"I think he's a pro," Ray said.

No one disagreed

"Camera caught him again coming back down the hall after he killed Selena," Harby said. "Nobody looked at him twice, especially since he had a bouquet. He was looking confused in all the chaos."

"He'd become invisible," Levi said. "Just some old man behaving exactly as you'd expect him to."

"Until he got to the elevator," Harby said. "He paused, looked directly at Juli, and gave her that little salute."

"He wanted the nurse to see him?" Levi asked.

"Of course, he did," Ray said. "He knew she'd be the one to make the call to lock down the hospital, but there isn't much security in a hospital like this. He wanted her to realize he was the killer. That's why he paused."

"It worked. She put out the alert for an old man—even described his clothes," Harby said. "He'd now successfully focused half the security shift in the hospital towards the west elevator on the first floor."

"And he got out on the second floor," Levi said.

"But he didn't take those stairs down next to that elevator," Harby said. "He walked clear to the other end of the second floor, smiling at the people he passed in the hall, playing the harmless old man."

"Went down another staircase to the first floor," Ben said.

Harby nodded. "And right at the bottom of that staircase is the only door in the hospital that doesn't have a security camera outside, so we don't know how he got away once he left the building—but it's a fire door with an alarm."

"And what was security doing when that fire door alarm went off?" Levi asked.

"By then, the elevator had opened on the first floor—empty, other than the bouquet of daisies in a glass vase sitting on the floor," Harby said. "So four security guards burst into the stairwell and rushed up to the second floor, realizing he'd gotten off there."

Ray shook his head. "But he was long gone. He'd made his escape from the east end of the building through the fire door while most of the security guys were stumbling up the steps to the second floor on the west end of the building. You've got to hand it to him. It was pretty slick. He's a pro."

"Any idea how he made his escape once he left the hospital?" Levi asked.

Harby shook his head. "Your guess is as good as mine My guess is there was a car waiting for him."

"Something bothers me about this," Ben said suddenly.

"What?" Ray asked.

"I know you believe the guy is a pro, but doesn't the execution seem sloppy to you?" Ben said. "Single shot through a pillow with a small caliber handgun. That just seems sloppy. Wouldn't a pro have a silencer? And don't hit men usually employ the classic double-tap? Two shots to the head just to make sure."

Ray and Levi glanced at each other.

"What caliber was it?" Harby asked, looking at Dr. Jackson.

"The autopsy hasn't been completed, but I've seen enough gunshot wounds over the years to say with some certainty it was a .22 round. The spent bullet was in the pillow under her head. Very small entry wound and barely enough velocity to go all the way through her skull."

Everyone was quiet for a moment.

"How long had Selena been under your care when she was murdered?" Levi asked, breaking the silence.

"She got here about nine yesterday morning through emergency. We ran a bunch of tests, and she was in her room by maybe noon. Ben was right behind her. He needed more work," Dr. Jackson said. "By the time I was done with Ben, the results of Selena's tests were back. It was nothing but bad news. I didn't talk to her until mid-afternoon yesterday about what we'd found. She was dead by two this afternoon."

"So a day and a half," Levi said.

"Yes," Dr. Jackson replied.

Levi glanced at Ray, who was leaning back in his chair, deep in thought as he subconsciously rolled up the corners of his mustache with his fingertips.

"So what we have is a clever escape from the hospital after a sloppy amateurish execution?" Levi said.

Ray sat up straight. "You know, there was nothing sloppy about it. That round was dead center in her forehead—through a pillow. Whoever did that has done it before. I'm still saying it was a pro. But that hit was planned fast, and he probably used what he had access to on short notice."

Levi nodded. That made sense.

"I want this case, Harby," Ray said.

"I don't have a problem with that. It started in your town, and the answers probably lie in your town. The River County Sheriff's Office will provide you with support as requested," the sheriff replied. "Let me know what you need. It's all yours, Chief Billings."

Ray stood. "Let's go, Deputy."

Levi sat in his chair, frowning as he thought about Selena's murder.

"Deputy?" Ray said again.

Levi didn't move.

"Deputy Garvey?" Ray said tersely. "You ready?"

"Oh," Levi said, snapping to attention and climbing to his feet. "That's me. I'm the deputy."

"No, you're not," Harby barked. "Listen, I'm only going to say this once. I've put up with this Twin Rivers nonsense for years. I don't know when it started, but it's going to stop right now. The sheriff has deputies—that means I have deputies. Chiefs of police do not have deputies. They have officers. It's about time Twin Rivers got it right. Am I clear on this point, Chief Billings?"

"Crystal clear, Sheriff," Ray said.

"Are we clear *Officer* Walker?"

"Absolutely, Sheriff Harby," Ben replied.

"Is that clear *Officer* Garvey?"

"Without a doubt, Sheriff Harby," Levi said.

"I don't want to hear that deputy crap again," Harby fumed as he walked out of the room.

Ben, Ray, and Levi exchanged glances after Harby left.

"Damn," Ray remarked. "I guess that really steams him."

"Glad he told us now," Levi said, "since we're ordering new uniforms."

"Maybe we ought to order officer badges to replace our deputy badges," Ben added.

"Definitely," Ray said as they walked towards the door. "Would you have Tori look into replacing our badges at the same time she's picking out the new uniforms?"

Dr. Jackson watched the men exit the waiting room and listened as they continued talking in the hall. A devote Christian man, he said a little prayer for Ray, Levi, and Ben—or maybe it was for himself. He prayed that the next time he saw them, it wasn't in the emergency room of St. Anne's Hospital. But knowing the men as well as he did, he realized it was probably an empty prayer. There was something evil lurking in River County again—he felt it. In thirty-five years, nobody had ever been assassinated in a hospital bed in Calloway.

Chapter 18

Levi pulled the cruiser door closed and started the car. Ray climbed into the passenger seat. Levi pulled out of the parking lot onto Wilm Boulevard and headed across Calloway to the Twin Rivers slab.

"You still convinced this is a professional hit?" Levi said.

"Absolutely."

"And you think Peter Long is behind this."

"You bet," Ray said. "Who else would it be? Who else even knew she was alive?"

"It could've been her drug dealer."

Ray was quiet for a moment. "That actually crossed my mind earlier—that maybe her death has more to do with her suppliers than with her husband. It's still possible, I guess. But that really makes no sense on the face of it. First, if you're a drug dealer, would you let Selena run up a huge tab?"

"That's a good point," Levi said.

"But let's say you're just that stupid. I mean, you're a drug dealer not a rocket scientist. What would the motive be for killing her?"

Levi nodded. "So instead of getting a little something every week, you get nothing."

"Right. That's just not it. Drug dealers are more about cash up front, especially from somebody like Selena who obviously has very little income."

"She knew something," Levi said.

"She did," Ray said. "I think Jay knows it, too. I think Jay spooked Pete, and Pete reacted. He hired a pro, but the pro had little time to plan. He used a gun he had access to and came up with a plan to get out of the hospital. The single shot to the head is evidence that the guy knew what he was doing. He's done it before, and he was confident a single shot would get it done. Nothing sloppy about it as far as I can see. It went off exactly as he planned it."

Levi nodded. "So we're looking for an old man who's an acquaintance of Peter Long."

"What old man?" Ray said.

Levi looked at him blankly. "The assassin, Ray. The guy with the flowers."

"That wasn't an old man," Ray said.

"You saw the security video," Levi said.

"I saw the same video you did, but obviously we didn't see the same thing."

Levi knew that very often Ray was two steps ahead of him. He was beginning to feel that way again.

"Okay, what did you see?"

"I saw exactly what I expected to see," Ray remarked. "I had to ask myself, after talking to that nurse, why that old man had given her a little salute from the elevator. He should've been long gone, but he paused."

"It was part of his escape plan. He wanted her to know," Levi said. "He wanted her to know he was the killer. It focused most of the security in the hospital on the wrong side of the building."

"That's right," Ray said. "And we know he went down the stairwell on the other side because we have video surveillance showing him in that stairwell. Without a doubt, that guy is our murderer, and every cop in River County is looking for that old man."

Levi glanced at him. "I'm not following you. Are you saying the old man didn't murder her? He was part of some kind of deception?"

"Nope, he did it without a doubt. That's not the deception I'm talking about. He wasn't an old man."

"I saw him, Ray, on the video," Levi said. "The nurse spoke to him. He was an old man."

"Not so. Apparently, you didn't see the way that old man skipped down those steps in the stairwell. He was leaping down three at a time swinging on the handrails. An old man wouldn't do that."

It suddenly hit Levi.

"Now that you've mentioned it, I don't think I could do that," Levi said.

"That wasn't an old man. You remember that bank robbery case a few years ago where the old man kept robbing banks? It was on some television show the other night."

"I saw that," Levi remarked.

"The FBI finally noticed something about that old man in the bank videos. He didn't move like an old man."

"Yeah," Levi said. "He was wearing some kind of high-end old-man mask."

"The FBI realized they were looking for a much younger man. Those masks can be purchased from any costume store. As a matter of fact, the FBI finally found their suspect's face in a costume catalogue and tracked him down through the purchase. I'm willing to bet we can find our suspect's face in the same place. I intend to find out."

Levi was silent as they rounded a curve on the Twin Rivers slab. The lights from town could be seen on the horizon.

"So this was without a doubt a professional hit. And we start with Pete Long?" Levi said.

"Oh, yeah," Ray said. "I still think that's our best bet. But we've been wrong before, so let's keep our eyes open."

"Let's go talk to him."

"I like the way you think, Officer Garvey. Let's go over and have a little chat with him first thing in the morning."

Levi grinned. "I'll stop for donuts."

Ray sighed. There had been a number of times he'd questioned his decision of making Levi his deputy—or rather, his officer. This was one of them.

Suddenly, Levi pulled off the slab and stopped in front of the bar, the Beer Chaser.

At least Officer Garvey can read minds, Ray thought, as he swung his door open and walked towards the entrance. When he looked through the front window, he saw Ed, sitting at the bar in his police uniform, talking to Joyce.

"We're going to have to talk to Ed about being in the Beer Chaser while wearing his uniform," Ray said as Levi walked up next to him.

Levi glanced down at what he was wearing. Ray noticed and glanced down at his own uniform.

"New policy—no sitting in bars in uniform. We'll begin it tomorrow," Ray said with a grin as he held the door open. "After you, Officer Garvey."

Chapter 19

"It was clean," the assassin said as he sat down in front of his employer's desk and put his feet up on the edge.

He'd done what he'd been paid to do, and he felt confident in the job he'd performed. The lights were low in the library of the mansion. The fire in the fireplace had burned down to glowing embers.

"You put your feet up on my desk?" the man said harshly, slapping the top of his desk violently.

There were few men the assassin feared. This was one of them. His temper was known to cause funerals. Quickly, he put his feet down.

"And the gun?" he demanded.

"It was untraceable. And it's gone," he said. Having lost his confidence, he now feared he could lose his life for simply placing his feet on the edge of an antique desk. "They'll never find it. I tossed it off the top of the Olton Lake Dam. They won't think to look for it there. Even if they do, that water is a hundred feet deep. And if they manage to find the gun, it won't matter because it was stolen two years ago out of the glove box of a car in a mall parking lot."

"A job well done," the employer said as he opened his desk drawer.

The assassin twitched—perhaps expecting to see the barrel of a revolver. The terror the employer caused in this man pleased him. He removed a thick envelope and tossed it onto the desk.

The assassin picked up the envelope and opened it, thumbing through the bills inside. Then smiling, he tucked the envelope into his jacket. He began to relax again. Little did he know his employer had no intention of allowing him to leave the estate alive. It had been arranged. The employer would soon have his envelope back.

"Have a safe trip home," the employer said.

The words chilled the assassin. Sweat broke out across his forehead. He sensed danger in his employer's words. If he was going to get out of the mansion alive, he'd better play his ace. He leaned forward, looking into the blue-gray eyes of his employer.

"There might be one more problem. I'd be happy to handle it for you."

The employer looked at him. Then leaning forward, he placed his chin in his hand. "And what would that be?"

"Another possible witness."

"Jay Snider?" the employer said.

The assassin nodded.

"He's crazy," the employer said, unconcerned.

"He was close to Selena," the assassin said. "Seventeen years he took care of her. If she told anybody, she told Jay. Is that a risk we can afford to take?"

"We?"

The assassin tried to swallow, his mouth suddenly dry.

The employer finally sighed. His assassin was trying to get off the estate alive. He was grasping at straws in a desperate attempt to preserve his life. But he had a point.

"The police have already questioned Jay from what I understand," the assassin added.

That caught his employer's attention. His eyes focused on the assassin, trying to pick up any deception in the man's countenance.

"What police? Chief Billings? As far as he knows, Selena was murdered by her drug dealer. That will lead nowhere. And his deputy is out for the time being. What's his name?"

"Ben Walker," the assassin said.

"Oh yeah," the employer said. "I'd forgotten. Mark Walker's little brother. He was in Iraq or somewhere like that."

"Afghanistan," the assassin said. He always did his homework. "I wouldn't underestimate Chief Billings. That slow Georgia lawman routine works well for him, but he doesn't miss much. Smart enough to call on his friend Levi Garvey for help in his time of need."

"Levi Garvey?" the employer said, surprised. "What's Levi Garvey got to do with this?"

After seeing the look on his employer's face, the assassin suddenly felt better about his chances. His employer hadn't known that detail. That's why he always did his homework.

"Well, before he was a writer, he was a cop—Illinois State Police—for ten years."

"I know that," he snapped, "but he isn't a cop now."

"Maybe you haven't heard," the assassin said, smiling—his chances of survival had just increased ten fold. "Levi Garvey is a duly sworn-in Twin Rivers police officer, who hit the ground running. Levi questioned Jay Snider first thing this morning. Chief Billings also called in Ed Garvey to help out. He's been sworn in as an officer, too."

"Damn," his employer said.

The news sent a chill run up his spine. His pulse race. Suddenly, it was very warm in the room, and sweat beaded on his forehead.

Levi was onto Jay Snider way too fast for comfort. He knew the Garvey reputation well. He'd rather have the whole of the FBI investigating him than have the Garveys on his trail, especially Levi. His employee had made another good point. It would be in his best interest not to underestimate Chief Billings. He couldn't let the Twin Rivers P.D. get anywhere close to this. He had to make sure there were absolutely no leads to follow. And Jay Snider, as unlikely as it was that he knew anything, was now too much of a risk to overlook.

"So what would you do?" he asked.

"We have to move fast. You know accidents can happen at any time," the assassin said, "and Jay lives in this little house right on the edge of a very steep cliff."

"Does he?" the employer said, leaning forward, suddenly interested.

The assassin nodded. "I'll make sure he has an accident. Maybe he falls off the edge of that cliff and bashes his brains out on the rocks along the Calloway River."

"I don't like it. What if he doesn't die?"

"You haven't seen that cliff," the assassin said. "There's no chance he'll survive a fall. He'll die all right."

It was risky, but perhaps it was riskier letting Jay Snider live.

"Same fee," he finally said.

"Double the fee," the assassin said. "And when you pay me next time, it will be on my terms. I won't be coming back here to collect the money."

The employer glared at him, but he knew he didn't have much choice. The assassin had realized at some point that his employer had never intended to pay him for the first job. The first rule of hiring a hit is that sometimes it is necessary to take out the hit man, too. No witnesses.

"Fine. Double the fee," he said. "Now do it fast. If he isn't dead by sunset tomorrow, you're going to have a huge problem."

"I'll take care of it," the assassin said.

The employer picked up the glass from a coaster on his desk and took a long sip of scotch as he looked intently at the assassin.

"I'm beginning to like you. If you manage to pull this one off, your reputation will be made. You'll find no shortage of work."

"I'm interested," the assassin remarked, smiling to himself.

"Take care of Jay Snider," he said harshly. "If you don't screw up, we'll talk again. There's just not enough new talent coming up through the ranks, and some of the best in the business are getting a little long in the tooth."

"Consider it done," the assassin said. "And I don't screw up. The key is doing the homework and being well prepared."

Suddenly, two men appeared from the darkness of the library. They stood on either side of his chair. The assassin had not heard the door open behind him, nor heard their feet on the floor. The employer had summoned them with a hidden switch under the edge of his desk.

"See him to the door," the employer said.

The taller of the two bodyguards glanced at him questioningly. "To the door?"

"To the door," he repeated.

It wasn't the order the bodyguard had expected. He'd assumed he would be escorting the assassin "to the gate." As the bodyguard escorted the assassin from the library, he glanced back at the man behind the desk, just to make sure. The man nodded at him again. He hadn't misspoken. It was "to the door."

One word was the difference between life and death.

Chapter 20

The bell jangled over the door as Ray walked into Harv's Grill. The restaurant was busy. April was delivering a breakfast order to the farmers' table as Harv dinged the bell in the order window. Another breakfast order was up.

"I'll be right with you, Ray," April said.

"Where's Nichole?" Ray asked, glancing around for the waitress.

"Flu," April replied. "She's been out two days."

When he started towards the counter, he was stopped.

"I would like to issue a complaint against one of your deputies," Floyd said from the farmers' table.

"Right now?" Ray said.

Floyd was about to make things interesting. He always did. He considered it his new job since he'd retired and closed the Twin Rivers Hardware Store a few years earlier. He didn't consider it a good day unless he'd been told to shut up at least half a dozen times. But beneath that comic veneer, there lurked one of the finest men Ray had ever met. Floyd had saved his life two years earlier—his life, Ed's, Levi's, and Tori's. It was the only time Ray had ever seen the real man, not the comedian, as Floyd had glared over the barrel of a shotgun which was pointed at the back of a murderer's head.

"Yes, right now," Floyd said stubbornly. "And don't you dare tell me to shut up."

"Fine, let's have it then," Ray said.

Floyd cleared his throat as everyone in the diner listened. "I was pulled over yesterday afternoon by a man proclaiming to be a duly appointed deputy in this community, and he gave me a ticket."

"You mean Ed," Ray said. "He's not a stranger. Everyone in here knows Ed Garvey well. Especially you, Floyd. You've known Ed since you were both in grade school—right?"

"Well, I'm not paying that ticket," Floyd said.

"What is it for?"

Floyd fished the ticket out of his pocket and handed it to Ray, who read it and then handed it back.

"I'd pay it," Ray said, grinning. "He had you dead to rights."

"He can't write somebody a ticket for this," Floyd argued.

"Obviously, he can," Ray argued back, "and he did."

"What was it for?" April asked as she refilled coffee cups.

"I was pulled over at 10:15 in the morning. The weather was clear, the road was dry, my vehicle was in good working order, and I had current vehicle registration, license, and insurance," Floyd said, reading the information off the ticket. "I was pulled over in front of the church and written a citation for 'being an asshole.'"

The patrons in the restaurant exploded into laughter.

"You could fight it," Ray said, wiping tears from his eyes as he sat down on a stool at the counter. "Take it to the Village Board."

"They'd find me guilty," Floyd said as everyone in the restaurant laughed again.

"You might want to talk to Ed," April said to Ray, fishing a ticket out of her pocket. "I got one, too."

Ray looked at her ticket. It was for slow service and rude conduct towards a valued customer.

"Yeah," Harv said from the order window. "That jackass wrote me one for breaking the yoke on his egg yesterday morning. It was $100 because he noted that I'm a repeat offender. He keeps this up, and he's going to have to learn to cook himself, which would be next to impossible since I've been feeding him three times a day for forty years."

"I also got one," Jerry Davis said, waving his ticket.

He was one of Levi Garvey's best friends since grade school and the editor of the *Twin Rivers Times* newspaper. If Floyd ever retired as town comedian, Jerry would be the next in line for the job.

"Mine is for 'insufferable arrogance.'"

"I could see that," Ray remarked as everyone laughed.

"I got one for reneging in a euchre game in 1977," Curt Anderson added.

"Did you?" Ray asked.

"I didn't mean to," Curt admitted.

"Rip them up," Ray said. "Even though you're all probably guilty, I'll talk to Ed about what he can write tickets for."

Ray swung around on his stool as April set a cup of coffee in front of him.

"What is today?" Ray asked. "Coconut or butterscotch?"

"Coconut," April said, smiling.

She knew it was his favorite. She knew what everyone's favorite pie was.

"I'll have a couple of eggs and bacon and a slab of pie," Ray said as April wrote down the order. "I'll have that pie while I'm waiting for the eggs."

"Of course," April said as she pulled a piece from the carousel at the end of the counter.

She put his order up in the window, but she knew her husband had put Ray's eggs and bacon on the second he walked in. Like just about everyone in town, Ray always ordered the same thing.

When the bell over the door jangled again, the customers in the restaurant began booing. Ray turned around on his stool. Standing in the doorway in his uniform, Ed Garvey was being pelted with wadded up napkins and pink citations.

"What?" Ed bellowed with a giant grin on his face. "This is the thanks I get for trying to make this town a better place to live?"

Turning back around on his stool, Ray said to April, "You know, I do love this town."

As he forked off a big piece of pie, April smiled at him and said, "I do, too."

Chapter 21

"What is this?" Levi said, picking up a pink ticket off the table in the breakfast nook where the mail and newspapers seemed to accumulate during the week.

Adam was sitting next to him in the high chair, eating Cheerios, with Rosco nearby, waiting patiently for a few to fall to the floor. Tori was standing in front of the microwave as Adam's cereal warmed.

"Ed wrote me a ticket yesterday," Tori said.

"I can see that," Levi said. "What's 'improper equipment usage' mean?"

"I needed a tow, so I called him," Tori said. "Mrs. B. was watching Adam while I ran to Calloway to look at tile samples for the Twin Rivers Library renovation."

"In Pappy?" Levi asked. "What's wrong with Pappy?"

Pappy was Tori's red 1950 Ford pickup. Ed and Levi had spent a year restoring it. They called it Pappy because, according to Ed, it was Old Blue's daddy. But Pappy had proven to be less reliable than Old Blue. Ed suspected that it wasn't the truck's fault but the driver's.

"I barely made it back to Twin Rivers when it finally clunked out in front of the post office," Tori said.

"And the problem?"

"So I walked home after I called Ed. He got his tow truck and hauled it to the carriage house," Tori said. "He said he'll have it running again in a few days. Can you believe it's only February and nearly sixty degrees outside? It was a nice day to walk."

"And what's the problem with Pappy?" Levi asked again.

"Mrs. B. really likes the tile samples I brought back," Tori said. "She's very excited about the renovation at the library."

"Tori," Levi said, "what's wrong with Pappy?"

"I found the exact same tile pattern that was put in the library when it was built. Did you know that the Twin Rivers Library was a Carnegie Library?"

"It was the clutch, wasn't it?" Levi said.

"I found the plans with all the original specifications. In the basement, I even found some of the original tile that was in the foyer before the library was remodeled in 1970. Why in the world would anyone take out that beautiful tile and replace it with linoleum? I'm going to bring the library back to the way it was when it was first opened. The statue is going to have to be moved—the duplicate of the war memorial statue. There's no way to get that huge statue out of the foyer without removing the entire triple doorway frame, but that can damage the door, so I'm planning to suspend the statue from the wrought iron frame in the ceiling and tile under it while it hangs."

"It was the clutch, wasn't it?" Levi repeated, chuckling.

"Yes," Tori snapped. "It was the stupid clutch!"

"Is that three or four clutches you've burned up now? No, wait, it's three. Two in Pappy and one in Old Blue. In what, two years? That's impressive."

Tori glared at him. She'd always driven an automatic until a couple of years ago. It was something she still wasn't good at unless, as Ed had put it, the purpose of a manual transmission was to make horrendous gear-grinding noises.

She pulled the cereal out of the microwave, stirred it, and then stuck her finger in it to make sure it wasn't too hot. She placed it in front of Adam and went back for one of his rubber-coated spoons. Before she could get back, Adam banged his fist down on the edge of the bowl, flipping cereal all over himself and the floor. Rosco looked up at Levi with a huge glob of cereal between his eyes.

Calmly, Tori sat down across from Levi. She began scraping cereal off Adam's face and spooning it into his mouth. But Levi felt the dangerous undercurrent lurking, just under the surface.

"I'm sorry, Levi," she said, looking at him. "You were asking me something? Something about a clutch?"

"I don't remember now," Levi said, reaching for the *Twin Rivers Times*. "Did you say it was almost sixty degrees yesterday? The paper says there's a huge winter storm coming this way. Should be here this afternoon."

"Not remembering—a very wise choice," Tori remarked with emphasis on *very*. "Come here, Rosco."

Using Adam's spoon, she removed the large glob of cereal from between his eyes, picked out a couple of dog hairs, and spooned it into Adam's mouth. Levi suppressed a grin.

"Something funny?" Tori said, looking at him with that untamable loose spiral of hair in front of her face.

"I saw nothing."

Tori smiled and then laughed. "Yesterday, I caught Rosco chewing on one of Adam's teething rings while Adam was chewing on one of Rosco's chewie toys. I'm done doing the 'perfect mom' thing. I'm starting to think that Rosco will get chicken pox from Adam long before Adam gets fleas from Rosco."

"I tend to agree," Levi said, glancing at the kitchen clock.

"What's on the agenda today?"

"We're going to question Pete Long."

"Should I be worried about this?" Tori said, glancing at his shirt.

She knew he'd been a state trooper for a decade, but seeing him in that uniform was something she just couldn't get used to.

"I'm not," Levi said.

"But there was a murder."

"We're investigating a murder," Levi said. "We're not personally involved this time. It's not like before. This crime has nothing to do with us. Selena was murdered to cover a crime. The bad guys aren't going to go after the investigators. I don't see us being in any personal danger."

"You think it was a professional hit?" Tori asked.

"It definitely looks that way."

"And the assassin wants everyone to believe an old man killed her," Tori said, trailing off.

"What are you saying?" Levi asked.

"It just seems familiar to me."

"You're talking about Tony O'Malley and his Four Horsemen?" Levi asked.

They'd met a professional and survived the encounter—one of the most notorious Chicago gangsters in American history, Tony O'Malley, the head of the Chicago Outfit, whose history went back to the time of Al Capone and prohibition. Tony O'Malley and his Four Horsemen had even been in their home. Somewhere in Chicago, the old man had a copy of Levi's book with a bullet hole in it from Levi's Webley revolver.

"You've got to admit that there are a lot of ways to conceal your identity from security cameras. Why the old man costume?"

"I'm not following you," Levi said.

Tori sighed. "People in town are already whispering. They know Tony O'Malley was here a couple of years ago. After all, he had pie at Harv's with his Four Horsemen. They also know something happened between us and the Chicago Outfit, just not exactly what. As soon as it got out that the man who murdered Selena was an old man, everyone began wondering if Tony had something to do with it. It's not a huge stretch of the imagination— an old man, a professional hit, and something to do with illegal activities. That adds up to Tony O'Malley as far as most people are concerned."

Levi's face blanched. "O'Malley will hear about it."

Tori nodded. "It'll piss him off that somebody tried to implicate him."

"Shit," Levi said. "And you know what happens when Tony O'Malley gets pissed off."

"People disappear," Tori said.

"Why would Peter Long do that intentionally?" Levi asked. "It's suicide."

"He wouldn't," Tori said. "It makes no sense for him to have done that. Are you sure he's behind this?"

"I'm not so sure now," Levi admitted.

"It's pretty clear Ray believes he is. When Peter Long gets murdered or just vanishes, everyone is going to know exactly what happened," Tori said.

"They'll assume that Tony O'Malley got him," Levi said. "And they'll be right. I can't imagine, knowing his reputation, that once Tony hears about this, he won't do anything about it."

"That's your headline—Tony O'Malley Implicated in Local Homocide," Tori remarked.

"And if Peter Long didn't actually kill Selena—" Levi said.

"Nobody is ever going to know who did," Tori said, finishing his thought. "You'd only implicate Tony O'Malley if you believed without a doubt that nobody will ever suspect your involvement, and you're framing the very person everyone already thinks is guilty. Tony kills Peter Long, and everyone, including law enforcement, is going to assume Tony killed Selena, too."

Levi stared at his coffee cup.

"This could get very dangerous," Tori remarked.

"I know. I need to talk to Ray," he said, rising.

"Levi?"

Levi turned to look at her. "I know what you're going to say, Tori. If this gets dangerous, I'll turn in my badge. I promise. And Ray will understand."

Tori looked at him doubtfully.

"I promise," he added again.

She stepped into his arms for a hug.

Then Levi walked quickly through the doorway.

"Come on, Rosco! Time to go to work!"

Chapter 22

"Let me handle this, Levi," Ray said as they pulled to a stop in Pete Long's driveway.

It was an enormous house built into the side of a hill. Ray had seen it only from the other side, the lake side where it was all glass and wooden decks. But on the street side, the house looked deceptively small, since only one level was visible.

They parked in front of three large garage doors and walked up a flagstone walk to the huge heavy wooden door. Leaded glass panels on either side and a large rounded stained-glass piece overhead let in light.

Suddenly, Rosco barked from the car window. Levi looked back at the car. Two huge German shepherds were leaning out of the open front and back windows.

"Rosco, no barking! And you keep quiet, too, Bo."

"I'm starting to question the wisdom of bringing those two today," Ray said as he reached for the doorbell.

"Okay, how are we going to play this?" Levi asked. "What am I—the bad cop or the good cop?"

Ray glared a Levi. "Are you going to be a problem today?"

Levi shook his head quickly.

Ray was reaching for the doorbell again when the door suddenly opened.

"Chief Billings, I was just getting ready to go out for a little cruise around the lake," Pete Long said, his hand moving to emphasize his casual dress— jeans, tennis shoes, and a windbreaker. "Of course, I heard what happened. Are you here to arrest me?"

"No," Ray said, "but I would like to ask you some questions if you don't mind."

"Of course," Pete said, opening the door wider.

Rosco started barking from the car window. Pete glanced at the cruiser in his driveway.

"Beautiful dogs. Are they friendly towards other dogs?"

"Very friendly," Ray said.

"Bring them," Pete said. "I love dogs. I've got a big, dumb St. Bernard. He'd probably enjoy some company while we talk."

Levi whistled. The two dogs bailed out of the windows and ran up the sidewalk, tails wagging.

"I don't think I've met your friend, Chief," Pete said.

"This is Officer Levi Garvey."

"The novelist? Are you researching a novel or something?"

"No, I'm a trained police officer, and Chief Billings has asked for my assistance since he has another officer out on medical leave."

Ray suppressed a grin. The remark had obviously annoyed Levi. He wondered if Pete Long hadn't intentionally taken a poke at Levi.

"How interesting," Pete said. "Please, come inside."

They walked into an entry way, which wasn't much more than a ledge at the top of the house. The enormous timbers that supported the roof crisscrossed overhead, and there was a broad staircase that led down to two levels below. The bottom level was open. From the rail in the entrance foyer, they could see a huge stone fireplace and library shelves. The far wall of the house was solid glass windows. The view of the lake was stunning with Olton Lake Dam, about four miles away, clearly visible at the far end.

"That's a lot of stairs," Ray said, looking down.

"There is an elevator," Pete said, pointing to one end of the entry way where there were two wood-paneled elevator doors. "I don't use it much, but it will undoubtedly come in handy one day. I'm not getting any younger."

Levi glanced at Pete, who was definitely polished in dealing with other people, but it was a polish that made Levi want to see what was underneath it. Ray, who was chomping on the bit to talk to Pete again, seemed to maintain his tough veneer despite Pete's friendly demeanor.

"Come on," Pete said, starting down the stairs.

Rosco and Bo bounded down in front of him.

From the rail at the landing at the bottom of the first flight of steps, Pete shouted, "Tinker! Come here, boy!"

A huge St. Bernard appeared at the lowest level. Rosco and Bo, who'd made it nearly to the bottom, skidded to a stop on the staircase—their ears up.

"Holy crap," Levi said.

"He's a big boy," Pete said, "and he's only two years old."

The St. Bernard's tail began wagging, and he barked at the two dogs on the stairway. Rosco and Bo cautiously walked down the rest of the steps, then circled the enormous dog, checking him out.

"Tinker?" Ray asked.

"That's what they called him at the pound where I rescued him last winter," Pete said. "He'd been badly injured by a snowplow. No tags. Never found out who owned him. So I have no idea why they called him Tinker, but he responded to the name, so I kept it."

When they reached the bottom of the stairs, Levi walked over to Tinker, dropped to one knee, and held the back of his hand out to the dog. Tinker licked his hand, and then Levi rubbed his ears. Suddenly, Levi was petting three dogs as Rosco and Bo came over for attention as well.

"His head is the size of a mailbox," Levi said.

"He weighs about 160 pounds, and he's still considered under-weight," Pete said. "The vet would like to see him at about 200. He was apparently badly neglected by his previous owner and then injured. He's gained 50 pounds this year. He'll probably gain another 50 as he reaches adulthood."

"I thought Bo was big at 90 pounds," Ray said.

Pete touched a button on his phone. "Shelia, please bring coffee for three into the library."

"Yes, sir," she responded.

"I love these things," Pete said as he tucked his phone back into the pocket of his windbreaker.

Levi realized they were supposed to be impressed with his newest generation phone, but they weren't since, thanks to Amber, they had the same phone he had.

Pete waved them over to a table in front of the glass windows. The morning light was blinding as Levi and Ray joined him. Shelia entered, set a tray down on the table, and poured three cups of coffee. Then she departed quickly.

"That sun is a little bright this morning," Pete said, leaning over to touch a panel on the glass wall. The windows suddenly darkened.

"Wow," Levi said. "That sure would be handy in my breakfast nook."

"It's special glass. I can adjust the light that comes in. Good thing, or in the summer it would be so hot in here I'd never be able to cool it. I can also black them all the way out for privacy. At night, you can see this house clearly from the other end of the lake, and if it weren't for that glass, you could see right in."

Levi sipped his coffee and glanced at Ray. Pete had said that for a reason—likely to indicate to Ray that he knew Ray had been watching him a couple of nights earlier.

The dogs were chasing each other up and down the stairs, barking and wrestling on the landings. The men drank their coffee silently. Finally, Levi cleared his throat.

Pete smiled as he wiped his pencil thin mustache with a napkin. "I think your deputy is ready for you to begin asking me questions," he said.

Ray took another sip of his coffee, then looked at Pete Long.

"You lied to me," he said finally. "I don't like being lied to. And you're good at it."

Pete leaned back in his chair. His expression never changed. If what Ray had just said impacted him, he didn't show it.

"So we're going to do this again," Ray continued. "And I would strongly advise you to tell me the truth this time."

"Am I a suspect in Selena's murder?"

"Absolutely," Ray said.

"I didn't kill her," Pete said calmly, sipping his coffee as his diamond ring glinted in the morning sun. "And I didn't have anyone else kill her."

"You expect me to take you at your word? You're one of the most gifted liars I've ever met."

"Then ask your questions again," Pete said. "I'll either answer truthfully, or I won't answer at all. How's that?"

"Let's start at the beginning again. How did you meet Selena?" Ray asked.

"She was a stripper in my club in Peoria," Pete said. "She was young with a perfect body. She packed the joint every night she worked, but she had problems. Even though she was already on drugs when I met her, I thought she had great potential in video."

"So you helped her advance her career," Levi said.

"I'd already started my studio, Passion Video, and I thought she'd be a natural. I gave her a screen test, and the camera loved her. She was seriously beautiful and uninhibited, so I started casting her in my video productions in secondary roles. Before long, I realized she was outshining the stars. In a short time, she was the star in most of our productions. Those videos sold like hotcakes. She was my first mega-star. And I might point out that we had a relationship at the time, too. She was seriously in love with me, but I can't say the same. Things were going great at Passion Video, and then we found out something that threatened the entire studio."

"You found out she was underage," Ray said.

Pete nodded. "I honestly didn't know. She had a very good fake I.D. I knew about another studio in the porn industry that got caught with a star who was also underage. That studio was sued into oblivion. I had no desire to lose everything I'd built because of an honest mistake."

"So you married her," Ray said with a shake of his head.

"I did," Pete said. "If anybody found out, she wouldn't have to testify against me. It's just that simple. But nobody found out. Then Selena's drug problems got worse and worse. That part of the story was true. I did everything I could to get her straight."

"But her problems didn't stop you from casting your wife in adult movies, did it?" Levi said.

Pete glared at him, color rising in his face. "We went from making tens of thousands, to hundreds of thousands, to millions in a few short years because of Selena. And not only that, we attracted a lot of new talent because of our success. After some years, Selena's time in the business was coming to a close. She was starting to look too thin and strung out, but I didn't kick her to the curb. I continued to take care of her. You can argue about the way I did it, but I did take care of her."

"You make me sick," Ray said. "How do you sleep at night?"

"I think we're about done here," Pete said.

"I'll let you know when we're done," Ray said.

Pete looked as if he'd been slapped. It was the first reaction Ray had managed to get out of him.

"I've got a question," Levi said. "If you didn't kill her, then who did?"

Pete looked at him for a long moment, then shook his head. "I really don't know."

"There are a lot of ways to make money in porn that don't involve selling porn movies, aren't there?" Levi said.

That was something Jay Snider had said to him. Levi wasn't sure what it meant, but he thought he'd see how Peter Long reacted to it.

After Pete regarded Levi for a moment, he said, "Yes, there are. We don't sell many movies anymore. There are pay-per-view channels on your dish. There are websites. There are even live chats with your favorite stars, and they'll take certain requests. There's an entire industry in sex toys. Both our male and female stars cast various body parts to make all kinds of interesting latex things. We have huge porn shows where thousands of fans come to meet our stars and buy these things. We even auction off chances to be in a porn movie with a favorite porn starlet. There are a lot of ways to make money in this business, and we work to find new ways all the time."

Ray shook his head. "And it's a multi-billion-dollar-a-year business."

"We're only one studio of many," Pete said, "but we're one of the largest."

"What do you make a year?" Levi asked.

Pete shook his head. "That's one I'm not going to answer."

"Do all these girls come from your strip clubs?" Ray asked.

"Very few," Pete said. "All you have to do is run an ad in a newspaper in a college town, saying that you're looking for young models. You'd be surprised how many show up. Then you tell them what it's really about and how much they can make. Many leave, but enough stay. You'd be shocked at how many young women put themselves through college like that. These aren't drug-addicted strippers. They are very smart . . . entrepreneurs."

"I'm sure not all of those who stay are ever cast in a video production," Levi said.

"Porn watchers don't like ugly girls," Pete said with a grin. "Those are out. The ones who make the cut basically do a demo for us. After we see those demos, we decide who we'll be able to use in our videos. Many of the prettiest never get a call. They're shy in front of a camera, or they won't do some of the things we need for them to do. We can't really use girls that are inhibited. Men want to watch women who are . . ."

"Willing?" Levi said, finishing Pete's sentence.

Pete nodded.

"What happens to those bad demos?" Ray said. "Do you use those for anything?"

"Of course not," Pete said. "If they're bad, they're bad. Nobody wants to watch bad porn."

Ray appeared to be having a difficult time with this interview. Levi doubted that Ray had ever watched a dirty movie—let alone buy a sex toy or get on a live chat website. Ray poured himself another cup of coffee from the carafe.

"What were you doing in Twin Rivers when you got into that confrontation with Jay Snider?"

"I was having dinner at Harv's," Pete said.

"Had you done that before?" Ray asked.

"Not in a long time. I think I'd been there maybe thirty years ago."

"Why that night?" Ray said. "Just seems like a hell of a coincidence to me. You show up for the first time in decades. Jay Snider shows up for the first time in years. And you two get into a disagreement."

Pete rose, walked over to the bookshelves beside the huge fireplace, and removed a book from the shelf. Returning to the table, he tossed it down. It was a copy of Levi's book *The Devil Within*.

"Levi is one of my favorite authors. I'd been wanting to try April's pie for a long time," Pete said. "I read all about it in the book. I finally decided to go try it out. Jay saw my car and stopped to confront me. That's the story."

"Is that the truth?" Ray said.

"That's the truth."

"And you have no idea why somebody would want Selena dead?" Levi said.

"Why would I want her dead?" Pete snapped. "She was out of my life. There was no way she could've hurt me at this point. I had no motive to kill her. What I paid her and Jay is a pittance, considering the money she made for me." He paused and swept his arm in front of him to indicate the luxury surrounding him. "Besides, I could've killed her any day I wanted to—with cash."

Ray and Levi exchanged glances. That much was true. They'd already had that conversation.

Pete leaned back in his chair, a smug grin on his face, obviously satisfied with himself. The look annoyed Levi, who hadn't liked him from the moment he'd set eyes on him.

Pete saw the look on Levi's face. "Something you want to say, *Officer* Garvey?"

"Yes, actually," Levi said. "I don't think you had anything to do with Selena's murder even though about half of the people in Twin Rivers do, including Chief Billings. I think somebody else did it, somebody who doesn't like you very much, and I think you know who that might be."

"And what's the basis of your theory?" Pete said with a snort.

"It's obvious," Levi said. "You may not realize it yet, but whoever killed Selena has also murdered you. You're already dead."

"What do you mean?" Peter said, leaning forward.

"Selena's assassin cleverly framed Tony O'Malley—made it look like the assassin was one of his Four Horsemen. The other half of Twin Rivers citizens think that one of them pulled it off. Even the Calloway newspaper mentioned that possibility. Unfortunately for you, it must've been a slow news day because a reporter for the *Chicago Sun Times* caught the story and repeated that theory. It was a small story on page three of the *Sun Times*, but you can bet that Tony O'Malley has already heard about it. I would imagine that's going to make him very angry. He gets really annoyed when his name appears in a Chicago newspaper and police knock on his door."

The color drained from Pete's face.

"Tony is going to think you did that. He's going to find you. If I were you, I'd be pretty anxious to help us figure out who did this because I can't imagine what fate Tony will come up with for you. You can sit there, all smug and satisfied with the clever answers you've given us, but I don't think you're going to be so calm when those four old men show up here to talk to you."

"You can't be serious," Pete stuttered. "What possible motive could I have to kill Selena? And why would I be so stupid as to frame Tony O'Malley?"

"It doesn't have to make sense," Ray said. "That's just the way it looks. Now do you want to help us come up with a few more suspects or not?"

"I can't," Pete said, sweat flowing freely down his temples. "You don't understand. Some of the people I do business with are just as dangerous as Tony."

Ray stood up from the table. "That's too bad, then. Looks like your chickens are about to come home to roost. And I can't say I'm very upset about it. It's difficult to protect somebody who lies and refuses to answer questions honestly. We've done what we can. You can work it out with Tony. Thanks for your time."

Suddenly, they heard a huge crash below them. Rosco appeared at the top of a stairway towards the back of the large room they were in. Neither Ray nor Levi had noticed that staircase until they saw Rosco. He barked down the stairs, and Bo responded. Rosco ran back down again. There were some thumps and some barking and then another crash.

"You have a basement," Levi said.

"There's another level below this one," Pete said, mopping sweat from his brow with a handkerchief—his hand shaking as he did so.

"What's down there?" Ray asked.

"It's my personal office and a den. It's where I work during the day and watch television in the evening."

"Can we get a tour?" Ray asked.

"No," Pete said flatly. "Nobody goes down there but me."

Ray shrugged.

When Levi whistled, Rosco and Bo bounded up the lower level steps and skidded to a halt on the wood floor in front of them. Their ears were up, their tails banging on the floor. Both were panting. Tinker lumbered up the stairs after them and flopped down on the floor. Obviously, all three had had a marvelous time.

"Shelia, see these men out," Pete said into his phone.

"Yes, sir," she responded.

Moments later, Shelia appeared. As they walked up the stairs, Ray glanced back down. Pete Long didn't look so well. In fact, he looked like he needed to see a doctor.

* * *

"I'd give a year's salary to know what is in that basement," Ray said as he backed out of the driveway.

"Can we get a warrant?"

"I don't think we have enough, but that was bullshit about an office and a den. Judging from the size the house, there's got to be at least 1,800 to 2,000 square feet down there— a pretty big space for an office and a den."

"I know somebody who's been down there," Levi remarked.

"Who?"

"Rosco, what was down there?" Levi said, turning to look into the backseat.

Leaning over the seat, Rosco licked his face. Levi rubbed his ears.

"You know, Levi, sometimes you really piss me off."

"It's a gift."

"We need to talk to Shelia," Ray said. "I'll bet she knows what goes on down there."

"You want to go back and talk to her?" Levi asked.

"Nope," Ray said as he fastened his seatbelt and pulled onto the road. "We'll get back to her. We're going to Calloway now."

"What's in Calloway?"

"Remember last Halloween?" Ray said.

"Why, yes, I do. Our Senior Warden showed up in lodge dressed as Darth Vader," Levi said with a chuckle.

"You know where I rented that costume?"

"There's only one place. Simpson's Magic and Costumes in Calloway," Levi said.

"Exactly," Ray said.

"We're back to the old-man mask, aren't we?" Levi said.

"We find the man who bought that mask, we find the man who killed Selena Long."

"You've changed your mind. You don't think it was Peter Long, do you?"

"You saw the look on his face when you mentioned Tony O'Malley," Ray said. "The guy is a gifted liar, but I don't think he's that good an actor."

"Let's find the mask," Levi said. "But seriously, do you think we're going to be able to solve this?"

"I don't know yet," Ray said. "I don't think we'll be able to solve this without Peter Long's help. He knows what this is about, and I think he knows who killed Selena. The problem is Peter Long is just as afraid of our killer as he is of Tony O'Malley."

Levi remembered something from years before, back when he lived in Savannah—the way Ray had always seemed to be two steps ahead of him, the way he used to know what was going on with Levi. Actually, Levi used to think of himself as Dr. Watson to Ray's Sherlock Holmes. Ray's powers of observation were far above and beyond those that Levi had. It was like magic. But, because he'd solved two cold cases in Twin Rivers, Levi had foolishly believed when Ray had brought him into the case, he'd been called on because Ray wanted him to solve the case. But Ray hadn't asked for Levi's help because he needed him to be Sherlock—Ray needed a Dr. Watson who faithfully helped his friend Sherlock Holmes track down the bad guys. Then, when things got dangerous, he could always be counted on for one specific purpose. Dr. Watson always had his trusty service revolver in his pocket when it was needed. Levi suddenly understood that was his role—not the investigator but the protector.

Chapter 23

Ray pulled into a parking space in front of Simpson's Magic and Costumes in Calloway.

"I'll tell you what," Ray said. "You go find out if Mr. Simpson can help you find that mask. I'm going to go see Russ Martin."

"About what?" Levi asked.

"Another little hunch I've got."

Levi sighed. He had a feeling that Ray was a lot further in understanding what was going on than he was saying. There was no sense in asking because he wouldn't tell until he was ready.

"I'll take the dogs with me," Ray said.

Levi swung his door open and climbed out. The temperature had dropped twenty degrees since that morning.

"Hey, keep an eye on the weather. We need to be back in Twin Rivers by lunchtime," Levi said.

A big snowstorm bringing eight to twelve inches of snow was forecasted to start in just a couple of hours. When Ray had heard the morning weather report, he'd had a little difficulty believing the prediction since it had been nearly sixty degrees at the time. But his opinion was beginning to change. It was closer to forty now, the wind had picked up, and the western sky was filled with shaggy dark clouds.

"Call me if you're done before I am, and I'll come pick you up," Ray said.

Levi slammed the door shut, crossed the sidewalk, and disappeared inside the store.

Ray backed out of his space and headed to C & S Locksmiths, just a couple of blocks further up Main Street. He parked in front of the store and called the dogs. They leaped over the back seat and jumped out after him. C & S had been in the hundred-year-old building since it was built. The initials C & S were spelled out in green and white mosaic tiles on the threshold. Above the locksmith shop was the Calloway Masonic Lodge, a stately old lodge, not dissimilar to the Twin Rivers Lodge. Actually, all the Masonic lodges in that part of Illinois had been built about the same time, using very similar designs. Ray had been in this one only once—when Sheriff Harby had invited him and Levi to his installation as Master a couple of years earlier.

When Ray whistled sharply, the two dogs ran up to him. They'd managed to sniff their way to the corner while he'd been daydreaming in front of the building.

Ray entered the dimly lit shop, and the dogs followed. There was nobody at the counter. Ray could hear Russ Martin, who ran the shop by himself, banging around in the back room. Ray dropped to one knee and rubbed the dogs' ears.

"Okay, boys, go get Russ."

With their ears up, they sniffed the air. Neither had been in the shop before, but they knew the familiar scent. They bolted around the counter, dog nails clattering on wooden planked floors, and raced into the back room.

"Shit!" Russ exclaimed from the back. A loud crash followed. "Come here, you two rotten dogs!"

There was some growling and barking, followed by another crash. Rosco ran out of the back, tail wagging. Russ—a big muscular guy with dark curly hair pulled back in a pony tail, a face framed by giant mutton chops, muscular arms covered with tattoos, and thick Buddy Holly glasses—lumbered through the doorway. Bo was gripping his pants leg and vigorously shaking his head back and forth. Even though Russ was a big guy, he was having a little trouble walking while dragging the ninety-pound dog that was trying to bring him down. Russ grinned at Ray. He knew the dogs well since he often joined Ray and the Garveys for pool in Ray's basement.

"These two mutts belong to you?" Russ said with a chuckle. "You know, I could lock these dogs up in a cage nobody would ever be able to open."

Ray laughed. Russ was one of the best locksmiths in that part of the state.

"Let go, Bo," Russ said, leaning down to rub his head. Bo released him.

"So what brings you here," Russ asked, wiping his hands on his t-shirt.

"I've got a hypothetical question for you."

"You never learn," Russ said. "The first time you asked me one of those I wound up running you to Dr. Jackson's office to have your hand stitched up."

"Yeah, I remember," Ray said, flexing the hand he'd crushed in a lock smashing tool. "I'll just ask you some direct questions then, and if you don't want to answer me because of some kind of professional confidentiality, you don't have to."

"That's better," Russ said, resting his elbows on the counter.

"Do you know Peter Long?"

"I do," Russ said. "He's a customer."

"Does he have a safe?"

Russ regarded him for a moment, then said, "That's the kind of question I'm not comfortable with. My customers expect me to keep the details of their security systems and safes to myself."

Ray smiled. He knew that Russ had just indicated that Pete Long had both a safe and a security system, and Russ was familiar with both of them.

"Okay," Ray said, thinking about how to frame the next question so Russ could answer it. "If I were to get a warrant to search Pete Long's house, would you have any trouble getting into that safe he may or may not have?"

Russ laughed. "You're about as subtle as a baseball bat to the side of the head."

"Well? Would you?"

Russ sighed. "Let's just drop the pretense. I sold him a wall safe about five years ago and a much larger floor safe about two years ago. I could open either one without any difficulty."

Ray smiled. "That's all I really wanted to know."

"But there's something else you should know," Russ said. "There's a vault, too."

"There is?"

"It's an unknown element," Russ said. "A vault can be a challenge to open. I don't know much about it because I didn't install it—vaults are a little out of my league. Some big security company from Chicago installed it about seven years ago."

"Then how do you know about it?" Ray asked.

"A vault is just a strong room with a massive impenetrable door," Russ said. "I know the contractor who built the vault room. It's pretty large for a residential installation—about twenty by twenty with a ventilation system and the whole nine yards. The walls, floor, and ceiling are ten inches of reinforced concrete. The inside is fireproofed and lined in steel paneling. I'm not sure what kind of steel, but I can tell you the First National Bank of Calloway's vault isn't built that stout. And as an added security precaution and to make it even more impenetrable, it's in a basement, so it's well protected."

"Could you get into it if you had to?"

"I can't tell you. I don't know what kind of vault door it is," Russ said. "My friend finished his work, and the door was installed later. He never saw it. Vaults can be very sophisticated. I'm guessing his vault would be a real challenge to open. You don't spend that kind of money building a vault room and then cheap out on the vault door. There are any number of ways that a vault door can open. It could be a time lock or a security code or even a biometric scanner. Who knows? But it won't open easy. I could probably open it eventually, but it's unlikely I'd be able to open it without destroying it—who knows how long that could take."

"So unless we find it open—" Ray started to say.

"It could be a real bitch," Russ said as his phone rang in his pocket. "Excuse me, Ray."

Ray looked out the window at Main Street as Russ took his call. It was beginning to spit sleet. Actually, it was more rain than sleet. Tori called it sneet—not snow and not sleet.

After Russ ended his phone call, he said, "You know, it's pretty well known what Pete Long does for a living."

"Yeah," Ray said. "I just wonder what in the hell he keeps in a vault."

"I've been thinking about that. Installing a vault like that in a house is a little odd. You'd have either of two reasons. Theft or fire. I'm guessing Peter Long had his built for both those reasons. He probably keeps the masters of all his movies in there along with his business records."

"That seems like a lot of vault for that purpose," Ray commented.

"It does, but he's got more money than God, so who knows."

When the shop door opened, Russ cursed quietly. The elderly man who stomped up to the counter was obviously in a bad mood with a full head of steam up.

"Morning, Mr. Fritz," Russ said in a tone that fell well short of cheerful.

"Don't 'good morning' me, Russell Martin," the old man snapped in a gravely voice. "You know exactly why I'm here."

"I'm sure there is something wrong with the work I did," Russ said with a sigh.

"You're damned right!" he said, pounding his fist on the counter. "I asked you for a good quality deadbolt on my garage. You installed a cheap piece of crap, and you skinned up the paint on the door and the doorframe besides."

"I did no such thing," Russ shot back. "That door was skinned up like that when I got there, and you know it. It was probably you trying to remove the old lock and install some generic piece of junk from Home Depot."

"You'll either replace that door you damaged, or I'll take you to court. And look at this," he growled, holding up a broken key. "First time I used it, the key broke off."

"I'll see you in court," Russ said. "That's not the new key I gave you yesterday. It's well worn. That's an old key you probably broke yourself so you'd have something to gripe about like you always do."

When the old man started to reach across the counter for Russ, Ray stepped in between them, accidentally knocking off the old man's ball cap.

"Who in the hell are you?" the old man said.

"I'm Chief Billings," Ray said calmly as he scooped up his hat from the floor and returned it to him.

Mr. Fritz snatched it out of his hand and jammed it onto his head.

"You should probably leave. You're not accomplishing anything here. Settle the matter in court if you want, but let's avoid a brawl. You know as well as I do that Russ could easily twist you into a pretzel."

Mr. Fritz was peering at his badge. "Twin Rivers? You've got no jurisdiction here," he growled, flashing a perfect row of white dentures at him.

"I didn't say I had jurisdiction here. I'm just giving you some friendly advice."

"And if I don't leave?" he said, glaring up into Ray's face with his deep-blue eyes.

"You want him to leave?" Ray asked Russ.

Russ nodded.

"Mr. Fritz," Ray said, looking him squarely in the face. "I'd rather not tangle with you today, but the owner wants you to leave. That means you're trespassing."

"You're not in Savannah anymore, Ray," the old man hissed. "We do things a little differently here in the Midwest."

The comment surprised Ray. He stared at the old man. How in the hell did he know I was from Savannah, Ray wondered. And how did he know my first name?

Ray looked at Russ, who had a strange look on his face—not irritated or upset but amused. In fact, it looked like Russ was trying not to laugh.

The old man glared up at Ray stubbornly. Then when he pushed his glasses up on his nose, something caught Ray's attention. He grabbed the old man's hand and stared at the Freemason ring with the red stone on the ring finger of his right hand. Ray wore one exactly like it. Then Ray noticed something else. For an old man in his eighties, he certainly had young hands.

Next Ray stared at Mr. Fritz's face as a glimmer of humor appeared in the old man's blue eyes. Finally, Ray noticed Rosco, who was standing beside Mr. Fritz, licking his left hand which was hanging at his side.

"I think he's getting it," Russ said.

"I think so to," the old man said as he stood straighter, seeming to grow four or five inches taller.

His voice had changed, too. It wasn't the gravelly voice of an old man anymore. Suddenly, Ray realized he'd been had.

"Levi?"

Chapter 24

Levi and Russ were still laughing as Ray stared. It was almost impossible to see anything familiar about Levi besides his blue eyes.

"That's amazing," Ray said, still looking at Levi's face intently.

Levi nodded as he pulled the fake dentures, which had fit over his real teeth, out of his mouth. He wiped them on his shirt and set them on the counter.

"The mask is silicon," Levi said.

"Even the neck," Ray said. "You've got an old man's neck."

"Kind of like yours," Russ said with a snicker.

Ray glared at him.

Levi unbuttoned his shirt to the waist. "This mask covers my shoulders and chest down to about my nipples."

"You've got gray chest hair," Russ said with a smile.

"It's creepy," Ray said.

"The mask is glued on," Levi said. "Across the forehead, around my eyes, under my nose, on the cheeks, around my mouth, and on my chin. The glasses help hide any transition line between the mask and my eyes. But as you can see, I can talk easily. I can even change my expression since the mask is stuck to my face. I can wrinkle my forehead, smile broadly, and laugh. I could even drink coffee or eat breakfast—although Mr. Simpson strongly recommended that I not do that."

"Why's that?" Ray asked.

"This mask costs seven hundred dollars. I'd rather not buy it if I damage it."

"Has Mr. Simpson sold any of those?" Ray asked with a glimmer of hope in his eyes.

Levi shook his head. "He's never sold one of the high-end silicon masks. He rents this one—with a huge deposit. It's the only one he owns, and it's not the face of our assassin, but I found that mask in one of his costume catalogues. Get this. The mask that our assassin wore is even more expensive than this one—it runs over a thousand dollars."

Ray whistled.

"How are you feeling now, Sherlock," Levi said with a laugh.

"Stupid." Then, glancing at Russ, Ray said, "Let me guess. That was Levi on the phone earlier."

Russ laughed as he nodded.

"You two should be on stage," Ray said. "That was a fine acting job."

"Not really," Levi said. "It was easy to trick you because you allowed yourself to be tricked. You saw what you thought was a grumpy old man, and you didn't pay much attention to the details. You even knew I was going to check out old-man masks, and it still never clicked with you. You didn't no-tice my hands when I reached over the counter and when I put the ball cap back on my head. I was just an old man. You didn't notice the dogs weren't alarmed when I got threatening. Normally, Bo would've been between you and whoever was threatening you. They knew who I was even if you didn't."

"I've got to be honest," Russ said. "I knew you were coming in here dressed like an old man, but when you walked in, I wasn't sure it was you. I thought maybe some other old dude got here before you did."

"It was a good plan," Ray said. "We also know another reason why the assassin wore gloves."

"To cover his young hands," Levi said. "My hands were what finally tipped you off."

"Actually, it wasn't your hands," Ray said, shaking his head. "It was your Masonic ring first. I was wondering what lodge would let an ass like you in."

"The standards aren't what they once were," Russ said, pointing to the newest tattoo on his right forearm—an all-seeing eye with a ribbon be-neath it that said "Brotherly Love, Relief & Truth."

Russ had petitioned the Twin Rivers Lodge the year before and had been raised a Master Mason a couple of months ago. The Calloway Lodge had come over to help with his degrees, including Sheriff Harby. They had no problem with their tenant downstairs petitioning a lodge in the next town over. They knew Russ had good friends there—Ray, Ed, and Levi.

"You know, most of us just buy a ring and a bumper sticker for the car," Ray remarked, looking at the newest tattoo.

Russ laughed. "I'm not most people."

"No, you're not," Ray admitted.

"Back to the mask," Levi said. "It seems to solve one big question."

Ray nodded. "No amateur buys a mask that costs a grand."

"We find where he bought that mask, and we find our assassin," Levi said. "That mask is sold by only one company in the world, Diablo Ef-fects in Los Angeles. I called them from Mr. Simpson's shop. According to their records, it's a new mask out just this year. They've sold only about fifty in the Midwest—mostly special orders from costume shops. The young lady I spoke to is going to send me the entire list of buyers by the end of the week."

"We've got him now!" Ray said with a laugh.

"Unless he paid cash," Levi said.

"Oh, look," Russ said. "It's snowing."

Huge fat flakes were floating to the ground, melting as soon as they touched, but the snow was coming down so heavily that the businesses across the street were almost invisible.

"That's never going to stick," Ray said.

"The guy from Georgia is a snow expert," Russ said.

He dug his phone out of his pocket, pushed on the screen, and handed it to Ray, who looked at it and handed it to Levi.

"Oh, boy," Levi said. "We might want to head home."

The weather map on Russ's phone showed a huge blue mass, indicating snow, just west of the green pin which marked Calloway on the map. It covered the entire western part of the state and parts of Missouri and Iowa. Twin Rivers, which was just eight miles south, couldn't be seen at all on Russ's map—it was already under the edge of the storm that was quickly approaching.

Chapter 25

Jay stood in front of the easel, smiling at his work. Then he leaned forward with his paintbrush and daubed a few more strokes around the eyes. He always started with the eyes when he painted people. He didn't have to. He just always did. Even before he picked up his brush, he knew exactly what the painting would look like when it was finished because it was imprinted in his memory like a photograph.

When he was satisfied that what he'd painted matched his memory, he stepped back to look at the two eyes floating in the center of the canvas. They were soft and wise and a shade of blue somewhere between corn flowers and the sky reflecting off a lake on a summer day. He'd wanted to paint this person for a long time, and he knew just who he was going to give this portrait to when he was finished.

Suddenly, a thump on the outer wall of his workshop took him out of his work and back into the real world. The snow outside the wall of windows was falling so heavily he could barely see the other bank of the river from his studio at the top of the bluff.

Something thumped on the outside wall again. Probably a branch knocking into the side of the building, he thought. When he walked out of the entry door, the strong winds that had whipped up in the last hour or two buffeted him. He pulled his jacket up snuggly around his neck and walked around the building to look at the side of his workshop where he'd heard the noise.

There was no branch near the building, but curiously, there were two clumps of snow stuck to the siding. He grinned. It looked like somebody had thrown a couple of snowballs at his workshop, but probably snow had blown out of the trees where it had settled in a fork before the wind picked up.

As he started back towards his house, he saw something out of the corner of his eye—something bright red caught in a tree and fluttering in the wind near the edge of the bluff. He turned to investigate. When he got close to the tree, he realized the object was a bright red balloon. That's odd, he thought. He'd reached out to pull it from the branches when he noticed something else strange. The balloon hadn't caught there in the wind. It was tied to the branch.

As he stared at the red balloon, he heard footsteps rushing up behind him. Before he had a chance to turn around, two palms slammed into his back, propelling him towards the edge of the cliff.

* * *

The two young hikers were trudging through the snow up the far bank of the river, moving as fast as they could. The storm had come up suddenly. They weren't dressed for a blizzard, and they'd been five miles from the truck when it hit. At times, the wind blew the snow so hard they couldn't see anything. As they'd stumbled through the undergrowth, their fear had increased until they'd found themselves along the banks of the Calloway River. Suddenly, they'd known exactly where they were.

Jim could hear little other than the whistle of the wind through the trees, the crunch of their footsteps, and his raspy breathing inside his hooded sweatshirt, which he'd pulled up over his face. He and Nat hurriedly began to scale the steep embankment. Freezing cold and wet, they were looking forward to the warm cab of their vehicle, just another half-mile away. They were nearly to the top when Jim stopped suddenly and turned back towards the river. Nat stopped at the same moment and turned in the same direction.

"Did you hear that?" Jim asked.

Nat nodded, shivering against the cold, his hands in the pockets of his light jacket.

"What did that sound like to you?"

"Like somebody screamed," Nat said, peering into the blinding snow.

They looked at each other for a minute—fear in their eyes.

"I don't hear anything now," Jim said.

"What should we do?"

"If we stay out here, we'll freeze to death," Jim said. "We'll call Chief Billings once we get back to the truck."

They'd taken a few more steps when Nat reached up and grabbed Jim's shoulder, stopping him again.

"What?" Jim said.

"Shhh . . ." Nat said, listening intently.

A tremendous screech rang out through the blinding snow.

The boys exploded into laughter.

"That's a red-tailed hawk," Jim said with a smile. "Scared the crap out of me."

"Yeah," Nat said. "Me, too. It sure sounded like a scream."

"Let's not repeat this story, okay?" Jim said as he started back up the embankment.

"Well, if I do," Nat said, "I'm going to claim I knew it was a hawk all along."

"That's fine," Jim said, glancing back at his friend. "Just remember who has the keys to the truck."

"Good point," Nat said.

Chapter 26

"Hang on," Levi said as he reached the four-way stop in front of the Beer Chaser.

The snow was coming down in huge fat flakes, and the wind had picked up. In less than an hour, the Calloway slab had all but vanished under the snow. Ray was hanging onto the passenger door with his right hand and bracing himself against the dash with his left. It was hard to believe that just a couple of hours earlier, they'd travelled this same road at seventy miles per hour with not even a trace of snow on the ground.

Ray had no idea how Levi knew exactly where the road was, but he was from Georgia. He didn't have much experience with snow, especially since the last two winters in Illinois had been very mild ones. The other thing that made Ray nervous was the depth of the snow. In a few places, the wind had drifted snow over the road so deep he was convinced the cruiser wouldn't get through it.

"Uh, that's a stop sign," Ray said as he firmed his grip on the dash.

"I stop now," Levi said, "and we're done."

He stomped the gas as he blasted through the stop sign into the deeper snow in the intersection. Then he eased off and cranked the wheel sharply, letting the car slide sideways.

Levi grinned. He thought Ray was saying some kind of prayer in the seat next to him.

When the car had slid halfway across the intersection, Levi snapped the wheel in the direction he was sliding and gunned the accelerator again. The rear of the car whipped around, but after a few sharp turns of the wheel, the car straightened out, and they were driving towards Main Street.

"Piece of cake," Levi said.

"Where did you learn to drive like that?" Ray said, daring a glance out the windshield.

"After about the fiftieth time you put your truck in the ditch, you start to figure out how the physics of snow and momentum work. And I clocked a few thousand hours on a snowmobile, too. The experience came in handy when I was a state trooper."

"Nice," Ray said, sounding just a bit sarcastic.

"I'm just going to run you by your house and then take the cruiser home. In another half an hour, these streets are going to be impassable," Levi said. "Why don't you call Amber and tell her we're back."

Ray nodded. He pulled his phone out of his pocket as Levi skidded out into another intersection and repeated the same maneuver.

"No signal," Ray said.

Levi pulled his phone out of his pocket. His was dead, too.

"I'll call her from the house. The land line should still be okay," Ray said—it was more a question than a statement.

"Most likely," Levi answered as he slowed to a stop in front of Ray's house. "I'll see you in a couple of days."

"A couple of days?" Ray said.

"Yup. This will last a good twenty-four hours, and it'll take a day to clear the streets."

Ray sighed as he looked at the house. Bernice was standing in the large living room window.

"Something wrong?"

"No," Ray said, shaking his head. "Just remembering a movie I saw once—"

"*White Christmas*?" Levi asked.

"No," Ray said, "*The Shining*."

Levi laughed as Ray opened the car door.

"You know you can always stay with us," Levi said.

"Thanks, but I've got to deal with this at some point," Ray said. "Let's go, Bo."

Bo bounded over the seat and plowed through the snow towards the house.

"Call me if you need anything," Levi said. "Do you have my house phone?"

Ray wasn't sure he'd ever called the house phone. Actually, he didn't even know Levi had one. He checked his phone contacts, and sure enough, it was there. "I've got it. Be careful."

Ray slammed the door and climbed through the deepening snow in his driveway. He glanced back towards the street when he heard the engine of the cruiser rev and the tires spin. Levi was in the process of cutting an impressive donut in front of the house. Then he went roaring back up the street in the direction he'd come.

"You could've called," Bernice said peevishly from the front porch step.

"No service," Ray said, holding up his cell phone.

"Naturally," she huffed as she stepped back into the house, leaving the door wide open behind her.

Ray trudged up the steps. He was thinking about that movie again—about how Jack Nicholson went crazy during the blizzard, went after his wife, and chopped down the door with the axe. I can see how something like that could happen, he thought.

"Here's Johnny!" he quoted from the movie as he walked into the house and pushed the door shut.

* * *

Levi stepped back from the fireplace to admire the job he'd done. The fire was crackling to life and bathing the library in reds and oranges. The power had flickered a few times. It would go out pretty soon. They had an old back-up generator. Sometimes it kicked on, and sometimes it didn't. Every time it stormed and the power flickered, they said they'd replace it, but then they always seemed to forget. Either way, with power or without, they were ready now.

"Here you go," Tori said, handing him a cup of coffee.

"I'd rather have a beer," Levi remarked.

Tori smiled and sipped her coffee.

"We do have beer," Levi said—a statement that was actually a question.

Tori looked at him nervously.

"Tori, please tell me we have beer."

"I forgot. There's a six pack in there, but that's it. Better enjoy it sparingly."

Levi sat down hard in his chair and shot her a look.

"I'm sorry, Levi. It totally slipped my mind. I got milk, batteries for the flashlights, and diesel for the generator, but I totally forgot to get you beer."

Levi shook his head, then smiled.

"What?"

"I was just thinking about this old movie Ray reminded me of earlier."

"*White Christmas*?" Tori asked.

"Yes," Levi said, rising, "that's exactly the one. I think I'll go write awhile in the den."

Tori sat down in the wingback chair he'd just left and picked up her Nook.

"Well, don't work too hard. You know, all work and no play makes Jack a dull boy. All work and no play makes Jack a dull boy. All work and no play makes Jack a dull boy."

Levi laughed out loud as he left her in the library. He could still hear her, repeating the same thing over and over again.

Chapter 27

The old man's eyes were heavy as he sat in front of the fireplace in his library, a book from his massive collection of rare volumes in his lap. He was fighting the nap he knew he'd be taking shortly. The wind outside howled, and the blowing snow rasped against the window panes of the mansion. Tony O'Malley glanced at his watch. It was only two o'clock, still a little early for a nap.

When the library door opened, he heard his nephew Carl's familiar footsteps on the parquet floor. Carl had been groomed his entire life to take over the family business. Even though Tony was in his nineties, he wasn't about to retire yet. His health was good, his mind sharp. He figured his retirement would come about two days before his funeral. But even Tony wasn't sure how many years he had left, so gradually he was letting Carl take the reins of the Chicago Outfit.

"Who was at the door?" Tony asked as Carl plopped down in the other chair in front of the fireplace.

"It was Jake," Carl said.

"And," Tony said, setting his book on the small table between the two chairs and holding out a liver-spotted hand.

Carl chuckled as he handed him the two file folders Jake had just delivered. Tony glanced through Jake's handwritten notes in the first folder—notes about a marijuana operation downstate.

"Who the hell was running that?" Tony growled.

"Oh, we're going to find out," Carl said grimly. "DEA is all over it. Sounds like whoever it was knew what they were doing, and the investigators are clueless so far. Jake will have it figured out before they do."

"There's never just one operation," Tony said from experience. "So many new players in the game these days. You find them and step on their necks and let them know who runs this state. Make sure they understand the necessity of respect."

Carl nodded. He knew what Tony meant. They'd soon be partners in what was obviously a lucrative, well-organized drug operation—and if their new friends weren't open to sharing the wealth, the Outfit would simply wipe them out and take it from them.

"What's in this other one?" Tony asked, handing the first folder back to Carl and opening the second one.

"Jake thought you might find that interesting," Carl said. "He ran across something else while he was in River County and wrote up a short dossier. It might be part of the marijuana operation, and it might not be. Jake doesn't think they're related."

Carl sat silently for a few minutes as Tony read. The second report was actually a lot longer than the first. When Tony got to one part of the report, his head snapped towards Carl, and he grinned before returning to his reading. However, when he got towards the end of the report, the smile faded and his jaw grew tight.

Finally, Tony closed the folder and stared into the fire for a couple of minutes. Carl knew better than to say anything. Tony O'Malley was working, and when he was working, only a fool would interrupt him.

"Jake was right," Tony said sharply, breaking the silence. "That is very interesting indeed—something worth looking into in more detail."

"I thought so, too."

"And how is Officer Walker?" Tony asked.

"He'll recover."

"And Chief Billings and his new officer, Levi Garvey?" Tony asked.

The Chicago Outfit's Four Horsemen, the enforcers in the organization, had butted heads with the Garveys not long ago. They'd come away not exactly friends but certainly not enemies. Tony respected the Garveys and the new chief in Twin Rivers. There was an unspoken agreement between Tony and his new acquaintances in Twin Rivers to leave each other alone.

"Ray and Levi seem to be making good progress," Carl said. "Actually, they've made more progress on the dead porn star than the DEA has on the drug operation. That's for sure."

"What's our exposure in this?" Tony asked.

"As you know, we've had a mutually beneficial relationship with Peter Long over the years. He's a club owner, and we've been of some assistance in some of his related endeavors in Peoria and up here in Chicago. We own a small interest in several of his clubs—untraceable. And there are a few other areas we've been involved with—mostly small-time prostitution. But he's a big-time porn guy. We're not involved in that, of course."

Tony O'Malley had rules about porn. It was lucrative, but Tony found it distasteful. And Carl had no interest in changing that rule when he took over.

Carl paused, then continued. "I'm not too concerned about our relationship with Peter Long. It would be hard to make a connection, but, of course, we are talking about Levi Garvey. Even so, I'd say our risk is minimal."

"So let's summarize this," Tony said. "Walker stumbles onto the marijuana operation while answering an unrelated police call. The woman on the call is a drug addict who winds up in the hospital. Walker winds up shot by the drug dealers. Then the woman, one of Peter Long's old porn stars, is murdered in the hospital."

"And I should point out, she was also Peter Long's wife," Carl said.

"And it looks like a professional hit," Tony added.

"Yes, pulled off by an old man," Carl added.

"The timing is interesting."

"It is," Carl said.

"Before the porn queen is murdered, Chief Billings, down an officer, has already tapped Levi and his Uncle Ed to help out."

"That's what makes it interesting," Carl remarked.

"Professional hit by an old man," Tony said tersely. "I'm sure nothing will jump into Ray's or Levi's mind based on that fact alone."

Carl glanced at Tony. Sarcasm wasn't something Tony did well. Sometimes it was hard to tell exactly what his point was.

"The assassin did that on purpose," Tony said. "He knew what Levi Garvey would think, didn't he? The assassin seems to have done it in such a way that Ray and Levi might believe it was a hit organized by you and pulled off by one or all of your infamous Four Horsemen."

"Little do they know we retired those old men," Carl said with a chuckle.

For more than forty years, Tony had depended on Carl and his three trained thugs to do his dirty work. They had terrorized those that got in the way of the Chicago Outfit, and more often than not, his enemies and any witnesses against him simply vanished like magic. But the Four Horsemen had grown old—the youngest was sixty-five, and the oldest had turned eighty last fall. Their leader, Carl, was no spring chicken himself. He'd just turned seventy. Their last trip to Twin Rivers had demonstrated that it was time for a change of the guard. Tony was glad the stand-off with the Garveys had ended peacefully since he wasn't sure how the aging Four Horsemen would've done against them. Not well, he suspected. Of course, he wasn't sure how well the Four Horsemen would've stood up against the Garveys even thirty years ago when they were in their prime.

Last fall, Tony had suggested that it was time for Carl to start putting together his own team—to start thinking about the next generation. It was time for Carl to pick his own right-hand man and his own group of enforcers.

"What do you think we should do?" Tony asked.

"Nothing," Carl said without hesitation.

"Why not?"

"Ray and Levi aren't stupid," Carl said. "They're not going to buy that. They'll see this as an attempt to frame us. Whoever hired that hit knew what he was doing. It was pretty ballsy trying to shift the focus of the murder onto us, but I don't think that ploy is going to fool Levi and the chief for one minute."

Tony looked at him with his pale-blue eyes. For a moment, Carl thought it was the wrong answer.

Then Tony nodded. "That's exactly right. But I'll make you a bet."

"What's that?"

"I have a feeling we're going to get a visit from Twin Rivers eventually."

"Levi or Ray?"

Tony chuckled. "Maybe both?"

"I'll tell you one thing. I really want to know who murdered that porn star. That's a problem for me. That's very . . ." Carl paused, looking for the right word. Then he finished, "disrespectful towards the Outfit. We can't let that stand."

"That right. Somebody's got to pay for that," Tony agreed. "We'll be paying a little social call when we find out who that was because it was very stupid to try to link that hit to us. I assume we're trying to find out exactly who that was."

"I've got Jake working on it," Carl said.

"And once he finds out who it was?"

Carl chuckled ominously. "Sounds to me like a job for the Four Horsemen."

Tony frowned angrily. "You'd pull them out of retirement for this? That's insane. They aren't up to the challenge."

"I'm not talking about *your* Four Horsemen. I'm talking about *mine.*"

The anger on Tony's face faded. "Really? You've got a team hired?"

"I've made my selections," Carl remarked, "but you still do the hiring around here, Uncle Tony."

"And who have you chosen as a right-hand?"

"Angelino," Carl said.

"The mercenary?" Tony asked as a small smile appeared at the corners of his mouth.

Carl nodded. "His family has worked for the Chicago Outfit since Capone ran it. He's highly trained in special ops, and he knows the importance of respect and family values. He can be trusted. He's young, but I can't think of anyone I'd rather have."

Tony smiled. He'd hoped that Angelino would be Carl's choice. He certainly would've been his. The sober-faced young man had impressed him the only time they'd met. There was something chilling about him. Tony liked hard men because it was a hard job, and Angelino, although young, was a very hard man.

"You picked all four Horsemen yourself?"

"Of course not," Carl said. He knew that question was a test. "It's Angelino's team and his job to pick the men. I've done it the same way you did it with me. He made good choices. They'll do what they're asked to do. Of course, you have the final say."

"Do you think Angelino could run this outfit one day? That's where the job leads. And you're a lot older than I was when I took it over."

"I think he could run it now," Carl said. "He's smart, and he's earned a certain reputation. In fact, there are a few of our associates that have been very interested in hiring him away from us."

"That's good," Tony said. "And what does Angelino think about these offers?"

"There's not enough money in the world to make him consider ever leaving the Chicago Outfit. He's our boy and always will be. It's a family tradition with him."

"I've been hearing about him for several years, and I certainly liked him when we met. But what does Angelino go by? Please tell me it isn't Angie . . ."

"He goes by Angel," Carl said with a smile. "I guess that makes him the Angel of Death."

Tony looked at him shrewdly. "That should strike fear into the hearts of those that cross you in the future."

"The nickname isn't nearly as frightening as the man it belongs to. Are you ready to talk to the Four Horsemen, Uncle Tony? They're in the hallway. And we just might be needing them soon."

"I'd like that very much," Tony said.

* * *

The four men in dark suits stood at the end of the library as Tony walked up to them. They towered over him, not one under six feet tall. Though they looked like young, innocent college frat boys, every one of them looked Tony right in the eye—secure in the knowledge they had nothing to fear from one of the most notorious gangsters in American history—unless they crossed him.

"You know why you're here," Tony said as he walked in front of them, regarding each in turn. "You know what the job is. You know the dangers. You've all come from families with long ties to our organization. You've all been to funerals where the casket had to be left closed. You're replacing four of the best and most feared enforcers in the world. Those are big shoes to fill. They've all retired—not because they were lucky but because they were that good. Even so, they all bear the scars to prove this job isn't easy.

"There's a good chance you won't be so lucky. Your job is to clean up the big messes. You're often going to be our last line of defense. And these jobs are always going to be dangerous. There's a good chance you won't be as lucky as those men you're replacing. Good chance one or all of you will be killed doing what you've volunteered to do. And if you're caught by the police or the FBI or whoever, you'll never have to worry about going to prison. I promise that you'll never see the inside of a courtroom."

Carl added, "Because if you're stupid enough to get caught, I'll have you killed."

"I think they got that," Tony said harshly.

Carl's face paled. Suddenly, the four men looked a little nervous. They were more afraid of Carl than they were of Tony. They'd experienced Carl. To see him react to Tony in a fearful way made a big impression on them.

"This is your last chance out," Tony said. "You're all hired, but you have twenty-four hours to accept the job. If you want out, you'll go back to what you're doing today, and there will be no repercussions. If you show up here tomorrow at this same time, you're Carl's Four Horsemen. And nobody ever resigns from that position. So you'd better damn well think about it. If you show up here tomorrow, the only way you leave this job is in a casket."

Tony walked to the far end of the library, about forty feet away, and looked at a portrait on the wall. Almost everyone in the Chicago Outfit knew Tony "The Shotgun" O'Malley was a history buff.

"Anybody know who the man is in this portrait?"

Three of the Horsemen looked puzzled, but Angel, standing at the end, just smiled.

"Angel knows. Do any of the rest of you?"

The other three shook their heads.

"Anybody want to guess?" Tony suggested.

"Is it Paul Revere?" one of them asked.

Tony smiled at him. "Is that your final answer?"

The young man shrugged. "I was guessing. Is that right?"

"No," Tony said. "That's wrong. Tell him, Angel."

"It's Benedict Arnold."

"A traitor," Tony said as he stepped in front of the portrait. "What happens to traitors in this organization, Angel?"

Tony barely saw the revolver drawn from his jacket, but he clearly heard the two gunshots and felt the bullets whiz inches over his head. Tony reached up and ran his fingers through his hair, checking to see if it was all there. Turning, he looked at the portrait. There were two bullets between Arnold's eyes, only inches above where Tony's head had been.

Tony glanced at Carl, who wasn't sure what to think. That certainly wasn't the answer he'd expected, and from the look on Tony's face, not the answer he'd expected either. Carl happened to know that portrait was worth a small fortune.

Slowly, Tony walked back towards the men. Angel re-holstered his gun and looked at Tony squarely.

"That's exactly right, Angel," Tony said, trying to act as if what Angel had done hadn't surprised him in any way. He wasn't sure he did a very convincing job.

Then stepping in front of the Horseman who'd guessed incorrectly, Tony growled, "That was stupid. Why did you guess? You think this is a guessing game? Your job is based on facts you know and abilities you possess. We don't guess. There's no room for guessing."

"Yes, you're right," the young man said, swallowing hard. "I'm sorry."

"You're sorry," Tony said, poking him in the chest and looking up into his terrified face.

Tony walked a few steps out into the library, then turned back to him. Carl knew the young man was in trouble. He just didn't know how much trouble yet. It wouldn't surprise him if Tony pulled his revolver and shot the young man in the head. Carl had seen him do it before.

"What's your name?" Tony asked.

"Scott," he replied.

"Are you afraid of me, Scott?" Tony said, looking at him with his pale-blue eyes.

Scott cleared his throat. "I know you have little patience for stupidity, and I'm afraid I didn't make a very good first impression."

"So you were just a little nervous, meeting me for the first time?" Tony said. "Thought I might just pull my gun and take you out. You've heard stories, I'm sure."

Scott nodded.

"You won't make a bad second impression," Tony said.

"No, sir, I will not."

Tony stared at him for a moment, then nodded and walked back to his desk.

"I'll see all of you here tomorrow. Think about the job carefully. Think about what it means. If you show up here again, there's no backing out."

Carl stepped forward. "You're dismissed."

The Four Horsemen began to walk towards the door.

"Angel," Tony said. "I'd like to have a word with you before you leave."

After the door closed, Carl poured himself a bourbon from the side-bar and asked, "You want a scotch, Tony?"

Tony nodded. "What do you drink, Angel?" he said, looking at the young man.

"I don't drink," Angel replied. "I never have."

"Have a seat if you like," Tony said, waving to one of the wingback chairs in front of his desk.

"I'll stand if you don't mind," Angel said.

Tony glanced at Carl. There was a glimmer of a smile in his eyes. Carl knew he'd made a good choice in Tony's mind.

"I think Carl has something for you to do," Tony said.

"We don't deal with stupid," Carl said off-handedly as he stirred an ice cube around in his bourbon with his finger.

"I made a bad choice," Angel said. "Scott has got impressive skills, just not any brains."

"That will wind up being a problem eventually," Tony said as sipped the scotch.

Angel grinned tightly. "Perhaps we can turn Scott's error into a teaching moment. Perhaps the other members of the team can benefit from an example."

"Do you have any doubts that all three of them will show up here tomorrow?" Tony asked.

"They know what they're signing up for," Angel said. "They'll all be here tomorrow."

"All of them?" Carl asked.

"All of them except Scott," Angel said coldly. "I have another candidate to replace him."

"Get with the other two and take care of it," Carl said. "Tonight. And be sure your replacement candidate is a good one, or the next one I replace could very well be you."

"Understood," Angel said.

Regarding Angel with his eyes tight, Tony added, "Don't make another mistake, Angel. Get your team together. I have a feeling we're going to need you very soon. And by the way, you owe me for that portrait. You have no idea how rare it is. I just got it last month. I didn't expect you to shoot it full of holes."

"You asked the question," Angel said, a faint hint of a smile on his face.

"You could've just answered it," Tony shot back.

"Horsemen are about action, not words," Angel said. "At least, that's the way I read the job description."

"You read it right," Tony said, gazing at his ruined portrait. "I think you have a job to do."

Angelino nodded, walked across the library, and exited.

"He knew it was a duplicate," Tony said.

Carl grinned. "Only a fool would hang a two million dollar stolen portrait in his library where the police, the FBI, or even the Secret Service might bust in at any time. And I'm pretty sure Angel doesn't think you're a fool."

Continuing to gaze at the ruined portrait, Tony said, "It's still a forty thousand dollar reproduction."

"Which will hang there for the rest of your life with two bullet holes in it," Carl said. "You love stuff like that."

Tony looked at a copy of one of Levi Garvey's books on his desk. It had a bullet hole in it, too—from the Webley revolver that belonged to Abe Garvey, Levi's great-grandfather.

"Make sure they get Scott taken care of," Tony said.

Carl shook his head. "You've never checked up on me, and I'm not about to start out by checking up on Angel. You can consider the job done."

Chapter 28

Tori was asleep in the wingback chair in front of the fire, dreaming of a summer day from long ago. She was sitting in the run-down Comet Theatre with Levi, watching an old movie and eating popcorn—their feet propped up on the row in front to keep them off the sticky floor. There were long rips in the old movie screen and stuffing hanging out of some of the theatre seats. Tori was in love with Levi even then, back in high school. Actually, each loved the other, but neither said anything for fear of losing the friendship if rejected as a lover.

But there was something wrong with the dream. Unlike most people, she almost always knew when she was dreaming. Most often, she just enjoyed the dreams—she could even change them if she wanted. But there was something off about this dream, and she found she couldn't change it. Somebody was running a vacuum cleaner in the lobby of the old theatre. They didn't do that during a movie. And in the old Comet Theatre days, it was unlikely anyone ever ran the vacuum since the place wasn't exactly known for cleanliness. The sound grew louder and louder until finally Levi looked over at her with that shrewd look that often said he'd just pulled off the best prank ever and nobody knew it yet. When Levi got that look on his face, Tori always said the same thing, "What did you just do?"

Just then, Rosco's head popped up from the floor between them, and he barked towards the lobby doors. They always took Rosco to the movies. Wait a minute, Tori thought. We take Rosco to the movies today. We didn't even have Rosco back then.

Suddenly, she woke up with a jerk in the library wingback. With his feet up on the ledge, Rosco was barking out the window. The sound she'd heard wasn't part of her dream but a part of the real world that had seeped into her dream. Her first thought was a motorcycle, but as she got up, she remembered the blizzard.

There was a loud knock on the front door. As she stepped into the foyer, Levi opened the door.

"Hey, thanks," Levi said. "I sure appreciate it. Here you go. Keep the change."

"Wow! Thank you, Mr. Garvey," the voice outside said.

Levi chuckled as he shut the door. When he saw Tori standing behind him, his smile withered. He had two twelve-packs of beer, one in his hand and the other tucked under his arm.

Outside, the engine cranked up. Tori glanced out the foyer window. A red snowmobile was heading down the driveway, the red taillight disappearing into the blowing snow.

"A case?" Tori said, shaking her head.

"Well, I wasn't going to have him go to that much trouble for just a twelve pack."

"You know, you're an evil genius," Tori said as a small smile crossed her face.

"Want one?" Levi asked. "I'm telling you, these are ice cold!"

"They should be," Tori said with a laugh. "They just traveled several miles on the back of a snowmobile during a blizzard."

Levi shook his head. "I would never ask a young man to venture out for beer during a blizzard. It's been downgraded to a severe winter storm. Besides, he was already running up and down the road and across the fields before I flagged him down."

"I'm sure you made it worth his while."

"All I had was a hundred dollar bill."

Levi headed towards the kitchen. Tori followed him. He put the beer in the fridge as she sat down on one of the stools at the kitchen island. Levi pulled out two beers, cracked one for Tori, then leaned against the fridge as he cracked his.

"You're right. It's definitely cold. It's almost a beer slushy," Tori said, sipping hers.

"Oh yeah," said Levi, sipping his.

"Adam will be up soon," Tori remarked.

"About any time now," Levi said, glancing at the clock on the stove. "This storm is winding down. It's no longer expected to be nearly as bad as originally forecasted. We should be out in the morning."

Since it was just past four o'clock in the afternoon, Tori wondered for a moment why, if Levi knew the storm was blowing itself out, he'd just spent $100 on $30 worth of beer.

"So why did you . . ." She stopped because she knew the answer.

Next time there was a blizzard, some kid would bang on the front door, his snowmobile idling, and say, "Is there anything you need, Mr. Garvey? I was just riding by and thought I'd check on you folks."

When Tori laughed, Levi tapped the side of his head and said, "Evil genius. You always say we need to have an emergency supply plan in place."

They looked at each other for a moment. Then Tori looked down at the beer sitting on the island counter. The silence grew long. Levi sensed that she wanted to say something—probably about his role as Officer Garvey and the case. She'd listened to Levi's accounts intently. Tori loved a puzzle as much as he did. She was more methodical in her thought processes than he was. She was analytical while he was more creative.

"I've got a couple of ideas about that Selena Long deal," Tori said finally.

"It's about time. And?"

"Nothing makes sense about this whole thing."

"No, it doesn't," Levi admitted. "It seems that Ray and I are official-ly stuck."

"I think the answer lies in who would want Selena Long dead," Tori said.

"She was probably a pawn in this," Levi said.

"I agree," Tori said. "What could she possibly have known at this point that would make her a target?"

"She'd been out of the picture for a long time. The only information she might've had could only hurt Peter Long now," Levi said.

"But do you think if Peter Long murdered her for some reason, he'd make it look like Tony O'Malley did it?"

Levi shook his head. "I saw the look on his face when Tony's name was mentioned. It was the only honest emotional response we got out of Pe-ter Long—and it was pure terror. There's no way he would've done that."

"The only reason the murderer dressed up as an old man was to get Tony O'Malley's attention," Tori said.

"There's somebody else behind this," Levi said. "And it isn't Peter Long, and it isn't Tony O'Malley."

Tori smiled. "There are two reasons for the murderer to do that."

"Two?" Levi said.

"The first reason is that once it looks like Tony O'Malley is involved he becomes the focus of the investigation and the focus of the media cover-age. Most people already know that Tony is famous for doing things just like that," Tori said.

"And the second reason?" Levi asked.

"We've already talked about that one," Tori said. "Once Tony O'Malley hears that somebody tried to implicate him, he's going to get angry about it. And when Tony gets angry, he has a way of getting involved."

"Tony is going to assume that Peter Long did this," Levi said.

Tori sipped her beer and nodded. "That's exactly what he's going to think. That's why I think our murderer was after Peter Long from the begin-ning."

"So our murderer is very smart," Levi said. "He's after Peter Long for some reason. He kills Selena, implicating Tony."

"Then Tony gets pissed off. He sends his thugs down here, and bad things happen to Peter Long," Tori added. "It's brilliant."

"Why go to that much trouble?" Levi said. "Why not just murder Peter Long if that's the guy you want dead?"

"I've been thinking about that, too," Tori said. "There are two rea-sons for that as well."

"What's the first reason," Levi said, impressed that Tori had obviously gotten a lot further with her thinking than he and Ray had.

"Our murderer would likely be an obvious suspect," Tori said. "I'm sure Peter Long has made a lot of enemies, so he set it up so that Tony O'Malley will commit the murder for him."

Levi smiled. "That's very good, Tori. That actually makes sense. What's the second reason?"

"That vault," Tori said. "Why would Peter Long have such a huge vault in his basement?"

"It suggests he has a lot of valuables," Levi said.

"Or a lot of valuable information," Tori said, "information that during a murder investigation would come out and could point at the murderer."

"But if Tony O'Malley kills Peter Long," Levi said, "there could be a thousand prime suspects uncovered in that vault, and it wouldn't matter because we already know exactly who murdered Peter Long."

"Tony O'Malley," Tori said. "And nobody has ever managed to get a murder charge to stick to Tony."

"We've got to find out who Peter Long's enemies are," Levi said.

"That's who you're looking for," Tori said. "And you need to move fast."

Levi glanced up at her, suddenly understanding what she meant.

"You can be sure that Tony knows about this," Tori said. "It's already been in the papers, so it may already be too late. Tony is going to have Peter Long killed without a doubt."

Both Levi and Tori glanced up when they heard a light thump on the floor upstairs. Whining, Rosco looked up at the ceiling, too.

"That little jail breaker did it again," Tori remarked with a grin. "He's climbed out of his crib. I'd better go catch him before he gets to the top of the stairs."

Levi watched her and Rosco make a hasty retreat out of the kitchen. Levi wasn't worried. Even though Adam wasn't walking yet, he was crawling everywhere. As far as the stairs went, Levi had watched Adam slide down more than once on his belly feet first, using his hands to control his descent and laughing all the way down.

As he listened to Tori's muffled voice, Rosco's barking, and Adam's excited shrieks, something Tori said began to sink in. It's one thing to have it rumored Tony O'Malley is involved, he thought. It's something very different when he actually gets involved. Levi leaned against the counter and rubbed the side of his head. Maybe there's a way to stop that from happening.

Chapter 29

"Where in the hell is Levi?" Ray said as he banged in through the door of the Twin Rivers Police Department. "I've been trying to call him for two hours."

Ray was wet up to his knees. He'd walked the three blocks from his house to Main Street.

"I have no idea," Amber said with a shrug. "He's not answering his cell, and April said he never showed up for pie. It's chocolate."

"What the hell? Levi never misses chocolate," Ray said, even more worried.

"I may have overreacted," Amber said. "When he didn't answer his cell, I called Tori. I couldn't reach her either."

"Then what did you do?" Ray asked.

"I sent fire and rescue," Amber said. "When they heard the name, all the emergency vehicles, including the ambulance from Calloway, went racing to the house. There was no problem. They found Mrs. B. watching Adam. Levi had called her so that he could leave. Tori had left at sunrise to run errands for the library project."

"Did he tell Mrs. B. where he was going?"

Amber shook her head. "No, he didn't." She sighed. "I'm going to be catching shit from the fire department for the next six months. But what could be more important to Levi than chocolate pie?"

Amber was right on two points. Those guys at the fire house would hound her mercilessly for months for calling them because Levi Garvey hadn't shown up for pie. And secondly, something was definitely wrong.

"They'll turn up," Ray said.

"I was trying to contact you, too. I just got a call from Merle Reid. I couldn't reach you, so I was about to call the County Mounties to go check."

"What's going on?"

"Do you know Merle?"

Ray shook his head.

"He lives out along the Calloway River. He was out filling his bird feeders this morning when he noticed a bunch of turkey vultures circling about a quarter of a mile up the river."

"And?" Ray prodded. Sometimes it took people from the Midwest a long time to get to the point.

"He's in his eighties, but he walked out to the edge of the bluff and looked with his binoculars. He said there's something dead on the rocks down beside the river."

"Maybe a deer?"

"It could be," Amber admitted. "But he said it's right beneath Jay Snider's place. He thinks it looks like a man. Merle also mentioned that a couple of kids were out stomping around in the woods yesterday right before the storm hit. I tried to reach Jay Snider, but he doesn't answer. I was going to ask if he could identify what Merle was seeing."

Ray felt the hairs on the back of his neck rise. "Where's Ed Garvey?"

"Haven't we already been over this? It's chocolate," Amber said, pointing out the windows towards Harv's Grill.

Ray turned suddenly and walked out the door. Amber watched him stomp through the snow to the restaurant.

Chapter 30

Levi pulled up in front of the gate in Old Blue. It'd been a long drive even though the roads were pretty much cleared. A few times, he'd wondered if Old Blue would pull through the snow, but the old truck had made it just fine. Unsure of exactly how to get to where he was going, he'd stopped once for directions. When he'd shown the young clerk in the gas station the address he was looking for, the clerk had simply shaken his head and walked away. As a result, Levi knew he'd have to find it on his own. After he thought to plug the address into his cell phone, the map had taken him right to the gate. Sometimes he forgot he had that tool at his disposal. Amber would be pleased to know he'd finally used it.

As Levi cranked down the window by hand, Rosco stepped over his lap and hung his head out the driver's side window.

"Would you get off me?" Levi said, pushing at the huge dog who responded by licking his face and knocking off his felt trooper hat.

"I've said it before," Levi said, glaring at the dog as he reached behind his head to retrieve his hat before it fell into the narrow gap behind the seat and the back of the cab. "If anything ever happens to you, Rosco, I'm seriously thinking about never getting another dog."

Levi snugged the hat back on his head. Then he looked at the heavy gates in front of him, wondering how many who'd driven through them had never left.

Levi pushed the red button on the speaker post beside the driveway. Then he waited.

"Yes?" a voice said.

"My name is Levi Garvey. That's Officer Levi Garvey from Twin Rivers. I'm here to see Tony O'Malley."

There was no response. Levi waited. Then, just about the time he thought there'd never be a response, the gates began to roll open.

"Okay, Rosco," Levi said, "here we go."

Levi followed the long winding drive until the stately mansion appeared in front of him. He rolled around a huge fountain with the figure of a naked female Greek goddess on top. Water wasn't running because it was winter, but Levi thought it was probably pretty impressive during the summer months. He pulled under a covered carriage port at the front door and stopped. Rosco jumped out right after him. As he raised his hand to knock, the door suddenly opened.

"Mr. Garvey, Tony is expecting you," the young man said, waving him into the expansive marble-tiled foyer.

A huge chandelier hung overhead, and a staircase wound up one side. Levi knew he wouldn't be climbing those stairs. He glanced at the double doors off to the side, figuring that was where he'd meet with Tony O'Malley. Levi noticed one lump created by the butler's shoulder holster and another one at his ankle. The entire scene was exactly as Ray had described it after his visit there a couple of years earlier with the exception that Carl had answered the door then. This butler was obviously a new hire.

"Let me guess," Levi said. "You'll need my gun."

"Are you planning on shooting somebody?" the butler asked.

"No," Levi said. "My dog is far more dangerous than my gun."

Glancing at the dog, the butler was obviously unimpressed by what he saw.

"Yes, he looks terrifying," he remarked blandly.

"You have the advantage," Levi said. "You know my name, but I didn't catch yours."

"I'm Angelino," he said.

"Nice to meet you," Levi said, holding out his hand.

Angelino looked down at Levi's hand but didn't take it.

"Mr. O'Malley is waiting," he said as he crossed to the library door and tapped twice.

The door opened, and a familiar face appeared.

As Levi looked up at the massive frame of the man in the doorway, a lump suddenly rose in this throat. The first time he'd seen Carl was in the open doorway of the carriage house. Carl had opened fire was an AK-47, turning the inside of the Garveys' carriage house into a war zone of blue smoke and wood splinters. He'd saved Levi's life. The second time, at the Twin Rivers Masonic Lodge, was even less pleasant. Carl was a trained killer—the most feared enforcer in Chicago organized crime.

"Levi," he acknowledged coldly.

"Hello, Carl," Levi replied.

"Tony is delighted you're here. He's just getting ready to have coffee. He'd like you to join him."

Rosco had already scooted past Carl. Rosco's tail thumped on the wooden parquet floor as Tony greeted him. Rosco knew both Tony and Carl. They'd had beers on the Garvey front porch one evening not so long ago after their last tense encounter at the Twin Rivers Masonic Lodge.

But we aren't old friends, Levi thought to himself, because when you meet old friends your heart doesn't thud in your chest, sweat doesn't trickle down the back of your neck, and your palms don't get all sweaty.

Carl opened the door wider, and as Levi walked towards it, Angelino bumped into him.

"Sorry," Angelino said.

"No problem."

"Levi!" Tony exclaimed from behind his desk in the huge library. "I'm so happy you're here! My favorite author finally stops in for a visit. We were just having coffee. I think you know my friend here."

Levi stepped in through the library door. His gut knotted when he heard the door close behind him and the lock click from the outside.

Chapter 31

"How do you know where the road is?" Ray said, gripping the door handle and bracing himself against the dash much as he'd done the day before when Levi was driving them back to Twin Rivers through the storm.

Ed's tow truck, with a plow on the front, was clearing a path down a winding river road, heading toward Jay Snider's house.

"You can just kind of tell. You can see where the snow has settled in the ditches sometimes, and when you can't see that, like now, you look at the trees that line either side of the road and aim straight down the middle. Sometimes it's telephone poles. Sometimes it's farm fences. You know, years ago I used to plow snow for the township during the winter months."

"So it's mostly guessing," Ray said.

He knew just how deep some of the ditches along these rural roads were, but he tried not to think about what falling off the edge of the road would feel like as the truck slammed into one.

Ed chuckled. "I guess you could call it guessing." Then, changing the subject, he asked, "What do you think is going on?"

"I'm not sure."

"You think that's Jay down at the bottom of the bluff?" Ed asked.

Ray glanced over at Ed. He didn't need to answer that question. Ed saw the answer.

"Damn," Ed said. "Jay was misunderstood, but he's actually a very intelligent man. He's just different. It's his brain that records every detail he sees. People think he's nuts, but he's not. He just gets overloaded and then panics. Then he winds up acting like an idiot and gets locked up in the Twin Rivers jail."

"I hope I'm wrong," Ray said.

Suddenly, Ed cranked the wheel to swing around a hairpin curve. Ray sucked in his breath as the back of the truck began to skid. With a few graceful maneuvers of the steering wheel, Ed had the truck back under control.

"Didn't see that turn coming," Ed said with a chuckle.

Ray let out his breath and relaxed his grip on the door.

"What's that?" he remarked, pointing at a large pile of snow in the shallow ditch on the right side.

As Ed crept by it, he said, "Abandoned car."

"You think they're still in it?"

"No, they most likely slid off the edge yesterday when the snow started. After they got out, the snow drifted and buried the car. They probably had somebody come pick them up, or they hiked out. You don't have any missing person reports, do you?"

"No," Ray said. "Just Levi."

"And Jay," Ed added.

"And Jay," Ray said with a nod.

"Here we are," Ed said.

He swung the tow truck into Jay's driveway, rolled down the long lane, and pulled to a stop next to Jay's Jeep. Ray's eyes widened as he looked at the other driveway that went up the steep hill which Levi had told him about.

"That's the driveway Levi took down," Ray said, shaking his head.

Ed chuckled. "Yeah, and back up again. I can't believe he made that. That's a trail made for Jeeps and four-wheel drives. Jay's house used to belong to his parents, and years ago they spent summers here. After he moved out here, Jay cleared this new driveway which is a lot less treacherous to get in and out of."

Ray swung his door open and stepped out into the quiet. In the distance, he could hear the river running over rapids far below. Ed joined Ray beside his door. He pointed up in the air where half a dozen large turkey vultures circled overhead just above the edge of the bluff.

"We'd better go have a look," Ray said, firming his resolve.

"What's that?" Ed said, pointing at something red, which was fluttering in the branches of a tree right at the edge of the bluff just beyond the garage.

"It looks like what's left of a balloon," Ray remarked as he walked towards the tree, "and it's tied to a branch."

Ed swung his arm around the trunk of the tree and leaned over the edge to look down at the river below. Since he wasn't very fond of heights, he quickly stepped back.

"I think we found Jay."

Ray peered over the edge. About fifty feet below was the river with enormous sandstone boulders, worn smooth over centuries, along the banks. A body was lying spread-eagle on one of those huge boulders, the surrounding snow stained red with blood.

"Damn," said Ray.

Ed sighed and shook his head. "I wonder what that balloon's doing here?"

"It lured me to the edge of the cliff," a voice said from behind them.

Ed and Ray spun around and stared speechlessly. Jay Snider was looking at them curiously. There was a large bandage on the side of his head.

"Boy, I'm glad to see you," Ed said, finding his voice and grinning broadly.

"Me, too," Ray said. "Are you badly hurt, Jay?"

Jay touched the bandage. "I banged my head pretty good and got a nasty scrape. Other than that, I'm fine."

"Who in the hell is that?" Ed asked, cocking a thumb towards the edge of the bluff.

Jay shrugged. "Your guess is as good as mine. I never saw his face."

"What happened?" Ray asked.

Jay sighed deeply and closed his eyes. Ray and Ed realized he was accessing his strangely wired brain and pulling up every single detail of the encounter.

"The snowstorm has obliterated all the tracks now," Jay finally said, "but I worked it out while I could still see them. I was working in my studio, painting. When I heard a couple of thumps on the side of the garage, I walked out to see what it was. I thought it was a branch rubbing on the side of the building. Then I noticed this bright red balloon in the tree and walked over to the edge of the cliff to check it out. It was odd. It didn't belong. About the time I noticed it was tied to a branch, I heard somebody running up behind me. Never had a chance to turn around before he hit me hard from behind. I just about went over, but I managed to hook my arm around that tree trunk—the one with the balloon in it. The guy began punching me in the back, but I held on. He grabbed my arm and started trying to pull it free from the trunk."

Jay stopped for a moment and walked over to the tree. He stared down at the lifeless body below.

"Finally, he pulled my arm free and swung me around. I was looking right at him, but he wore a ski mask, so I never saw his face. He was trying to walk me backwards over the edge. I felt one of my feet slip off the edge, but both of my hands were free, so I was able to grab that branch overhead," he said pointing to a heavy branch that forked off the trunk over the precipice. "He kept pulling and pushing on me, trying real hard to break my grip. I was kicking at him with my legs, but I didn't have a great hold on that branch, and besides, it was wet on top from the snow. My hands were slipping. I was pretty sure I was going to fall, but I decided I wasn't going alone. I took one hand off the branch and grabbed the sleeve of his jacket. Then I pulled back on him as hard as I could. He managed to get a grip on my leg, and I knew I couldn't hold both of us with one arm if he decided to hang on. But he panicked when he realized he was leaning over the edge and let go of me. He made a grab for the same overhead branch I was holding onto, but he missed, and gravity took him right over the edge. Once he fell, I reached up and grabbed that branch with my other hand. Even with both hands on the branch, I thought I wasn't too far behind him. The bark was slick, and my grip wasn't that great."

"And it looks like it's broken," Ray remarked.

"Yeah," Jay said. "My plan was to swing back and forth a couple of times and then let go, hoping to land on the edge. But then the branch cracked. I got lucky because when it cracked, it sagged closer to the trunk of the tree, so I decided to make a jump for it. That didn't go very well. I smacked right into that tree trunk, knocking the air out of me and skinning up my face, but I had a death grip on the tree trunk. After my wind returned, I was able to pull myself the rest of the way back up on solid ground."

"You're very lucky," Ed said, venturing another glimpse over the edge.

"I'm glad it was a maple tree rather than an oak," Jay said. "If it'd been a hardwood tree instead of a softwood tree, that branch would've just snapped off clean, and I'd have been on the way to the bottom, still hanging onto it."

"His plan was very simple," Ray said. "Hide behind that big bur oak tree, make a few snowballs to lure you out to see the balloon, then shove you over the cliff."

Jay got an amused look on his face. "I kind of screwed up that plan."

Ed chuckled.

"I should've seen the tracks in the snow when I walked up to the balloon," Jay said. "He'd made no effort to wipe them out. But I was so focused on the balloon that I just didn't pay any attention. I'm guessing he was going to make it look like an accident. If he'd succeeded, he would've taken his balloon, the storm would've wiped out the tracks, and everyone would've assumed I got too close to the edge of the cliff—perhaps I got turned around in the blowing snow and simply walked off the edge."

"Why didn't you call in?" Ray asked.

Jay pulled his phone out of his pocket. "It fell out of my coat pocket during the struggle. I found it in the snow later. They don't work so well when they're wet, and I quit the house phone four or five years ago." Jay cocked a thumb towards his Jeep parked beside the garage. "That's dead, too. If you ever checked the messages at your shop, Ed, you'd know I called you for a tow two days ago."

"Sorry, Jay," Ed said, shaking his head. "I've been playing cop the last few days. I told you about that battery six months ago."

"Yeah, you were right about the battery," Jay said, shaking his head. "Deader than a hammer. Wouldn't even hold a charge when I hooked it up to my charger."

"I think you should get your head checked out by Dr. Jackson," Ray said. "I'll call Amber to get Jeff and the coroner out here."

"You'll probably need rescue out here, too," Ed remarked. "Our dead guy isn't going to be easy to retrieve."

"I'll stay here," Ray said with a sigh. "You take Jay to see Dr. Jackson."

Ed nodded. "Have Jeff check out that car we passed along the side of the road. I'll bet anything it belongs to our dead guy. Let me know if you want me to tow it."

"The house isn't locked and neither is the studio," Jay said to Ray as he climbed into the tow truck. "Don't stand out here and freeze. Make yourself at home. There's plenty of coffee in the kitchen, a wood stove in the studio, and wood along the garage. Build a fire and fix coffee for the emergency crew if you want to. It's butt-ass cold out today."

"Thanks," Ray said. "I'll do that."

Chapter 32

Levi knew Carl had stayed in the library—he sensed his presence behind him. There were two wingback chairs in front of Tony's huge mahogany desk. One was occupied, but Levi couldn't see who was sitting in the chair.

He started to cross the library. The size of the space was intimidating. The library shelves holding Tony's rare book collection filled every inch of wall space on both sides of the library. And ten feet above, there was another level of the library with a walkway all the way around, accessed by a wrought iron spiral staircase in one corner. Bright morning light spilled in through towering windows. Several nooks cut into the library shelves featured photos. Levi paused at one collection which Ray had told him about. Actually, it had given Ray the clue that told him the combination to Tony's private safe—12-07-41. The photos were from Tony's time in the Navy—he was a Pearl Harbor survivor.

With his fingers tented under his chin, Tony sat at his desk, watching Levi's slow approach. He was taking great delight in watching Levi's appreciation of his collection. Levi spent a few hours almost every day in the small library in Twin Rivers. He could spend a lifetime in this one without even scratching the surface.

"World War II," Levi said, glancing at the volumes that surrounded that alcove.

"Older to the right, newer to the left," Tony remarked.

Levi wandered a few steps to the right. "World War I," he said, glancing at the spines of the books.

"Yes, including a first edition, author autographed copy of Eddie Rickenbacker's autobiography."

"Signed by Eddie Rickenbacker," Levi stated, obviously impressed.

"I met him in the late 40s."

"He was a Mason," Levi remarked.

"I have something of his which relates to that affiliation. It would look very nice on the wall of your beautiful Masonic Lodge in Twin Rivers. It's a signed 1920s dues card from his lodge in Detroit. I'll send you home with it if you'd like it."

Levi said nothing as he walked on past the WWI section. Tony wasn't surprised. There was nothing he could offer Levi Garvey that he would accept under any terms.

"Civil War," Levi said, stopping. "This first section is biographies."

A slow smile crossed Tony's face as he realized Levi was looking for something in particular, and he was about to find it. "That's right."

"You seem to be missing a book," Levi said, placing his finger in a gap between the volumes neatly lining the shelves. It was the only gap he'd noticed in Tony's entire library. Tony chuckled.

"It's right here between the three-volume first edition of *The Memoirs of Ulysses S. Grant*—"

"All three volumes signed by both the author and the original publisher," Tony added.

Levi's head snapped toward Tony. If that were true, those volumes alone were worth a fortune. Carefully, Levi removed the first volume, opened the cover gently, and looked at the signatures of none other than Ulysses S. Grant and his publisher—a man named Samuel Clemens.

"Holy crap," Levi said with a chuckle.

"But you were saying . . ." Tony said.

Levi placed the book back on the shelf.

"I was saying there's a gap here between Grant and this biography of Colonel A. J. Garrison," Levi said. "I'm not familiar with A. J. Garrison."

"Garrison served the Confederacy," Tony remarked, waving his hand. "It's not that remarkable—more fiction than fact. Just another sad volume written by a Confederate officer trying to rewrite the historical facts."

"What's interesting is that a rare book was donated by an anonymous donor to the Twin Rivers Library just over a year ago. It would fit right in that spot between Garrison and Grant."

"*From Gettysburg to Twin Rivers: A Memoir of Captain William Garvey*," Tony said. "I knew you'd enjoy it, but I also knew you'd never accept it as a gift from me. It belongs in the library of the town he founded. I didn't give it to you. I gave it to your town. It's the only copy I've ever seen. You can return it if you like."

"No, I agree with you," Levi said. "The book is where it belongs. And I have accepted a gift from you—a very, very rare gold coin, the sale of which will do a lot of good for generations to come."

"I didn't give that to you either, Levi," Tony said. "I gave that to the Freemasons."

"True," Levi said, glancing at the gap on the bookshelf again. "But I had a feeling you were behind that rare book showing up in the Twin Rivers Library. In fact, I bet my wife $100 you were behind it. That would pay for the case of beer I bought yesterday, wouldn't it, Tori?"

Levi heard Carl chuckle from the shadows of the second level walkway.

Levi walked over to the occupied wingback chair in front of Tony's desk. Tori flashed an angry look up at Levi, but she said nothing.

"Let me guess," Levi said. "This was on your way to Home Depot to pick out wood trim or something for the library?"

"How did you know?" Tori asked.

"I smelled it," Levi said, grinning.

He pointed at the chocolate meringue pie, sitting on Tony's desk next to the coffee service. As Carl emerged from the shadows of the second story walkway, Levi poured four cups of coffee, dished out servings of pie on the plates, and handed them out.

"Those pies are made by only one person, Tori."

"April Jenkins," Tony remarked, picking up a fork. "Fabulous."

No one spoke as they savored the pie.

Finally, Levi set his empty plate on the desk. "We have business to discuss, Tony," he said as he stroked Rosco's head which lay in his lap.

"We were just getting down to business when you arrived," Tony remarked. "Surely, you're not worried about your safety. We're just talking here as old friends do."

Tony chuckled as he leaned back in his chair, causing the hairs on Levi's neck to rise again.

Levi glanced at Tori. Her eyes slowly drifted to the edge of the huge desk. Taking the hint, he followed her gaze. Lying there was a copy of Levi's first book with a large bullet hole in it. Of all the rare books in his massive collection, there was only that one book on his desk. Levi had shot it with his Webley at Tony's request. There was no doubt in Levi's mind that Tony liked him for some reason, but he wondered if being liked by Tony O'Malley was enough.

Suddenly, Carl sat on the corner of Tony's desk and said, "So let's talk about why you're here."

Levi and Tori exchanged glances. They couldn't remember Carl ever saying much—other than threatening to beat Uncle Ed's ass for smashing his nose with a broom handle years earlier. Suddenly, Rosco's ears went up. Levi knew without looking that somebody was standing between them.

Levi looked up. Angelino was there, staring down at them. Levi glanced at Tori whose eyes were suddenly fearful.

Tony chuckled. "Something wrong, Levi?"

"I think the Garveys are starting to figure things out," Carl said.

"You've met my nephew Carl a few times before," Tony said.

"Your nephew?" Levi said as he leaned forward in his chair, suddenly alarmed.

"He usually doesn't say very much. He's a lot like his mother, my sister, Peg. As you know, I'm not getting any younger. You've got to have a succession plan in any family business, and you've got to start grooming them young to take over. Carl will soon replace me."

"So let's talk," Carl said, glaring at them. "You both had some reason to visit today, right? Officer Garvey in his police uniform, no less."

Tori and Levi knew they were in trouble.

Levi reached down to stroke Rosco's head. As he did so, he glanced at his holster, making sure he had the clearance to pull out the Webley if he needed it. But his holster was empty. Suddenly alarmed, he started to stand up, but Angelino's strong arm shoved him back down into the chair hard.

"Something wrong, Levi?" Carl said with a chuckle.

Suddenly, Levi remembered how Angelino had bumped against him as he'd walked to the library door. Angelino was good—Levi had never felt the gun leave his holster.

"I think he's looking for this," Angelino said, laying the revolver onto the desk in front of Tony.

The blood drained from Tori's face as Angelino placed the rounds he'd unloaded from Levi's gun in a neat pile beside it.

"That leaves you with the dog," Angelino said. "He's way more dangerous than the revolver, right?"

"Well, shit," Levi said. "I was trying to do you a favor, and now I'm really screwed."

"I think that's what Carl is wondering about," Tony said, wiping the corners of his mouth as he laid his fork down. "Why in the hell are you and Tori here? You think we're friends? You think you can barge in here any time you like?"

"I think we're both asking ourselves that same question," Tori said.

"Well, that, and who's going to raise our son," Levi said with a chuckle.

Tori glanced at him in amazement. There was nothing funny about this situation. She couldn't believe he was joking. Maybe he really was an evil genius. She decided to follow his lead.

"And you just bought a case of beer and drank only one," Tori remarked. "That's just wasteful, Levi."

"I forgot to pay my lodge dues," Levi said, looking at Tori.

"Well, there goes your Masonic funeral rites," Tori said, shaking her head.

"Don't even start with me," Levi said. "Did you pay April for this pie?"

"No, I promised April I'd pay her for that pie when I got back. Tony, would you make sure that a wealthy anonymous donor pays April for this pie after we're gone."

Tony glanced at Carl, who did something neither of them thought he was capable of. He grinned.

"You two are idiots."

Levi and Tori looked at each other and shrugged.

"Take your gun back," Carl said. "Give him his bullets, Angelino."

"Don't bother," Levi said. "I don't need that gun. I wouldn't have driven up here and through those gates if I'd thought for one minute I was doing anything other than the right thing. Neither would Tori. We're both here for a good reason. We just want to make our case and get the hell out of here. You can take it or leave it. I sure didn't know Tori had the same idea, but I think you should give us a listen. If you don't like what we have to say, we will sit patiently with our feet in buckets of concrete, waiting for it to dry."

Tony leaned forward. "We never actually did that, you know. The whole concrete shoe thing."

"Really?" Tori asked.

"Really," Tony said.

"Wood chippers are far more effective for disposing of bodies," Carl remarked.

Levi and Tori looked at him in alarm. Suddenly, a glimmer of a smile appeared on his face. Angelino snorted behind them.

"Would you like a piece of pie, Angelino?" Levi said, standing suddenly.

Angelino glanced at Carl. That look spoke volumes about the succession plan. Angelino worked for Carl. He was Carl's right-hand, not Tony's.

Carl gave an almost imperceptible shrug.

"Sure," Angelino said.

"So what's going on in Twin Rivers?" Carl said, pouring himself another cup of coffee.

"I'm sure you already know. Somebody murdered a porn star and made it look like you or one of your Horsemen did it," Levi said, leaning back in his chair with a second piece of pie. "I'll share everything I know as long as you promise to share everything you know about Peter Long and the huge marijuana operation outside Twin Rivers."

Carl looked at Tony.

"Nope," Tony said. "That's not going to happen. You tell us what you came up here to say, and I'll decide what questions I'm going to answer—if any at all."

Tori looked at Levi. He shrugged.

"I guess that will have to suffice," Tori said. "So you already know what's going on in Twin Rivers. Here's what Levi and I think . . ."

Chapter 33

"So you're saying it's a rental," Ray said.

He'd just arrived at the scene of the abandoned car after leaving the bluff where they'd winched the body up, using the ladder of the Twin Rivers fire truck as a crane.

"Yes," Jeff said.

Having finished processing the inside of the car, he climbed out of the back seat and stretched his back.

"There's not much there, not a receipt or anything. And I just got a call that the body is clean as well, no ID or any other item so far to help us identify him. But we'll have the name of the person who rented this car in a few minutes. Maybe that will give us something to work with."

"So you think he was a pro?" Ray asked.

"It looks like it to me," Jeff remarked. "Very clean. No identification on the body, no paperwork in the car. I'm down to processing the trunk, but it's frozen shut."

"I think I've got something for that," Ed said as he headed towards his truck.

He'd dropped Jay off in Calloway and then returned. He walked back with a large crowbar.

"With your permission, Jeff."

"Do it."

Ed leaned down and squirted the lock with something from a small aerosol bottle he had in his jacket. He tried the key Jeff had given him. The lock turned, but Jeff was right. The trunk lid was frozen tight.

"Yup," Ed said. "It's frozen."

"I've been doing this for fifteen years, Ed," Jeff growled. "Don't you think it occurred to me to try that? I have that same lock deicer in my kit. However, you've got something in your hand there I don't have. Why don't you give that sucker a try."

Ed chuckled as he stuck the edge of the crowbar under the lid. As he turned the key, he pushed down on the crowbar sharply. The lid popped open on his first try.

He stepped back, looking satisfied with himself. "Fifteen years— shit, I've been doing this for almost fifty."

Ray raised the trunk lid. "Holy crap!" he yelled, jumping back.

"What?" Ed said.

Ray pointed at the open trunk, unable to put what he'd seen into words.

Jeff looked in and jumped back as well. "Oh, my God!" Then he cocked his head to one side and stepped a little closer. "Wait a minute," he said. He pulled out his flashlight and shined it inside. Suddenly, he laughed.

"What is it?" Ed asked, keeping a distance.

"Not what I first thought," Jeff said. "And obviously not what Ray first thought either. Have a look."

Ed walked up slowly. "What the hell?" he said.

The three of them stood, staring down at the gruesome sight—a face staring up at them and part of the torso.

"We've found our assassin," Ray said matter-of-factly.

"Unfortunately, he's not going to be able to answer very many questions," Ed said.

All three men burst out laughing. They were looking at the old-man mask.

"We'll get something on this guy. Don't worry about that. You'd be surprised about what we'll be able to tell from the body," Jeff said.

Jeff's phone rang. After a brief conversation, he said, "We've already got a name on the person who rented this car—John Galt."

"I'll bet he paid cash," Ed said, shaking his head.

"We'll soon know who John Galt is," Jeff said.

"I already know," Ray said. "You don't read much, do you, Jeff?"

"No time," he remarked. "Why?"

"John Galt doesn't exist," Ed said. "You ever hear of Ayn Rand? John Galt is a fictional character in her novel *Atlas Shrugged,* one of the few books I've ever read. A guy in my company in Vietnam had a copy of that book, and I think all of us read it while we were over there."

"I think we're stuck again," Ray mumbled.

"Not necessarily," Ed said. "One thing is much clearer. Somebody wanted Selena Long dead and hired a professional assassin to murder her. That same person wanted Jay Snider dead as well. His hired killer went after Jay next, trying very hard to make the death look like an accident, and it might have if he'd succeeded. But who would want both Jay and Selena murdered, and why? That's a brand new and very interesting question."

"There's a common denominator there," Ray said. "Can it be that simple?"

"Sure," Ed said. "Peter Long. It keeps coming back to Peter Long."

Ray rolled the ends of his mustache between his fingers as he looked down at the mask in the trunk of the rental car.

"That seems to be the best physical evidence we have right now. I want to know who bought that mask and where," Ray told Jeff. "Levi found out that they are manufactured by only one company, so it shouldn't be hard to find out. Most of them are sold as special orders directly from the company. Call Amber. I can't remember the name of the company right off, but she'll have it. And as soon as you have an ID on that body, I want to know everything about him. Every damn detail."

"You bet," Jeff said.

"You want to take a little drive?" Ed asked.

"I sure do," Ray said as they walked back to his tow truck.

Chapter 34

Tony leaned forward and placed his elbows on his desk as the exchange of information wound down. Levi and Tori were a little surprised at just how much Tony already knew. He'd chimed in a number of times during the discussion. Now there was a long, uncomfortable pause as he regarded Levi and Tori in turn.

"Is that it?" Carl asked as he set down his plate. He'd polished off two pieces of pie as they talked, and Angelino was eyeing the last piece.

"That's all we know so far," Levi said.

"So what's the favor you're doing for us again? I think I missed that part. You haven't added anything new to what I already knew. As a matter of fact, it seems like you're here to ask a favor from us."

Levi glanced at Tori.

"You're right, Tony," Tori said. "We're very much aware that whoever did this will eventually be subject to . . . repercussions."

"But I'd like to solve it first," Levi said.

"And you can solve it?" Tony said.

"I can solve it."

"I have long arms and very good ears," Tony said. "The one question you had, about the marijuana operation . . ."

"Yes?" Levi said.

"I'll tell you this much. We've got nothing to do with that, and unfortunately, we don't know who does—yet."

"So you intend to find out," Levi said.

Tony shrugged. "I don't think that's a question I'm going to answer."

"But it's likely you'll go after them," Tori said.

Tony's gaze narrowed as he leaned forward. "If I do, and I'm not saying I will, it's unlikely to ripple the quiet town of Twin Rivers," he said harshly. "Let's just get down to brass tacks. You want time, and I may give you that since it seems like it might be good for both of us actually. How long?"

"Give me a month," Levi said.

"A month?" Tony laughed. "At my age, who even knows if I have a month. You've got ten days to wrap this up. That's it."

"Then what are you going to do?" Tori asked.

"Use your imagination," Tony said, his voice rising slightly. "You'll have to. There's little chance you'll ever know. But there will be corrective action taken."

"Ten days?" Levi said.

Tony nodded.

"Any chance you'll share anything you might uncover?" Levi asked. "It's obvious you're looking into it."

"None," Tony said flatly.

"I'll take the ten days," Levi said.

"It's not a negotiation. That's what it is," Tony said, leaning back in his leather chair and tenting his fingers under his chin. "Thank you for the remarkable pie."

Carl stood, and suddenly, Angelino appeared between them. The meeting was over. Levi reached over and picked up his Webley off the desk along with the pile of bullets. He reloaded the antique revolver and holstered it.

"Thank you," Levi said as Tori stood up and started towards the door of the library. Rosco followed her.

Levi paused in front of Tony's desk.

"Is there something else?" Tony asked.

"Could I have a private word with you? It's about something totally unrelated."

Stopping, Tori said insistently, "Levi? We should go. Now."

"Carl can hold my revolver," Levi said.

"Not necessary," Tony said. "Close the door behind you, Carl."

"Levi," Tori said.

"I'm right behind you. I'll call you a few minutes after I leave. Would you take Rosco home with you?"

Tori looked at him fearfully. She knew once Levi made a decision, he wouldn't be swayed.

"Come on, Rosco."

The door closed. Tony looked up at the Levi, who was still standing in front of his desk.

"I'll split the last piece with you?" Levi said, glancing at the pie on his desk.

Levi divided the pie and scooped the larger piece onto Tony's plate.

"Something's bothering you, Levi," Tony remarked as Levi filled their coffee cups.

"It's an academic question," Levi said. "One historian to another."

"It's that book your great-great-grandfather wrote, isn't it?" Tony remarked. "Captain William Garvey."

"I've read it over and over again," Levi said. "There's something missing."

"Ah, yes," Tony said. "You were friends with Reverend Guy Garvey, and you're wondering how his African-American family and how your Anglo-Saxon family are related. Both lines of Garveys seem to have begun about the same time in Twin Rivers—right after the end of the Civil War. I remember you saying something about that in an interview I saw once."

"He mentions a few names in the book," Levi said, "but there are no details about the relationships."

"It could have gone back to slavery," Tony remarked. "Sadly, slaves often took the names of their masters."

"That seems the most likely origin, but I've noticed that the memoir has a lot of exact details and dates. It's hard to believe he would've remembered that much nearly fifty years later when he began writing his memoir," Levi said.

"I noticed that, too," Tony admitted. "He probably had a field journal. Most officers during the Civil War did. He referenced it when he wrote his memoirs years later. You've come to that same conclusion."

Levi nodded. "The question is—where is it? I've searched the library in Twin Rivers from the rafters to the basement. I've searched our house, the carriage house, and even the old records at the Masonic Lodge. I've searched the Masonic archives at the Illinois Lodge of Research, hoping to find it. Both families were involved in Freemasonry. I've found nothing."

Tony smiled. "You think I have it."

"Do you?"

"I'm sorry to tell you that I do not," Tony said. "It may be lost forever."

"I knew it was a long shot," Levi said, sounding disappointed.

"I think we have something in common, Levi."

"What's that?"

"Family. It's obviously important to me," he said with a chuckle. "There you were just a couple of years ago, the last male in your family line with little thought about marriage and family. Look at you now. You've brought back the Garveys in Twin Rivers, and with your little boy, there will be another generation after all."

"Is that your family?" Levi asked, pointing to an old black and white framed photo on a shelf behind Tony's desk.

Tony swiveled in his chair. "It is. I had four sisters. I was the only boy. That was taken in the mid-20s." He smiled as he touched the glass. "That's me in front. I was about three at the time. I'm holding my baby sister, and my three older sisters are behind me. All are gone now, except my baby sister. She's still alive and well."

"Would that be Carl's mother?"

"Yes, my sister Peg."

Levi smiled. He couldn't believe he was having this conversation with Tony "The Shotgun" O'Malley. Just a short time ago, he wasn't so sure he was going to leave this house alive.

"You know, Levi," Tony said, "I'm the last O'Malley in my line. I had sons, and they had wives, and they had children. Back in the mid-50s this house was full of O'Malleys. I thought the O'Malley name would live on forever in Chicago. But all the Chicago O'Malley's are gone now—except me. This house is a museum of empty bedrooms."

"Family business?" Levi asked cautiously.

"Yes," Tony admitted. "My sons have all been killed over the years. And my three grandsons as well. The last was killed in '82. I lost my wife, and one of my daughters. It's not like it once was, but it's still an ugly business."

"You've got Carl," Levi remarked.

"And now you know why I've kept that a secret all these years," Tony said. "He's blood, but he's not an O'Malley. He's my sister's boy. But he's all that's left of this family. If my enemies had found out who he was to me, he'd have been a target, so I've protected him, and I've groomed him to take over. Not that my enemies haven't tried really hard to kill off the Horsemen a time or two, but every attempt failed—guppies trying to kill sharks."

Levi looked down at a ring on his finger and smiled.

"What are you thinking?" Tony asked.

"You know, I've got a great-aunt," Levi said. "She gave Tori this ring that had belonged to Abe Garvey. It's his Master Mason's ring. He was a member of my lodge—joined back in the early 20s. Not that long before that picture of you and your family was taken."

"Abe was your great-grandfather," Tony said.

He knew all about Abe Garvey. His father was the Civil War Captain William Garvey, and his son's exploits during WWI and afterwards were part of William's memoir, including the part about the Webley he brought home from WWI—the same revolver Levi was carrying in his holster.

"I know what you're thinking," Tony added.

"If she had Abe's ring, she might have a few other things that belonged to him."

"Maybe his father's journals?"

"Reverend Guy Garvey told my Grandma Lucille a story about the Garvey families," Levi said. "He told me that, and then later regretted telling me. He said there was a part of that story that he didn't think I'd want to know."

"Maybe Lucille, knowing the story, didn't want you to know part of it," Tony remarked. "Maybe she gave those journals to her sister along with Abe's ring—to protect you from it."

"I think I'll go visit dear Aunt Maggie," Levi said as he reached over the desk to shake Tony's hand.

"Tell your wife I really enjoyed the pie," Tony said.

"I will."

Levi walked to the library door and turned the knob. It was locked. He looked back at Tony.

"Is there a signal you have to give or something?" Levi asked.

"I'll give it. But first, there's just one more thing I want to tell you," he said from across the huge library. "I've enjoyed our conversation, Levi, but don't ever come back here again. Not ever."

Levi looked at him blankly.

"I think you're a gifted writer." Tony reached over and touched the copy of Levi's book on his desk. "But we live in different worlds. Don't come back into mine again. You have ten days, Levi. If you haven't solved this little problem in Twin Rivers in ten days, you'd be well advised to take a step back. It would be a very bad idea to get in my way."

"I won't," Levi said. "Take care, Tony."

Tony reached under the edge of the desk. Instantaneously, the lock on the door clicked, and the library door opened. Angelino was standing at the entrance.

Levi paused and glanced back at Tony O'Malley. They wouldn't be meeting again. Then he turned and followed Angelino out of the library.

Tony walked to the window and watched Levi climb into his old blue Ford truck. Carl slipped up beside him as the truck disappeared down the winding drive.

"You really going to give him ten days?" Carl asked.

Tony nodded. "I always keep my word. Do you disagree with that decision?"

Carl sighed. "I think you're playing a dangerous game. I'm not so sure we shouldn't just steer clear of that whole town, especially the Garveys and Chief Billings."

"Let it go?" Tony said, turning towards his nephew.

Carl nodded.

"Maybe you're right. But I still want to know who was running the marijuana operation. When they legalize that crap, and I think they will soon, we'll be on the ground floor of a very lucrative business that will be totally legal."

Carl grinned. "I agree. And if there are more than one of those operations, we'll soon know. Hopefully, those won't be anywhere near Twin Rivers or Chief Billings or those damn Garveys."

"Let's just wash our hands of the whole thing," Tony remarked.

Carl breathed a sigh of relief.

Angelino knocked twice, then opened the door, and walked over to the window.

"What is it, Angel?" Carl said.

"There's been a development in Twin Rivers," Angelino said. "Jake wants you to call him."

"Spit it out," Tony snapped. "Jake told you what he had to tell Carl, so don't act like you don't know."

Angelino looked at Tony nervously. "He didn't say much. Just that the hired assassin who killed that porn star is dead. They found him early this morning. That's all he said."

Carl was already dialing Jake's number.

"That son of a bitch," Tony hissed. "Levi seems to have left out that part of the story. He knew I was interested in who the assassin was, and he intentionally left out the fact he's dead." Tony slammed his fist on his desk. "Lock the gate. Stop him, and bring him back!"

"Why are you still standing here?" Carl snapped at Angelino with the phone at his ear, waiting for Jake to answer.

Angelino's face blanched. He turned and bolted towards the library door.

"You and your boys lock that gate. Tear ass down there and bring him and his truck right back here," Tony shouted after him.

Tony walked over to a cabinet beside the fireplace, opened the glass door, and pulled out his favorite—a double-barrel ten-gauge shotgun. He snapped it open and, satisfied it was loaded, snapped it closed.

"He played me. Levi Garvey played me. He's about to learn a lesson—his last lesson. And it's too bad," Tony said, glancing at the book on his desk. "He was a really gifted writer."

It wasn't lost on Carl that Tony had used the past tense.

Chapter 35

Ray waited patiently at the door with Ed a couple of steps behind him. He'd both rung the bell and knocked several times. He was just about to knock again when he saw Shelia's face in the side window and heard her working the lock.

"Good morning," Ray said. "I'd like to have a word with Pete if I could."

"He's not here," she said, looking around him at the man standing at the edge of the stoop.

"This is Officer Ed Garvey," he said by way of introduction.

"I thought that was Ed," Shelia said, brushing her wet blonde hair out of her face and tightening the belt on her robe. "I'm sorry if I kept you waiting. I didn't hear you. I just got out of the shower."

Taking a few steps closer and looking at her intently, Ed said, "Do I know you? I'm afraid I don't recognize you."

"It's been a few years," she said. "You taught me how to cast with a fishing pole."

"I did?"

She smiled at him. "Mostly, your bait wound up hooked in trees, but I got fairly good at casting. I hit the water more often than you did. I caught more fish than you did, too. It's no wonder since there aren't that many fish in the tree branches along Olton Lake."

"Shelia," Ed said, searching his memory as he rubbed his face. Nothing was clicking yet.

"You used to call me J.J.," she said.

"No," Ed said as a broad smile crossed his face. "You aren't Jabber Jaws, are you?"

Shelia grinned. "That's right. Twenty years ago, I used to go fishing with you and Dad."

Ed nodded. "I miss your dad. What's it been, five or six years now?"

"It'll be ten years this April."

"Ray, this is Shelia Carter. Her dad and I used to get into a lot of trouble back thirty years ago or so. She used to come fishing with us every so often, right here at Olton Lake. Her dad had a little cabin over on the north side up the spur. When she was with him on the weekends, we'd all get out on the lake at the crack of dawn. She'd start talking the minute we got in the boat and never take a breath all day. Yak, yak, yak, yak, yak . . ."

"That's why he called me J.J.—Jabber Jaws," Shelia said with a smile.

"So you grew up around here," Ray said.

Shelia nodded. "Mom lived in Twin Rivers, and Dad lived here at the lake."

"Divorced?" Ray asked.

Ed laughed. "Nope, they just preferred it that way. They'd realized shortly after they were married they didn't like living together and were way happier back when they were dating, so they kept separate residences."

"It worked for them," Shelia said. "Quite well, apparently. I have two younger brothers."

"Do you know when Pete is going to be back?" Ray asked.

"Not sure. He went to Atlanta on business. Sometimes he's gone a day or two, and sometimes it's a couple of weeks. He took the dog with him, so I'm thinking he might be gone awhile. He only takes Tinker down there when he's planning a longer stay."

"He has a place there?" Ed asked.

"Pretty nice, from what I understand," Shelia said. "He has a place in L.A. as well. On the beach."

"I couldn't talk you out of a cup of coffee, could I?" Ray asked.

Shelia looked at him from the doorway. "Mr. Long has been very clear about that rule. He doesn't like people in the house while he's away."

"I understand," Ray said. "You're very dedicated, and you obviously enjoy your job a great deal. I wouldn't want you to get into trouble. Thank you, Shelia."

Ray started to turn when Shelia opened the door wider. "Actually, I was just going to make some coffee. Promise not to tell him?"

"Of course not," Ray said. "It's just that I got up early and have been busy all morning. I missed my morning cup."

"Well, come on then," Shelia said.

Ray and Ed followed Shelia down the long flights of stairs to the ground level of Pete Long's enormous lake house.

"Boy, that sun is bright this morning," Ed remarked, squinting out through the wall of windows towards the lake.

"Check this out," Ray said, walking to the panel beside the window. When he touched a button on the panel, the glass darkened several shades in a couple of seconds. "It's special glass."

"Never seen that before," Ed remarked, walking up to the darkened windows. "Sunglasses for your house."

"I'm going to go into the kitchen now," Shelia announced. "I'm going to make some coffee for all of us. I'll be gone at least fifteen minutes. Make yourself at home."

Ray glanced at Ed.

Shelia walked up the hall, looked back at them when she reached the kitchen at the end, and pulled the door closed behind her.

"That was an invitation," Ray said.

"It was," Ed said. "But, of course, anything we might see or find would never be admissible."

"Probably not," Ray said.

"And it would be wrong," Ed said.

"I've been wrong before, but maybe a little peek might tell us if getting a search warrant would be in order," Ray said as he started walking towards the basement steps he'd seen when he'd visited with Levi.

"You're walking a fine edge," Ed said. "You sure you're not letting your feelings get in the way of your responsibilities to the law?"

"That's exactly what's going on," Ray admitted, "but she did say to make ourselves at home."

"Well, let me help you then," Ed said, flipping a switch on the wall that lit the basement. "Tada!"

"Don't touch anything," Ray said. "We're just looking."

Ed glanced at him doubtfully.

"Just don't touch anything, okay?" Ray said more emphatically as he started down the steps.

* * *

"No, I'm fine," Levi said as he drove down the winding driveway. "I wanted to ask Tony about the book he donated to the Twin Rivers Library."

"That was really stupid, Levi," Tori snapped.

"I think we're tied when it comes to stupid moves today," he said.

Tori was quiet on the other end.

"I'm going to run a few errands. I'll see you at home later," Levi said.

"Promise me we won't do anything this dumb again."

"I can't promise that, but Tony made it very clear it would be very unwise to ever visit him again."

"I think that's good advice," Tori said. "I'll see you later."

Levi hung up the phone and stuck it in his pocket. He started to say something to Rosco before realizing Tori had him. It was strange, being in the truck without him. Stupid damn dog, he thought as he smiled.

When he rounded a curve, his heart leapt into his chest. Four large men in dark suits and overcoats were standing shoulder to shoulder across the road about two hundred feet in front of him, each holding an AK-47 pointed right at him. Shit, Levi thought.

His first impulse was to hit the accelerator. The truck sped up. Immediately, one of the men stepped forward and opened up, spraying a line of bullets across the road not far in front of Old Blue. It was a warning.

Knowing he had no chance against one of those weapons, let alone four, Levi locked the brakes. The line of men never moved—never even flinched—as the truck slid to a stop in front of them. As the stern-faced, square-jawed men stared at him through the windshield, Levi recognized one face in particular—the butler. Sweat broke out across his forehead, and his jaw dropped as he suddenly realized what he was seeing. My God, he thought. These are *Carl's* Four Horsemen.

Levi glanced down at the Webley. When he looked back up, he saw a slight smile on Angelino's face. That's what he wants, Levi realized.

Angelino walked to the window of Old Blue. Levi kept his eyes forward. Angelino tapped on the glass. When Levi glanced at him, Angelino raised an eyebrow. He wasn't amused. Levi rolled down the window.

"Step out of the truck," Angelino said.

"Why?"

"Tony wants you."

"I can drive back," Levi said tersely.

"I have my instructions. You want to do this the easy way or the hard way?"

Levi looked at the other three stern faces over the hood of his truck. Then slowly, he opened the door and stepped out onto the snowy road.

"The keys are in it," he said.

"I'll need your gun and your phone."

"Like hell," Levi said.

"Have it your way," Angelino said.

Levi saw a blinding flash as pain blossomed at the back of his head. The ground rushed up at him as the black edges of unconsciousness closed over him.

* * *

"I thought you said not to touch anything," Ed remarked as he watched Ray lean over a computer on the desk. Ray had already looked through all the file cabinets.

The basement wasn't like any basement Ed or Ray had ever seen. It was set up like a business office. Right at the bottom of the stairs was a receptionist's station and a waiting area. There were potted plants and art like you'd find in any high-end executive office. To the right and down a short hall, fully visible from the waiting area, was a large office area with a dozen cubicles for employees. Behind the receptionist's desk was a large wooden door, obviously to the executive office.

Ray and Ed started there.

The executive office was huge with a massive wooden desk and a plush leather chair behind it. There were two luxuriously padded leather chairs in front of the desk for guests and a small seating area off to one side with a few more chairs, an overstuffed leather couch, and a coffee table. One door on the left led to a bathroom, and the one on the right—that door was locked.

At the executive desk, Ray tapped a few keys on the computer and shook his head. "What in the hell is this place? It makes no sense."

Ed had been walking around the room, taking in the furnishings and art as Ray went right for the desk, the file cabinets, and the computer. Ed was standing in the center of the office now, looking at himself in a round fisheye mirror in a gilt frame behind the executive desk. The mirror looked expensive, and it probably was. The whole office felt expensive.

"Interesting," Ed said.

He picked up the phone on the desk, held it to his ear, and smiled before returning it to its cradle.

"Glad you think so," Ray said. "We've got a desk that doesn't have even a pencil in it. We've got totally empty file cabinets. We've got a computer that doesn't have any files on it and an inbox on the desk loaded with file folders filled with blank sheets of paper."

"The phone isn't hooked up either," Ed remarked.

He walked over to a sidebar which had three crystal liquor decanters sitting on it. He picked up one of them, pulled the cut glass stopper out, and held the bottle under his nose.

"Let me guess," Ray said. "It's not liquor."

Ed picked up a glass and pour a couple of fingers of the amber liquid into it.

"I'd better check," he said as he swigged it down, smacking his lips. "Nope, that's definitely whiskey. Very good whiskey, in fact. Of course, it makes sense that the liquor would be real."

"What do you mean?"

"Don't you realize what this is?"

"Not really," Ray admitted.

"You ever see the movie *The Sting*?" Ed asked.

"Of course," Ray snapped. Suddenly, a light went on. "This is designed to trick people. This is a con."

"Not exactly. But I think it's designed to trick young women into going into porn. This whole room is fake, but what's real are the cameras. I've seen at least half a dozen cameras in here," Ed said, walking over to a picture over the leather couch and pointing to a small, nearly invisible hole in the corner of the frame. "That's one there. There's another one in the ceiling. There's one in that plant on the coffee table. There are probably more. I'll bet cameras cover every square inch of this office from various angles."

"So how does he work this?" Ray asked.

"I can guess. I think he runs ads for modeling in college newspapers, and his people audition the girls at some hotel nearby. Maybe he gets them to do a little nude modeling to make sure they have all the necessary attractive physical attributes. He might get a few of them to do a little more—who knows. Then Pete goes through those videos from the hotel rooms and finds some promising young talent. He brings them up here to Olton Lake, probably as part of a group, for a whole weekend maybe. Of course, that will impress those young women right off the bat. He takes them out on the lake on his party barge, wines and dines them. They get very comfortable with him."

"Eventually, he makes the pitch, right?" Ray said.

"Sure, he probably introduces them to his director who, he claims, works right here on the property. This guy is probably an even better con artist than Pete is. This director brings those girls down into the basement headquarters of Passion Video. And all those desks are full of employees working, probably actors or people who work other jobs for Peter Long. And maybe it's Shelia playing the part of the receptionist. One by one, they meet the director for a real porn audition with some male talent who's probably on hand. Now those girls know exactly what they're getting into, but they think they're going to get rich doing it. They believe Pete will continue to lavish attention on them."

"So they want to get into porn," Ray said. "They learn how much they can make. And this place convinces them it's obviously not some sleazy operation."

"You're getting it," Ed said. "And before you know it, they're auditioning on that couch with some male performer so the director can see if they're what the studio is looking for."

"And do they know they're being recorded?" Ray asks.

"You don't hide cameras unless you need to hide cameras," Ed said, walking over to the locked door and rattling the knob. "I'm guessing they don't know. They probably believe it's just a private audition."

"You think that's the control room?"

"You might want to look away from this door for a minute."

"Just open the damn door," Ray growled.

Ed chuckled as he dropped to one knee in front of the knob. He removed a small leather pouch from his back pocket, selected a couple of small picks, and went to work on the lock. The door swung open in a few seconds.

"There we go," Ed said.

"I didn't know you could do that," Ray said.

"You know how many calls I've had because people have locked their keys in their vehicle. That's way easier than jimmying the door."

They walked into the dark room. There wasn't a switch, but there was light streaming in through a window. Suddenly, Ray realized it wasn't a window. It was the fisheye mirror over the big desk.

"One way glass," Ed remarked as he peered through the round window into the office.

Ed had suggested there might be a dozen hidden cameras in that room, but there were more than that. Ray was looking at a bank of more than twenty monitors, each labeled with the location of the hidden camera.

"There are even cameras in the floor," Ray said, pointing at one of the labels. "Why would you need cameras in the floor?"

Ed sighed. "Think about it."

Ray considered it for a moment, then shook his head.

"You've never watched a porn movie, have you?" Ed asked.

"Of course not," Ray said. "Have you?"

"No," Ed said. But after Ray glanced at him, he added, "Well, not a lot. But I've seen this office before."

"In a porn movie?" Ray asked.

"It's adult entertainment," Ed said, correcting him. "And yes, I've seen that couch before. Some of those first auditions are released later once a new porn star becomes popular. It's a series produced by Passion Video called *The Casting Couch*."

"I don't know what disturbs me more," Ray remarked. "The fact that stuff like that exists or the fact that people I know watch it. So do you have favorite porn actresses? Is that how it works?"

"I don't think I want to have this conversation with you, Ray," Ed snapped. "But that's probably why those auditions are recorded here. If one of these newbies makes it in the business and becomes a big star, those first audition videos become very popular commodities years later."

"But they don't know they're being filmed," Ray said.

Ed reached over a control panel and pressed a button on a DVD unit. The drawer slid open. There was a DVD lying in it. Ray knew what Ed was thinking. They were crossing a line, but Ed picked up the DVD and held it out to Ray anyway.

"Maybe you should watch one and decide for yourself if the young woman on the couch knows she's being recorded."

Ray looked at the DVD in Ed's hand, then took it, and slid it into his pocket. Then he pushed the button and watched the small drawer retreat into the machine.

"We're about out of time," Ed said.

"There's one more thing I want to see," Ray said as he walked back into the office. "Make sure you lock that control room door."

Both looked around the office to make sure they hadn't left anything out of place. Ed wiped out his whiskey glass and returned it. Then Ray turned off the light, and they pulled the door shut.

"I'll bet it's down here," Ray said, walking up the hallway past the cubicles.

"Ray, we need to be going," Ed said.

"It'll just take a second," he said as he stopped at a door at the end of the hall.

He twisted the knob, but the door was locked. He glanced at Ed and waved at the knob.

"Step aside," Ed said, dropping to his knee.

When the door was open, Ray stepped through it into the dark. Ed felt along the wall around the door for a switch. When he found it, he flipped it on.

"Wow!" he said.

"There it is," Ray said, smiling broadly. "I didn't tell you about this part."

In front of them was a monstrous vault door with a huge locking mechanism on the front and a control pad to one side—a vault that looked even larger and more imposing than the one at the First National Bank of Calloway.

"Well?" Ray said.

"Well, what?"

"Open it," Ray said, waving his hand towards the vault.

Ed stared at Ray, a blank expression on his face. Ray stared back impatiently. Then a smile played beneath his mustache.

"You got me," Ed said.

Ray pulled his smart phone out of his pocket and flashed away with the camera, taking at least a dozen pictures of the door and the electronic panel and the room itself.

"Let's go. I've got what I need in here," he said, tucking his phone into his pocket.

Chapter 36

"Wake him," Tony snapped as he climbed off the elevator into the basement of the mansion.

Carl stepped off the elevator behind Tony, who had the short-barreled shotgun on this shoulder. Tony was famous for favoring that particular weapon over his long career. Seeing him with it caused even Angelino to feel a tickle of fear creep up his spine.

The basement, called the armory, was the clubhouse of the Four Horsemen. It had a soundproof shooting range, a game room, and a media room featuring the latest in home entertainment technology. It also had a kitchen, bedrooms, and a gym with a Jacuzzi and a sauna. And, of course, it had a giant vault filled with the tools of the trade—every kind of weapon imaginable. The collection, which went back nearly a century, even included four beautifully maintained Thompson machine guns with the round drum magazines that had made them famous—Tommy guns, they were called. That was the weapon of choice in the 20s when Tony O'Malley's father worked for Al Capone, the founder of the Chicago Outfit. The armory had everything a paid assassin would ever need for comfort.

But the room where Levi Garvey and the Four Horsemen had assembled wasn't the game room or the media room or the gym. It was the dungeon.

After Tony looked down at Levi Garvey and then at Angelino, he said, "What did I just say?"

Angelino looked at Carl, who gave a signal that was almost invisible to Tony.

"Wake him," Angelino snapped at one of his Horsemen.

"No, wait a minute," Tony said, glaring at Angelino. "That's the second time you've paused when I've given you an order and looked over at Carl. Who do you work for?"

"I work for you," Angelino said.

"I'm not dead yet," Tony said with the emphasis on *not*. "Next time you pause, I'll show you exactly how alive I still am."

"Wake him," Angelino said.

Though Angelino's face gave no indication that he feared Tony, his wavering voice betrayed him. It gave Tony tremendous satisfaction to hear the fear in Angelino's voice.

One of the Horsemen grabbed a pitcher and splashed water on Levi's face.

When the ice cold water hit him, Levi's eyes flew open, and he took in a deep gasping breath. He tried to look around the room, but his vision was blurry, and water was running down his face. When he reached up to wipe his face, he realized he couldn't move his hands because they were cuffed to the arms of a heavy wooden chair. His legs were also cuffed to the chair. His head throbbed, and a wave of nausea seized him. The edges of consciousness were starting to slip away. His eyes rolled back as he passed out again.

"Hit him again," Tony snapped.

Angelino grabbed the pitcher without hesitation and flung more icy cold water onto Levi's face.

Levi gasped audibly a second time. He blinked his eyes rapidly, trying to focus on the man in front of him.

"Good morning, buttercup," Tony snarled.

Levi's eyes widened as Tony took the shotgun off his shoulder.

"Any last requests?" he said, aiming it right at Levi's head.

Levi stuttered as he looked first at Tony and the barrel of the shotgun, then at Carl standing beside him with a smug grin on his face, and finally at Angelino, who was looking a little pale and unsure. Levi had never been more frightened in his life. His fear doubled when he assessed the situation. He was cuffed to a sturdy wooden chair, both hands and both feet, and he had a shotgun in his face, held by a man known for using it. But what scared him the most was the fact that Tony had already decided his fate. The chair was sitting on top of a huge sheet of plastic. It didn't take a genius to figure out its purpose.

"Well?" Tony said, pulling back both hammers on the ten-gauge.

Levi heard the hammers lock into place. It actually helped him relax, knowing the hammers were locked. If Tony's ninety-year-old hands had slipped, both shells would've gone off, and they'd have found little of Levi's head.

"Speak now, or forever hold your peace."

"I'd like to know what I did," Levi said, his voice breaking.

"You lied to me," Tony said.

"I didn't," Levi said, shaking his head.

"You failed to mention that the assassin who killed the porn star is dead," Tony snapped.

Levi's face fell. When Tony saw his expression, he thought that either Levi was the most gifted actor in the history of the world—or he really didn't know.

"You didn't know that?" Tony asked.

Levi shook his head. "I didn't. I left early this morning to come up here. Tori left earlier than I did. I don't know what time this happened, but I swear to you I didn't know."

"Who has his phone?" Tony barked.

"I do," one the young Horsemen said without hesitation.

"Have you looked at it?"

"I'm looking at it now," he said, his hands shaking.

"I turned that phone off this morning, knowing I was coming up here," Levi said. "I knew Amber at the Twin Rivers Police Department might be looking for me at some point, and I didn't want anyone to know where I was, obviously. She can find the phone if it's on. I turned it on only once after I left—to find your house. Then I turned it off again and left it in my truck while I was in with you. I turned it on again after I left you—to I call Tori. I saw I had a few messages from Ray—I assumed he was pissed off and looking for me. I didn't listen to them. I turned the phone off again after I talked to Tori."

"He's got five messages on here from Chief Billings," the Horseman commented.

"Let's hear all of them," Tony said. "You'd better be telling the truth. The second one of those messages betrays you, I'm going to kill you, Levi. You sure you don't want to change your story?"

"I don't have to," Levi said. "I'm not lying."

* * *

Ed and Ray had barely sat down at the table in front of the windows when Shelia banged out of the kitchen door.

"Sorry for the delay," she said apologetically. "It took me nine minutes longer than I said—*nine* whole minutes longer."

Ed knew what that meant. She'd waited in the kitchen until they came back up, and they'd been down there a lot longer than she'd wanted them to be. Likely, she knew what they were doing. She might even have been able to watch them on hidden cameras as they searched the basement.

"I'm sorry to have to rush you," Shelia said as she handed them two foam cups of coffee. "I'm afraid I've got a family emergency, and I'm going to have to ask you to leave so I can attend to it. Right now!"

"Well, thank you," Ray said as he rose.

"We appreciate it," Ed parroted as he stood.

Quickly, they climbed the long flights of stairs to the top of the house where the door was. Ed was well-winded by the time he reached the top. Placing his hands on his knees, he tried to catch his breath. Ray looked down over the railing at Shelia, who was standing beside the table in the library below, bathed in the muted light from the wall of windows. She was scared. Even from the top of the stairs, he could see the insistent look on her face.

Looking up, she mouthed, "Go!"

"Come on, Ed," Ray said, pulling on his arm.

"Give me a second," Ed snapped back. "You know I'm twenty years older than you."

"No, we have to go now," Ray whispered. "If we don't, I think J.J. is going to have a problem."

Ed glanced down at his friend's daughter. He recognized that look. He'd seen it before. It was panic. He rushed out the door behind Ray.

After Ray pulled the cruiser door closed, he glanced over at Ed, who was wiping his forehead, and said, "You okay?"

"I will be," Ed answered. "Let's go."

Ray backed down the driveway, then pulled onto Olton Lake Drive that wound its way around Olton Lake. Not far from Pete Long's house, they saw a large van coming towards them.

"That's a security van," Ray said as it passed them.

"Don't hit your brakes," Ed said. "They've seen our squad car, and they'll be watching in the rear view mirror. Just keep driving."

"Please tell me you saw the name on the side of that van," Ray said.

"I didn't," Ed said. "It went by too fast."

"I'll bet we triggered a silent alarm when we went into the vault room."

"That would be my guess," Ed said.

"You think Shelia is okay?" Ray asked.

"She broke the rules, but I don't think she's in danger right now, but she could be when Peter Long returns from Atlanta."

* * *

They'd all listened to the new phone messages. Levi had told the truth. He hadn't listened to those messages from Ray. The first couple indicated that Ray was looking for him. Later, he'd called with the news they'd found the assassin, dead at the bottom of a cliff.

"Everybody out," Tony said.

The Four Horsemen quickly left, but Carl lingered behind.

"Everybody," Tony snapped, glancing at Carl. "And shut the door behind you."

After Carl left, Tony pulled a folding chair over and placed it right in front of the chair where Levi was bound. He sat down, uncocked the shotgun, and laid it across his knees.

"So now what?" Levi said.

"Every instinct I have says you should never leave this house alive," Tony said.

Levi's face paled. "I'm hoping there's a *but . . .*"

"But I'm considering letting you go," Tony said.

"I think there's another *but*," Levi said, pulling on the restraints that held him in the chair.

"You're not going to like the conditions."

"Let's hear them," Levi said.

Tony pulled a small notebook out of his pocket and wrote something on one of the pages. Then he ripped it out, folded it, and stuck it into Levi's shirt pocket.

"What's that?" Levi asked.

"You're working for me now," Tony said. "You're going to call me every day and update me on the investigation. And you're not going to tell anybody. Not Tori. Not your Uncle Ed. And certainly not Chief Billings. You're going to tell me about every break in the case. You're going to tell me if you find out who tried to make it look like one of my Horsemen killed that porn star. You're going to tell me anything you might learn from the State Police or the DEA about who was running that marijuana operation. You're not going to leave any details out."

"That seems extremely unlikely," Levi said.

"If you want to leave here alive, those are the terms," Tony said.

"Only through the end of the investigation?"

"Yes. Ten days. After that, I don't ever want to see you or hear from you again."

Levi sighed as he nodded.

"I know what you're thinking," Tony said. "It's written all over your face. Get out of here alive and then play me for a fool. That's a mistake, Levi. You think we have something, don't you? We both love history. We both love to read. You think we're friends, but we're not. I'll do whatever it takes to protect my interests. You should know that."

"I know that," Levi said.

"We're not friends, Levi. And if you try to fool me, you'll be sorry. I'll find out. You're not the only set of eyes and ears I have on this."

"I know your reputation. You'll kill me," Levi said. "I get that."

"I wouldn't kill you, Levi," Tony said. "That's not how you hurt somebody. I know that better than anybody, living in this museum of empty bedrooms. You'll suffer the same fate I have. Your life will be shot to hell because I'll kill your wife. I'll kill that little boy. I'll burn down your damned house after I kill your Uncle Ed and your friend Ray Billings. I'll torch Harv's Grill and the Beer Chaser just for good measure. And I'll make sure my Four Horsemen run over your dog just for fun when they leave Twin Rivers. I'll turn your quiet little town into a tragedy, and you can scream all you want, but there won't be one piece of evidence linked to me, and if there happens to be a witness foolish enough to come forward, even April Jenkins or that fool Floyd—well, they'll just vanish like witnesses against me so often do. I've been doing this for a long, long time. If you take this offer, you'd better know I play for keeps. If you can't do this, then I suggest we just end this right now and avoid that horror."

Levi's face had gone pale. He believed every word Tony had just said. Levi had never feared danger, but he still feared death—more so in the last few years when he'd gotten so much more to live for. Right at that moment, he wanted nothing more than to go home to his wife and son and to live the life he'd been enjoying until they'd made the very foolish mistake of coming to see Tony O'Malley.

"Well?" Tony said. "What's it going to be?"

"How about one condition?"

"You think you're in a position to negotiate?"

"If I didn't have something you wanted, I'd be dead already."

Tony leaned back in the metal chair and nodded.

"I'll do as you ask, but I still want those ten days to solve this without you being involved in any way," Levi said. "Even if I call you tomorrow with the name of the person behind this, you stay out of it for those ten days. After that, if there's something you need to take care of, I don't want to know anything about it."

Tony ran his fingers over his mostly bald head as he thought it over. "Ten days, and you call me every day and leave nothing out. If I find out you're holding back—"

"Yeah, I got it," Levi said.

"Agreed. After ten days, I make no promises."

"What time should I call you every day?"

"I've been reading a lot about the Freemasons since I met you. Let's see, what do you call it—high twelve?"

Levi nodded. "High twelve it is. I'll call you at noon every day. And I'll give you a full report whether there's anything new to report or not. But if I solve it before then, those calls stop."

"If you solve it today and tell me tomorrow at noon, you're free of me forever."

Levi nodded reluctantly. "It's a deal. You have my word."

Tony rose, walked to the metal door, and rapped twice. Carl opened it.

"Release him, get him cleaned up, and send him on his merry way," Tony said.

"What?" Carl said.

"Did I stutter, Carl?" Tony said with narrowed eyes.

Carl shook his head. Turning quickly, he said, "You heard Tony! Get him cleaned up and bring his truck around."

Chapter 37

They were standing around the pool table in Ray Billings' basement. Jeff had just finished telling Ray what they'd learned from the crime scene and the body at the bottom of the ravine.

Ed was circling the pool table with a cue, shooting pool balls into various pockets in rapid succession. He was the only one playing. In some part of Ray's mind, he noted Ed hadn't missed a single shot in a long time. He'd racked the balls over and over again and then, as they discussed the case, cleared the table rapidly, one shot at a time.

"So what you're basically saying," Ben Walker said from a barstool, his arm in a sling, "is that you have very little to go on."

"Not even that much," Ray said with a sigh.

"We'll get more eventually," Jeff said, walking to the fridge and pulling out a beer. "But we've got no ID on the body, and the car told us nothing. The way I see it, we're at a dead end until we're able to learn who that guy was, which will hopefully lead us to whoever hired him."

"Peter Long hired him," Ray said.

"I still think you're looking at this thing the wrong way," Ed said as he began racking the balls again. "There's more to it. I still have my doubts that Peter Long hired the hit man."

"Then who did?" Tori said from behind the basement bar.

Ed fired the cue ball at the balls at the end of the table. They exploded in all directions with a thunderous clack. Two dropped—one solid and one stripe.

"I've been thinking a lot about that today," Levi said as he suddenly appeared in the doorway at the bottom stairs that led from the garage into the basement.

"Where in the hell have you been all day?" Tori snapped.

Levi reached down and scooped Adam up off the basement floor, where he was playing.

"I told you two weeks ago I was going to the U of I today. I was invited to have lunch with the Illini High Twelve club—that's a Mason lunch club that just started there. After that, I went over to visit with a few of my old professors while I was in town."

"Oh, yeah," Tori said, smiling sheepishly. "I totally forgot."

"I didn't think I'd make it because of the snow storm, and you left early without bothering to tell me where you were going, either. I had to call Mrs. B to watch Adam."

"Sorry," Tori said.

"And your phone?" Ray snapped. "I've been trying to call you all day!"

"I forgot it at home," Levi said. "Sorry, I thought I'd told you, too."

Levi glanced at Ed, who'd stopped shooting balls. He looked back and forth between Levi and Tori a couple of times before walking around the table to take another shot. Ed didn't say anything, but Levi was pretty sure he knew that what he'd just heard was total bullshit, that both of them were lying for some reason. Ray didn't seem to notice.

"You may have," Ray said. "So what is it you've been thinking about today?"

"Well, what do you think started this whole chain of events?"

"I think it started when I sent Selena to the hospital," Ben said. "Obviously, somebody wanted to silence her. She'd been kept in hiding for a long time, and the first time she leaves that house, she's murdered."

"Ray?" Levi asked.

"I tend to agree," he said, rolling up the corners of his mustache with his fingertips. "That seems to be the point when everything blew up. Peter Long gets nervous and has her murdered."

"And Jay?" Levi said, walking across the basement to get a beer out of the refrigerator.

"Well, we're both certain he knows a lot more about this than what he's said," Ray remarked. "We're just not seeing the whole picture yet."

"Wait a minute," Jeff said, pulling his iPhone out of his pocket.

They all waited for him to get to his point. Suddenly, he grinned.

"What is it?" Tori asked.

"I should've noticed this earlier," Jeff remarked. "Selena went to the hospital on Wednesday, the same day Ben was shot."

"That's right," Ray said impatiently.

"She was murdered on Thursday," he said.

"Get to it, Jeff," Ed said shortly as he shot the cue ball hard at the purple nine ball and missed.

"The assassin's car was rented on Tuesday morning in Bloomington," Jeff said.

Ed stopped and grounded the pool cue. "Are you sure?"

"Very sure," he said with a nod.

"Peter Long argued with Jay Snider Tuesday night," Levi said. "Selena was safe at home, and nobody even knew that pot shed existed at that point."

"What the hell?" Ed said, sitting on the edge of the pool table and leaning on the cue.

Ray sighed. "This thing was already in motion before Selena came into it and before the pot shed was discovered. The assassin probably didn't live in Bloomington. He was obviously a professional, so he probably traveled here from God knows where to do this job."

"You still think it's Peter Long?" Tori asked Ray.

Ray glanced over at her. "I still like him for this. I think he planned on killing Jay long before they argued at Harv's. It was a done deal already. Then Jay went to jail. Pete didn't anticipate that. Selena ran out of groceries and called 9-1-1."

Ben nodded. "That scared the hell out of Pete. I'll bet Selena knew the same thing he was willing to kill Jay over."

"So while he's got his assassin in town, he has him hastily plan the murder of his wife as well," Levi said.

"And he makes it look like Tony O'Malley might be involved?" Tori said skeptically. "That really doesn't fit, does it?"

"Why not?" Ben asked.

"We've all said the same thing," Tori said. "Whoever killed Selena in that old-man mask meant to make it appear as if the Four Horsemen were involved. They wanted that detail to make the papers and muddy up the waters. But whoever did that and tried to frame Tony would be in deep shit with him, right?"

"Yeah, it's a death wish," Ed remarked.

"Does that describe Peter Long?" Tori asked.

Everyone glanced at Ray, who sighed. "It doesn't at all. Pete was the first suspect and the most obvious. You should've seen the look on his face when we mentioned Tony O'Malley's name. It was terror."

"He's the last guy that would've pulled a stunt like that," Levi said. "Let's say it was him. He had to know the police would come knocking on his door first. And they did. You think he's going to drag Tony O'Malley into this if he actually did it?"

"And what does Peter Long do?" Ed said.

"He ran," Tori said.

"He took a sudden trip to Atlanta," Ray added.

"And I'll bet you a hundred dollars, he's not in Atlanta," Levi said. "I'll bet he's somewhere far, far away from here, but I'll bet it's not Atlanta, I'd be hiding out in a barn somewhere in Montana, praying."

"Do you think Peter Long was the intended target all along?" Ray asked. "Somebody hired that hit man to kill him?"

"I do," Levi admitted. "And I think once the plan was put into place, it got really messy. That assassin had to take out a couple of other problems first—Selena and Jay. There is still something here we're not seeing. But my money is on the fact that Peter Long was the intended target, and he knows it. Otherwise, why would he vanish?"

"And he's not coming back here for a long, long time," Ed said, pounding a ball into the corner pocket.

"Actually, I have a thought about that," somebody said from the doorway.

Everyone in the basement looked at Russell Martin, who was standing in the entrance, his dark eyes swimming behind his thick lenses.

"And what might that be?" Ed said.

"He never left," Russ said.

"How's that?" Ray said.

"I've been looking at the pictures of his vault you gave me. It's very interesting. First, it's huge. I knew that before I saw these pictures. Now that I've seen the door, I'd be willing to bet he's got a lot of secrets hidden in there."

"Like what?" Ray asked.

"Like Peter Long," Russ said with a grin. "You ever hear of a panic room?"

"Sure," Tori said. "Rich people have them. If anybody tries to rob them or kidnap them or whatever, they go into the panic room and lock the door. It's basically an impenetrable room."

"That's right," Russ said. "That's one huge vault. I was looking at something on one of your pictures—one of the shots you took in the wrong direction."

"Well, I was nervous," Ray said shortly.

"I'm not complaining," Russ said, walking over to the pool table and setting down his iPad. "That picture was a lot more telling than those of the vault door. Come look."

Everyone crowded around him to see the picture on his iPad.

"It's kind of blurry and sideways, but look on that far wall. There are shelves. You see what's on them?"

Tori squinted at the screen and then laughed. "I do!"

"It looks like gallons of water and maybe canned goods?" Ed commented.

"And there's toilet paper, too," Levi said, pointing to one corner.

"Exactly," Russ said. "He never left. He's in the vault along with whatever secrets he's got that have put his life in jeopardy. After looking at that locking mechanism and the door, I can tell you that nobody's getting in there any time soon."

"We'll never get him out of there," Ed said.

"I don't know," Ray said, smiling.

"You have an idea, don't you?" Tori said.

"Oh, yeah," Ray admitted. "Ed, I think you and I need to take another drive to Olton Lake in the morning. And Levi, I'm going to need a big favor from you."

Levi glanced at them both and shrugged. "Sure," he said.

Chapter 38

Ray knocked on the door and waited. Ed was standing behind him. They waited a long time before the door opened.

"Morning, Shelia," Ray said.

Shelia shook her head. "You shouldn't be here. You know you tripped a security alarm yesterday. Pete knows you were here."

"I know," Ray said as he handed her a piece of paper.

She started reading it.

"We just wanted to apologize. I hope you didn't get into trouble because of us," Ed said. "The last thing we wanted was to get you into any trouble, J.J."

Shelia looked up from the piece of paper, her face ashen and her eyes wide. Nodding toward the police cruiser, Ray held up a finger to his lips.

"Well, thank you for the apology. I'm not in any trouble, but I can't ask you in."

"We'll be leaving then," Ray said.

"We'll have to go fishing some time, huh?" Ed added.

"Sure, goodbye," Shelia said, looking back and forth between them, wide-eyed.

Ed reached over, guided her out of the doorway, and pulled the door shut loudly behind her. Then he put his fingers to his lips again as he looked at her intently.

"I sure hope we didn't get J.J. in trouble," Ed announced into the air.

"She said she wasn't," Ray said. "I'm about ready for lunch."

"Yeah, me, too. Let's get out of here."

The three of them walked to the car. Shelia climbed into the back. As soon as the door closed, Ray started the car. Then they both turned around to look at Shelia in the backseat.

"I'm in danger?" Shelia said. "You think somebody bugged the house, too?"

"We're not sure if anybody was listening or not, but it was better to be safe than sorry. But make no mistake, we believe you are in danger," Ray said. "We're going to take you somewhere safe right now. There's no time to pack a bag."

Ed smiled at her. "You'll be fine. I won't let anything happen to you."

"We know Peter Long is in the vault, and we know why," Ray said. "The same men that want him dead may very well be after you as well. You know what's going on here."

"I don't know exactly," Shelia said with a stutter.

"But you have a damn good idea, don't you?" Ed said.

"I'll bet you know a hell of a lot more about it than Selena Long did," Ray added, "and she's been gone from here a long, long time. She's dead now. Murdered."

"And I'll bet you know more than Jay Snider does," Ed said, "and they damn near got him, too."

They drove several miles in silence before Shelia spoke quietly.

"It's some kind of blackmail, but I don't know who is after Pete, but he does. It goes back long before my time working for him, I think."

"Do you want to go with us," Ed asked, "or would you rather stay here?"

"I'm done here," Shelia said. "Where are you taking me?"

"I think you'll enjoy the accommodations," Ed said. "You'll be perfectly safe. All the arrangements have been made."

"Let's get out of here, then," Shelia said anxiously.

"Just one question?" Ray said. "Does Pete ever come out of that vault?"

"Yes, in the mornings. He took his boat out early today, as a matter of fact, with the two heavily armed security guards who are staying in the guest rooms. I think Pete is feeling a little safer the more time that goes by. Pete has got everything he needs in that vault to stay for a long time if he needs to."

"Where were those guards yesterday when we searched the basement?" Ray asked.

"He sends those gorillas out on errands," Shelia said. "He doesn't like seeing them standing around, doing nothing. He sent them over to Peoria yesterday to pick up a better mattress for the vault and some sort of expensive coffee maker."

"I think we saw them as we were leaving," Ray said.

"They got back minutes after you left," Shelia said. "It's unlikely Pete will ever send them out on errands again."

"This information is good to know," Ed said. "Let's get you to the airport."

"Airport?"

"Yup," Ray said. "Your flight leaves in two hours."

No one noticed a small white car following them out of Olton—or the beat-up Chevy pickup that replaced it fifteen miles further down the road.

* * *

Levi shut the bathroom door at Harv's and locked it. Then he pulled his phone out of his pocket. It was 11:58. The face in the mirror above the basin was pale with dark circles under the eyes. Levi had slept fitfully for the last couple of nights—nagged by a bad feeling that this was not going to turn out well in the end. He'd never been more fearful in his life. Turning his back to the mirror, he leaned against the basin as he dialed the number.

"Hello, Levi. Right on time again," the familiar voice said on the other end.

"I don't have much to tell you."

"Let's have it."

"As I told you before, we don't think Peter Long hired the hit man. We think he's the target. He's still holed up in his panic room. Uncle Ed has been watching his house every morning, and he hasn't seen him yet. But we're sure he's there. When they can, they're going to try and grab him. Not sure how. He has two heavily armed security thugs there."

"And the girl?"

"I said before that she's safe."

"She's safe where exactly?"

Levi paused for a long moment.

"Levi, this isn't going to work if you hide things from me. We have a deal. Where's the girl?"

"Shelia is staying at my townhouse on Pulaski Square in Savannah."

Tony chuckled. "Very clever. I didn't know you still have a residence in Savannah. Any idea who is behind that marijuana operation yet?"

"None. The DEA is investigating that with the State Police, but they haven't told us anything."

"Any idea who Peter Long is blackmailing, or what it's about?"

"Nothing yet."

"You're running out of time, Levi."

"I'm well aware of the time, very aware. We're just not making any progress."

"Listen, I'm going to share something with you. Consider it a favor. Peter Long had some investors in his porn business early on. A few of them went on to become very reputable individuals. If I were guessing, I'd say one of them is the person you're looking for. There's one in particular that would have a lot to lose if it came out that he was ever the partner in a porn studio."

"Really?"

"A certain television evangelist back in the 80s made a small fortune from his partnership with your boy, Peter Long. He's making millions today—more than enough to hire a world-class assassin. And he'd be the perfect target for the brand of blackmail Peter Long is undoubtedly involved in. My money is on Reverend Richard Palmer."

"Are you kidding me? Reverend Ricky started out in porn?"

"He sure did."

"If that's true, how do I bring that to Ray's attention?"

"That's your problem, isn't it?"

"And there's every possibility that both Selena Long and Jay Snider knew him back in the day," Levi said. "So if it is Reverend Ricky, he'd have every reason to take them out as well."

"Let's just say the four of them were together when things really started happening for Peter Long. Rev. Ricky bailed out early. Gone by the 90s. He's found it far more lucrative to sell absolution rather than sin."

"Thanks," Levi said.

"Seven days, Levi.

"I know. Then we're done, right?"

"We'll see," Tony replied.

"What's that supposed to mean?" Levi said in a panic.

But the phone was dead. Tony had hung up.

* * *

"Anything else you need, Shelia?"said the tiny white-haired woman standing in the doorway.

"No, Anna," she replied. "I'm fine, thank you."

"Sure you don't need a jacket? It's a little nippy this morning," she said.

"It's seventy degrees," Shelia said with a laugh. "I just left a foot of snow on the ground."

"Well, let me know if there's anything you want," Anna said before the screen door clacked shut behind her.

Shelia smiled and leaned back in her chair. A fresh cup of coffee steamed on the small table beside her. She could hardly believe where she was. She gazed out into Pulaski Square from the porch of Levi Garvey's Savannah townhouse. She'd never even met the famous author, and here she was—staying in his home.

The morning light filtered down through the live oaks draped in Spanish moss. The people were different here. The dog walkers strolling by all waved, and she waved back. Many of the men were wearing Panama hats like the one Levi Garvey wore in the pictures on the backs of his books. She looked up at the palm trees, which she'd never seen before. For some reason, she'd thought that palm trees grew only in Florida and California.

When her phone buzzed, she glanced at it. She didn't recognize the number, but she recognized the area code—it was Twin Rivers. Her heart fluttered as she tried to decide whether she should answer it or not. Finally, she decided she should since it was a new phone that Ray Billings had given to her. It was unlikely anybody else would have the number.

"Hello?" she said tentatively.

"So how is everything? You enjoying your stay in Savannah?"

She didn't recognize the voice.

"Who is this?" she asked.

"It's Levi Garvey," the voice on the other end said with a chuckle. "If you haven't yet, you should have breakfast on the front porch. It was my favorite thing to do when I lived there."

"That's what I'm doing right now. Thank you so much for this!"

"Let Anna know if there's anything you need."

"Don't worry about me," Shelia said.

"Hopefully, you won't be there too long," Levi said.

"It's okay. I could quickly get used to this."

"I'm kind of jealous," Levi said. "Remember, it's a bed and breakfast now, so you might come into contact with other guests. If you do, remember the story Ray gave you. We don't want anyone to know who you really are or where you're from. Anna doesn't know who you are either. You're just a guest."

"I know. I'm Shelia Sullivan on an extended vacation from St. Louis," she said.

"Don't get elaborate. Just keep it simple," Levi said. "Make sure to take in all the local cuisine and visit Bonaventure Cemetery, one of my favorite places. It's a beautiful city. Enjoy it."

"I will. Thanks, Mr. Garvey," Shelia said.

"It's Levi," he replied. "I'll check on you every so often. And if there's any sign of trouble, you let Ray know. Even if it's just a feeling, okay? He's got a lot of friends there in the police department, so you should be perfectly safe. And remember, don't call anybody—not friends, not family—until this is over. If there's anybody you want to contact, let Ray know and only Ray."

"I will," Shelia said.

"We'll call you when it's safe to come back," Levi said.

Chapter 39

At just past two in the morning, Tori walked down the stairs. Levi had never come to bed. He'd been having trouble sleeping. The truth was, so had she.

Levi was asleep in front of the television in the library. An old black and white film was playing on the screen. When she reached down to wake him, she saw his phone sitting on the coffee table. I shouldn't, she thought. But she knew something was very wrong. In the back of her mind, she had a feeling she knew what.

After looking at Levi to be sure he was sound asleep, she quickly picked up his phone and browsed through his call history. Three days in a row, he'd called Chuck E. Cheese Pizza right at noon. Her heart thudded. She recognized the number—the same number that was in her phone as "Aunt Linda." She'd been making her call each day at three in the afternoon. Tony had called her shortly after she'd gotten home that day. You don't say no to Tony O'Malley. Tori had had no idea that Levi was caught in the same trap. Her heart pounded harder. She only hoped that Levi was being honest because she had been completely honest during her calls. If Levi lied, Tony would know. He'd know because she'd told him the truth.

"My God," Tori gasped as the realization sunk in.

"What are you doing?" Levi said, rising up on an elbow on the couch and staring at his phone in Tori's hand.

"Please tell me you've been honest when you call Chuck E. Cheese at noon each day," Tori said, tears in her eyes.

"What are you talking about?" Levi said as he snatched the phone out of her hand.

"I've been calling Chuck E. Cheese every day at three o'clock, and I've been totally honest," Tori said. "Have you?"

"Oh, my God," Levi said, sitting up to face her. "I've been totally honest. I haven't lied to him."

"What in the hell were we thinking?" Tori said.

Levi reached for her hand and gently pulled her down beside him.

"I don't see a way out of this," he said.

"We're going to have to go through with it," Tori said.

"If we don't solve it, Tony gets involved," Levi said, "so you and I will continue being completely honest with him. Then what happens, happens."

"That's heartless. Not to mention that we're lying to everyone," Tori said.

"Do you have another idea?"

Tori shook her head.

"When this is over, we'll tell them the truth," Levi said. "But honestly, I'm not going to lose any sleep over the fact one stone-cold killer may or may not kill another stone-cold killer."

"Well, here's something that might keep you up then," Tori said. "Do we tell Tony we know about each other?"

Levi sighed. "Oh, crap. What do you think?"

"If we lie and he finds out . . ." Tori said, not finishing her thought.

"Then we'll tell him," Levi said. "And we'll tell him exactly how we figured it out. I'll do that tomorrow when I call him at noon."

"Agreed," she said, relieved to share her burden with Levi, to feel safe in his arms.

Chapter 40

Ray stepped out onto the dock, adjusted his hat, and snugged his jacket under his chin.

"Catching anything?" he said as he walked to the end of the short fishing pier and sat down beside Ed. Their legs dangled off the end.

"Pneumonia," Ed remarked with a shiver that made all the fishing lures dangling on his hat jiggle.

"Yeah, it's a bit nippy, isn't it?"

Ray picked up a pole and cast the line into the water without bothering to bait the hook.

"There's coffee in the thermos," Ed said.

"I'm fine," Ray said. "Seen anything?"

"Nope," Ed said, nodding down towards the end of the lake where Peter Long's massive home stood. "I've been here since dawn. No sign of him. You sure he's in there?"

"It makes sense," Ray said. "He'll come out. He loves that boat, and it's supposed to be warmer today."

"Ever occur to you he saw us and didn't fall for the fisherman routine?"

"That's possible," Ray admitted.

They were quiet for a few minutes.

"There's something that's been bothering you the last couple of days," Ed said, regarding Ray with his deep-blue eyes. It wasn't a question. It was a statement. "Ever since that conversation in the basement, something has been up with you."

"Bernice left," Ray said.

Ed snorted. "I knew that. Everybody knows that. I would've thought you'd be pretty happy about that."

"Actually, I am," Ray said with a shrewd grin.

"So are you going to tell me what's bothering you?" Ed asked.

"You know what's bothering me," Ray said. "Don't play stupid with me. You've noticed it, too."

"Levi and Tori," Ed said.

"Levi and Tori," Ray repeated. "They lied. And not very well. The Illini High Twelve meets on the third Thursday of the month, not the second Tuesday. I checked. And there wasn't one single word in the *Daily Illini* newspaper about a famous author visiting the campus either. I don't know where Levi Garvey was, but I'm pretty sure I know where he wasn't. Do you have ideas where Levi and Tori actually went the day after the snowstorm?"

"I have a bad feeling I do," Ed said.

"Tony O'Malley?"

"Yup," Ed said. "Probably went up there to urge him to stay out of it."

"Then why lie about it?"

"Because I think something went really wrong with that plan," Ed said. "I hate to say this about my own nephew, but I think we should be careful what we say around him."

"You think he's compromised?" Ray asked. "And Tori, too? You think Tony got to them?"

"I do," Ed said.

"I'm going to take his badge," Ray said. "We can't trust him."

Ed turned quickly towards him. "I wouldn't do that. I think he's in a dangerous place. Doing that might put both their lives in danger. If Tony has those two willing to do his bidding, there's a threat there that has scared them both, and you know them well enough to know that scaring those two wouldn't be an easy thing to accomplish."

"So what do we do?" Ray asked.

"We keep him on the edges of the investigation until this is over," Ed said. "Maybe we have him work on tracking down that old-man mask. Jeff sure hasn't had any luck with it."

Ray reached behind Ed for the coffee thermos, twisted off the cap, and poured himself a cup. Steam flowed out of the cup like fog as Ray raised it for a sip.

"Okay," he finally said. "That's a good idea. We'll give him busy work until we figure this thing out. I'll call Levi and have him track down that mask."

"Well, lookie there! I think I've got one finally," Ed said, grinning, as he began reeling in his line.

"You're actually fishing?"

Ed glanced at him as if that was the stupidest thing he'd ever heard.

* * *

"What are you looking at?" Peter Long said as he walked up behind one of his bodyguards who was scanning the lake with binoculars.

Pete was immaculately groomed, even in heavy flannel-lined blue jeans and an insulated shirt.   "Have a look," the bodyguard said as he handed the binoculars to Pete and pointed at the fishing dock several hundred yards up the east side of Olton Lake.

"Hmmm, interesting," Pete said. "Kind of a cold day to be fishing. And they're fishing into the wind, so they're either terrible fishermen, or they aren't really fishing."

"That's what I thought," the bodyguard said.

Pete fiddled with the knob on the binoculars. Then he chuckled as the image zoomed into focus more clearly.

"Well, well, well. If it's not Chief Billings and Officer Ed Garvey. They must know I'm here."

"What do you want to do about it?" the bodyguard asked.

"Let's go say hello," Pete said as he grinned from under his pencil-thin mustache. "It's a nice day for a boat ride even if the water is a little choppy. I'm tired of being cooped up."

"You sure about this?" the bodyguard asked.

"Let me go get my coat and my hat," Pete said. "I'll meet you down at the boat. Don't forget your gloves this time."

* * *

"Look!" Ray said, nodding toward Pete Long's house.

The two bodyguards were bounding down the steps that descended the front of the bluff. Then they walked out onto the boat pier and began to untie Pete's motorboat.

Ed dialed a number into his phone. "Yeah, Sheriff Harby? I think Peter Long is about to take a little ride out on the lake. Can you get your deputies out here? Grab him on the dock once he goes back."

Ray grinned. "I knew he was in there!"

Peter Long skipped down the stairs and climbed into his boat. As soon as the two bodyguards had sat down, Pete started the giant motor. After revving it a few times, he eased away from the pier. Once the boat was clear of the mooring, it immediately picked up speed. The acceleration surprised both Ed and Ray. In seconds, the boat was zooming across the lake, the front bouncing across the choppy water, sending out fans of spray from the nose each time it slammed down.

"Holy crap, that thing is fast," Ed said with a grin.

Ray was laughing as he watched the boat skim over the water on the far side of the lake. Then it turned around in a wide arc.

"Boy, he sure knows how to navigate that boat," Ed said.

"Yeah. You'd think that boat would flip right over in a turn at that speed, wouldn't you?" Ray said.

"That's what they're made for—speed, speed, and more speed."

The boat turned again. The engine screamed as Pete kicked it into an even higher gear. Suddenly, Ed and Ray had the same thought—Pete was heading right towards them on the little fishing dock.

"What in the hell is he doing?" Ed asked nervously.

"I don't know," Ray said as the boat roared towards them, the speed seeming to increase by the second.

"I don't like this," Ed said. "Let's get off this dock."

"Agreed," Ray said as they scrambled to their feet.

By the time they were on their feet, the boat had closed the distance. It was barreling right at them. In that split-second, Ray seriously considered diving off the dock. The boat was going to crash into them. There was no way it could miss.

"Shit," Ed said, also ready to jump.

Suddenly, the boat veered sharply to the left, sending a huge sheet of water flying towards them. The wall of water smashed into both of them, drenching them from head to toe. Ed slipped backwards, and his foot went over the edge of the dock. He fell into the lake.

"That son of a bitch," Ray fumed as the cold water soaked down clear to his skin.

"I'm going to kill him," Ed sputtered as he began splashing through the waist-deep water towards the shore.

Even over the retreating sound of the motor, they could hear Peter Long and the two bodyguards' laughter echoing across the lake.

"You okay?" Ray asked.

"I'm fine," Ed said as he climbed back up onto the fishing pier.

As the boat began to make the same turn it'd made before, Ray said, "Let's get out of here. That asshole is going to do it again."

Suddenly, there was a huge flash, followed a split second later by a tremendous boom. Even from halfway across the lake, they felt the shockwave and the heat from the explosion. Both of them had instinctively turned their backs. When they turned back around, all that could be seen of the motorboat were a few pieces burning on top of the water. The thick billowing clouds of black smoke from the burning fuel and oil rose into the sky.

Ed and Ray stared at each other in stunned silence.

"That was no accident," Ed said finally. "I think Peter's enemies just found him."

"Ray? Ed?" a voice called from behind them.

"Down here, Sheriff," Ray called back.

Harby stepped out of the woods and onto the dock.

"What happened?" he said, looking at the black smoke and smoldering remains of the boat floating near the center of the lake.

"Peter Long just met his maker," Ray said. "And I'd be willing to bet it wasn't an accident."

"Ah, geez," Harby said, taking off his hat and running his fingers through his thinning hair. "So much for getting any answers from him."

"Things just got a lot harder," Ray admitted.

"You two are soaking wet," Harby said. "Did you fall in?"

"Long story," Ed grumbled.

"We're fine," Ray said.

"Listen, I'll call Jeff and get a team out here," Harby said. "You two had better get out of those wet clothes before you catch your death. The State Police divers are going to love this one in the icy water. You know this lake better than anyone, Ed. How deep do you suppose it is out there?"

Ed scratched his head. "It's deep, and it's winter, so the lake is at its fullest. This finger of the lake used to be a deep wooded ravine before they built the dam, so the bottom drops out about forty feet from the shore. I'd guess in the middle where the boat exploded it's at least fifty feet. It gets even deeper as you get closer to the dam—ninety-five at its base."

Harby sighed. "You two go get some dry clothes and come back. I've got this right now."

He unclipped his cell phone, punched in a number, and walked to the end of the pier.

Ed and Ray climbed the trail to the road above where Ed's old Cadillac—his mother's car—sat. Ray's cruiser was hidden quite a ways off the road on a barely visible lane.

"Let's take my car. It's closer. Our wet butts won't hurt the seats in that old bomber," Ed said. "We'll pick up the cruiser when we come back."

Too cold to protest, Ray slid into the old car. Ed started the engine, flipped the heater on full blast, and let the car idle. In just a minute or so, heat poured from the vents.

"You can't beat the heater in these old Caddies," Ed remarked.

"It's a Chevy, right?" Ray said.

Ed shot a glance at him and said, "You want to walk back to your cruiser?"

Ray shook his head.

Ed pulled onto Olton Lake Drive, which wound its way around the lake to the point where it met up with the Calloway Slab. As they rounded a bend, a guy walked out of the woods and climbed into a small white car. He was wearing khaki pants, a sweater, and a light jacket.

"That's odd," Ed remarked. "He's not really dressed for the woods, is he?"

"No, he's not," Ray agreed. "You got a pencil?"

"Check the glove box."

As they passed the car along the edge of the road, Ray jotted the plate number down on the back of Ed's vehicle registration card.

"Worth checking, don't you think?" Ray said.

"I do."

Chapter 41

Levi was working in his den when the doorbell rang. It was mid-afternoon. He'd been trying to track down that mask, without much luck, since Ray had called him several hours earlier.

"Get that, would you?" Tori yelled from the kitchen.

Levi walked out into the foyer. Rosco was looking out the front window, his tail wagging. Levi opened the door. Ray and Ed were standing on the porch.

"Is Tori here, too?" Ray said shortly.

"Kitchen," Levi said as Ray brushed by him and headed towards the kitchen.

Ed stepped in and stood beside Levi as he shut the door.

"What's going on?" Levi asked.

"I'll let Ray tell you."

Levi walked down the hall and stepped into the kitchen. Tori looked at him with a disturbed expression on her face. Opening up the refrigerator, Ray pulled out a beer and cracked it open.

"Have a seat, you two," he said, taking a long drink from the can.

Tori reluctantly took a seat at the kitchen island on one of the tall stools. After looking at both Ed and Ray in turn, Levi took the other one. Ray leaned against the stove as Ed leaned against the sink. Ray looked at them both for a long moment.

"I don't want either of you to say anything, okay?" Ray said. "Just listen."

They both nodded.

"You both lied to us the other night," Ray said. "Levi, you didn't go to Champaign the other day. I checked. Tori, you never said where you were, but I know where, and I know why. And I know it didn't go like you planned, and now both of you have a big problem."

Tori started to say something.

"Don't," Ray snapped angrily. "It's pointless."

Ed saw the angry flare in Tori's green eyes fade.

"Just listen," he repeated calmly.

"I did something today I've never done before. I asked somebody to break the law. I had Amber hack your phone records. Both of yours. Levi, you've called the same number four days in a row at noon. Tori, you've called the exact same number every day for the last three days at three o'clock sharp. Amber couldn't identify that number because it's an unregistered burner phone. But if I call that number from one of your phones, I'd bet my house I know who'll answer it."

There was a long pregnant pause as the truth of the situation soaked in.

Levi sighed. "Could I have a beer?"

Ray opened the fridge.

"Me, too," Tori said.

Ray glanced at Ed.

"Might as well," Ed remarked.

Levi started to say something.

"I'm not done yet," Ray snapped, cutting him off. "I don't know how you got into this mess. Maybe he threatened to kill you."

"Nope. I'd live, but he'd kill her and Adam and you and Ed and pretty much everyone else I care about. And he meant it."

"Good God," Ed said. "What in the hell were you two thinking?"

Levi shook his head.

"It's about to get a lot worse than it already is," Ray said.

"How could it get worse?" Levi said.

"Peter Long is dead," Ed said. "Somebody put a bomb on his boat with probably a pound of C4. Killed him and his two bodyguards, and there isn't a piece of any of them left that's bigger than a fingernail."

"If that bomb had gone off a few seconds sooner, it probably would've killed Ed and me as well," Ray said.

"But here's the kicker," Ed said. "We're leaving the lake after the explosion, and we see this guy come out of the woods near a white car. He wasn't really dressed for a hike, so Ray wrote his plate number down."

"The car is registered to Jake Pierce," Ray said.

"I don't know who that is," Levi said, glancing at Tori, who shrugged.

"Well, the FBI sure as hell does," Ray said. "His family has a long history with the Chicago Outfit. He is a well-known associate of Tony O'Malley. He's worked for him for more than twenty years. He was a prime suspect in a mob hit in Chicago back in '96. Of course, there was never enough to charge him because the one witness apparently committed suicide—a left-handed witness who shot himself in the head with his right hand."

"No witnesses. That's Tony O'Malley's signature," Ed said.

"I don't know if this makes your situation better or worse, and I don't expect you to tell me," Ray said. "To be honest, I really don't want to know. The bottom line is that the FBI now firmly believes that Tony O'Malley is behind the murder of Peter Long. Since organized crime falls under their jurisdiction, we're out of it."

"But this gets even uglier," Ed remarked.

"I'm stuck in a tough position," Ray said. "If Tony O'Malley did kill Peter Long, you and Tori may be accomplices in the homicide."

"My God," Levi said.

"You told him, didn't you?" Ed said. "You told Tony O'Malley where we thought Peter Long was."

Levi nodded.

"I did, too," Tori admitted. "Didn't have a choice."

"Damn," Ray said. "You two told Tony where Pete was, and now he's dead. You know, if the FBI tracks this back to you, I can't help."

"I know," Levi said, "and you've made it even worse, Ray."

"I know. Because if I don't report this, I become an accomplice after-the-fact."

"We both are," Ed said.

"So what are we going to do?" Tori said.

"We're all going to be accomplices together," Ray said. "And we all may just go down together."

"You're not going to report it?" Levi asked.

"Nope."

"We might as well jump all the way in then," Tori said, looking at the clock before fishing her phone out of her pocket. "It's either prison or concrete shoes for us all. Which is it?"

"Speaking for myself," Ed said, "the idea of prison is more appealing than getting on the bad side of Tony O'Malley."

Ray shrugged. "Let's do this."

Tori laid her phone on the counter, turned on the speaker, and dialed the number.

It rang a number of times before it was answered. "It's a little early for you, Tori. Is something wrong?"

Ray felt a cold chill run up his spine when he recognized Tony O'Malley's voice.

"Total honesty, right?" Tori asked.

"That's the deal," Tony replied.

"I'm here with Levi, Ed Garvey, and Chief Billings," Tori said. "Ray and Ed figured it out."

There was a long silence on the other end.

"This isn't good, Tori," Tony said curtly.

"I'm afraid it gets a lot worse," Ray said.

"Are you recording this call?" Tony asked.

"No," Levi said. "That would be really stupid. You see, Tony, we're all accomplices in a homicide."

"How's that, exactly?"

"Let me tell you," Ray said.

* * *

After Ray finished the story, Tony said, "Interesting predicament we've found ourselves in, huh?"

"How do we work this out, Tony?" Levi said.

"Looks like I'll be dealing with the FBI," Tony said with a chuckle. "Those keystone cops haven't got a chance of putting together a case. They've been trying to put me away for seventy years and haven't managed to come even close. I'm not too concerned about the FBI. But since the Twin Rivers Police Department is out of it, let's just say our association has ended."

"We're done?" Levi asked.

"You did what I asked you to do," Tony said, "so erase that number out of your phone, and our association is ended forever. Understand?"

"I'm sorry, Tony," Tori said. "But I just don't believe you. We're witnesses in a homicide you committed, and we all know how you feel about witnesses. They have a tendency to vanish."

Tony chuckled. "You're not witnesses because I didn't have Peter Long killed. I had him watched. I've had the same guy watching you all to make sure you made good on your promise, but he certainly didn't kill Peter Long. Actually, he was just as surprised as Ed and Ray were when that boat exploded this morning. As usual, the FBI has this entire thing wrong."

Relief washed through Levi, and a broad grin crossed his face.

"And Levi?" Tony said.

"Yes?"

"Why don't you go back to writing books," he said.

"This case is closed for us," Ray said. "Ben Walker wants to come back to work on Monday, and before I leave this house, I'm going to fire two of my police officers—the ones named Ed and Levi."

"I think that's wise," Tony said. "I'll stay out of River County, and you idiots stay out of Chicago. Got it? Next time one of you comes barging in here, all hell is going to break loose."

The call ended abruptly. The four of them looked at each other. Then Tori picked up the phone and stuck it back in her pocket.

"Well, that's that. I need another beer," Ed said.

"I need another half dozen," Ray said.

"Are we all okay, then?" Tori said.

"Tomorrow is another day," Ray said. "Let's just get back to normal and never speak of this again. Ever."

"You going to pass out a few more beers or just stand there like a big dope?" Ed said to Ray.

Ray pulled the fridge door open. "Looks like Levi has most of a case in here. That should be enough."

"There's some Red Stripe in the back," Tori said.

"Perfect," Ray said.

"Now," Tori said, "what I want to know is what happened with Bernice?"

"So the whole town knows," Ray said.

"Of course," Levi said with a grin.

* * *

Tony pressed the end button on his phone. He'd been on the speaker, too. Carl poured himself a bourbon and Tony a scotch. He handed the glass to Tony, who took a sip, then set the glass down on his desk, leaned on his elbows, and tented his fingers under his chin. Angelino stood silently nearby. Both men knew better than to say anything while Tony was thinking.

"Kind of a mess, isn't it, Angel?"

Angel nodded.

"What would you do?" Tony asked.

Angel shook his head. "I'm not paid to think."

Tony smiled tightly.

"How about you, Carl?"

"You're still the boss," Carl said.

"I'd like to hear your opinion," Tony said. "I could keel over any day, and these decisions will be your decisions."

"Okay," Carl said. "We pull out of Twin Rivers. I'm no longer that interested in who framed us in the murder of that porn star. I personally think that Peter Long did that—why, I don't know or even care to know anymore. And that marijuana operation isn't lucrative enough, in my opinion, to risk getting entangled with the FBI."

Tony nodded. "Then who killed Peter Long?"

"One of the people he was blackmailing," Carl said. "Maybe it was that TV preacher you liked for it—Reverend Ricky. He does have a lot to lose if his association with a porn guy ever comes out. It doesn't involve us, and, frankly, I don't give a shit. I think we cut our losses and get the hell out of there. I'm not very fond of the Twin Rivers Police Department or the Garveys. It won't be the FBI that eventually busts us. If we stick around there, they'll be the ones who'll finally take down the Chicago Outfit."

Tony laughed. "You've hit the nail right on the head," he said picking up his scotch. "Twin Rivers has just advanced to the very, very top of my I-don't-give-a-crap list. We're out of there."

"And Jake Pierce, getting caught out like that, using his own car, for God sake. He really screwed the pooch on this one," Carl said.

"Yes, he did," Tony said. "Too bad he got both complacent and dumb since he's been such a faithful and trustworthy associate all these years."

"Yes, he has been," Carl agreed.

"Angelino," Tony said. "When you kill Jake Pierce, make it fast. Surprise him. We owe him that much. But do it tonight if you can. Make it clean. Don't take any unnecessary risks since the FBI is snooping around our doorway again."

Angelino nodded, rose from his chair, and started towards the door.

Carl cleared this throat and looked at Tony with a raised an eyebrow.

"Oh, yes! I almost forget," Tony said with a smile. "Angelino, we have a little tradition we'd like to pass onto you. Would you like to use my shotgun on this job? I let Carl use it when he went out on his first assignment as my head enforcer many years ago."

"That would be a great honor," Angelino said, almost smiling.

Tony nodded towards the case along the edge of the room.

Angelino walked to the case, opened it, and removed the old shotgun. Carefully, he snapped it open to ensure that it was loaded. Then he snapped it closed again.

"Thank you, Mr. O'Malley. I won't make him suffer."

"And if you can arrange it, don't do it in front of his family," Tony added.

"I'll do the best I can," Angelino said as left the library, closing the door behind him.

"Don't kill him in front of his family? Really? You're getting soft, Uncle Tony," Carl said, smiling at him.

"I'm old, and I'm trying to get into heaven."

Carl grinned. "You think you've got a chance?"

Tony picked up his scotch glass and drained the remainder.

"Nope," he said, holding up his glass. "How about just one more?"

Carl took the glass and returned to the sideboard.

"I'm with you on one thing though," Tony said.

"What's that?"

"I'm really glad to be done with the Garveys."

Carl laughed. "Let's drink a toast to the Garveys," he said, handing the tumbler to his uncle.

Tony held up his glass. "To the Garveys, the biggest pains in the ass in the state of Illinois. May they never darken our door again."

"I'll drink to that!"

Chapter 42

Levi sat down on the front porch with his coffee and snugged his jacket around his neck as he leaned back and propped his feet up on the porch rail. It was a cold morning. The heavy frost on the tree branches glistened in all the colors of a prism in the morning sun.

It was his habit to start every morning on the front porch, summer and winter, but it'd been a while since he'd done so. It felt good to get back into his regular clothes and his regular routine. He certainly wouldn't miss those itchy uniform pants. Steam puffed out of his mug as he took a tentative sip.

Rosco was already down the front steps, sniffing around the bushes in front of the porch. Rabbit tracks covered the snow. It would be only a minute before Rosco would flush one out and chase it across the yard. He was good at finding where they were hiding but not so good at catching them. He was more a skunk dog than a rabbit dog. Truth be told, he wasn't good at catching skunks either, just good at getting sprayed by them.

Tori walked out onto the porch with the flag. Adam was still sleeping.

"Well, look at you," she remarked. "Going to fall right back into your usual routine, huh?"

"You bet," Levi said as he watched her insert the pole into the bracket on the porch post.

The flag went out every morning and in every evening—a tradition that went back generations. In the attic, they'd found an old box of Lucille Garvey's photos of the house going back to the 30s. There wasn't one photo of the porch without the American flag mounted in the bracket on the post beside the steps.

Tori picked up the paper off the steps, sat down next to Levi, took the coffee mug out of his hand, and took a long sip. She didn't hand the mug back.

"Really?" he said.

She smiled, took another sip, and handed it over.

Suddenly, both looked towards Rosco. A very young rabbit had just run out from under some bushes by the porch. Rosco was right on its tail as it fled, bobbing and weaving to avoid the snapping teeth of the German shepherd.

"Oh, no," Tori said, squeezing Levi's arm. "He's going to catch it."

"Just wait," Levi said with a smile.

The terrified rabbit suddenly shot up the side of a snow drift that had formed around the base of a maple tree in the front yard. In hot pursuit, Rosco bolted after him, but outweighing the rabbit by a hundred pounds, he broke through the crust on top of the drift. Buried up to his belly in the snow, Rosco struggled to free himself from the trap—totally humiliated by the rabbit, which actually stopped to look back at the dog before leisurely hopping off into the tall weeds by the edge of the road.

"See? I wasn't worried. Rosco will catch a rabbit the same day Wile E. Coyote finally catches the Roadrunner," Levi said.

Tori laughed as Rosco, covered in snow, slowly returned to the porch and plopped down at the top of the stairs—his head down on his paws in utter defeat.

Levi grinned. "You'll get him tomorrow, Rosco."

"So I take it you'll be heading up to Harv's for pie and coffee and then to the library for a long read?" Tori said.

Levi looked over at her. She'd managed to get his mug again when he wasn't paying attention, and she was in the process of polishing off his coffee. That wild strand of kinky blonde hair was hanging loose in front of her face as it had since the day he'd met her back in the sixth grade. He wondered momentarily if it would still do that when they were both old and gray-haired. He was well on his way there now. In another ten years or so, he figured he'd have snow-white hair like his Uncle Ed's.

"I think I'm going to skip the pie," Levi said. "I could barely get these pants buttoned and zipped this morning."

"It's all those donuts you've been eating the last week or so. You should seriously work on your diet, Levi. Too many meals at Harv's and not enough fruits and vegetables. I won't even mention the beer."

Levi sighed.

They sat quietly for a few minutes, taking in the beauty of the morning.

"Do you think Tony is really done with us?" she asked finally.

"I do," Levi said.

He'd been awake late, staring at the ceiling, wondering the same thing. Finally, he'd decided that there was little benefit and a lot of risk involved if Tony did come after them. Tony O'Malley wasn't a stupid man. They'd done exactly what he'd asked. And for some reason, Levi had never truly believed Tony wanted to harm them.

"You think Ray will leave this alone?" she asked.

Levi shrugged his shoulders. "I hope so. He doesn't really have a choice since the FBI has the case now. They'll be all over Tony, but I honestly don't think that bothers him one bit. Ray knows this isn't a local matter. It's not like last time when we knew the murderer was right here in our midst."

"So life returns to normal," Tori said.

"That's my plan. I'm going to run over to Olton today to visit Aunt Maggie. I got one good idea from Tony. Aunt Maggie had this," he said, holding up his hand. The morning sun glinted on his gold Masonic ring. "It belonged to my great-grandpa Abe. Aunt Maggie isn't a Garvey. She is my Grandmother Lucille's sister, so Grandma must've given it to her for safe keeping. If Aunt Maggie had this, maybe she has a few other things that belong to the Garvey family."

"Like your great-great-grandfather William's Civil War journal?"

"Exactly," Levi said. "It could be that simple."

"Do what you want, Levi," Tori said, "but Lucille didn't want you digging around in the family skeleton closet. And Reverend Guy Garvey, in his final days, seemed to realize she was right. I know your inquiring mind, but I wonder if you'll be happy once you find the answer you're looking for or if you'll wish you'd never learned the truth."

"I know," Levi said. "I've been over and over this in my mind. What in the hell is the big secret?"

"And come hell or high water, you've just got to know, don't you?"

"I'm sure that when I learn that secret and regret it, you'll be right there to say 'I told you so.'"

"That's my job," Tori said, leaning over to kiss his cheek before rising and walking back towards the door. "One more thing, Levi."

"What?"

"Those aren't your pants. They are mine," she said as she turned to enter the house.

Levi glanced down at his jeans. He'd known there was something wrong when he put them on.

"Well, that explains all the extra room in the seat," he said, glancing at Rosco.

"What did you say?" Tori asked, suddenly reappearing in the doorway, her green eyes flashing.

"I didn't say anything," Levi said.

"I didn't think so," she said as she closed the door behind her.

Levi glanced over at Rosco, who was looking at him with his ears up.

"That was a close call," he remarked, "but I'll bet you a week's worth of treats she just locked us out."

Rosco whined and plopped his head back down on his paws.

Chapter 43

April was making coffee when the bell over the door jangled. Moments later, all the customers in the diner began to applaud. Turning, she smiled immediately.

Officer Ben Walker was standing in the doorway in his police uniform, his arm in a sling. He looked around sheepishly as Chief Billings walked in behind him.

April was so happy to see Ben back on duty that she almost failed to notice their new uniforms. The khaki shirts and pants were gone along with the brown felt trooper hats. Ray and Ben were both in black, their new gold badges gleaming from the pockets of their winter jackets with black fur collars. On their heads, they wore black ball caps with "Twin Rivers PD" in gold thread on Ben's and simply "Chief" on Ray's.

After the applause ended, they both walked to the counter and took stools. April set coffee and pie in front of them. Before Ben could pick up his fork, she reached over the counter, took off his hat, and planted a kiss on his forehead, her lipstick leaving a smear. She popped his hat back on his head, looked at him over the top of her glasses, and grinned.

"Thanks," Ben said.

"I didn't get a kiss with my pie," said a man from the farmers' table. "I have pie here every damn day, and I've never gotten a kiss."

Ben turned on his stool and said, "I've never enjoyed saying this more. Shut up, Floyd."

The diner erupted into laughter.

Floyd leaned back with a huge smile on his face. "What's up with the new uniforms?" he asked.

"Ask Tori Garvey," Ray said, turning up the corners of his handlebar mustache. "She told me it was time to replace the old uniforms. She got our sizes and apparently ordered them. They showed up yesterday. We've got summer uniforms and winter uniforms, heavy jackets and light jackets, ball caps and cold weather fur lined caps with ear muffs. What do you think?"

"I think they look great," Harv said from the kitchen door, wiping his hands on his kitchen whites. "Should have gotten rid of those old ones after—"

April glared at him. There were some names they just didn't say anymore in Twin Rivers. Doug Malone was one. Alan Haig was another. And most definitely, the third was the name of the man who'd befriended them all and fooled them all for decades—the former bank robber, cop killer, and long-time Twin Rivers Chief of Police, Clifford Craig.

"Hopefully, Ben won't bleed all over that uniform," Floyd said with a cackle.

Ben glared at him.

"Don't say it," Floyd said, putting his hands up. "I know, I know. Shut up."

The bell jangled again, this time followed by boos. Ed Garvey stood in the doorway, wearing a denim coat with fleece lining.

"Oh, pipe down, you ungrateful citizens. I got fired last night."

Cheers and exaggerated whistles filled the diner as Ed worked his way to the counter and sat down next to Ray.

"So now what, Chief?" Ed asked.

Ray sipped his coffee, then said, "I've got hours and hours of paperwork to catch up on, and considering your reception, I should probably write a number of apology letters, too."

Ed chuckled. "You know they're not really mad, right?"

"Yeah, I know," Ray said, smiling back, "but it'll be fun to apologize for your stupid ass."

"What are you going to do on your first day back, Ben?" Ed asked.

"Well, I've got to go confiscate some illegal fireworks from a few ornery boys over on the western front," he said. "Apparently, a number of mailboxes were blown off posts last night. I guarantee it's those same boys who did it last time. You'd think they'd change their M.O., wouldn't you? Other than that, I'll just work my patrol as usual."

"Nothing ever happens in Twin Rivers," April remarked as she filled cups.

"You know, April," Ed said. "Maybe we ought to stop saying that. I'm not sure it was ever true."

"I tend to agree," Harv said as he banged through the swinging door back into the kitchen.

Chapter 44

Jay set his paintbrush down and stepped back to look at the portrait. He'd been working all night. He always knew when he was done because the picture on the canvas matched the picture in his strange brain perfectly. The problem with his work was that sometimes painting things perfectly was unflattering, even ugly. There might be a wart or a cold sore or a little sleep crust in the corner of the eyes.

But this painting, which was to be a gift, was very pleasing, he thought—the clear titles of the books on the shelf, the angelic old woman, the perfect light of a fall morning, streaming through a window. It was Lucille Garvey, just as he'd seen her thirty years ago in her library. Her blue eyes were focused on him, and her white hair radiated the light from the turret room windows. Her gentle, almost inquisitive smile started at her mouth and worked up into the crinkled edges of her eyes with that one raised questioning eyebrow.

Jay remembered that one second from thirty years ago in every detail. Since he remembered every second that way, the moments he decided to put on canvas were always remarkable in some way.

Thirty years ago, he'd awakened suddenly in that library after a very drunken night with her son, Ed, who was still snoring on the settee. Lucille had snapped open the blinds, flooding the room with light. He sat up on the couch, rubbing his head. When he looked up, she was standing there, looking at him, just as he'd painted her for her grandson, Levi.

Jay and Ed had been playing pool the night before. It wasn't often he could beat Ed, but he'd had a very good night that particular evening at the Beer Chaser. Ed refused to quit until he won his money back. He didn't, and Joyce threw them out at 2 a.m. They stumbled out together. Jay got into his El Camino, threw in into drive instead of reverse, and launched his car over the concrete bumper, hanging it up on the frame. Ed suggested he spend the night at his house, have a little something to eat, and maybe down a couple more beers. He promised to pull the car off the bumper in the morning when they were both sober enough to do so.

They'd gone over to the Garvey house in Ed's old red tow truck. Ed owned his house even back then, but he rarely stayed there. He preferred staying in the basement room at his mother's house. They let themselves in the basement door. It'd taken a long time for Ed to find the right key and the lock. They were both extremely drunk. Once inside, they climbed the steps up from the basement into the kitchen. Ed put a finger to his mouth as they reached the top of the stairs. He twisted the knob on the kitchen door.

"Shhh... my mom and my nephew will be asleep, and the last thing we want is to wake up Mother," Ed said, trying to speak softly but failing.

Ed tripped on the top step of the basement stairs and fell into the door, which banged against the wall with a loud thump. After listening for a moment, they stepped into the kitchen. A minute later, Ed finally found a small light over the stove, but only after he'd knocked the tea kettle off the top onto the floor. Ed froze in the dim light and listened again. Then he smiled.

"Mom is a very sound sleeper," he said with a slur.

Ed rummaged around in the refrigerator and found some leftover spaghetti. Then, after more searching, he pulled a pan from the cabinet, but not before a large lid rolled out and clattered around and around on the floor like a coin on a bar top. Ed dumped the contents of the Tupperware dish into the pan he'd found. Then he stood in front of the stove, stirring it with a large metal spoon. After a few minutes, he got some plates from an upper cabinet. When he returned to the stove, his elbow hit the spoon handle, flipping it to the floor and leaving a long red stripe of sauce down the front of his shirt and pants. He grabbed a wooden spoon out of a crock nearby, knocking it over, too. All the utensils spilled across the counter.

Suddenly the kitchen lights came on. Lucille Garvey was standing in the doorway, dressed in a robe and slippers, obviously agitated.

"What in the hell are you doing, Ed?"

"I'm warming up some spaghetti for me and Jay," he said, waving the sauce covered spoon at Jay.

"Good evening, Mrs. Garmen," Jay slurred from the kitchen table.

She sighed, shaking her head.

"You're making enough noise down here to wake the dead," she said. "It's a school night, and you'd best not wake Levi."

"I won't," Ed snapped. "Just turn off the lights and go back to bed. I'm almost done here."

"Fine," Lucille said, flipping off the lights and leaving them in the semi-darkness.

"Sorry about that," Ed said as he continued to stir the spaghetti.

Suddenly, the lights came on again.

"One more thing, Ed," Lucille said.

"What?"

"You might want to turn the burner on," she said.

Ed reached down and angrily flipped the knob on the stove. Blue flame whooshed to life under the pan.

The lights went off. As Lucille walked away, her laughter filled the hallway.

"Sometimes she really ticks me off," Ed muttered as Jay covered his mouth to stifle a laugh.

As promised, there was leftover spaghetti plus a few more beers. The next thing Jay remembered was waking up on the couch in the Garvey library.

Looking at the portrait, Jay smiled. He promised himself never to tell Levi the story of how he'd come by that amazing moment in time. If Levi ever heard it, he'd have to hear it from Ed. But Jay knew that most likely Ed wouldn't remember the story at all. Sometimes the memory of a single moment was more enjoyable without the story that went along with it.

Chapter 45

Shelia ended the call and tucked her phone into her pocket. Then she sat down on a bench near a famous grave—the grave of musician Johnny Mercer. Little did she know that a few years earlier, it had been the spot Levi Garvey favored. He'd often sat on that bench as his German shepherd, Rosco the Brave, explored the area. Of course, that was before the dog had lost his life in Twin Rivers and become Rosco the Brave. Levi was still calling the sleepy dog Rosco the Lethargic back then in Savannah.

Shelia had been having a nice walk through Bonaventure Cemetery when her phone startled her. Only two people had her number—Chief Ray Billings and Levi Garvey. Chief Billings had called.

What he'd had to say was shocking. Peter Long was dead, and she could safely return to Twin Rivers. Gently, he'd given her the full account. Little did he know that she actually hated the man and everything he stood for. His death was a relief to her, but it also scared her.

Somebody had killed him and Selena Long. Somebody had tried to kill Jay Snider. She knew Pete had earned many dangerous enemies through his sleazy business dealings. She also knew there was one person who knew more about those dealings than either Selena or Jay.

She was that person.

When Shelia had told that to Chief Billings, he'd suggested that perhaps she should stay in Savannah a while longer after all. Maybe the FBI would figure it out, he'd said.

She knew they wouldn't. The answers were well-guarded behind the door of the giant vault. Eventually, they'd try to break into that vault, and they might get through the door, but they'd never get the contents of that safe out intact. That vault was a lot of things—a safe, a panic room, and a crematorium of sorts. If somebody tried to defeat that door, it would trigger a security system that would incinerate everything inside. The only way into that vault was having the combination and knowing the protocols required to open the door. Shelia didn't know all the details, but she knew that even the booby traps had booby traps. What was inside that vault was meant to stay inside that vault. Peter Long had gone to great expense to make sure of that—whether he was alive or not.

But Shelia knew something about that vault she wasn't supposed to know—an overheard conversation, once overheard but never forgotten. She just couldn't decide what to do with that information. If she called the FBI, she'd have no control over it. Sadly, one of the secrets that vault held was the reason she worked for Peter Long, the reason she could never leave his employment.

Shelia had to think this through, but she also knew time was short. It wouldn't be long before the FBI would try to cut into the vault. Perhaps that wouldn't be such a bad thing since everything inside would be destroyed. But the destruction of the contents would only help her in one way. Whoever had killed Selena and Pete was still out there. Even with her secret safely destroyed, she'd still be a target. The assassin who'd killed them would still assume she had first-hand knowledge of what that vault contained.

Should she talk? And if she did, to whom should she talk? She thought she could trust Chief Billings, but she didn't know him very well. However, there was another she could trust unconditionally. She pulled her phone out of her pocket, remembering the number she'd called so often as a child. Her life might never be the same if she dialed it, but she'd never be safe if she didn't.

"Hello?" the familiar voice said.

"Ed?" she asked.

"Yeah?"

"It's Shelia."

"Shelia?"

"J.J."

She heard the familiar laugh. "J.J., how are you? How's my nephew's house in Savannah?"

"Listen, Ed. I need for you to help me figure out what to do."

"Okay," Ed replied. "Talk to me."

"There's a way into Peter Long's vault," she said, "but there's something in there I'd rather nobody sees—"

Her breath caught in her throat.

"I kind of wondered why you worked for Peter Long. I assumed he was holding something over you," Ed said after a long pause. "I'll do everything I can to protect you."

Shelia looked out at the rows of gravestones, all blurred through her tears.

"I just don't know who to trust. I think I can trust Chief Billings, but if I give him the instructions on how to open the vault . . ." She paused, then added, "The thought of the FBI getting in there—" She didn't finish the thought.

"Why don't you tell me, and I'll decide what to do with the information," Ed said. "You know they'll get in there eventually."

"Not without my help, they won't," Shelia said, her voice cracking. "That's my problem. If I say nothing, my secret is no doubt safe. But even with my secret safe, I'm in danger from the murderer."

"And if you tell me," Ed said. "Your secret is at risk, but we might be able to figure out who the murderer is and take him down."

Ed Garvey often played dumb, but he was anything but dumb.

"That's right."

"So how about this?" Ed said. "You give me the information. Trust me to be discrete. I'll get in there and destroy your secret first thing."

"You'd do that?"

"Of course, but the down side is you're going to have to tell me what I'm looking for."

"I don't know."

"Shelia, I'm the last person who can judge others for mistakes they've made," Ed said. "I've made more than you can possibly imagine. And I have a few secrets of my own that I've hidden well. It's your decision."

A glint of sunlight on metal caught Shelia's eye. A dark sedan was moving slowly down one of the winding paths of the cemetery. It stopped behind her rental car. Her heart began pounding as two men climbed out and looked into the windows of her car.

Quickly, she ducked behind a large headstone.

"Shelia? You still there?" Ed said in her ear.

"Listen closely," she said.

Suddenly, keeping her secret was no longer her primary concern.

"I'm listening," Ed said. "Is there something wrong?"

"No, I'm fine," Shelia said. She said sitting on the ground, leaning against the back of the headstone. "But if anything happens to me—"

"You're in trouble," Ed said, sounding alarmed.

Shelia smiled as tears coursed down her cheeks. She'd always known her mistake would lead her to a bad end.

"Not even the police can get here in time, Ed," she said.

"What's going on?"

She knew she had time either to describe her killers, who were pros unlikely to ever be caught, anyway, or to tell Ed how to get at the information he needed to solve the crime.

"Not your problem. It's mine," she said, glancing over the headstone.

The men were splitting up. One was walking away. The other was heading her way.

"There are six security protocols required to open that vault, including Peter Long's thumbprint. And the biometric scanner can tell if that thumb is alive or dead."

"I've heard of that," Ed said. "The scanner has to detect a pulse as well as a fingerprint. Unfortunately, there are only tiny pieces of Peter Long left at this point."

"So you can't open the vault that way, but there's another way. I overheard him talking to the CEO of the security company that installed the vault. You know, Pete thought I was stupid, so he frequently talked in front of me as if I wasn't even there. Anyway, there's a backdoor into the system. I don't think he ever trusted anyone enough to give it to them, but it's built in. There is only one minute every day that the vault can be opened using a simple ten digit code, but you have only sixty seconds and one chance to open it. If you miss that window or punch in that code wrong, everything inside will be destroyed. I know what time that code will work, and I know what Peter Long used as the code number."

"I'm listening," Ed said.

"There's a display on the front of the vault . . ."

Chapter 46

The little white poodle jumped onto the back of the sofa and began barking at the window.

"Quiet, Sandy," the old woman said as she walked over to peer out.

An old blue pickup truck was parked in her driveway. Her great-nephew climbed out, and his huge German shepherd jumped out after him. Suddenly, Sandy streaked across the small parlor and squeezed under an overstuffed chair by the fireplace.

Levi stood, wearing his Panama hat, and looked at the house for a minute. The old woman thought it was a ridiculous hat to wear with a foot of snow on the ground. When a car with a yellow flashing light on top pulled up to her mailbox, Levi waved. Then he went to the end of the driveway to retrieve the mail. As he walked towards the kitchen door, his dog at his heels, she moved to an old roll-top desk, took a long flat metal key from a drawer, and tucked it into her robe pocket.

Without knocking, Levi opened the door a crack and yelled, "Aunt Maggie?"

"Come on in, Levi," she said, leaning on the doorway between the kitchen and the parlor.

"I've got my dog with me," he said, peering at her through the narrow opening in the door. "Surely you still don't have that annoying little poodle, Candy, do you?"

"Heavens, no," she said with a laugh. "I've had Mandy, Brandy, and now Sandy since then. But come on in. She'll be fine. She's already seen your dog, so she'll never come out from under that chair."

"Be nice," Levi said to Rosco as he opened the door and walked into the overly warm kitchen.

He tossed the mail on the kitchen table. Then he took off his coat and hung it on one of the hooks behind the door beside his Panama. His aunt was, after all, his grandmother's sister, and she had the same rule—no hats in the house, ever.

"There's coffee on the stove," she said as Rosco began sniffing around the tiny kitchen. "Bring me a cup, too. I think it's done."

Levi walked over to the old gas range with the Pyrex percolator on the burner. He hadn't seen one of those in thirty years. The coffee was perking, and it was dark. He turned the flame down low and grabbed two mugs from a little mug tree beside the stove.

"Black, right?" he said as he poured.

"Of course," she said as she smiled, showing her teeth that were the color of old parchment paper.

"In here or in the parlor?" he asked.

"In here," she said, shuffling from the doorway to the kitchen table.

Sitting down across from her, Levi watched as she took the coffee mug in her gnarled hands and raised it to her mouth. Even though she appeared to be fragile, her hands didn't shake at all as she sipped. Then she leaned back in her chair, the mug between her hands.

"How have you been?" Levi asked, loosening his collar. It was sweateringly warm in the kitchen.

"Better than you'll be when you're ninety-eight," she said with a grin. "Still have my teeth. Still live alone. Still make my own coffee and my own breakfast, lunch, and supper. And I still play the organ at church every Sunday morning even with these miserable, old hands. The congregation is very forgiving of my clunkers these days and amazed that I still drive myself up to the Church of Christ, I suppose. A couple of months ago, I was a little under the weather and missed church. They sent an ambulance!"

Levi grinned broadly. "Well, better than a hearse from the funeral home."

The old woman leaned back and laughed loudly, sounding so much like his grandmother that a lump formed in his throat. She even looked like an older version of Lucille.

Levi sipped his coffee and winced. It was almost as strong as the stuff his grandmother had made. She'd made great pie but lousy coffee. Ed used to try to get up first so he could make coffee in the morning, but he rarely succeeded because Lucille Garvey had been a very early riser.

"Nice ring," Margaret said.

Levi glanced down at his Masonic ring.

""Where'd you get it?" she asked innocently.

"My wife got it from this old crone," Levi said, smiling.

She laughed again. "It looks a lot better than when I gave it to Tori. She obviously found a jeweler who could restore it. Do you like it?"

"I do. I wear it every day. Having it means a lot to me. Thank you," Levi said.

"Something wrong with your coffee?"

"No, it's almost good enough to be three cups," Levi said.

"Lucille's father-in-law used to complain about my coffee, too."

"Abe?" Levi asked, glancing at the ring on his finger.

Margaret nodded.

"I can't imagine why," Levi said, taking another tentative sip.

"Not for the same reason you want to complain about it," she said. "He said it was as weak as water."

"Maybe that explains why you could stand a spoon up in Grandma's coffee."

Rosco walked over and put his muzzle on Margaret's leg. She reached down to stroke his head.

"You're over here for a reason, so why don't you just ask me?"

"I always forget you actually knew Abe," Levi said, shaking his head.

"I knew his father, too. William."

"You did?" Levi said, his eyes wide.

"That's right. I attended his funeral, the funeral of a great American Union captain. He died young, in his late eighties, and he was a young captain—in his early twenties when he received his commission, I think."

Levi smiled. He'd caught the humor in the remark—"died young, in his late eighties."

"I was probably a teenager when he died in the early thirties," she said, thinking back.

"That was a long time before Grandma married Grandpa William," Levi said.

Levi had never known his grandfather who'd died fifteen years before he was born.

"Our families had been friends for years—starting back with the first William, Captain Garvey, and my father. Early on, Dad farmed for the Garveys. Later, William and Dad start an ice business at the turn of the last century—they were partners. They harvested ice from several small ponds in the winter and stored it in ice houses. The demand for ice quickly outgrew those little ponds they'd been harvesting. In fact, that's why there's a dam at Olton Lake. My father and William Garvey dammed the Olton River. In the beginning, that dam was about ice, not drinking water as it is today. As soon as the ice formed, they worked day and night, cutting blocks and storing them in sawdust. Then all summer long, they delivered that ice in twenty-five pound blocks all over Olton, Twin Rivers, and Calloway. They employed over a hundred men back then. In fact, when we were girls, Lucille and I both worked in the office of the ice company. Our families made a fortune together, and it wasn't just the ice company. We were in several profitable ventures together back in those days—especially in the 20s and 30s."

"I didn't know that," Levi admitted.

Margaret smiled. "In the 20s, my Uncle Clarence and Abe Garvey also went into business together. In fact, they were so successful they built the theatre in Twin Rivers which Tori restored—the Comet. You might not know this, but when that theatre was built, movies were still fairly new. Nobody expected them to take off like they did. In the beginning, most of the features at the Comet were vaudeville performers—they'd show movies on the weekends. Not talkies, but silent movies. You know, I saw Al Jolson at the Comet Theatre when I was a little kid and later, Red Skelton, too. And I saw a guy who later became really famous on television in the 50s. He performed with a vaudeville troupe as a song and dance man. He played Lucy and Ricky's neighbor. Fred Somebody?"

"Fred Mertz?" Levi said, unable to come up with his real name.

"That's right, Fred Mertz." Then snapping her fingers, she said, "Ah, his name was William Frawley!"

She leaned back in her chair, smiling, satisfied that her ninety-eight-year-old brain had retrieved that bit of trivia.

"I never heard of Uncle Clarence," Levi said.

"Lucille named one of her boys after him," Margaret said.

"I don't have an Uncle Clarence."

"A nickname for Clarence is Larry. That's what they called him."

Levi tensed at the mention of his father's name. Margaret changed the subject.

"So why are you here, Levi?" she asked again.

Levi glanced down at his ring.

"Wondering how I managed to have that, huh?"

He was amazed at his elderly aunt's grasp of more modern speech. She'd kept up. She may have been a teenager during the Al Jolson years, but when visiting her back in the early 80s, he'd watched MTV with her in the parlor. She'd particularly liked the Stray Cats and Huey Lewis then—not a far stretch from the Elvis and Jerry Lee Lewis songs she'd enjoyed during the 50s when she was closer to his age.

"Yes, I am curious," he admitted. "How did you get this old ring?"

"Lucille gave me that," she said. "You were in college, and she didn't think you were coming back. Ed was a train wreck at the time. She thought he was well on his way to drinking himself to death. Frankly, I'm surprised he's still alive. So Lucille was faced with the end of the Garvey family line since she didn't see you ever getting married and having a family. She figured that after she was gone, the house would go up for sale. She wanted to keep a few things safe. I have a son, and I had a daughter at the time, but she's passed on now. Since our families were so close, she wanted me to keep those things in case you ever came looking for them."

"A few things," Levi said.

"I have a box in the attic that belongs to you," Margaret said. "You'll have to go up to find it. I don't do attic stairs anymore. It'll be easy to find because it has 'Levi' on it in your grandmother's handwriting."

Levi nodded as his eyes clouded. He couldn't speak.

"The journal isn't in it."

Levi's head snapped up.

"I know why you're here," she said. "It's not there."

"What happened to it?" Levi asked.

"It's safe. You'll have it soon. I feel pretty good, but I'm ninety-eight. In time, it'll fall right into your hands," she said, reaching into her robe pocket.

She handed him the long flat metal key.

"Not before then," she said. "That was Lucille's wish."

"Did you read it?" Levi asked.

Margaret nodded. "You can probably guess how the black Garveys and the white Garveys are related. That's what you're interested in. But there's a lot more in that journal. What she didn't want you to know about was the River County War."

"River County War?" he repeated.

"Let's just say that my family, the Garveys, and several other families that are all still around today behaved very badly back seventy or eighty years ago," she said, shaking her head. "You'll inherit that journal eventually. You already possess the key. But if I were you, I'd never use it. You know better than anybody that sometimes things that are in the past are better left in the past. What the journal contains will poison you. I think Reverend Guy Garvey told you basically the same thing. Sometimes ignorance is bliss."

Levi looked down at the key. The thing he'd been obsessed with finding for the last couple of years was contained within the very safety deposit box that key opened. His first impulse was to learn the secrets in that journal, but the past had been speaking to him—his grandmother, Reverend Garvey, and now his Aunt Maggie.

Handing the key back to her, he said, "Seems like you have two or three or even four years left, so you decide if I open an empty box or find that relic from the past."

It was a plea. She took the key and tucked it back into her robe pocket.

"So I'm stuck between honoring my sister's wish and your desire to know," Margaret said.

Levi said nothing.

"So be it. I'll make the choice for you. Either way, whether it's in there or not, I think you'll curse me in the end."

"I trust your judgment."

"Do you?" she asked sharply. "You don't trust Lucille's."

"I'll accept your judgment," he amended.

"You won't have a choice. If I leave it, you'll regret it. If I take it, you'll feel cheated."

"So what's the answer?" Levi said.

She leaned over the table and held her hands out. "I'll pray about it."

Chapter 47

Ed rushed into Ray's office, the door slamming into the wall.

Ray looked up at Ed's ashen face.

"What's wrong?"

"You need to call your friends on the Savannah Police Department."

"Shelia?"

Ed nodded, trying to catch his breath. "I have no idea where she is, but they need to find her right now."

"You should've called me," Ray said, reaching into his pocket for his phone.

"I tried," Ed snapped.

Ray searched his pockets, but he didn't come up with his phone. "I must've left it in my car."

Suddenly, the phone on his desk rang.

"Twin Rivers Police Department, this is Chief Billings."

He looked at Ed as he talked. When his face fell, Ed knew what was being said on the other end.

"I understand," Ray said. "I appreciate the call, Captain Harper."

After Ray hung up the phone, Ed sat down in the chair across from his desk. Ray rubbed his temples and stared at his desk top for a long moment.

"Damn," he said.

"I promised her she'd be safe," Ed said.

"How did they know she was there?" Ray said. "Only the three of us knew and a few on the Savannah Police Department."

"I have no idea," Ed admitted. "Actually, one other person knew where she was, thanks to Levi and Tori."

"Tony O'Malley," Ray growled.

"We need to put Jay into protective custody," Ed said as Ray rose from his chair and grabbed his black jacket and cap from the coat rack.

"I hope we're not too late," Ray said.

Chapter 48

Tori walked into the kitchen with Adam on her hip. She'd been shopping. Levi was sitting at the table, which was covered with old papers and photographs. He was peering at one photo in particular.

"What's all this?" Tori said as she set Adam on the counter to take off his coat.

When she let him loose on the floor, he made a beeline for his box of toys in the corner of the kitchen.

"Stuff that Grandma Lucille left with Aunt Maggie—stuff that belonged to Grandma and Abe, and even a few things that belonged to Captain William Garvey."

"So she did have the Garvey things. Is there a Civil War journal in there?" Tori said as she slid into the booth across from him and started to look at some of the papers on the table.

"Nope, but I know exactly where it is."

"You've found it!"

"I'll inherit it after Aunt Maggie passes—unless she changes her mind and destroys it. She's praying about the decision. She knows how Grandma felt about me seeing the journal."

"Oh," Tori said, "so what are you looking at?"

"It's a picture of my mother and a baby," Levi said, handing it to her. "I'm trying to figure out who the baby is."

It was one of those small square snapshots that were so common in the sixties—probably taken with the same kind of Kodak camera everyone had back then. Tori recognized Levi's mother without a doubt. She was standing in a front yard with several other people who seemed familiar, but Tori didn't recognize them right off. There were a lot of sixties hairdos with hair pomade and horn-rimmed glasses. Everyone was dressed up for a special occasion.

"That's you, Levi," Tori said with a smile.

"That's what I thought but look again, closely."

Tori looked again, but she didn't see anything that would make her change her mind. She'd seen other baby photos of Levi. Obviously, he wasn't much more than a couple of weeks old.

She flipped the snapshot over. Written in pencil in Lucille's tidy handwriting were the words "Easter Sunday."

"It's Easter," Tori said. "I guess I'm not seeing it."

"Easter Sunday! That's part of it," Levi said. He pointed to the edge of the photo where the processing date was stamped in blue ink.

"Ah," Tori said, suddenly getting it. "It says April 1967, and you were born at the end of May 1967. So it's not you. The picture was taken and processed before you were born."

"It can't be me. I just noticed that a couple of minutes ago," he said. "I just can't figure out who that baby is. It must be somebody on Grandma's side of the family. I think all these people in the picture are her relatives."

"Your dad isn't in this picture," Tori said.

"I noticed that. Dad probably took it," Levi said. "They were married in 1966, so I'm sure he was there. There's probably another photo in this box with him in it. Don't you remember how family snapshots were done back then? You'd take turns so everyone could be in at least one of the photos."

"You know any of these other people?" Tori asked.

Levi took the photo back. "I kind of remember that tall guy," he said pointing to the man wearing a suit which seemed a little short for his tall frame. "I think that's Aunt Maggie's son. When Grandma and Aunt Maggie's dad died, I was about six. He took me to see a movie at the Comet Theatre while they did the whole visitation thing. It was *Herbie Rides Again* with Helen Hayes and Stephanie Powers, I think, and maybe Ken Berry. He didn't like the movie, and I didn't like him, so I decided to be a pain in the ass. When we got back to the house, he made me go to bed so he could watch Columbo on television. That was back when we had the big huge antenna on a tower beside the house. We had two TV's, one in the den and one in the basement. Since Uncle Ed watched the most television, the antenna control was in the basement. While my babysitter was watching Columbo, I sneaked down the stairs and through the kitchen and down into the basement. I clicked the big plastic dial around until the antenna pointed in the opposite direction."

Tori smiled. "I haven't thought about an antenna box in years."

"Anyway, by the time I got back up from the basement, he was standing in the hall. I guess Columbo had gone to snow. He looked pretty mad, having figured out exactly what I'd done, and I was already regretting having done it. As luck would have it, Aunt Maggie and Grandma Lucille walked into the foyer at that moment and saved me."

"He looks kind of familiar to me, too," Tori said, peering at the photo more closely. "He looks like he's in his twenties there, so he'd be in his seventies now."

"Please tell me that's not Floyd," Levi said with a chuckle.

"Oh, he does kind of look like Floyd. He's not a relative, is he?"

"I never knew much about Grandma's family. You don't suppose that's the huge family secret, do you? She didn't want me to know Floyd is related."

Tori laughed.

"Who is the little short guy?" she asked. "He looks familiar, too."

"I remember him," Levi said. "That was my great-uncle. He was Aunt Maggie and Grandma's brother. He was very funny and very smart. He didn't like most kids, but for some reason, he liked me. He used to read Sherlock Holmes stories to me when I was really little. Years later, when Reverend Guy read Sherlock Holmes stories to us every so often in Sunday School, I already knew a few of them. He also read me stories about Horatio Hornblower. I remember those, too. But I think he died a long time ago—like when I was in grade school."

Tori was looking intently at the photograph again. "When was Easter in 1967?"

"Hmmm," Levi said, pulling out his phone. He tapped on it and waited for the Google search to come back. "In 1967, Easter was on March 26."

"So you would've been at least ten months old at your first Easter Sunday," Tori said.

"Right. My first Easter Sunday would've been in 1968—a year later."

"I don't know," Tori said, handing the photo back. "Why don't you ask your Aunt Maggie? That baby sure looks like you, though."

Levi tossed the photo back into the old shoebox.

Tori slid out and said, "You want some coffee?"

"Yeah, I do."

Tori poured water into the back of the coffee maker and reached for the coffee in the cabinet. Suddenly, she stopped.

"Wait a minute."

She walked back to the table and retrieved the picture from the shoebox.

"What is it, Tori?"

"You sure that's your mother?"

"Positive, why?"

"Because she's not pregnant," Tori said, handing the picture to him.

Levi looked at the photo closely. "You're right."

"On March 26, 1967, your mother would have been seven months pregnant—with you!"

They looked at each other for a long moment. Then both burst out laughing.

"You're older than you thought, Levi."

"They lied," Levi said, becoming serious. "I was born in March, not May."

"I'd guess a date change was common enough back then. There was a real stigma attached to getting pregnant out of wedlock," Tori said. "So your parents get married real fast. Then she goes off to have the baby in March, but she tells people you were born in May. Wonder what the story was that Easter with the family?"

Levi said with a shrug, "That also explains the unlikely story that my parents met, became engaged, and then got married in two weeks' time."

"Who told you that story?" Tori asked.

"Grandma did," he said, "so she knew."

"Wonder what else is in here," Tori said, looking at all the stuff laid out on the table.

"Not sure I want to know now," Levi said with a wry smile.

Tori walked back to the counter to continue making coffee. She had a grim look on her face.

"I know what you're thinking," Levi said.

"What am I thinking, Levi?"

"The same thing I am," he admitted.

As the coffee was running through the filter, Tori slid back into the booth across from him. "Lucille didn't seem to mind you learning you were born in March instead of May. That wasn't a big deal in her mind. But she didn't want you to see what is in that journal, did she?"

"No, she didn't," Levi said with a sigh. "It's like the key to Pandora's box, isn't it? Once I open it and learn what there is to learn, there's no way to unknow it. What in the hell could the secret be?"

"You'd better think long and hard on that," Tori said. "The time will come when you'll get your hands on the journal. You'd better think before you open it. We've already opened a couple of those Pandora boxes, haven't we?"

Chapter 49

Ray pulled the cruiser to a stop beside Jay's Jeep and climbed out. Ed followed him as he strode towards Jay's workshop. After peering through the window of the workshop door, they pushed the door open.

"Jay!" Ray called.

There was no answer. Jay wasn't in the workshop.

"He's not too far away," Ed said, pointing at the propane heater mounted on the wall. "He left the heat on."

"Probably in the house," Ray said.

Ray followed Ed towards the house. As they approached the front door, Ed's arm shot out, stopping Ray. The door frame was splintered, and the door was ajar. Ray drew his weapon. Ed wasn't licensed to carry a firearm, and since he was no longer a cop, he shouldn't have been armed, but Ray knew he probably was. Ray nodded. Ed reached into his jacket and pulled his Smith & Wesson Model 10 from a shoulder holster. Each took a place on either side of the door. When Ed nodded, Ray pushed the door open a bit further.

"Jay? Are you home?"

No answer.

Then something crashed inside. Ray slammed the door open wide and rushed in with Ed right behind him. There was nobody in the front room. They paused, listening. Suddenly, a door creaked.

"That's the back door," Ed yelled as they dashed towards the kitchen.

Jay was lying face down on the linoleum floor, blood pooling around his head. Ed stepped over the body and rushed towards the open door.

"There!" Ray shouted, pointing at the man who ran by the kitchen window.

Ed burst through the kitchen door. As he rounded the corner of the house, two slugs slammed into the siding near him. Quickly, he retreated back around the corner. Two more shots were fired. He waited a moment, then ventured another quick peek around the corner. There wasn't anyone in the front yard, but the gunman had flattened two tires on the police cruiser. Suddenly, he heard somebody running through the dry leaves. Ed ran towards the sound. As he rounded the corner, he saw a man scurrying up the steep hill towards the road above.

"Stop!" he yelled.

He was answered by two more shots. Both wild.

Ed leveled his revolver and fired at the man as he neared the top of the hill. The slugs kicked up puffs of snow just in front of and behind the running man, neither hitting him. As Ed started up the steep embankment, he heard in quick succession, a car door slam, a motor start, and the spin of tires as the car sped off.

"Damn," Ed said as he stopped.

It was pointless to continue up the hill since the shooter was long gone, so Ed returned to the kitchen. Ray was stooped down by Jay's body, one hand on his neck, the other grasping his wrist. He looked up at Ed and shook his head.

"What's that?" Ed said, pointing to a large canvas, which was lying face down on the floor near Jay's body.

Ray examined the back of the canvas closely and said, "You'd better have a look at this."

Written on the back in charcoal pencil were the words, "For Levi Garvey."

"Jeff is going to kill us for messing with his crime scene," Ray said.

He picked up the canvas and flipped it over. It was a beautiful portrait of a old woman with striking blue eyes. Ed sucked in his breath.

Noticing his reaction, Ray said, "Who is this?"

"It's my mom," Ed said as he shoved his revolver back into his shoulder holster. His eyes were suddenly shiny with tears. "Levi's grandmother."

"What do we do, Ed? This is not good. Do you think this portrait has something to do with the murder?"

"Are you asking me if we should leave the portrait or remove it?" Ed said.

Ray shrugged. "It wouldn't be hard to prove, if somebody looked hard enough, that both Levi and Tori were mob informants. Did the information they gave Tony O'Malley lead to this murder and the one in Savannah? Will this portrait take that investigation right to their door?"

"We're involved, too," Ed said. "There's a good chance Tony lied to us. There's a good chance he did kill Peter Long. And Selena. And Shelia. And now Jay. Who else has the reach to coordinate a hit in Savannah and in Twin Rivers at almost exactly the same time?"

Ray sighed. "When this is over, I'm turning in my badge and resigning."

Ed nodded.

Ray handed the canvas to Ed. "Go to the workshop and swap this with another canvas the same size. Then I'll call Jeff. Wipe all the prints off that one and leave it in the workshop and don't leave any on the one you bring back."

"You sure you want to do this?"

"I'm just getting started. We're going to figure this out, one way or another. When we get done here, we're going to break a few more laws."

Ed took the canvas. He knew exactly what Ray was going to do.

Chapter 50

"You know if we get caught, we're going to prison, right?" Ed whispered as they walked up the driveway.

"I know," Ray hissed. "We've talked this thing to death, so are we doing it or not?"

"I don't see what choice we have," Levi replied, glancing at his phone. It was 1:45 in the morning.

"We don't have time to be talking about it, so let's either do it or turn around now," Russ Martin whispered.

No one turned around. At the door, Ed tried the knob. Then he nodded to Russ, who walked up to the door, dropped to one knee, and opened his bag. With a small flashlight between his teeth, he worked the picks. In a few seconds, he twisted the doorknob.

"It's open," he whispered.

Ray stepped up, cut the police tape, and pushed the door open. There was a beep as soon as the door opened. Russ walked directly to the electronic keypad behind the door, pulled a card out of his pocket, and punched in the code he'd written down. The flashing red light on the pad went to solid green. All four men entered the foyer.

"Close the door," Russ said to Ray.

Quickly, they descended the staircase down into Peter Long's house. When they reached the bottom, Ed pointed to the top of another flight that led to the basement level.

"We're going down there, Russ," he said.

Russ nodded and flipped the switch at the top of the stairs, illuminating the way down. When they reached the bottom, Ray flipped another switch, lighting the waiting room and the reception desk. Behind the desk, where Shelia had no doubt played a part in the elaborate ruse, was the wide mahogany door of the executive office, every square inch of which Ed and Ray had learned was wired for sound and video from multiple angles. Ed, Levi, and Russ followed Ray past that area and down a long hallway lined with cubicles.

At the end was an ordinary metal door. Ray glanced at Russ and nodded towards the door. Ed had opened it the first time, but Russ had tools that could open it more gently. Ray didn't want the FBI to notice any new jimmie marks on the lock. Russ had the door open in seconds.

The small room beyond was well illuminated with fluorescent lights. It was hard not to notice the huge bronze-colored vault door that took up the entire wall across from the door.

"Shut the door," Russ said as everyone entered the vault room.

Russ studied the vault door—every detail from the hinges to the geared mechanisms to the small control panel with a keypad beside the door.

"You're sure about this?" he said to Ray.

Ray nodded.

"What time is it?" Russ asked.

Levi glanced at his phone. "I've got three minutes until two."

"I hope Shelia was right about this," Russ said.

"She said it could be opened with a ten-digit code between 2:00 a.m. and 2:01 a.m.," Ed said. "You have only one shot at it. If the code is wrong, everything inside will be incinerated."

"And we're sure about the code?" Russ said, rubbing his hands together.

"She overheard the conversation," Ed said. "It was a number Peter Long knew well—his mother's phone number. Ray had Amber look for it. Pete's mother had the same phone number from 1968 until she died in 2001. It has to be the code."

"I sure hope he didn't change the code at some point," Levi remarked.

"I asked Shelia about that," Ed said. "She said he wouldn't have done that. He wasn't good with electronic stuff. She had to change the clock in his car when the time changed in the spring and fall, and he used the same pin number and password for everything. Of course, we'll know for sure in a minute."

Russ shot a glance at him. "Sometimes you're not helpful, Ed."

"Sorry," Ed remarked.

Russ thumbed through a small notebook. Then he pressed a couple of unlabeled buttons on the top of the keypad. It lit up.

"That's a good sign. That worked like it should. Now say a little prayer for me because we need to know what time the vault says it is."

"What do you mean?" Levi asked.

"I need to bring up the clock function," Russ said. "As you can see, all the keys are unlabeled except on the number pad. If the safe is a minute faster or slower or if it's still on daylight savings time, we'll be in trouble when we punch in that phone number to open it."

Levi glanced at his phone again. "Well, you've got about two minutes to do that."

Russ looked through his notebook again and said, "Cross your fingers."

He pressed four buttons and leaned back.

"That's a problem," Russ muttered.

Nothing had happened.

"We should get out of here," Russ said nervously. "That should've brought up the clock, and it didn't. If you punch in the wrong function, you'll either shut it down for twenty-four hours, or you'll trigger a security protocol."

"The booby trap," Ed said. "You're right. We should go!"

As they started towards the door, the keypad suddenly blinked to life and beeped loudly.

"Wait," Russ said, smiling broadly.

The beep clicked off the seconds—119, 118, 117 . . .

"Okay, it's counting down to when we can enter that code. We've got less than two minutes before we can try the code."

Ed wiped a hand across his sweaty forehead. They all were staring at the changing numbers. Levi thought it sounded a lot like a time bomb in a movie. Maybe they were waiting for a bomb to go off. Maybe Russ had triggered a booby trap.

As the last ten seconds clicked down, Levi glanced at Ray whose white face was rigid. Even Russ backed away from the keypad. 5 . . . 4 . . . 3 . . . 2 . . . 1 . . .

They all winced and braced as the zero came up. But nothing happened. The display panel showed sixty seconds. 60 . . . 59 . . . 58 . . .

"Okay, that's good. Let's try the code," Russ said, wiping his hands on his pants.

"Don't screw up," Ray said.

"Shut up!" Russ said, glaring at him.

Russ wiped his hands again. Then holding the card with the phone number in a hand that trembled a little more than Ed would've liked, Russ began punching in the digits. Ed counted the beeps. Nothing but asterisks appeared on the display, so he had no way of knowing if Russ had made a mistake or not.

"That's it," Russ said, leaning back.

The clock kept counting down—10 . . . 9 . . . 8 . . .

When the clock got to zero, nothing had happened. Seconds passed as they all stared at each other. Suddenly, there was a giant metallic clunk. The men all startled. Gears began to turn, and the bars began to recede from the thick walls of the vault. Seconds later, the hydraulic door started to swing open, revealing the black interior of the vault yawning before them. Suddenly, the lights on the inside of the vault clicked on.

Russ grinned. "We're in. I wasn't worried."

"Like hell," Ed snorted.

"Move fast," Ray said as he walked inside.

In the massive interior, there were rows of metal shelving loaded with thousands of DVDs. Ray knew exactly what he was looking at. Ed pushed by Ray and began looking at the rows of DVDs, running his index finger down the rows of sequential numbers on the spines.

"Ed, we're not after the movies. We're looking for some kind of ledgers or records," Ray snapped. "Maybe a laptop or an iPad."

"You get what you need, and I'll get what I need," Ed growled back.

"I don't see anything but DVDs," Levi said nervously, looking around.

"I don't either," Ray called back.

Behind the shelving units, they found an open area with a toilet and shower, a kitchenette, and a recliner in front of a television.

"It's not the Hotel Carlyle," Ray said, "but he was living in here obviously."

"I think I got it," Russ said.

He pulled a cloth skirt off a table next to the recliner. It was actually a large black safe.

"I'll bet the records are in here. I sold him this old safe. It's from the 1930s—a great safe. Fortunately, I reset the combination for him when I sold it to him."

Russ thumbed through his notebook, then dropped down in front of the large dial on the front. His fingers moved quickly, spinning the dial one way and then another.

As Levi walked towards the safe, he saw Ed pluck a DVD off a shelf and stuff it inside his jacket.

"What was that?" Levi said.

"Don't worry about it," Ed said. "I made a promise."

"Shelia?"

Ed nodded.

"Crap! I overshot that one," Russ said as he began to spin the dial again.

The lights flickered in the vault.

"What was that?" Ed asked.

"I don't know," Levi said.

Russ continued to focus on the dial.

"You smell that?" Ed remarked.

Levi sniffed the air. "I do smell something."

Suddenly, they all smelled it very strongly.

"That's propane!" Ray said.

"Let's go!" Ed yelled, remembering what Shelia had said about there being booby traps inside of booby traps.

"Wait," Russ said.

"No, we've got to go," Levi said.

"I almost have it," Russ said, spinning the dial.

Levi glanced behind him. The vault door was closing slowly.

"The door!" he yelled.

At that moment, Russ hit his last number, cranked the lever down, and pulled the door open. The safe was full of bound records.

"Grab what you can and run!" Ray shouted.

Russ scooped up an armload of ledgers and dumped them into his bag. It wasn't nearly all of them. Ray grabbed the back of his jacket and pulled him up.

"Out!"

Levi reached the door just behind Ray, Ed, and Russ. He tried to edge through the quickly narrowing opening. As he did so, he heard something from inside the vault—something very familiar but something he couldn't quite place—chink, chink, chink. Suddenly, he knew what it was. The stove—it was the sound made by the electric igniters which sparked the gas when he turned on the burner. His heart pounded with panic, his knees felt weak. The smell of propane was overwhelmingly strong now. Still trying to squeeze through the narrow opening, knowing he was about to be roasted, he tripped and fell in the entrance, half in and half out. The vault door, weighing thousands of pounds, would probably cut him in half. Damn, he thought.

Reaching down, Ed yanked Levi through the door just as it boomed closed. A split second later, the explosion within rocked the basement. Ed, the Vietnam veteran, instinctively hit the floor beside Levi while the other two men ducked low. A single burst of brilliant blue flames flashed across the ceiling of the vault room as the propane gas that had escaped from the inside of the vault ignited outside the vault door.

Shakily, Ed rose from the floor, patting himself to be sure he wasn't on fire.

"Okay?" Ed said to Levi. "Still got everything."

"I think so," Levi said, slowly climbing to his feet.

"We need to get out of here," Ray said, looking nervously at the vault door.

There were no flames or fire outside the vault, but they felt the intense heat emanating from the vault door. They all understood there was an inferno raging just on the other side of that door, and the air in the vault room seemed thin.

"We've got to get out now!" Russ said.

They looked at each other for a split second before suddenly realizing what Russ meant. They'd escaped the vault, but they hadn't yet escaped the danger. The men dashed up the steps and outside to Tori's Impala in the driveway. About two minutes later, as they sped along Olton Lake Drive, they heard two more loud explosions in quick succession.

"Oh, boy," Levi said, looking through the back windshield.

"What?" asked Ray.

"I don't think we have to worry about anybody finding out we broke into Peter Long's house."

Quickly, Ray pulled off onto the side of the road. They all climbed out to look. The sky at the end of the lake was glowing. The lake reflected the flames, which were rapidly growing to engulf the large house.

"Wait for it," Russ said.

"Wait for what?" Levi said.

A huge explosion suddenly blasted all the windows out of the front of Peter Long's house, sending glass, wood splinters, and debris splashing across the lake. They stood in stunned silence as the heavily timbered roof of Peter Long's house slowly shifted and collapsed, crashing down in a bloom of flame and sparks.

"I guess we can add arson to the list of our crimes," Ray muttered, leaning on the roof of the car.

"You knew the house would explode," Levi said, glancing at Russ.

"I had a feeling," Russ said. "We got in using the back-door protocol, but I'll bet there was something we were supposed to do once we were inside to verify we were authorized to enter. Probably a hidden keypad where we were supposed to re-enter our access code. We didn't do that, so the vault went into destruct mode as it was designed to do. But once the contents were destroyed along with whoever broke in, the next protocol was to make sure anyone outside the vault didn't get out alive either."

"We may have a tough time explaining why we're here, reeking of propane and looking slightly singed, when the fire trucks start arriving," Levi remarked.

"Good point," Ray said. "Let's go."

Chapter 51

"Well?" Levi said.

They were gathered around the kitchen island. Tori was examining one of the bound books they'd taken from Peter Long's vault. The rest were stacked next to her. Ed was looking over her shoulder, and Levi was standing across from her, trying to read upside down. Ray and Russ were leaning on the counter drinking beer.

"Just hush," Tori said, running a finger down one of the columns and comparing it to another of the bound books.

Finance was her specialty. She'd been the president of the First National Bank of Calloway for over ten years. She'd worked in finance for a large insurance company before that.

"There are no names in there," Levi said with a sigh.

"Nope," Tori said, "but there are millions and millions of dollars recorded in these books."

"And these ten aren't all of them," Russ remarked. "Only about half of what was in the safe."

"So what can we learn from these, if anything?" Ray asked.

"It looks like these ledgers are the most recent, judging by the dates recorded in the first column," Tori said. "Last month alone, he recorded income of more than eight hundred thousand dollars. I think I get the system. In the first column, he writes the date. In the second column, there's some kind of number—looks like an account number. He probably kept a separate list of who those accounts belong to. The third column is a code of some kind—I don't know what it means. There's a column that shows how much the payment is, and the last column is the amount received."

"What kind of code is that?" Levi said, pointing at the third column.

"I don't know. There are two numbers, a dash, two numbers, another dash and then five more numbers," Tori said.

"I know what that means," Ed remarked, looking over her shoulder. He had the DVD he'd removed from the vault in his hand. "This one is 96-12-00158. That was the filing system for all the DVDs in the vault. Most of them weren't porn movies. They were porn audition tapes of young women who wanted to make porn movies. Peter Long was blackmailing those women who auditioned. He's referencing the actual recording in the ledger. The one I just mentioned—it was made in December of 1996. And it was the 158th audition made that month."

"How do you know that?" Tori asked him.

"Shelia told me," Ed said flatly. "I promised her I'd retrieve and destroy this one. I failed to keep her safe like I said I would, but I can keep this promise."

Ed dropped the DVD on the floor and ground the heel of his boot into it. No one spoke for several minutes.

Then Ed spoke again, "A lot of those girls were college-aged. They were paid a pretty good fee to audition, and they would've made much more if they made the cut and actually were in movies produced by Peter Long's studio. It was a talent market Peter Long was very familiar with."

"I'm beginning to see the whole picture," Levi said. "He kept track of those girls long after most had forgotten about that mistake back in college."

Ed nodded. "They didn't even know the audition was being recorded."

"That's sick," Ray said as he twirled the corners of his mustache thoughtfully.

Russ Martin shook his head. "Ten or fifteen or even twenty years later, they've got their degrees and have become successful doctors or lawyers or scientists or CEOs or college professors or soccer moms. Then, out of the blue, they get a copy of that audition in the mail with a little note. It's something that could ruin their reputation, their career—"

"Their marriage," Levi added.

"And they pay," Ed said. "They pay and pay and pay."

"Like Jay Snider said," Tori remarked, "there are a lot of ways to make money in porn."

"Exactly," Ed said. "And these might not be just women who auditioned. They could be strippers in his clubs, prostitutes, call girls—anybody who worked for Peter Long who had a secret worth paying to keep hidden. But we don't have the key. We don't have the ledger that links the account numbers to the names of the individuals. But I'll bet anything our murderer is one of the people in the ledgers."

"So we've gained nothing," Levi said, running his fingers through his hair, which he figured was much grayer after the ordeal at Peter Long's house—maybe even a bit singed on the ends.

"Not necessarily. We know one thing—our murderer is a woman," Tori said.

"That's true," Ray said.

"Each of these ledger books represents a year," Tori continued. "Look at this one number in 2003," Tori said, pointing at various placed down the pages. "She is paying ten thousand each month. That's the largest amount here."

Tori picked up the 2005 ledge. "Now she's paying fifty thousand a month."

Ed opened the 2008 book and whistled low.

"Wow! A hundred thousand," he said, pointing to the January line. "That would be 1.2 million a year."

"She's our murderer," Tori said, looking at the ledger for the current year. "No one else was paying anything like that. Obviously, she has wealth—a lot of it—and a life that could be destroyed by the revelation of a porn tape."

"That's a bit of a leap, don't you think," Levi said.

Ed looked over Tori's shoulder again. Suddenly, he smiled. He got it, too.

"What is it?" Ray asked.

"Tell him," Ed said.

"Three months ago, the payments ended," Tori said. "Pete continued to record the payments as due, but there's no income recorded.

"She called his bluff," Russ said.

"Yeah," Ray said. "She decided to stand up and see if he'd actually expose her."

"Would Peter Long be likely to actually do that?" Levi asked. "I mean he's making millions on this even without her, and if she decides to turn the tables on him and threatens to expose him—"

"It could bring his whole lucrative blackmail business down," Ed said, finishing his thought. "She's obviously extremely successful and wealthy. Maybe she's finally at a place where that old secret can no longer hurt her, so she tells Peter Long to take a hike."

"Or," Tori said, "she decides to better invest the money she's paying by killing him and anyone else who could expose her secret."

"That's what she did," Ray said. "She quit paying him to see what he'd do. She's smart. He probably threatened her, and she decided to take him out."

"I don't know," Levi said. "She had no way of knowing about that vault. She'd be worried about the evidence surviving. Killing him doesn't get rid of her secret. It just gets rid of her blackmailer."

"There were thousands and thousands of DVDs in that vault," Ed said. "Maybe this happened so many years ago she wasn't worried about anybody recognizing her today."

"It was more important to kill the blackmailer and anybody living who might be able to make the connection," Tori said.

"That's it," Ray said. "And maybe when Selena surfaced, she decided to take her out. Maybe it went back far enough she thought Selena would remember her. And Jay might've been around then, too. We never really got the whole story about the work he did for Peter Long in the beginning. But we're stuck. We know the line item but not the 'who,' and we're unlikely to ever know that."

"I'll bet Shelia knew," Levi said. "She was Peter Long's assistant for at least the last three or four years."

"The murderer decided to kill them all, starting with the easiest two first," Tori said. "And she did a pretty good job of making it look like Tony O'Malley was involved. The police would naturally assume that when an old man murdered Selena, it was one of his Horsemen and that a slime ball like Peter Long probably had mob connections."

"I'm sure he did at least on one level or another," Levi said. "He had clubs all over, including Chicago, and you don't do business there without rubbing elbows with the Chicago Outfit. Anyone looking too hard at Peter Long is going to come up with at least some connection to Tony O'Malley."

"That certainly seems to be the focus of the FBI investigation," Ray remarked. "Maybe, just maybe, Tony did kill Peter Long." Ray looked at Ed. "You remember his associate—the one we saw at the lake after the boat exploded?"

"Yeah, Jake Pierce. We wrote his plate number down," Ed said.

"He'd been an associate of Tony O'Malley's for years," Ray said, "and guess who vanished this morning?"

"Jake Pierce?" Tori asked.

Ray nodded. "The FBI isn't sure if he's dead or just on a paid vacation somewhere without an extradition treaty. But he is gone. I got a call this afternoon."

"He's dead," Levi said.

"Of course, he is," Ed said.

"So now what?" Russ Martin asked, peering at each of them in turn through his thick lenses. "We've gone so far over the line, all of us, we could be charged with crimes with mandatory sentences—most of them federal at this point."

There was a long silence.

"I have to resign," Ray said. "I can't be a cop since I no longer have a clear conscience. I'm now just as dirty as the last two chiefs. I'll wait an appropriate period of time after the FBI finishes the investigation, but I'm done. We're never going to solve this. Ben is clean. He'll make a good chief."

"So we bury this and hope nobody digs it up?" Levi asked.

"The only person in Twin Rivers who ever solves old cold cases is you," Ed said.

"I'm not looking into this one."

"So we're done here," Ed said. "This isn't a local matter. We won't be solving it."

"And we hope the FBI doesn't discover our involvement," Tori said.

"Right," Russ said.

"But if they do track it back to us," Levi said, "we don't lie. Our motives were clean. It was our actions that were criminal. They knock on our door, we tell the truth. Right? Most of the criminal actions were committed by Tori and me. We're the ones that got caught in Tony's web. But even then, we were in a tough spot and had little choice in the matter."

"We might be able to justify our actions," Ray said, "but the only way we do that is to bring Tony O'Malley into it. We'd become witnesses against Tony, and we all know the outcome there. So don't kid yourselves. It's either prison or Tony's wrath for all of us."

"So we walk away now," Ed said. "We don't say a word, and we leave it alone. If it should happen the FBI finds out what we've done, we do the right thing. We tell the truth, the whole truth, and nothing but the truth. Do we all agree?"

They all looked at each other and nodded in turn.

Chapter 52

Levi was sitting in the archive room of the Twin Rivers Library, reading digitized copies of the *Twin Rivers Gazette* from the 1920s. For the last few months, he'd been thinking about an idea for a novel—a 1920s murder mystery based on a fictionalized version of the Garvey family history in Twin Rivers. A historical fiction novel would be very different from what he'd written in the past. He was thinking about empire building in the age of powerful industrialists like his great-great grandfather, who'd made his fortune during that period.

Several weeks had passed since they'd managed to burn down Peter Long's house on Olton Lake. Everyday he'd waited for the FBI to materialize on his doorstep. An agent had shown up ten days ago to talk to Levi about Shelia. It seemed odd to them that a woman from Twin Rivers, using an assumed name, was staying in an East Coast home which belonged to another person from Twin Rivers. First, Levi had told the agent the truth. His Uncle Ed had known Shelia since she was a little girl. He'd been good friends with her father. Then, he'd told a slightly altered version of the truth. He said that when he'd been told that Shelia was in danger, he'd simply offered her sanctuary. Apparently, that story had checked out with the FBI. He hadn't heard from them again, but the lie had left him feeling ill at ease. He had a nagging feeling that he wasn't done with that agency yet.

He knew the FBI hadn't gotten very far with the case. The young agent had indicated that they hadn't been able to connect Tony O'Malley to the murders of Selena, Peter, Jay, and Shelia—or with the marijuana operation that Officer Ben Walker had stumbled upon. Now their investigation was headed in a totally different direction.

Oddly enough, they'd found a motive for Shelia's murder in Savannah—thanks to an anonymous call. They'd found a ledger book, believed stolen from Peter Long, among Shelia's possessions in her house on Olton Lake—the one she'd inherited from her father. The ledger showed what they believed was a long history of blackmail. The FBI now speculated that Peter Long had been murdered by one of the people he was blackmailing. Unfortunately, the ledger didn't list names. Therefore, the FBI was trying to match payments to bank withdrawals from a number of persons of interest.

Levi had been able to convincingly act surprised while hoping they'd wiped away all of Tori and Russ's fingerprints from the one ledger they'd decided to slip into the hands of the FBI.

Now, they'd all begun to relax a little. Ray was even thinking that since they'd managed to pass on at least some of the evidence they had to the FBI, maybe he could continue as the chief in Twin Rivers with a clear conscience. They'd acted criminally but with the best possible intentions. And since it was looking as if Tony O'Malley wasn't involved, Levi and Tori felt a little better at being caught in his trap and serving as his informants—but they all still had the blood of Jake Pierce on their consciences.

Even so, life had returned to normal. Coffee and pie at Harv's. Pool in Ray's basement. Meetings at the Masonic Lodge.

Levi smiled as he ran across a ninety-year-old ad in the paper for the Comet Theatre. A show was scheduled for a Friday and a Saturday night. Admission was two bits—fifty cents—which was a lot of money back during the Great Depression. Levi knew, for instance, that at that time, the Masonic Lodge dues in Twin Rivers for the entire year were $1.25 compared to $50 now. But the Depression hadn't hit Twin Rivers as hard as it had hit a lot of other places because so many of the residents were employed by the Garveys' companies—the railroad, the coal mine, the brickyard, the ice company, the electric company, and the budding phone service.

Levi read through the names of the performers, but only one of them rang a bell—a song-and-dance man named William Frawley, who wasn't even a headliner. He was listed among a number of forgotten names. It would be decades yet before William would meet Desi and Lucy. And several years before a song he first sang on stage would be made famous by another singer. The song was "My Mammy," and the performer who made it famous was another vaudeville performer, Al Jolson.

Levi leaned back and smiled—amazed at the treasures which could be found within the pages of a tiny newspaper few had ever heard of in the dusty, musty archives of a small town library.

When Mrs. B walked into the room, Levi quickly waved her over.

"Check this out, Mrs. B.," he said as the frail old woman gazed over his shoulder at the screen. "Fred Mertz performed at the Comet. And check out the headline. It was the same week they dedicated the war memorial statue. Look who Captain William Garvey got to come speak at that event!"

Mrs. B. grinned broadly. "I sure didn't know he ever visited Twin Rivers."

There was a photo of the shiny new bronze memorial. Captain William Garvey was in full Union uniform, standing next to the United States Speaker of the House of Representatives—Joseph "Uncle Joe" Cannon—another Illinoisan and Freemason.

"That's Abe Garvey," Mrs. B. said, pointing to a younger man standing off to the side of the picture. "That memorial was dedicated to the veterans of World War I. Abe and his buddies from that conflict raised the money to build it."

"Looks like his father, William, was taking center stage that day, however. And look," Levi said, pointing. "Abe is wearing my Webley on his hip."

"I think it was his," Mrs. B. said with a smile. "I'm guessing he'd be pleased to know a Garvey still owns it, but I'm not sure how he'd feel about what your wife did to that statue several times. He wouldn't likely find the 'Bikini Bandit' as humorous as we do today."

"Probably not," Levi admitted. "Did you want something?"

"There's a man at the librarians' desk asking for you," she said.

"Really?" Levi said, his face tight.

"He's waiting."

"Any idea who he is?"

She shook her head. "I have a bad feeling though because he wouldn't tell me what he wants."

Levi stood up and headed towards the door. The man standing at the counter was wearing a dark suit and a long black topcoat.

"Rosco is in the truck. Just so you know," Levi said to Mrs. B.

"Okay," she said, understanding that he might be leaving with the man.

Levi left the archive room and walked down the three steps to the library floor. The man wasn't the same agent Levi had talked to before. He was young with dark hair and dark brown eyes. When he saw Levi, he walked towards him.

"Mr. Garvey?" he said.

"I'm Levi Garvey."

"I'm sorry to have to do this," he said, glancing at the library patrons and staff. "Is there somewhere we could talk in private?"

Levi leaned towards him and whispered, "If you're here to arrest me, we can just walk out together. I have no intention of resisting."

A grin slowly crossed the man's face. "Arrest you? Are you making a joke?"

"Who are you?"

"I'm Pastor Keller from the Church of Christ in Olton."

Levi snickered. "I thought you were the FBI."

"Why would the FBI want to arrest you?" he asked.

"I don't seem dangerous to you?"

Pastor Kelly grinned at him broadly. "You are making a joke, aren't you?"

"Of course," Levi said. "Let's go out into the foyer."

Levi and the pastor walked down the marble steps into the round foyer of the Twin Rivers Library. They stood at the base of the statue—a duplicate of the one on the top of the war memorial.

"So what can I do for you?" Levi asked.

"I'm the assistant pastor of your Aunt Margaret's church and her very good friend. I'm sorry to say she has taken ill—very ill. She's not long away from her journey home."

Levi was stunned at the news. Even though she was old, she'd seemed to be in great shape when he'd visited her recently.

"She's dying?"

"I'm afraid so," the pastor said. "She has pneumonia. Dr. Jackson says it's a matter of time due to her advanced age. Her son is on his way here."

"Thanks for coming to tell me that. Is she at St. Anne's?"

"Yes," he said. "She wanted me to give you something. They told me at that little diner on Main Street that you'd be here."

Levi sighed, knowing that the pastor was about to hand him a long flat key.

"It's in my car," he said as he walked towards the door.

Somewhat annoyed, Levi followed him out into the parking lot, wondering why the pastor hadn't just brought the key into the library.

"This was of great concern to her. She wanted me to make sure I took care of it myself."

He pushed the button to unlock the door. As soon as the locks clunked, the little white poodle inside began to bark furiously.

"Oh, no," Levi said, putting his hands up and taking a step back.

Pastor Keller opened the car door and scooped up the little dog.

"This is Sandy. She's a sweet little girl. I've been keeping her the last couple of days, but Margaret thinks she needs a more permanent home with family."

He held out the dog, which looked at Levi and growled—that is, she growled as much as a small ball of white fluff can growl.

"If Margaret recovers, she'll take her back. She wants to make that clear. She still believes she will recover."

Levi took the little dog. Then holding her out in front of him, he glared at her snarling muzzle and tiny sharp teeth.

The pastor quickly climbed into his car. "She's a sweet little dog. It just takes a while for her to warm up to new people."

"Obviously," Levi said as the pastor started his car.

"Margaret is in room 306. She'd like to see you."

"I'll be over a little later," Levi said as the pastor backed out.

"You're kind of wishing I was the FBI, aren't you?" he said with a grin.

Levi laughed. Then tucking the wiggling, snarling little fur ball under his arm, he waved as the car rolled out of the parking lot.

Looking down at the angry little dog, whose teeth were trying to find a purchase on his arm, he said, "You bite me, you little bitch, and I'll feed you to Rosco. Got it?"

Levi walked over to Old Blue. When the little dog saw Rosco, she literally climbed into Levi's open jacket. Then with terrified brown eyes, she peered out at the giant German shepherd on the other side of the window. Rosco began barking at her.

"Hush, Rosco," Levi said firmly as he opened the door.

Rosco jumped out. He began sniffing all around Levi and as far up his jacket as he could without jumping up on him. The little dog was trying to climb up inside Levi's jacket onto his shoulders.

"You're riding in the back," Levi said to Rosco as he snapped the tailgate down.

After Rosco leaped in, Levi closed the tailgate behind him. Then he walked to the driver's door, opened it, fished the little poodle out of his jacket, and tossed her onto the seat. Rosco was peering in the back window at her.

"You starting to get it?" Levi said with a chuckle as he pulled the door shut and started the truck.

Sandy jumped into his lap and began to lick his face. Rosco, who didn't like that at all, barked loudly outside the window.

"That's what I thought," Levi said, looking down at the frantic little dog as he backed out of the parking space. "Starting to figure out I'm the only thing between you and being a snack, aren't you? To a big dog, you look a lot like a little rabbit, and Rosco hates little rabbits."

The small dog barked up at him and then put her paws up on the window sill on the driver's side.

"You know, Sandy, when Rosco does this, I make him go over to his window. But he weighs over a hundred pounds. What do you weigh? Maybe three?"

Levi rolled his window down, and the little dog stuck her head out.

"I think this could work out."

Chapter 53

Tori pulled up in front of the house. Adam was screaming in the backseat. Actually, he'd been screaming since they'd left the grocery store in Calloway. Eight miles of screaming. Her nerves were shot. It'd started over a box of animal crackers in the checkout lane. She'd said no, something Garvey men, young and old, weren't used to hearing. And young or old, they didn't like the word. She pulled Adam out of his car seat, walked up the front steps, kicked the door open, and set him down on the floor in the foyer.

Tori returned to the car for the groceries, popped the trunk with her remote, and grabbed as many of the plastic bags as she could. Both arms loaded down, she walked up the porch steps and kicked the door open again. Adam had finally quit screaming. He was laughing at something, instead. She struggled up the hallway with the first load, set the bags on the kitchen island, and turned around for the second load. On the way through the foyer, she glanced down at a now giggling Adam, who was playing with one of his stuffed toys. Back at the car, she pulled out the rest of the groceries. Carrying the two gallons of milk with one hand, handles of the plastic jugs together, and the case of beer under her arm, she returned to the house. Adam was still laughing and giggling with his toy. After she dumped the second load in the kitchen, she leaned against the counter, trying to catch her breath. There was still a case of bottled water in the car. Even though she'd have to get it before it froze, she had time for coffee now. She pulled a mug down from the cabinet, poured a cup left over from that morning, and popped it into the microwave.

In the foyer, Adam was still laughing. At fourteen months, he wasn't talking much yet. He was trying but had yet to say one word that sounded anything like English. But he laughed like his Uncle Ed and his father—kind of a baby guffaw. Suddenly, Adam stopped laughing.

"Hey, hey, hey, hey, hey!" he said, which was as close as he'd gotten to English. He used that word when he was trying to get someone's attention.

Who is he talking to, Tori wondered. Then she heard something strange—something skittering across the wood floors, something like a mouse late at night but bigger, something like a raccoon or a rat!

Suddenly, she panicked. What had Adam been playing with? She bolted across kitchen and into the hall. Running around the foyer was a little white poodle, wearing a hot pink collar. Her nails clacked on the wood floor.

"Hey, hey, hey, hey," Adam chimed as he crawled after the little dog which ran up to Tori and barked.

"Where did you come from?" Tori said, picking her up.

The little dog, obviously still a puppy, was a squirming mass. She licked Tori's face aggressively.

"Well, aren't you a sweetie," Tori said as she stroked her neck.

Hanging from her collar was a little heart-shaped metal I.D. tag. Tori read the name stamped into the metal—Margaret Clayburn. Suddenly, Tori understood.

"You're Aunt Maggie's little dog, aren't you," Tori said. "Clayburn must be her married name."

Tori hadn't known Aunt Maggie's last name. It'd never come up in their conversations. She'd met her only a few times when she was restoring the theatre in Olton. She remembered Maggie had once mentioned a son and a daughter who'd passed away. Now Tori wondered about something else. She walked to the table where the box Maggie had given Levi lay. It was trivial, but it bothered her that she didn't know the answer. Paying particular attention to the backs where many of them were labeled, she started looking at the photos in Lucille's box. Adam crawled into the kitchen and pulled himself up on her leg—he wasn't far from walking. While the ice cream from the grocery store melted on the kitchen counter, she looked through all the pictures in the box without finding the answer she was looking for.

"That's really odd," she muttered. "I'll just ask Levi."

She pulled her phone out of her back pocket and sent the question to him as a text. As she waited for the reply, she knelt down by Adam and the little dog, who looked up at Tori with big nervous brown eyes.

"Be nice to the little doggie. Pet her nice, like this," she said, running her hands down the length of the little dog's back.

Adam did the same.

Chapter 54

Levi stepped off the elevator onto the third floor of St. Anne's Hospital and walked to the nurses' station.

"Hi, Levi," Juli said, looking up at him.

"My Aunt Maggie is here in room 306," he said. "Is it okay if I go see her?"

"Certainly," Juli said. "I'm not sure if she's awake, but she has a couple of visitors now, her son and her brother."

"Brother? I didn't know she still had a brother living. Thank you, Juli."

Levi walked up the hall, paused at the door, and glanced in. Aunt Maggie was lying in the bed with one man on either side. The light above her bed was on low. Since he didn't want to butt in, Levi started to turn away, but one of the men saw him in the doorway.

"Come on in, Levi," he said. "She's sleeping."

Though he couldn't see the man clearly, the voice seemed familiar. Levi stepped into the room. As his eyes adjusted from the comparative brightness of the fluorescent lights in the hall to the dimness of the room, he focused on the peaceful face of his great-aunt. Her eyes fluttered open, and she smiled at him.

"You have Sandy?" she asked.

Levi nodded. "We'll take good care of her until you're well enough to take her back."

She nodded and drifted off to sleep again.

"I appreciate you taking care of that little dog," the man holding her hand said. "Mom obviously trusts you. Of course, you are family."

"I don't remember your name," Levi said to the back of his head. "I kind of remember you from when I was a kid. I'm that little brat that messed with the antenna when you were babysitting me years ago."

"I remember," he said. "You're lucky Aunt Lucille and Mom got back when they did."

Levi chuckled. "Probably saved me an ass whooping."

"Without a doubt," the man said, turning towards him.

Levi's eyes widened as he took a step back, stumbling over a chair beside the door and falling into the wall. That's when the older man turned to look at him.

Levi stared. This has got to be a dream, he thought as he slowly slid down the wall until he was sitting on the floor. A nightmare!

His phone chimed with an incoming text message. As he sat on the floor, looking up at the two men in the hospital room, he pulled his phone out of his pocket with a trembling hand. It was Tori—asking the question he'd just learned the answer to himself.

* * *

Tori looked at her phone expectantly. Unless he was driving, Levi usually texted back right away. It was a simple question. Shrugging, she started to look through more of the pictures. Maybe she could get an answer to her question without him. Not like it was a huge deal anyway—just a question that had never occurred to her before.

* * *

"Is it soaking in yet?" the older man said.

"It's starting to," Levi sputtered as he climbed up from the floor. "But I sure didn't see that one coming."

"You should have," the younger man said.

"You're Aunt Maggie's son?"

"Yes," he said. "There are obvious reasons you weren't told."

"And you?" Levi said, looking at the older man.

"I'm Maggie's brother," he said. "Of course, I've always called my sister Peg. Maybe you remember me, too. I used to read you Sherlock Holmes stories when you were just a little thing. I thought you'd recognize me when we met again, but you didn't. I seemed familiar to you though, didn't I?"

That was true. The old man had seemed familiar the first time they'd met. Looking down at his phone, he typed in the answer to Tori's question and punched send.

* * *

When her phone chimed, Tori read the message. The phone slipped out of her hand and clattered across the kitchen floor.

Such a simple question—"What was your Grandma Lucille's maiden name?" Such an unbelievable answer—not only unbelievable but also impossible.

Tori laughed nervously. Levi had played a joke on her. She rose shakily. Adam was again making happy noises at Sandy in the foyer. Methodically, she began to put away the groceries—the soft ice cream into the freezer, eggs and cheese into the refrigerator, mac and cheese into the cupboard.

Then she began wondering if Levi would joke about such a thing. He was known for his sometimes inappropriate humor, but there were some things even he wouldn't joke about. But his answer was impossible, she told herself.

Or was it? She remembered how calm Levi was all those times he'd taken on Doug Malone, how calm Uncle Ed was when he put a bullet in Doug's head, how calm Levi was when he killed Alan Haig with the Webley in the den, how calm he and Uncle Ed had been after all four of their attackers had been killed that terrible afternoon two years ago. Tori knew that the emotional detachment and calm that Levi and Ed possessed in the face of danger was something which bothered even Chief Billings. One evening at the Beer Chaser after they'd had one too many beers, he'd looked at her and said, "You know, Tori, there's a certain hidden darkness in Ed Garvey. And Levi has it, too. Sometimes those two scare me."

That calmness scared her, too, but she'd been able to overlook it because it'd surfaced rarely, and each time it had, it'd saved their lives. Even so, she'd lost sleep over Ray's remark. There was a darkness that ran in the family along with blue eyes and blonde hair.

Tori picked up the phone from the floor. It wasn't a joke. Levi would never joke about something like that. She looked at his answer again. "O'Malley."

That single word had shattered her world.

Walking into the foyer, she looked down at Adam. Oh, God, she'd done something that couldn't be undone. She'd married the last of the Garveys—Levi. They'd created a child, a child with the Garvey-O'Malley DNA. Adam pulled himself up on her leg again. The eyes looking up chilled her. Her son's eyes were a lighter blue than his father's, but they were the same steel-blue eyes of Tony "The Shotgun" O'Malley.

"Uncle Tony," Tori whispered as her heart hammered in her chest.

* * *

Levi had recovered quickly. He regarded the two men in turn. Then he focused on Tony O'Malley.

"You're a terrible uncle," Levi said. "Forty-six years and not one birthday card?"

Tony grinned at him. "I'm your great-uncle, and there's a reason this family connection was kept from you—several good reasons. First of all, Lucy and Peg didn't want you following me and your cousin into the business. The second reason was that we cut all family ties years ago to protect Carl when he was growing up. As I told you, most of my family is dead because of the family business. If my enemies had learned he was my nephew, he'd have never made it to his thirtieth birthday. Besides that, your family wouldn't have been safe either. There's no reason to change that now. The fact that you know the truth changes nothing. We won't be spending holidays together."

"Ed knows?" Levi asked.

Tony nodded. "Of course he knows. He kept it from you for the same reasons."

Margaret opened her eyes. "Tony thought you'd figured it out when you saw the picture behind his desk—the one of all of us as little kids back in the 1920s."

Levi shook his head. "I did see it. I even commented on it, but I didn't make a connection."

"I gave you too much credit," Tony said.

Levi looked at Carl. "So when Uncle Ed beat you up, he knew you were cousins."

Carl grinned. "You never wondered how Ed Garvey lived all those years with a multi-million dollar coin that belonged to Tony and the Chicago Outfit never went after him?"

"I did wonder," Levi admitted. "I just figured you were afraid of him."

Tony laughed, but Carl's jaw got tight.

"And you do know where William Garvey's journal is," Levi said, looking at Tony. "You lied to me."

"I didn't lie to you. I didn't know at the time, but I knew if Peg had the ring, she probably had the journal, too," Tony admitted. "I figured it out about the same time you did, and I gave you a hell of a hint where to look for it, didn't I."

Levi nodded.

"There's another little secret I've been keeping from you," Margaret said.

"I'm two months older than I thought."

She smiled weakly. "That's right. But let me tell you why."

"I think Tori and I have already figured that out," Levi said. "Obviously, she was already pregnant when she married my dad."

"Let me tell you the rest of it," Margaret said, closing her eyes.

"You should rest, Mom," Carl said, patting her hand.

"I need to tell this story," Margaret said. "I should've told it to you the day you came to see me, Levi, before I fell ill. You need to hear it."

Levi grabbed the chair by the door, the one he'd fallen over earlier, and sat down at the foot of her bed beside Carl.

"I'm listening," Levi said.

Chapter 55

Levi drove up the driveway and parked next to Ed's tow truck, which he wasn't surprised to see. Ed had a sixth sense when it came to things like that—he always seemed to be right there when he was needed. He wondered if Tori was packing her bags. He swallowed hard, trying to make the lump in his throat go away.

"Come on, Rosco," Levi said as he pushed the door open.

Rosco leaped out over his lap, and Levi followed him up the porch steps. He paused for a long moment before pushing the door open.

What he heard surprised him. Ed and Tori were laughing in the kitchen. Levi walked up the hallway to the doorway. They were sitting in the kitchen nook, looking at the old photos from the box Levi had gotten from Aunt Maggie. Adam was in his high chair at the end of the table, his face and the tray in front of him covered in something green and slimy. At its best, baby food nauseated Levi. This scene was positively disgusting.

The laughter stopped when Tori and Ed noticed him.

"Are you okay?" Tori asked.

Levi nodded. He walked to the refrigerator, pulled out a beer, and drained most of it.

"It's a lot to take in," Ed said.

Levi nodded and finished the can. Then he reached for another one.

"To be honest, I thought you'd be packing your bags," Levi said, glancing at Tori.

"That was my first reaction," Tori admitted. "So you found out just about the same time I asked the question?"

Levi took off his hat and tossed it on the counter. "Believe it or not, yes. Juli said Aunt Margaret's son and brother were in the room. Imagine my surprise when I walked in and discovered Tony and Carl. I about had a stroke."

"How is it you never knew your grandma's maiden name?" Tori asked, frowning. "For heaven's sake, Levi, she raised you."

"That's the question I asked myself all the way back from the hospital," Levi said. "I guess boys just aren't that curious. Except for Aunt Maggie, we didn't spend much time with her family. I guess it never occurred to me to ask."

"And Mother was very good at steering conversations away from the subject of her family," Ed said. "Not just from you but with everyone. Do you think there's anyone in Twin Rivers who knows that Lucille Garvey was Tony O'Malley's sister? Your Aunt Margaret did the same thing. But to give you at least a little credit, you did ask her one time about her maiden name. You were working on a family tree project in third or fourth grade."

"Oh, yeah," Levi said. "I do remember that, but I can't remember what she told me."

"She told you that she'd been a Garvey for so long that she wasn't even sure if she remembered," Ed said with a chuckle.

"Then she pulled out a box of Garvey pictures and started telling me about her husband, my grandfather William Jr., and his dad, Abe, and his father, Captain William Garvey. I did my whole project on the Garvey side of the family," Levi said.

"Uncle Tony used to come down and visit every so often up until the early 70s," Ed said. "He stopped doing that when it got too dangerous—they were very concerned about Carl and the Garvey family. That's when Tony took over the Chicago Outfit, and that change in leadership sparked a bloody gang war that raged until the early 80s. A lot of people died during those years, including most of the O'Malley family."

"That's sad," Tori said. "So they didn't see Tony for years after that?"

"They did talk on the phone," Ed said.

"Wait a minute," Levi said, glancing at Ed. "The annual shopping trip."

Ed smiled. "Every year, the week after Thanksgiving, Mom and Aunt Maggie went on their annual Christmas shopping trip to Chicago. They took the train up and spent a whole week there. It would be just me and Levi here at home."

"I called it hotdog week," Levi said with a smile. "That's all we ate— hotdogs and mac and cheese."

"That's when the O'Malleys got together for the holidays," Ed said. "Maggie and Mom didn't like what Tony did, but they remained a close family."

"So this changes nothing," Tori said, but it was more a question than a statement.

"Are you asking if we're moving to Chicago so I can take over part of the family business?"

"Something like that," Tori said.

"Nothing changes," Levi said. "But there's another little interesting part of the story."

"What's that?" Tori asked.

"Did you tell Uncle Ed we found out I'm two months older than I thought I was?"

"No, I didn't," Tori said.

"That's actually a much better story than learning my great-uncle is one of the most vicious mobsters in American history," Levi said.

"What it is?" Tori said.

"I'm not a very good story teller," Levi said, pulling out one of the barstools at the counter and glancing over at Ed. "Why don't you tell her the story, Dad."

Ed's face went slack.

"Dad!" Tori laughed.

Ed said nothing as he looked back and forth between Levi and Tori several times. He wiped a shaking hand across his face, which had lost all its color.

"Dad?" Tori said as the smile faded from her face. "Dad? Levi's dad?"

Ed nodded almost imperceptibly.

"Oh, my God, Levi," she said, her face knit with worry.

"I'm fine," Levi said. "I guess I kind of always knew that, too. But I sure can sympathize now with Luke Skywalker. Actually, he had it easy."

A smile slowly crossed Ed's face. "So you're saying I'm Darth Vader?"

"No," Levi said. "Darth Vader is my Uncle Tony. You're a lesser minion of the Dark Lord but just as dangerous."

"Let's have it," Tori said sharply. "No more secrets in this house. Let's have the whole damn thing, right now."

She slapped her hand down hard on the table top. Ed jumped.

* * *

Ed took a sip of his beer. Tori and Levi were sitting in the booth across from him. Tori was stroking the head of the little white dog in her lap. Rosco was at Levi's feet, growling low at the fluffy intruder. Adam was making a hellish mess—a green nightmare on himself and the tray in front of him—and laughing as he coated his hands in goo.

"It was 1966," Ed said. "I'd taken a hunk of shrapnel in my back and another big chunk in the back of my leg. I nearly died. By the way, you should take good care of your kidneys, Levi, because I don't have a spare, thanks to that injury. I spent weeks in the hospital stateside, but, believe it or not, I fought against a medical discharge. Instead, because I was such a valued commodity to the Marine Corps, I was given six weeks leave to rest and recover, so I came home. That was in May of 1966. I got that leave because, on top of needing the time to recuperate from my injuries, I'd planned on getting married."

"To April," Levi said.

Ed nodded. "I'd bought that little house long before then. April had been getting it ready to move into. She'd painted and decorated. When I got home, I put the linoleum down on the floor. Her decorating and what I did are about the last improvements my little house has seen. But something was wrong. I'd changed. I'd already seen too much over there, and I knew I was going back after my R&R ended. I was angry all the time. I drank too much. It wasn't long before April decided I wasn't the same man she'd wanted to marry."

"So she left," Tori said.

"Not really," Ed said. "She was assessing the situation, but then I screwed up. I did something she couldn't get over."

"You had a little fling, didn't you?" Levi said.

"I had a few little flings and one big one," Ed admitted. "I was a young man back then and far more handsome than you ever were."

"That's unlikely," Levi said.

"Anyway, the news got around," Ed said. "Small town and all. It was a different world then and a lot less forgiving of that kind of behavior. It didn't take long for April to hear about what I'd been doing up at the Beer Chaser. I went in there the very first time I was home on leave. About a week before I left, I met another woman at the Beer Chaser. Joyce warned me about her. Said she was bad news—a shameless gold digger. But she was wild, and she was beautiful, and it wasn't long before I was buying her drinks."

"Was her name Marie?" Levi asked. That was his mother's name.

Ed nodded. "We spent that entire last week together—day and night. Mostly drinking and—"

"I don't need those details," Levi said.

"Finally, I sobered up the last day I was home and saw things a little more clearly," Ed said. "I saw her for exactly what Joyce had said she was—a woman no doubt more interested in my last name than in me. At some point, I guess I'd promised her we were going to go to the courthouse and get married before I left. That's what she said anyway. I don't remember, but it's probably true. That had been her goal all along. She wanted to be a Garvey and attached to the Garvey money. To say she left angry when I didn't marry her is an understatement. She busted out all the windows in my car—well, your grandmother's car."

"Did Grandma know you'd had this little fling with Marie?"

Ed shook his head. "First time I showed up here drunk while I was on leave, Mom told me that if I was going to behave like that, I could do it in my own house. She'd also been hearing rumors about the whoring around and a couple of fights, too. I wrecked my truck that last week, which is why I was driving her old car. And I'd managed to spend at least two or three nights of my leave as a guest of the Twin Rivers Police Department—a trend I continued for a long time after I got out of the Marine Corps and came home for good. But I spent my last day sober at home with Mom. We parted on good terms. Then I went back to the jungle, took up as a sniper, and resumed collecting the brass shell casings of my victims."

Ed shook his empty beer can. "I could use another beer."

Levi got up and got one for each of them.

"Well?" Tori said.

"So the next April I get a letter from Mom," Ed said. "It took the mail a while to catch up with us in Vietnam. She'd written it in March. It said my little brother Larry had managed to find a woman who wasn't hideous to look at—those were her words. They'd gotten married just a few weeks after they met. Between the lines, it was pretty obvious Mom didn't like her at all, but the woman did have one thing going for her. She became pregnant very shortly after the wedding. Mom was thrilled at the idea of having a grandchild. She had a little boy, two months premature in March. An eight pounds and something preemie."

Levi chuckled.

"It was pretty clear to Mom that Larry had done a little work on that girl prior to the nuptials. Like I said, it was a different world back then. By the time I got home from Vietnam, little Levi's birthday was in May, not March. I missed that detail at first. I'd gotten the letter, but I hadn't really put it together yet. Levi was about three years old by the time I met him. My brother Larry was pretty proud of him, but he wasn't really liking the whole responsibility thing. That was hardly surprising since he never did like work of any kind. What was surprising was Levi's mother, Marie."

"I take it you'd met before," Levi said.

"Many times," Ed said with a grin. "Of course, you said you didn't need those details."

"No, I'm good," Levi said.

"Like I said, I didn't put it together at first," Ed said. "I was back to my full time job—drinking at the Beer Chaser, getting into fights, wrecking cars, and beginning the only successful relationship I've ever had in my life—with Joyce. That was also about the time I took over the towing business from my Uncle Fred. He was your grandpa's brother. I'd worked for him all through grade school and high school."

"I always wondered how you got started in that," Levi said.

"Uncle Fred was a nice man, devotedly Christian, but he drank almost as much as I did," Ed said, smiling at the memory. "But even dead drunk, he'd knock your teeth loose if you used the Lord's name in vain. Your grandmother didn't think much of Uncle Fred's drinking, but when he got sick, she moved him right into this house, and this is where he stayed until he died.

"It wasn't long after he died that I had a bad accident with that tow truck. I was trying to pull a truck out of a deep ditch with a cable, but that truck wasn't coming up. I was hung over, so instead of trying it from another angle, I just kept up with the winch. That steel cable snapped suddenly and shot back like a rubber band. Broke three of my ribs and my arm in two places."

Tori whistled low.

"I was in the hospital for three weeks," Ed said. "They don't let you drink there. It was nice being sober again. It had been a long time since I hadn't ended my day falling into bed after midnight, totally hammered. I was sitting in my hospital room one afternoon, watching reruns of *Gilligan's Island* on television, when suddenly it hit me. I had all the facts. I just hadn't put them together. You weren't born in May. You were born in March. The arithmetic was easy."

"March minus nine months is June," Tori said.

"Larry didn't even know Marie in June," Ed said, "but I did."

"Did you ask my mother?" Levi asked.

Ed nodded. "I cornered her here one day when Mom and Larry were gone. She denied it at first, sticking with the story you were born in May and were Larry's son. When I went home, I dug out those old letters. My memory was correct. I drove right back over here and showed Marie the letter Mom had written me in March. She finally admitted it—even cried a little and begged me not to tell Larry."

"And Grandma knew, too?" Levi asked.

Ed shook his head. "She didn't know at first, but she found out later—I don't know how. Probably the grapevine. Somebody probably told her I'd been spending time with Marie before she'd met Larry. Your grandmother was a smart lady, and like I said, the math was pretty easy to figure out."

"So my dad—I mean Uncle Larry—never did the math at all?"

"Let's just speak plainly here," Ed said. "My brother, Larry, isn't very smart, and he was never good at anything except sitting in front of a television set. If it weren't for Larry, none of the ugly girls at Twin Rivers High School would have ever been out on a date. Then Marie comes along, and she's gorgeous, and he falls head over heels for her. She was probably the first woman he'd ever dated he could get his arms all the way around."

"Ed!" Tori said with a frown as a smile played at the corners of her mouth.

"Sorry," Ed said with a grin, "but it's true. When he was a senior, Larry brought his prom date by here to meet Mom and Dad. My dad was a very funny man. After Larry left, he looked over at Mom and said, 'Well, she looks like two tons of fun.'"

Levi chuckled, and Tori shot him a glare.

"Marie was smart," Ed said. "She used him, and he's always been oblivious to it. They likely fooled around before they were married, and I'm sure he knew she was pregnant when they got married. When she changed the birthday, he probably assumed it was because he'd knocked her up before the wedding. And then there's the May birthday they gave Levi after he was born in March."

"What about my birthday?" Levi asked.

"They picked May 26th," Ed said. "Surely you know Larry's favorite movie actor."

Levi sighed. "John Wayne."

"You think it's a coincidence that you and the Duke share a birthday?" Ed asked.

"Mom probably let him pick the date," Levi said. "He'd never question it if he picked it himself."

"And I'll bet he never questioned the fact you were born premature either," Ed said.

"In March, at eight pounds, four ounces," Tori said, shaking her head.

"So what happened to my birth certificate?" Levi asked.

Ed laughed. "Your grandmother's best friend since grade school, Patricia England, took care of that. She worked at the courthouse. Oddly enough, when you needed a copy to apply to the University of Illinois, we all learned it was missing from the courthouse records. You got a new one made, based on a notarized letter from the attending physician, Dr. Gillespie. Probably not the first time he'd fudged a date slightly to protect the virtue of a young woman."

"I remember that," Levi said.

"So that's it?" Tori said finally.

"The whole sordid story," Ed said.

"Who else knows?" Levi asked.

"Well, your Aunt Margaret knows. Mom told her once she found out. Joyce knows, of course. April Jenkins had always suspected it. Sometimes she made remarks about how much you looked like me and acted like me. Then, when you came home finally, she flat out asked me for the first time. It was the night you called the diner from the airport in Atlanta—just before the whole Doug Malone thing blew up."

"And what did you tell her?"

"The truth," Ed said flatly. "Harv was standing there when she asked. He knows, too."

"So now what?" Levi said.

"No more secrets," Tori said.

"What about my mom and dad?" Levi paused, then corrected himself. "I mean, what about my mom and Uncle Larry."

"I tend to agree with Tori," Ed said. "It's time for the secrets to stop. I'll call Larry tomorrow. He wouldn't piss on me if I was on fire, so it's not like I'm wrecking our relationship."

"That's going to blow up his world," Levi said.

"Marie should have told him forty-six years ago," Ed said. "It's not as if he's ever lifted a finger to be a father. Why do you think your grandmother kept paying for all those trips and excursions of theirs?"

Levi shrugged.

"I know," Tori said. "She wanted to raise you right, and she wanted your father involved in your upbringing."

Ed nodded and looked at Levi. "I did the best I could. It just took me a long time to pull myself together."

Levi looked at him for a long moment. "You didn't do too bad."

"Darth Vader cut Luke's hand off before he told him he was his father," Ed remarked.

Levi grinned. "Well, there's that!"

Tori looked over at Levi and smiled. "You remember what you told me out at Kingery Pond that night after we graduated from high school?"

Levi shook his head. There were parts of that evening he remembered perfectly. He'd spent more than twenty years going over it again and again, but he didn't know what she was talking about.

"Your mom and dad didn't come home for your graduation," Tori said. "It hurt your feelings."

"Not the first time," Levi admitted.

"You said, 'Why couldn't Uncle Ed have been my father?'"

"We were drinking his beer at the time, I'm sure," Levi said.

Ed chuckled. "Why do you think I kept only a six pack in that fridge in the carriage house?"

"Because you knew we were stealing it?" Tori said.

"Have you ever known me to lose track of a single cold beer?"

"Nope," Levi said.

Levi's eyes clouded as he cleared his throat. How many times had he wished that Ed was his father. Ed was always there when Levi needed him. Ed had used that odd sixth sense he seemed to possess. His appearance at the house today had likely kept Tori from leaving. Even though Levi didn't remember ever saying it to Tori, he'd always wished his father was Ed.

Sensing Levi's thoughts, Ed said with a chuckle, "Your wish is my command. I am your father."

Levi glanced over at Adam, who looked like a baby swamp monster covered in green goop.

"Why don't you clean up your grandson then," Levi said, scooting out of the booth. "I'm not touching that."

Chapter 56

"No, not that one," Tori said, looking up the staircase as she checked her hair in the hall tree mirror. "Wear your black wool topcoat."

Levi returned to the top of the stairs moments later, held his arms out, and turned in a circle. She could tell he was about to lose his patience.

"That's the right coat, but don't wear that Panama, Levi. Wear the gray fedora. It's going to be cold."

Levi walked down the stairs and hung the Panama back on the hall tree. He took the old gray fedora off a hook and tried it on. As they looked at themselves in the mirror, Tori smiled. She liked that hat, which had belonged to her grandfather. Levi didn't wear the fedora often, but he looked good in it.

"You ready?" he asked.

She nodded. Sticking her head into the library, she said, "Call us if you need anything, Amber."

"Sure, have a good—" Amber stopped in mid-sentence when she remembered where they were going.

"Have a good time?" Levi said with a smile.

"Sorry," Amber said.

"We should be back in a few hours," Levi said. "We'll probably go have lunch afterwards."

"That's fine," Amber said.

Tori picked Adam up off the floor and kissed him on the head. Levi did the same.

"Come on, Tori," Levi said, holding out his arm. "Let's go put the 'fun' back in funeral!"

As Levi and Tori walked towards the kitchen to the back door, Levi smiled at her. It was a rare day when Tori, who didn't wear heels very often, clicked across the kitchen floor.

"What are you grinning about?" Tori said.

"You're kind of dressed up like a grownup," Levi said.

"I know. It's kind of scary, isn't it?" she said, glancing down at herself.

They walked across the yard and through the open doors into the huge interior of the carriage house. Levi opened Old Blue's door for her. After he made sure her coat was in, he shut the door and walked to the driver's side.

"You don't think . . ." he said as he fired the truck.

She shook her head. "Not a chance. I'm sure the O'Malleys arranged a private service."

They drove the short distance to Olton in silence. There weren't many cars in the Church of Christ parking lot. That was the problem with living such a long life as his Aunt Maggie had done. Many of your friends and family are already gone, leaving few to celebrate your life. Levi had seen that many times when attending Masonic Funeral Rites. The older the Mason, the fewer in attendance at the service.

Inside the church, Tori and Levi removed their coats in the coat room. After Levi put his hat on the rack above, he said, "All that fussing over the hat and coat, and nobody even saw them."

Tori elbowed him as they walked out into the large sanctuary. There were very few people there, and Levi didn't recognize anyone. Margaret's casket was closed on the dais in front of the pulpit. There were a few elderly men and women talking up towards the front of the church—probably friends of hers from the church. It was very quiet.

Suddenly, a man at the front of the church saw them and walked in their direction. Levi could tell it was the minister by the way he was dressed and the cross pin he wore on his lapel. He appeared to be in his mid-fifties with a pale complexion and sad eyes. He reminded Levi a great deal of the movie actor Peter Lorre.

"Glad you could come," he said, taking each of their hands in turn. "You must be the Garveys."

"Yes, I'm Levi, and this is my wife, Tori."

"I'm Bill Anderson," he said. "I'm the senior pastor here. I believe you've already met Pastor Keller. He'll be conducting the graveside service afterwards."

"Nice to meet you," Tori said.

"Peg said a lot of really nice things about both of you. She particularly enjoyed her conversations with you, Tori, while you were restoring the old Majestic Theatre here. I know you had a number of visits with her. And Levi, almost everyone in the congregation has read your books. Peg was very proud of your accomplishments. There's a photo that a member took up on one of the collage boards. It shows Peg sitting at the organ during a morning worship service, reading one of your novels while I was giving my Sunday sermon."

Levi and Tori both laughed.

Pastor Keller smiled. "Whenever you published a new book, it was impossible to get it out of her hands until she'd finished reading it—even if it meant reading it during the church service. She bought every single one of them in hardcover the day of release. I didn't mind because she loaned them to me once she was finished."

"I didn't know she read my books. Thanks for sharing that. I know this congregation meant a lot to her. She had many good friends here," Levi said.

"She did, myself included," he said. "I'm sorry we don't have a larger group today, just her close friends. We had a much larger turnout last evening at her visitation service. The whole congregation and half the town went through here to pay their respects. We have a younger congregation of working people, so weekday funerals are usually pretty sparsely attended, I'm sad to say."

"Sorry we couldn't attend last night," Levi said. "We have a young son."

"I understand," Pastor Anderson said. "I'm very glad you could come today. I don't know if you noticed, but usually we have music prior to a funeral service. Your great-aunt played the organ for so many years we decided that, out of respect, we weren't going to have any music today."

"That's very nice," Levi said.

The large pipe organ was off to the left of the pulpit. The bench had been draped in black silk, and there was a portrait of Margaret set up on a tripod beside it.

"Will you be coming to the cemetery afterwards?"

Levi nodded.

"Very good. I'll see you then. I've got to get ready to begin," he said, shaking both of their hands and slipping back to the front of the church.

"Hey, look who just walked in," Tori said, nudging Levi.

Nichole Larsen was standing in the doorway. She was in her early thirties and pretty in that small town cheerleader sort of way. When she saw them, she walked over.

"Where's your fiancé?" Levi asked.

She nodded towards the back of the church. "He's hanging up our coats. I thought you'd be here today. I thought a great deal of your aunt."

"I didn't know you knew her," Levi said.

"This has been my family's church for generations," she said. "Peg began teaching me the piano when I was just a little girl. When I got into high school, she started teaching me how to play the pipe organ. She was a wonderful teacher. For the last few years, she has played both of the morning services, and I've played the evening service. She used to play all the services, but it was getting harder because her hands hurt from arthritis. In fact, she asked me just a couple of weeks ago to take one of the morning services."

"Did everyone call her Peg?" Tori asked.

"Pretty much everyone here did," Nichole said.

"It seems odd that I didn't know she went by Peg," Levi said. "I always knew her as Aunt Maggie. My Grandma Lucille called her Margaret or Margie."

When Chuck Franklin joined them, Chuck and Levi exchanged grins. They'd gone to high school together. Chuck, who was the star quarterback of the Twin Rivers Comets the year they won the state championship, had been popular with the girls.

"Hello, Levi," he said, holding out his hand. "I don't think I've seen you two since the 25-year reunion."

Levi smiled as he shook his hand. Chuck was tall, his blonde hair perfectly cut, his teeth capped, his hands soft and warm with manicured nails. He'd been serving as a representative in Springfield for several years. If Levi's prediction was correct, after the next election, they'd be calling him U.S. Senator Franklin. In Levi's opinion, he was one of the few politicians who actually did what he said he was going to do, who spent time listening to those who'd elected him, and who never forgot a name.

"How did you two meet?" Tori asked.

Nichole smiled warmly. "I went to a town hall meeting in Calloway. Afterwards, he walked up to me."

Chuck flashed his election-winning smile. "When I saw her in the crowd, I decided I'd like to meet her. We had coffee afterwards."

"And then dinner the next night," Nichole said with a smile. "And a movie the night after."

"So when is the wedding?" Tori asked.

"We're thinking September," Nichole said. "We're going to get married at his father's farm. Of course, you'll be getting an invitation."

Chuck glanced towards the front of the church. "I think the minister is getting ready to begin. He just stepped up to the podium."

The two couples walked down towards the front of the church and sat together. The pastor, wearing a white robe and green sash, cleared his throat. Conversations subsided.

"I'm sorry if this beginning is a little awkward. Usually, it's Peg who tells the congregation by the music she plays that we are beginning the service. For more than sixty years, she played for thousands and thousands of church services, weddings, and funerals. I've been thinking this week about what a significant portion of Peg's life was spent playing that organ for our congregation. That's why we have no music today. When the faithful go to meet the Lord, they leave a hole amongst the living. The absence of music today is helping us remember our friend and her life-long contributions to our church. We come to celebrate a life well lived. Let us pray . . ."

As Levi lowered his head, Tori reached over and took his hand.

Chapter 57

Ray was sitting in his office—the one in a converted spare bedroom in his home, not the one at the police station. There was no way he could do what he was doing in his office there.

He pressed the eject button on the VCR, and the tape popped out. He put it back into the box, set it off to the side, removed another from a box, and pushed it in. He hadn't thought much of Naughty Nurses 1, 2 or 3. In a few seconds, the title screen for Naughty Nurses 4 came up. There were six in this series all together. Before this case, Ray had never watched a porn movie. Now he'd watched dozens, mostly fast forwarding through them. Several weeks ago, he'd gone back to Selena's house and boxed up the entire collection, every movie she was in. He was convinced that the answers lay somewhere in those tapes.

Ray was listing the names of all the stars and co-stars in Selena's film collection. The names and faces changed often since most of the actors and actresses appeared in only two or three of them. Every time a new actress appeared, Ray looked at her face carefully, expecting eventually to recognize somebody who'd later become famous for something completely different—somebody who'd be willing to pay to keep her involvement in porn a secret years later. So far, however, he'd discovered nothing.

Ray was a dozen movies away from having seen them all. Porn sickened him. He just didn't understand why it was such a huge business. The films depicted the same acts over and over and over again. He had watched Selena's movies in order from the beginning of her career. It was shocking how much Selena had changed from that first movie in 1983 to the ones from the late eighties that he was watching now. In less than ten years, she'd aged twenty years. Her eyes reflected her drug addiction. And it was obvious she was having a lot of plastic surgery done. Her boobs got larger every few years until she looked like a cartoon character.

Ray wasn't sure he wanted to watch the last dozen films. He was beginning to think he was wasting his time. There was nothing to indicate that the person Peter Long was blackmailing was ever in a full scale porn movie—at least not in this collection. That vault had been full of older tapes and DVDs, mostly auditions. There was a good chance the woman they were looking for had done only a porn audition, and only Peter Long knew about the mistake made in college, perhaps for a little money to help pay for tuition. Something immediately regretted and long forgotten.

Ray leaned forward and hit the fast forward button. There were some things they did in the movies that he just couldn't watch. He pushed play when that scene ended and another began. He leaned forward to look at the newest faces. He had seen this particular scene done a dozen different ways. There were a bunch of young topless girls around a pool—playing pool volleyball, of course. Selena Fine, the star, was amongst them. It wasn't long before the doorbell rang, and Selena went into the house to answer the door. It was probably the pizza delivery man. And she wouldn't have any money. Ray pressed fast forward, waiting for the next scene to begin. Then he pressed play again. He'd seen a lot of versions of this one, too. Dad came home early and found the babysitter helping herself to his liquor cabinet.

"Ray?" a voice called from the other room.

He jumped to his feet and walked quickly out into the living room. Ed was leaning against the doorframe between the living room and the kitchen.

"Sorry, I didn't mean to barge in. I knocked, and the door was unlocked."

"That's okay," Ray said. "What do you want?"

"Well, after all this time, it seems like Jay Snider's case is destined for the cold case file. I want the key to his workshop so I can retrieve that portrait of Mom Jay painted for Levi. I think he'd really like that."

"Sure," Ray said, pulling a wad of keys out of his pocket and fishing through them. "I'm not sure which one it is."

"Well, I can open it without the key."

"Yeah, I know you can, but you probably shouldn't do that," Ray said, removing one key from his keychain. "I think it's this one."

"What's going to happen with Jay's house?" Ed asked, taking the key.

Ray shrugged. "He mentioned a cousin—a photographer. I think that's the only family he had left. As far as I know, they haven't been able to contact her."

"You want to come along?"

"No, I've got work to do. I'll catch up with you later."

As Ed turned to leave, he paused. There were now sounds of grunting and moaning and ecstatic shrieks coming from Ray's office.

"What are you doing in there?" Ed said, grinning broadly.

"Not what you think," Ray snapped.

Ed chuckled. "I think you're watching a dirty movie. Now I'm really sorry I barged in. No wonder you didn't answer the door."

"You know exactly what I'm doing, and it's not that funny," Ray said, stepping into his office and hitting the stop button on the VCR.

When he reentered the living room, Ed said, "You're watching all those movies Jeff found at Selena's house, aren't you?"

Ray slowly nodded. "That's all I've got. All the audition tapes in the vault were destroyed in the fire."

"It's a long shot," Ed said. "You find anything? You recognize any of those girls?"

"No," Ray admitted.

"You got a warrant for those tapes?" Ed asked.

"You got a court order to retrieve that portrait?" Ray fired back.

Holding up his hands, palms out, Ed said, "Fair enough."

He was almost to the kitchen door when he turned and said, "You going to resign?"

Looking at the serious expression on Ed's face for a long moment, Ray couldn't believe that it had never occurred to him before that Ed could be Levi's father. Ed looked exactly like an older version of Levi.

"I have to, Ed. The citizens of Twin Rivers deserve to have an honest chief after having consecutive dishonest ones. And I haven't been. I've been just as lawless and dishonest as Malone and Craig."

"I think it's a mistake, Ray. The difference is motives, and yours were pure. You weren't hiding your crimes. You were trying to protect the town and your friends."

"That's not true," Ray said. "You knew Levi and Tori were in no danger from *Uncle* Tony. You knew it."

"I did not," Ed said. "Sure, I knew he's my uncle, but if you think Tony O'Malley wouldn't kill family to protect his organization, then you're a fool. And one fact you're missing is how much effort Tony has gone to in order to protect his successor—Carl. If his enemies had learned who Carl was when he was growing up, he'd be dead by now. And if they learn about the rest of his family ties, the Garvey family will be at risk, too. A war is going to break out in the mob when Tony dies. Tony's enemies are already preparing for it, and Carl is, too. I'd rather not be involved in the war as a member of the O'Malley family."

"You're probably right, Ed, but it doesn't change things. I just can't continue as the chief, acting as I have. I made a bad decision involving you and Levi. I made a bad decision climbing into bed with Tony. I made a bad decision breaking into an FBI crime scene."

"Do what you need to do," Ed said, "but just think about it. There's nothing black and white in this world. It's all gray. You knew that in Savannah. You knew then that sometimes you had to get past the badge and do the human thing. Sometimes to resolve a dangerous situation, you had to fall back on what you knew would work and damn the regulations. Didn't you get shoved into retirement because you sometimes crossed that line between what worked and what the regulations said?"

Ray looked down at the floor, saying nothing.

"Am I wrong?" Ed pressed.

Ray shrugged, then said, "But I'm so far over the line."

"So confess," Ed said. "Call the FBI and tell them everything."

"I can't do that," Ray snapped.

"You're right. You can't because what you did was the right thing to do. You had to do it to protect your community and your friends. If you confessed now, you'd kill us all. Right?"

"I have to think about this," Ray said.

"Then think about it," Ed said. "You're being a Monday morning quarterback. You didn't know then what you know now. Stick with what you knew back when you did it—stick with the reasons why you crossed the line to begin with."

"So I either learn to live with it, or I resign," Ray said.

"And who benefits if you resign?" Ed said.

Ray smiled wryly. Ed was a lot smarter than anybody ever gave him credit for being.

Chapter 58

"It's kind of like being on a date," Levi said as he turned Old Blue onto Main Street.

Tori laughed.

"I mean I love that little kid. Don't get me wrong. But he painted my dog," Levi said with a grin. "It's constant chaos in that house."

"Get used to it. You know Rosco loves Adam," Tori said. "If he didn't, he would've eaten him the first week, and he certainly wouldn't have sat still while Adam coated him from head to toe."

"I told you he was a little young for finger paints," Levi said.

"Actually, it was pudding," Tori said.

"It was a hellish mess," Levi said. "And where was Mom at the time?"

"I went to put a load of clothes in the dryer. I was gone for maybe two minutes."

"And when you got back, I had a chocolate dog."

"You want to talk about when you took an unscheduled nap, Levi, and Adam got his hands on the baby powder?"

"That was different," Levi said as he pulled to a stop in front of Harv's. "I was tired, and he was asleep on the floor."

"And when I got home, you were asleep, and the den looked like the scene of a bakery explosion. You were covered in powder, the floor was covered in powder, Rosco was covered in powder, and little Adam powder tracks indicated he'd crawled through just about every room downstairs."

Levi laughed as he turned off the truck. "And when Mommy got home, she yelled and cussed and put Adam down for a nap. A little later, Mommy was all covered in powder, too, rolling around on the den floor with Daddy."

"Yes, and don't forget that Mommy got a new vacuum sweeper, so it was worth it."

"Well, that old piece of crap didn't work very well," Levi said.

"On baby powder," Tori added with a laugh.

Levi sighed. "Are we going to sit out here in front of Harv's, or are we going in?"

"What else you got in mind?" Tori asked.

Levi glanced at his phone. "The matinee starts at the Comet in ten minutes. *The Bad and the Beautiful.* 1953. Lana Turner. Kirk Douglas. Walter Pidgeon. We could go up in the balcony."

"We just saw that one on TCM," Tori said.

Levi smiled wickedly. "Even better. We won't miss anything."

"Get out," Tori said. "I'm hungry."

When they walked into the diner, they knew something was wrong. It was absolute chaos. Harv was banging on the bell in the order window with his spatula. April was standing behind the counter with a young woman in an apron, pointing at various tables and booths as the young woman tearfully looked down at her order pad.

Tori and Levi slid into a booth.

"Hope you're not hungry," Floyd said to them from the farmers' table. "It's going to be a while. I've been waiting for my burger for fifteen minutes, and I still don't have coffee."

"What's going on?" Levi said.

"Another new waitress," Floyd said with a huff. "April is trying to teach her. It's been busy because school is out today. The boiler isn't working, and there's no heat at the school. Everybody came up here for lunch today. Normally, April could do this herself, but she's trying to teach Susan."

"Susan?" Tori asked.

"The newbie," Floyd said. "Damn good thing you weren't here five minutes ago, Levi."

"Why is that?"

"She just dropped an entire pie," Floyd said. "They ran out of pie in the carousel, so Susan went back to get the last one from the kitchen. Tripped coming out. It hit the floor and exploded like a giant egg."

Levi's face went pale. "Today is chocolate!"

"Take a deep breath," Tori said. "It's just a pie, Levi."

"Just a pie?" Levi said, looking at her wide-eyed. "Who *are* you?"

The new waitress suddenly burst into tears, jerked off her apron, threw it on the counter, and ran to the door.

"There goes number four," Floyd said. "They're never going to find another one like Nichole."

Tori slid out of the booth. "I'm going to help April get caught up."

Levi nodded. His focus was on the chocolate mess on the floor in front of the swinging door.

Tori put on Susan's apron. She was overdressed in her black skirt, jacket, and high heels. At the order window, Harv pointed to the customers the orders belonged to. Tori placed the first order in front of Floyd.

"If you bitch because this is cold—" Tori started to say.

"I'm sure it's fine," Floyd said, putting his hands up.

April was right behind her with Floyd's coffee.

When she placed a cup in front of Levi, she said, "You probably already heard."

Levi sighed. "No pie."

"Sorry, Levi," she said. "Breakfast or lunch?"

"Breakfast," Levi said.

He watched as she wrote the order down on the fly and placed it with Harv. He was sure it was only two words—Levi breakfast. Harv's translation: two eggs over easy, bacon, hash browns, and white toast with no butter.

"So that was number four?" he said to Floyd.

"Maybe it was five. They all left the same way—in tears."

Levi watched as Tori delivered several orders, apologizing for the wait—sometimes nicely to customers who smiled and sometimes with veiled threats if they were like Floyd. In Twin Rivers, there were more like Floyd.

"I didn't realize Nichole left so suddenly," Levi remarked. "You'd think she would've given some notice. I mean she's worked up here on and off since she was in high school."

Floyd had just taken a big bite of his cold hamburger. He held up a finger as he chewed. Then he said, "I think she meant to. The last night she worked was when she got engaged. Everybody in town came up to see that ring of hers. You were on the West Coast at the time, right?"

"Yeah," Levi said, sipping his coffee. "Ray told me about that when I got home."

"She got the stomach flu that was going around after that," Floyd said. "I don't think she ever worked another shift. You know, her fiancé probably didn't like her working up here after their engagement was announced—him being a politician. I doubt if part-time waitress should be on the resume for a senator's wife."

"We saw them just about an hour ago," Levi said. "Chuck and Nichole were at Aunt Maggie's funeral this morning."

"This burger is cold as hell," Floyd said, setting it down on his plate.

"What did you say?" Tori said, walking up behind him.

"I said I can't eat another bite."

"That's what I thought you said," Tori remarked as she filled a couple of empty coffee cups at the farmers' table before walking off.

"Wait a minute," Levi said.

"Is something wrong?" Floyd said. "You have the most peculiar look on your face."

Levi looked right at him. "That last night Nichole worked—the night she was wearing the engagement ring—was that the same night Jay Snider came in?"

Floyd shrugged. He looked at another man at his table. "Rich, was the last night Nichole worked the same night Ben Walker was here? The night he tossed old crazy Jay across the table and cuffed him?"

"I think it was," Rich said, wiping his chin with a napkin "Why?"

Floyd looked at Levi. "Why, Levi?"

Levi got up from the booth, pulled on his coat, and walked to the door.

"Where are you going?" Tori said.

Shaking his head, he said, "I'll be back."

Tori watched through the window as he walked to Old Blue and climbed in.

"Where is Levi going?" April asked her.

"I don't know."

"It was just a pie," April said. "Tell him I'll make chocolate tomorrow. They take pie way too seriously in this town."

Chapter 59

Levi sat in the driveway for several minutes, looking at the house. The car was in the driveway, so he knew she was home. Let's do this, he thought as stepped out of Old Blue and walked towards the door. The wind, which had picked up, just about whipped the fedora off his head. He grabbed his hat, snugged his jacket around his neck, and rang the bell. The temperature was dropping. It'd been cold and windy at the cemetery, but now it was frigid.

Nichole opened the door.

"Levi!" she said, looking surprised. "Come in before you freeze."

"Thanks," he said as he started to pull his shoes off inside her small house.

"Don't worry about your shoes," she said. "Come into the kitchen. I've got coffee made."

She waved him towards one of the stools at the counter that divided the kitchen and the living room. He tossed his coat across the back of the couch, parked his fedora on top of it, and sat at the counter. Nichole slid a cup of coffee in front of him as she'd done a thousand times before at Harv's.

"Thank you."

"Is there something wrong?" she asked, leaning against the sink, sipping on her own cup. "You're acting a little strange—even for you."

"I don't know exactly how to put this," he said finally. "It's about the last night you worked at Harv's."

"Okay," she said, looking at him questioningly.

"That was the night Jay Snider got into a fight with Peter Long, right?" Levi asked.

"I wouldn't call it a fight, but yes," she said. "Is there something you want to know about it?"

"You know what Peter Long did for a living," he said.

"I do," she said curtly.

"He made a lot of money making movies," he said, "but he made millions more blackmailing women who auditioned to be in them. He'd get these girls—many of them young and broke and in college—to audition. He'd pay them. Some of them later went on to be in his productions, but he kept track of the girls who'd only auditioned, too. Years later, when they were successful, that little mistake from the past would resurface and threaten to ruin their careers and their families."

"That's awful," she said, her face pale.

"We think one of those women murdered him and Selena Fine and Jay Snider and Shelia Carter," he said. "We think she had them murdered to protect that secret."

"How do you know all this?" Nichole asked. "I heard that all of Peter Long's records were destroyed in the fire at his lake house."

"A lot is just guessing," Levi said. "Most of the evidence is gone, but we have a ledger that belongs to Peter Long. No names, just numbers and payments. We need to find one of these women he was blackmailing and hopefully get her to shed a little more light on what was going on, maybe even lead us to the killer."

"Makes sense," Nichole said, sipping her coffee.

"Did you go to college?" Levi asked.

Nichole smiled. "I did three semesters at the University of Illinois. My grandmother died after the second semester. I couldn't afford it on my own, and my grades weren't that great. I just didn't want to take on huge student loans. It's bugged me ever since, but I never finished."

When Levi glanced up at her, her face suddenly reddened.

"Wait a minute," she said, setting her coffee cup down. "Where are you going with this?"

"I know why Peter Long was really at the diner that night," Levi said flatly.

"Why is that?" Nichole said, her voice rising slightly.

"We all make mistakes when we're young."

"Are you suggesting . . ." Nichole didn't finish as her eyes narrowed and she walked closer to Levi. "You think I made a dirty movie when I was in college. You think Peter Long was up at Harv's to intimidate me."

"Listen, I'm not judging you," Levi said. "But the same night you became engaged to Chuck Franklin, Peter Long showed up out of the blue. Chuck Franklin is powerful. He's successful, and his family is wealthy. All of that adds up to exactly what a blackmailer is looking for. If your indiscretion came out, it could ruin Chuck's career."

"And it couldn't be just a coincidence?" Nichole spat angrily.

"I don't believe in coincidences," Levi said.

"Well, let me tell you something, Mr. Garvey," she said, shaking a finger at him. "I was never involved in a pornographic audition or a dirty movie of any kind. Not ever. I've never even let a boyfriend take a picture of me naked. I know that's pretty common these days, but I don't do it. I have values I learned in my church and from my family and from the little town I grew up in. It didn't happen."

Levi looked at her doubtfully.

"You don't believe me?" Nichole shouted.

"I'm starting to," Levi said. "I'm sorry. I didn't mean to upset you. It just made sense that was why Pete was there. Running into you and Chuck today—"

"Get your coat and your hat, and get out of my house," Nichole said.

"I'm so sorry. I obviously had it completely wrong."

"Get out!" Nichole shouted.

Tears were now coursing down her cheeks and her hand shook as she pointed at the door. Quickly, Levi grabbed his hat and coat. At the door, he paused. He started to say something.

"Out!" she screamed.

Chapter 60

Levi beat Tori home. He was so rattled after his encounter with Nichole, it took him a minute to remember where Tori was. When he called her, she said she'd get a ride home later. He paid Amber for babysitting, checked on Adam, who was sound asleep in his crib, and made coffee. When he heard a car pull up in the driveway, he stepped out onto the porch.

"Sorry I left you," Levi said as Tori climbed the steps in her high heels.

"That's okay," Tori said, smiling up at him. "That was actually kind of fun. I made $35 in tips."

They waved as April backed out onto the road in front of the house. April honked twice and waved back.

"Where did you go?" Tori asked. "You looked like you were on a mission."

"I was."

Gazing at him thoughtfully—she could read his face like a paperback novel—she said, "What did you do? Let's have it."

"I really screwed up," Levi said. "I'm so embarrassed."

A Mercedes pulled into the driveway and came to an abrupt stop in front of the porch. The tinted windows hid the driver's identity.

"This have something to do with it?" Tori asked.

As Chuck Franklin climbed out of the car, Levi said, "Yup."

Chuck climbed the steps up to the porch as Levi tried to figure out what to say to him. One thing about Chuck Franklin was that he was always calm. He'd understand.

"Hello, Chuck," Tori said brightly.

"Hi, Tori," he said, glancing first at her and then at Levi.

"I guess we need to talk about what happened this afternoon," Levi said.

Chuck shook his head, pulled his arm back, and punched him in the face. Levi fell back against the siding and slid down the wall. Levi touched his nose. His fingers came back bright red with blood.

"Sorry, Tori, but he had it coming," Chuck said as he walked back down the steps.

Levi struggled to his feet. They watched as Chuck backed down the driveway and pulled away. They didn't wave.

"You've got such a gentle way with people," Tori said.

"It's a gift," Levi said, wiping blood from under his nose. "Why didn't you stop him?"

"I've known Chuck for over thirty years," Tori said. "I've never seen him do anything like that. I figured if he was mad enough to hit you, you probably deserved it."

"I did."

"Is it broken?"

"I don't think so," Levi said, touching his nose again and wincing.

"You'd better get some ice on that," Tori said, leading him to the door. "Then you're going to tell me what you did this afternoon."

Chapter 61

"That doesn't even make sense, Levi," Ed said as he pulled the triangle off the pool balls he'd just racked and took a step back.

"No, he just goes off half-cocked as usual," Tori said.

She leaned over the table with her pool cue and fired the white ball towards the end of the table. The balls exploded with an loud crack. Two balls fell into pockets, a solid and a stripe.

"We'll take stripes," she said, walking around the table to line up her next shot.

"It made sense at the time," Levi muttered, holding a cold beer beside his swollen nose, "but I guess I didn't think it through."

"It couldn't have been her," Ray said, curling up the corners of his mustache. "She's not old enough. The woman we're looking for had already paid Peter Long hundreds of thousands of dollars, maybe even millions, over a long period of time."

"And if our murderer is the number in Pete's ledger we think she is, the audition was made back in '89," Tori said. "Then she didn't start making the blackmail payments for ten years. It took her that long, apparently, to become successful. That's not Nichole. I made $35 in tips today, and April says that's a pretty good lunch. Between her hourly wage and her tips, Nichole made maybe $150 a day—tops."

When Tori missed her third shot, Ray lined up on a solid. It was a tricky shot, but if he made it, he'd leave the cue ball in a perfect place to knock in two more easily.

"I know what Levi was thinking," Ed remarked. "He was thinking it was Chuck Franklin making those payments—if it was Nichole and she'd made an audition back when she was in college."

"Nichole is still too young. She went to college in the late nineties, not the eighties," Tori added.

"That's right," Ed said, smiling as Ray made the tricky shot and lined up for his next two easy ones. "Nichole is a good ten years younger than Chuck. But if she'd made an audition, she'd be prime pickings for Peter Long. The Franklins have lots of money, and they would've paid. The last thing they'd want, right before Chuck's big announcement, would be for it to come out that his fiancé was in a porn movie in college."

Levi sighed. "But our murderer had been paying for years already— long before Chuck and Nichole started dating. We're looking for a woman who's Tori's age or older. I figured that out already."

"When was that?" Tori asked.

"When I was talking to Nichole," Levi said. "Suddenly, I realized I had it completely wrong—what made so much sense when I drove over to Nichole's house fell apart right before my eyes."

Ray missed an easy shot. Levi stepped up and eyed the table for his best shot.

Ray grinned. "Can you see okay?"

Levi was well on his way to having two very black eyes—one was swollen almost shut already.

"I can see just fine," Levi growled as he fired a stripe into the side pocket.

"You know what bothers me, Levi?" Ed said.

"Please tell me," Levi said, walking around the table to line up another shot.

"You thought you were right, and you went over there to confront her. Right?"

"Yeah," Levi said, pausing to look at him.

"You were convinced she was our killer," Ed said.

"I already said that, yes," Levi admitted.

"You don't share that with anybody. You don't tell Tori where you're going. You don't call me. You don't let Ray know. You just go over there. What if you'd been right, and Nichole had seen you coming?"

Levi nodded. He knew where Ed was going.

"This is a woman who'd murdered multiple times to keep her secret, and you go over to expose her all by yourself. She could've killed you, and nobody would've had any idea where you'd gone."

Levi shrugged. "Well, I didn't think she'd killed all those people herself. I thought it was the Franklins cleaning up her mess."

Ed laughed. "You should write fiction. The Franklins? There's been only one black sheep in that family, and he's been dead for decades. Seriously?"

"I do write fiction," Levi huffed.

"We've known Chuck Franklin since grade school," Tori said. "How in the hell do you cast him in the role of somebody who'd hire a hitman? He's squeaky clean!"

"I know," Levi said, shaking his head.

"Let's say you were right, and Nichole was in a porn film," Ed said. "What would Chuck Franklin have done?"

"I think the engagement would be over," Levi said.

"I agree," Ed said.

"And he would've done the same thing he did several years ago when he got that DUI after his staff Christmas party," Tori said.

"I wasn't here yet. I was still in Savannah, but I heard the story. Didn't he call a news conference?" Levi said.

Ed nodded. "He was barely over the legal limit, but he called a news conference and told everyone what had happened."

"Even though his family is loaded, he didn't want any special treatment," Tori said. "He didn't post bail and spent the entire weekend in jail. Then he went to court and pled guilty. He lost his license, paid his fines, did his community service, and went to the mandated DUI classes. Then he went back to his work in politics. That's Chuck Franklin. His honesty and the way he handled that situation actually boosted his career. That's why he's going to be our next senator. And you cast him as a murderer?"

"I've already said I didn't think it through," Levi said.

"It wouldn't surprise me a bit if he didn't call a news conference tomorrow," Ed said, "to tell everybody he assaulted you and why."

"I hope he doesn't do that," Levi said.

"I hope not either," Tori said.

"I don't think he will," Ray said. "Seems like it was a private matter—a matter of honor. I'd have knocked your block off, too. You basically called the woman he loves a slut."

A small smile crossed Levi's face. "I'll tell you one thing."

"What's that?" Ray said.

"I've been hit many times in my lifetime," Levi said.

"It's because of your gentle way with people," Tori said.

Levi glared at her. "You done?"

"I'll let you know," Tori said, pulling Adam out from under the pool table where he'd crawled and returning him to the corner where Ray kept the toys he played with. "You were saying?"

"I've been hit many times," Levi repeated, "but I've never been hit quite that hard before. It was like I stopped a bus with my face. Even so, he kinda pulled back on that punch a little bit. If he'd wanted to, I think he could've caved my face in."

"He was a football player," Ed said. "He's still in good shape—a lot better shape than you are and better shape today than Doug Malone was when he was regularly using your face as a punching bag back in high school. If you'd gone head to head with Chuck Franklin in your youth, instead of Doug Malone, we'd all still be mourning you."

"Please," Levi muttered.

"Are you going to shoot, or we going to stand here talking?" Ed said.

Levi leaned over the table and lined up his shot, an easy one. He not only missed it but also dropped the cue ball into the corner pocket.

"Well, thank you, son," Ed said. "That's a scratch. You can step back now and watch me finish this game. Watch me carefully—this is how you clear a pool table."

Ed lined up his shot. As he pulled back to shoot, Levi said, "If you start calling me *son*, I'm going to start calling you *father*."

Ed flinched as he shot. The cue ball sailed through the air and bounced across the basement floor. Adam squealed as the ball rolled over to him. He picked it up and laughed.

Chapter 62

"I just don't want to talk about it anymore," Levi said.

He carried Adam up the front porch steps as Tori opened the front door. When they stepped into the foyer, Tori took Adam.

"I think Ray is right. I think our murderer is either a very rich middle-aged woman who made a mistake in college, or it's the televangelist," Tori said.

"I agree, and either way, it doesn't have anything to do with us or Twin Rivers at this point."

After starting up the stairs, Tori paused and looked back at him. "Are you coming to bed?"

Levi shook his head. "I'm a little wound up. I think I'll ice down my face and do a little work in the den before I come up."

"I'll see you in the morning," Tori said. "I'm wiped out."

Levi walked up the first couple of steps and kissed her. Then he kissed Adam on the head. He watched as she climbed the stairs. Then he walked back down and went into the den. Rosco was snoring in the wingback chair beside the fireplace. Rosco never woke up when they got home, but if a car or truck that wasn't theirs pulled up in the driveway, he'd be at the window in two seconds. Aunt Maggie's dog, Sandy, was curled up in the chair with Rosco, staring at Levi with big brown eyes. Levi didn't care much for little dogs, but Sandy, who now seemed to be a Garvey, was beginning to grow on him. He walked over to the roll-top desk and turned on his computer. As he settled into his chair, he glanced over at the little dog, who was still staring at him anxiously—maybe sensing that she liked Levi, at this point, a lot more than he liked her. Levi snapped his fingers. Sandy bounded out of the chair, ran across the den, and leaped up into his lap. Rosco woke up briefly, then closed his eyes and began snoring again.

"I don't like little yipping ankle-biting dogs," Levi said as Sandy licked his chin before settling into his lap. He stroked her head as he began looking through his email.

It was a couple of hours later when Levi glanced at the clock over the fireplace. It was just after midnight. Another half an hour and I'll go to bed, he thought.

For several weeks, off and on, he'd been working on a story idea. Novels always started in his head. He worked them out, scene by scene, before the first word was written. He was almost at the end—it was almost a novel. That would mean some late nights coming up. In another week, maybe two, he'd start banging it out on the computer almost as if he were writing the whole thing from memory. That's the way writing worked with him.

Tonight he was surfing the internet, working on some story details—finding answers to little questions he had and verifying facts. Stupid
little things. For instance, what household product in the 1930s could be
used as a poison? What popular song would a British housewife be humming
as she vacuumed her carpet in 1938? Did they even have vacuums in 1938?
These were the little details that meant nothing to the story, but somebody
out there might realize they were wrong, and reality would crash down, ruin-
ing the realistic fiction he was creating.

Levi wasn't sure how much time had passed when he heard something and stopped. He looked up from the monitor and glanced at the clock.
Nearly two hours had passed. He'd totally lost track of the real world. He
wondered what had caused the noise which had interrupted his concentra-
tion.

It was Rosco. He was standing at the window, his paws on the ledge,
his tail rigid, his ears up, a low growl in his throat.

"What is it?" Levi said.

With Sandy under his arm, he walked over the window and looked
out. He didn't see anything. Obviously, Rosco didn't see anything either, but
he'd sensed something or heard something. He scanned the yard anxiously,
then ran to another window to scan the yard again. Levi was uneasy—Rosco
was rarely wrong. Something was out there.

"Coyotes?" Levi said, leaning in closer to the window pane.

He could hear some faint yips and growling far in the distance. Rosco was used to those common sounds. Maybe there was a pack closer than
usual.

Levi set Sandy down in his desk chair, walked out into the foyer,
and opened the closet door. He pulled out Granny's Howitzer, an ancient
ten-gauge shotgun. He snapped it open, reached up on the top shelf where he
kept a couple of shells, and loaded it. Coyotes had been running right
through the yard recently. He's seen tracks close to the house after the last
snow. It'd been a long, bitterly cold winter, and they were hungry—now obviously attracted to the bounty of rabbits that lived well-sheltered in the
bushes around the house and in the orchard on the back half of the Garveys'
six acres.

Levi opened the front door. Rosco tried to rush out around him, but
Levi blocked him from exiting.

"You stay in," he said.

Coyotes traveled in packs, and while they didn't often attack domes-
tic dogs, especially large ones like Rosco, it did happen. Closing the door
behind him, Levi stepped to the top of the porch steps and listened. He could
hear the pack more clearly now, probably from a mile or so away, yipping,

snarling, and growling. When one killed something to eat, it would call the whole pack in to share the meal. It was a spooky sound to hear late at night.

Satisfied they weren't near the house, Levi turned and walked back to the door. Suddenly, he startled when Rosco jumped up in the window, barking furiously and showing his teeth. His breath steamed the window pane. When Levi turned to look again, his heart leaped.

Somebody was walking across the yard.

"Hey," he yelled. "Who's there?"

The man just kept walking, his hands in his pockets.

"Stop!" Levi yelled. "You're trespassing!"

Without changing his speed or his direction, the man kept walking—never even glancing in Levi's direction. Rosco was barking frantically, his nails scratching at the door. The porch light came on—Tori was awake.

Levi walked to the top of the porch steps and raised the shotgun barrel into the air. His finger was on the trigger, ready to fire off a warning round, when he caught motion to his left. Somebody was standing in the shadows only a few feet away from him.

Suddenly, his head exploded in a bright flash of pain. As he fell down the porch steps, he heard Tori scream inside the house. Levi managed to get up on his hands and knees at the base of the steps. With blurred vision, he saw Tori wrestling with a dark shadow. As Levi tried to gain his footing, the heel of a boot smashed into his face.

He remembered nothing else.

Chapter 63

Ed flipped on the light next to his bed, jerked upright, and rubbed his face. It was just past one. He'd slept less than an hour this time. His light sleep had been tortured by strange images. Something had been nagging him ever since he'd left Ray Billings' basement. Something was wrong. Obviously, that feeling had followed him into his dreams. Every time he woke up, it seemed that if he could've dreamed just a few moments longer, whatever it was he was missing would be revealed. This time, however, he was left with one faint image. He struggled to grasp it as it faded away.

"Damn," he muttered.

The image, so clear seconds ago, was gone. Or was it. Suddenly, he snapped his fingers. One tiny piece of that dream surfaced for a second. He grabbed it, trying to recall more, but there was nothing else there—just that one brief image.

Jay Snider, he thought. That's what he'd seen. Jay Snider, painting in the sunlight in his studio.

Ed climbed out of bed, pulled on his pants, walked out into his small living room, and flipped on the light. Sitting on the arms of an over-stuffed chair was the portrait Jay had painted of Lucille Garvey. Ed kept telling himself that he just hadn't had a chance to give it to Levi, but the real truth was that he was procrastinating because he really liked the painting.

He looked at the portrait closely—every square inch. There was nothing there. But his mind was screaming at him that he'd seen something or heard something that he'd missed—something his mind had caught and his dreams were trying to reveal.

When he remembered that he hadn't returned the key he'd borrowed from Ray, he scooped his truck keys off the kitchen counter, pulled his coat off the hook behind the kitchen door, and left the house.

When Ed got to Jay's house, he found that the driveway was still covered by a huge drift, so he left his truck parked on the edge of the road, grabbed his flashlight, and walked to Jay's workshop. Inside, he searched the wall for a light switch, actually surprised when the light came on. Jay had been dead for a couple of weeks, but apparently he'd paid his bill before his demise.

Ed walked over to the paintings that were leaning against the wall in stacks. Even though he'd looked at all of them when he'd retrieved the portrait of his mother, he began thumbing through them again. After nearly an hour, he was finished—and frustrated. He'd seen nothing that meant anything to him.

Ed sat down on a folding chair in the center of the workshop. He smiled at the painting nearest him. It was Floyd, a much younger Floyd in his late thirties or early forties. Ed couldn't believe that Jay had wasted paint on such a goofy-looking grin as that.

Then Ed noticed something in the background—something familiar. Where in the hell was Floyd standing, he wondered.

Ed picked up the painting and set it on the easel in the full light. It didn't take him long to recognize the old gas station, which had burned down in the late 70s. A bunch of them used to go up there every morning for coffee. They'd sit in the garage and shoot the shit. Sometimes they helped old Bob change a tire or replace a muffler. When the gas station burned down, old Bob proved himself to be a pretty smart guy, considering he'd originally come from the hills of Kentucky. With the hefty insurance check he received, he built a new place, what they were calling a "convenience store" back then. No garage—just gas, cigarettes, beer, some groceries, donuts, and fountain drinks. The first Hillbilly Bob's had opened in Twin Rivers less than a year after his old gas station had burned down. Then a second one in Calloway and a third in Olton. After the fourth Hillbilly Bob's opened, he franchised the brand, and everybody was building them all over the state. By the time he died a millionaire in 1984, there were fifty of them statewide—and now more than three hundred, almost exclusively in small towns. In every one of them, there were a couple of tables and booths where guys could drink coffee and shoot the shit. Ed was still convinced old Bob got the idea from the bunch that used to show up in the old gas station every morning to do exactly the same thing.

Ed smiled. Suddenly, the light dawned. He walked back to the paintings and pulled out all the portraits. He set them up on the easel, one at a time, focusing on the background details instead of the subjects. The third one was a face he knew well, but he didn't immediately recognize the background though it seemed vaguely familiar. The portrait was obviously painted in the 80s, judging by the hairstyle and how young the subject looked, but what was the background?

Ed sighed as he tried to place the location. Then when he focused on one thing in the background, he knew exactly where Jay's strange mind had immortalized his subject. Ed stabbed that one detail with his finger.

"I gotcha!" he announced.

Snatching the portrait off the easel, he walked quickly to the door. Even though he wasn't leaving the workshop the way he'd found it, he didn't have time for that now. He flipped off the light, locked the knob, pulled the door closed behind him, and headed towards his truck in the snow which had just begun to fall.

Chapter 64

Levi felt numb as he slowly opened his eyes. He was looking up into the sky as a light snow drifted down. Unsure of where he was, he slowly sat up, gasping as pain shot through his head. I must have fallen, he thought as he glanced around.

When he started to brush the snow off his shirt and shoulders, he realized his hands were numb. He rolled onto his hands and knees, then rested until the crushing pain in his head passed. Carefully, he climbed to his feet. Once erect, he suddenly remembered what had happened.

"Oh my God!" he said as he staggered up the steps to the front door which standing wide open.

"Tori!" he yelled.

There was no answer. He leaned against the front door frame, fighting a wave of nausea. When it passed, he ran up the stairs, flipping on the bedroom light as soon as he reached the door. The bed was empty. He ran to the next door. The crib was empty, too. A sob escaped him.

Hanging onto the rail, Levi struggled to descend the stairs. When he entered the library, he gasped at the chaos before him. The library had been ransacked—the den, too.

As he weaved his way up the short hallway to the kitchen, he bumped into the walls, knocking several picture frames to the floor. When he flipped on the kitchen light, he saw nothing askew. His hands, which were beginning to warm, tingled painfully. He reached for the phone in his pocket. It wasn't there. When he turned to go back to the den to retrieve it, he saw the note, written in permanent marker on a sheet of paper ripped from the yellow legal pad they kept on the counter. It was stuck to the kitchen wall with a steak knife. Through tears that filled his eyes, Levi read, "Your family for the ledger. Do nothing until we call. No police. No tricks."

Levi snatched the note, leaving the knife in the wall, and laid it on the counter. He read it several more times. His heart was beating so hard with fear and rage that his breath came in ragged gasps. His head jerked up when he heard a faint scratching sound at the door to the basement. He grabbed a butcher knife out of the block on the counter and crept to the door. Carefully turning the knob with one hand, he swung the knife up over his head with the other. Then he flung the door open.

Rosco and Sandy were looking up at him. When they saw Levi, they began to whine and cry frantically. Levi dropped the knife onto the counter and sank down onto the floor. The dogs covered him with wet tongues.

When Levi rubbed Rosco's head and muzzle, he noticed blood on his hands. Rosco was hurt. Levi examined his head and neck. The blood seemed to be coming from his mouth. Rosco had a tooth missing on the side.

"Somebody kicked you, didn't they," Levi said, his voice shaking as he hugged the dog. "Somebody kicked me, too. But don't worry, Rosco. I kick back, and I know exactly whose ass I'm going to kick."

Using a nearby stool, Levi pulled himself up. Then he walked to the den. His phone was sitting on the desk where he'd left it beside his computer. He looked at if for a long moment before dialing the number.

Chapter 65

With the portrait held under his arm, Ed banged loudly on Ray's kitchen door. It wasn't quite five a.m., and there was no hint of color in the east to indicate that dawn was coming. When there was no response, Ed banged on the door again. The neighbor's porch light across the street came on, and an old woman peered at him through a slit in her curtains. Ed beat on the door a third time. Finally, the kitchen lit up. The curtain covering the door window was pulled back, and Ray's stunned, sleepy face appeared.

"Open the door, Ray," Ed said.

The knob jiggled, and the door slowly opened. Ed barged right in.

"What in the hell is wrong with you?" Ray said. "You know what time it is?"

"It's early," Ed said. "You've got to see this."

Ray laid his Colt .45 down on the counter as Ed set the portrait up on his small kitchen table, leaning it against the wall. Ed flipped the switch which turned on the light over the table.

"That's one of Jay's paintings," Ray remarked.

"You're sharp early in the morning, aren't you?" Ed said.

"Well, we all know who that is," Ray said, clearly irritated. "So what's the big deal? It makes sense that he'd paint him."

"True," Ed said. "The first couple of times I looked at it, I didn't see anything odd either. It's not the subject of the painting. Look at the background."

Ray stepped closer to the painting, pulled out a chair, flipped it around, and sat on it backwards. Ed said nothing while Ray stared.

After a minute of silence, Ed asked, "You got it yet?"

"No, but that background seems familiar, doesn't it?" Ray said, running a hand across his bald head.

"Let me help you," Ed said, stabbing his finger at the one detail in the background that had finally clicked for him.

Ray nodded. "It's a mirror."

"A fisheye mirror. Kind of expensive looking," Ed said.

"I've seen one like that," Ray muttered, leaning back.

"We both have. We discovered it wasn't a mirror. It was a window."

Ray's eyes went wide. He stared at Ed as it dawned on him where he'd seen the fisheye mirror.

"That's the weird office in Peter Long's basement—the one wired for sound and video, the one where those porn auditions were made!" He looked at the portrait again. "What in the hell was he doing there?"

"What do you think?" Ed said. "We've been looking for a woman because women wind up being the stars, but there are lots of men in those films—and they also would've auditioned."

"Peter Long was blackmailing him," Ray said with a wide smile. "That's our murderer!"

Ed laughed as he gave Ray a high five.

"Oh, yeah," Ed said, "we've got him all right. We have to tell Levi and Tori."

Ray glanced at his watch. "It's a little early. You want some coffee and eggs?"

"Sounds great," Ed said. "I'll make the coffee while you work on a couple of those omelets you're famous for."

"Then we'll go over and tell Levi and Tori what we've discovered," Ray said.

"It's about time we figured something out before Levi did," Ed said.

Chapter 66

Levi was sitting at the kitchen counter when Ed and Ray burst in through the front door.

"Oh, good, you're up," Ed said as he strode into the kitchen and made a beeline for the coffee pot.

"You might want to get Tori up for this," Ray said. "We've figured it out!"

Ray leaned the canvas against the wall, face in, for the big surprise once Tori joined them. Ed pulled two mugs out of the cabinet and poured coffee into them.

"Just took some good old-fashioned investigative skill," Ed said with a grin as he handed a mug to Ray. "I'll be happy to teach you my technique one day, Levi. You seem to be a few steps behind us these days."

"But don't get us wrong," Ray said. "We would never rub it in or anything."

Ed laughed his mule laugh. Suddenly, his laugh was cut short when Ray's mug shattered on the floor. His face had gone pale. Ed followed his gaze across the kitchen to where the steak knife was stuck in the wall.

"What the hell?" Ed said as both he and Ray turned to stare at Levi's battered face.

Levi was sitting at the counter, just as he'd been when they'd rushed in. When he glanced up at Ray, the look in his eye was one Ray had seen only a couple of times before. It was chilling.

"What's happened?" Ray asked.

Levi nodded to the note in front of him. Ed snatched it off the counter. Ray leaned over his shoulder to read it. In shocked silence, Ed and Ray looked at each other, then at Levi, who stared at them blankly.

"We know who it is," Ed said.

"So do I," Levi said thickly through his swollen lips. "They want that damned ledger. And until yesterday, only we knew about it—until I told Nichole Larsen, who told her fiancé—our murderer, Chuck Franklin."

Levi paused to let the lump in his throat dissolve.

"A DUI didn't ruin his career," Ed said. "That's forgivable. But porn? No politician can survive a revelation like that."

"So we have an advantage here," Ray said. "Chuck Franklin doesn't know we know who he is. We'll make the exchange, get Tori and Adam back, and then let the FBI bust them later."

Levi slowly shook his head as tears welled in his eyes. "They're not going to let Tori and Adam go. You know that. Look at what they've done to protect that secret already. They hired a hit man. Probably three, actually. One killed Selena in the hospital and ended up at the bottom of the cliff when he tried to kill Jay. Another one finally killed Jay and was likely the same guy that killed Pete, too. And then there was a hit man in Savannah who killed Shelia. That sort of criminal power got me thinking about the Franklins. Where did they get all their money? Then I remembered someone else. Bruce Franklin."

"Bruce Franklin," Ray said. "Now that's a name that rings a bell."

"That was our last case, Ray," Ed said. "Bruce Franklin was the guy Tony O'Malley hired to drive the getaway car in the robbery of the First National Bank of Calloway back in '71. He was killed at the scene by my friend, Deputy Jim Mathis, right before Cliff Craig killed him with a shotgun blast. Bruce was Chuck Franklin's uncle—his father's brother. Bad dude, that one."

"The Franklins were involved with the Chicago Outfit going back to Al Capone's day," Levi added. "Obviously, Uncle Bruce was still involved with Tony O'Malley when that bank robbery took place. But the story is that Chuck's father, Charles Sr., went legit back in the early 70s when he came of age—wanted nothing to do with his family's former line of work. Now it's beginning to look like Charles Franklin was just done with the Chicago Outfit. Maybe all his money came from building his own empire. His family certainly had the expertise to do that."

"Are you thinking they are behind that pot shed?" Ray asked.

Levi nodded. "Probably. But I'm sure that's just one small sideline, and I'm sure that's not the only marijuana outfit either. The Franklins sure have a lot of money and a lot of connections, and they certainly aren't afraid to have a few people killed to protect little Chuck's reputation."

"Wait a minute," Ed said. "Where did you get this information?"

"I made a decision," Levi said.

"What decision?" Ray asked.

"About how we're going to handle this," Levi said.

"Do you think the three of us are going to charge into the Franklin Estate and rescue Tori and Adam?" Ed asked. "Are you kidding me? I've been out there only once, back when I was sidelining in snow removal years ago. That's a big spread, and it's well known in Twin Rivers that he takes security seriously because he's made a lot of enemies as a capital investor. There's even a gate house with armed security. We'd never get on the grounds."

"Capital investor, my ass," Levi said. "He's the head of an organized crime syndicate."

"You didn't answer my question," Ed said. "Where did you get this information?"

"From me," a voice said behind him.

Ray and Ed spun around and looked at the man standing in the basement doorway with Rosco at his heels. It was Ed's turn to drop his coffee mug.

"What in the hell are you doing here?" Ed snapped.

Chuckling, Tony O'Malley walked across the kitchen. He pulled the steak knife out of the wall and tossed it onto the counter.

"A couple of years ago, we were all sitting on the front porch, drinking ice cold beer and talking after our tense encounter at the Twin Rivers Masonic Lodge," Tony said. "You remember that, don't you?"

Neither Ray nor Ed answered.

"Tori was pregnant. I thought it odd that she'd put her life and her baby's life at risk to save Ed from Clifford Craig. She never even thought twice about it. Neither did Levi or even you, Ray—even brought this useless dog, too," Tony said as he reached down to stroke Rosco's head. "You all charged to the rescue, even against me and my Four Horsemen. I was damned impressed with Tori, especially, so I asked her that night why she'd do such a thing in her condition."

Ed nodded. He remembered.

"You know what she said," Tony said, looking at Ed.

"I remember," Ed admitted. "She said that when you take on one of us, you take on all of us."

Tony smiled. "Like it or not, my dear nephew, we're family. I'm your mother's little brother. When Levi called me for help in the middle of the night, I didn't hesitate. And we're going to demonstrate this principle to the Franklins. When you take on one of us, you get all of us."

Almost on cue, Carl appeared in the kitchen door, followed by his Four Horsemen.

"Good God," Ray said fearfully as he saw the new Horsemen for the first time.

Ray remembered clearly just how quickly the old Horsemen had gotten the drop on them at the Twin Rivers Masonic Lodge. The young Horsemen were even harder looking than their predecessors and more intimidating because of their youth.

"What are we doing here? Have you lost your mind, Levi?"

"Not at all," Levi said. "Just ask Tony what he'd do if he were in Charles Franklin's shoes right now?"

"I don't think I need to," Ray said.

"We either go get Tori and Adam, or we get used to living without them," Tony said. "And I might mention, you won't have to get used to living without them for very long because you three won't survive either. He'll take you out one at a time or together. It's just the way it works in my world."

"Please tell me we have a plan," Ed said.

"As you already pointed out," Carl said. "We have the advantage because they don't yet know we've figured it out. My guess is they'll call Levi at some point today to lure him in with that ledger exchange. They didn't find it when they ransacked the house. But they have no intention of an exchange 'cause Levi knows too much. They'll kill him, then you two—probably today. Unless we do this, I doubt if any of you will see the sunset tonight."

Ray shook his head, hoping to wake up from this bad dream. But in his heart, he knew that Tony O'Malley was right. At the very least, Tori and Adam wouldn't be coming back home unless they struck first, and Tony was probably right about the rest of them as well. The Franklins were likely planning their demise right this minute.

"Of course, we're not waiting for the call," Tony said. "We're going to hit them right now because they don't expect it. And besides, they may be a little nervous about taking on the Garveys because of your reputation in Twin Rivers, but they have no idea just how interesting your family tree really is. Angelino!"

Angelino stepped forward and placed a computer pad on the counter. Ed and Ray stepped up to look down at the screen.

"This is a satellite view of the Franklin Estate six miles north of Twin Rivers . . ."

Chapter 67

Ray was sweating profusely—wiping his hand across the top of his wet head and then onto the leg of his blue jeans. Ed was leaning on the counter on his elbows, looking down at the iPad map intently, nodding as Angelino explained the plan.

Finally, Angelino straightened up.

"Well?" Ray asked.

Ed nodded. "This could work."

"Could work?" Ray said nervously.

"It should work," Ed said, "but there are a couple of things that bother me."

"Should work? Oh, that's much better, Ed. Good God." Ray sighed, shaking his head.

"What's your problem with it, Ed?" Carl asked.

Pointing at two different areas on the map, Ed said, "Right there and there. The first is that guard shack at the gate. If something goes wrong there, we don't even get onto the grounds. Then there's this building where the off-duty guards are probably housed. It's between the guard shack and the main house. It's been set up that way to prevent anybody from doing exactly what we're planning to do—which is ballsy to say the least."

"And I have a problem, too," Ray said. "This plan is too last-minute. It's not like we're looking at real-time maps from a military satellite. We've got nothing but a Google map that was taken six months ago—no direct information. We don't know if we're dealing with six armed security guards or a dozen or even more. And we don't know if they're rent-a-cops or a military-trained strike team like Tony has. If it's true that Charles Franklin is running an organized crime syndicate, I kind of think he'd have men trained like the Horsemen are—professional killers."

"I'm not concerned about that," Angelino said. "Either way, they're outmatched. We have a secret weapon that's going to even things up."

"What's that?" Levi asked.

Looking at Ed, Tony said, "We've got a military trained sniper. One of the best."

"Me?" Ed said, eyes wide as he shook his head. "No, what you have is an old man who was a sniper forty years ago."

"So you're too old?" Tony asked.

Ed looked back down at the map they'd been examining.

"I am too old, but it's my daughter-in-law and my grandson," he said, looking at Levi. "You can count on me to do whatever I need to do."

Levi seemed to have drifted off somewhere else. He was staring across the kitchen at the nook where he and Tori had eaten breakfast just the day before.

Ed looked at the overhead map of the estate again, considering it from a totally different perspective—through the eyes of a sniper. He was looking for his best vantage point. Nobody said anything as he thought. Finally, he pointed to a spot on the edge of the estate.

"Right there. That's the best spot for me."

Angelino nodded. "How long will it take you to work your way there through that scrub from say here?" he asked, pointing to another spot on the map. "That seems to be the closest place we could drop you off without drawing attention."

"How far is that?" Ed asked.

"Quarter of a mile? Maybe a little more."

"Hmmm," Ed said, rubbing his chin. "That's rough terrain. Not sure about the cover. Give me an hour just to be safe. I'm well past crawling in a yard at a time on my belly like in Vietnam. But they won't be looking for me from the back of the property since it borders the Kingery Mining Property. Looks like their security is focused mostly on that gate at the front of the property. We've got radios?"

"Of course," Angelino said.

"Okay, once I'm in place, how far is my nest from the guard shack and this outbuilding we're worried about?"

"Way too far for a Model 700 Remington .308," Angelino said. "That's well out of the effective range even for a dead shot like you."

"That's a problem," Ed said, taking another look at the map. "I'm going to have to get a lot closer then."

"Maybe not," Carl said.

He pointed to one of the Four Horsemen who vanished up the hall. The man returned moments later with a large black case, which Angelino set on the kitchen island. Ed stepped forward, flipped the latches, opened the lid, and leaned over to get a better look. Then he whistled low.

"You know what that is?" Tony asked.

"It's illegal. That's what it is," Ed said.

"What?" Tony said in feigned shock. "We have illegal weapons? I had no idea!"

Carl snorted.

"That thing looks nasty," Levi said, walking around to take a closer look.

"It is," Ed said. "Probably one of the finest sniper rifles in the world. It'll double the range of my old Model 700."

Ray took out one of the rounds that was stuck into the foam and held it up. Levi wasn't sure he'd ever seen a rifle shell that size. It was nearly four inches long—more than twice the length and diameter of the .308.

"That's a .50 caliber," Ray said.

"It's a cannon," Ed said. "It's an M107, which is a .50 caliber semi-automatic, effective to about 2,000 yards—well over a mile. And it weighs, what—thirty pounds?"

"That's close," Angelino said. "They call it a light .50 for a reason. And those rounds are armor piecing. It's amazing what they'll go through. Very effective at stopping vehicles since that round will go right into an engine block. No problem."

"I've never fired anything quite like this," Ed said.

"You have a place where we could put a few rounds down the barrel?" Angelino asked. "I think you'll find that somebody with your skill won't have much trouble adapting to it."

"With a round that large, it probably kicks like a mule," Ed said.

"Quite the contrary," Carl said. "It's an amazing piece of technology, and I'd be willing to bet it recoils about the same as your .308. And unlike your bolt action, it's a clip fed semi-automatic. You can fire as fast as you can squeeze off rounds."

Ed nodded. "I have a place close by where we can go to fire it—out on the Kingery Mining Property."

"I'll take you there," Angelino said.

"But there's another problem," Ed said. "A .50 caliber is loud. The sound of this rifle is going to echo for miles. When I fire this a few times out at the Franklin Estate, somebody is going to hear it. We might wind up with law enforcement issues."

"We're not too worried about that. Show him, Angelino," Carl said.

Angelino pointed at the iPad map. "Look right there. What does that look like to you?"

Squinting at a structure towards the back of the property, Ed said, "Looks like a firing range. Okay, I get it. There aren't any close neighbors, and anyone who happens to be around would most likely be used to hearing gun fire from the Franklin Estate. But having a rifle range right on the property still concerns me. That security force might be very well trained."

"I wouldn't worry about those guys. They're weekend warriors," Carl said with a derisive snort. "You know better than anyone that practice on a range doesn't translate into skill on the battlefield."

"That's exactly right," Ed said with a nod.

Tony said to Angelino, "Take Ed out and have him get familiar with that rifle. He's key in getting this to work. Be back here in one hour."

"Won't take that long," Ed said, grinning tightly. "You going to be okay with this, Ray?"

Ray nodded. "I can't believe I'm saying this, but Tony is right. It's life or death for all of us. I'm just a little worried about the aftermath."

Tony chuckled. "That's the easy part. That's my specialty. If I weren't good at the aftermath, I'd have gone to prison fifty years ago."

"All right, then. Let's go get Tori and Adam out of there," Ray said, looking at Levi.

Levi eyes clouded as he nodded.

Tony stood up. "We've got preparations to make while Ed and Angelino are gone. Let's go out in the carriage house. One hour, Angelino. No more. Then get Ed geared up and drop him off. Ed, when you're set up, let us know. You'll have a comm link."

"I've done this a few times before. It's just been a while," Ed said. "I know the drill."

Chapter 68

Tori stared at her captor—a huge, muscular man with deep-set dark eyes and a broad nose. He stood beside a window with a blind which kept her from knowing what time it might be. The man stared back at her, seemingly unconcerned that he was holding a woman and her small son hostage. She'd heard the instructions he'd been given just outside the door.

"Don't take your eyes off her for one second," the voice had said sternly. "Underestimating her would be a mistake."

Her captors had already gotten into the house before she'd been awakened by Rosco's furious barking and Levi's shouting. She'd rushed down the stairs. Whoever grabbed her was in the hallway. She'd been over-powered, handcuffed and blindfolded, then forced into a vehicle and whisked off. She knew they weren't far from Twin Rivers because they hadn't gone far when the car stopped. She'd been led up a few stairs into a house and then up two short flights of stairs. When he'd removed her blindfold, she saw Adam, still sound asleep, lying on the bed.

Tori had no idea where she was. The large bedroom had been stripped of most of the furniture. Indentations in the carpet indicated where pieces had once been placed. The wallpaper was a bit brighter where pictures had once hung. All that was in the room was a double bed and a wooden chair on which she sat.

At least she was fully clothed. She'd been so tired when they'd gotten back from Ray's that she'd fallen asleep in her clothes. That was lucky. Otherwise, she'd be sitting in the chair in her underwear.

Time passed as the man stared, Adam slept , and Tori sat, her heart pounding as she looked at her beautiful son.

"Are you afraid of me or something?" she finally asked her guard.

His impassive expression never changed.

"I have to go to the bathroom," she said.

He pointed to a door. She stood and walked over to it. After opening the door, she flipped on the switch. When she started to close the door, the man's foot stopped it.

"You're going to watch me?" she said.

He nodded.

"You must think I'm very dangerous," she said. "All that's in here is a sink, a toilet, and a roll of toilet paper. Is it the toilet paper that concerns you?"

He stared at her blankly.

"I don't have to go that bad," she said.

He shrugged and backed into the bedroom, never taking his eyes off her.

"You are afraid of me," she said, smiling as she returned to her chair. "I'm just a girl, you big sissy."

No reaction. She couldn't tell if he was intelligent or not. What worried her was that he was big, and he wasn't about to take his eyes off her, not even for a second. Coming up with a plan was going to be hard with his eyes never wavering.

"It's hot in here," she said, winking at him with her deep-green eyes as she pulled her kinky blonde hair back. "Is there a thermostat you could turn down?"

No reaction.

Reaching up to unbutton her shirt, she said "You don't mind if I take my shirt off, do you? I've got a bra on."

His eyes never left hers as she peeled off her shirt.

"That's better, but I'm still hot. Maybe the jeans? But I can't remember if I wore panties last night," she said with a giggle.

She reached down, unbuckled her belt, and pulled it through the loops. Then she slowly undid the top button on her jeans.

No reaction from her captor.

"Well, crap," she said, glancing down. "I didn't wear panties."

His eyes never left hers, but sweat suddenly popped up on his brow. There it is, she thought. He can be distracted. She rolled up her belt and placed it on the floor beside her.

"Well, I can't really take off my jeans, can I?" she said. "I'll just take off my shoes and socks instead."

As she slipped her feet out of her shoes and pulled off her socks, the guard wiped sweat off his forehead. His stare shifted from her face to her bra. She leaned back in the chair and let her eyes go heavy. She'd let him stare while she pretended to doze. She hoped that Adam would stay asleep. He'd been up late. Usually, he couldn't be awakened with a marching band until after nine in the morning.

Tori began to breathe in and out slowly and deeply. She could see the man's outline through the slits in her eyes. When Adam turned over, she saw the man's head move in his direction. He thought she was asleep.

Now she began to work out a crude plan. It was unlikely to work, but it was better to try than to— She stopped that thought, her heart thudding in her chest. She wouldn't think about what was likely to happen. She'd think only about a plan.

Chapter 69

When Ed reached the top of the ridge, he stopped to catch his breath. It was brutally cold, and the wind stung his nose. He couldn't yet see the Franklin Estate, but he knew it was below him. Slowly and methodically, he began working his way down the embankment, which was not only steep but also covered in a tangle of brush and briars. Ed stopped often to pull the branches loose from the white camo fatigue jacket he'd been given to wear. He glanced at his watch. There was no need to rush. One slip and the plan would be in serious jeopardy.

About half way down, the embankment became almost a vertical cliff he'd be unable to descend. He sat on a rocky outcrop from which he could now clearly see the back of the Franklin Estate. It looked to be too far away for his purposes.

But he was carrying a very different rifle now. He pulled the range finder out of his pocket and looked through it to the guard house at the gate. It was about 1,600 yards from his position, just shy of a mile. He smiled. That was well within the effective range of this rifle. The house was about three hundred yards closer, and what they believed was the guards' barracks was in between those two ranges.

I can work with that, Ed thought as slipped the rifle off his shoulder and flipped out the bipod legs. He lay down on his belly in the snow, flipped the scope covers open, and sighted all three of the areas where he was likely going to need to do his work. From his position, he could easily shift the rifle barrel to sight all three places without moving his body. Even with the new rifle and the excellent position with plenty of scrub to conceal him, Ed wasn't sure this plan to rescue Adam and Tori was going to work. So much could go wrong. Of course, there was little choice. Ed pulled several clips out of the cargo pockets in his jacket and laid them on the ground near his right hand. He seated one of the clips into the receiver and chambered a round into the rifle. He was ready.

Ed pulled his glove off and stuck his finger in his ear, pushing the tiny button on his earpiece that turned on his comm link. "This is Vader. I'm in position."

"I copy you, Vader," Tony said. "Skywalker, are you ready?"

"I'm not very fond of these handles," Levi said, "but I'm ready."

"Let's light this candle," Tony said.

"Roger that," Levi said.

* * *

Levi shifted down when he felt the tail of Old Blue slip on the snow-covered road. He was driving on what had once been an old access road on the west side of the Kingery Mining Property which abutted the Franklin Estate. Now the road was a solidly paved private driveway. As he rounded a tight curve, he saw the gate, which sent a ripple of fear down his spine. His stomach rolled. He felt naked, going into this situation without the Webley beneath his coat.

Rosco was sitting beside him on the seat with his head out the window. The heater was good in the old Ford F-100 but not good enough to overcome the air rushing in from the open window on the passenger side. Rosco was wearing a ridiculous sweater that Tori had given him. Rosco didn't like it, but the windchill was well into the negative numbers.

Levi rolled to a stop in front of the gate and honked. A white security van was parked along the shoulder of the road outside the gate, but nobody was in it. Levi started to honk again when the surprised face of a man appeared in the window of the guard house. He held a finger up—the universal sign for just a minute.

As Levi waited, he said. "You can still hear me okay?"

"I hear you," Ed said.

"I wish we'd fitted this ear thingy in my right ear. If the guard sees it, we're done," Levi muttered as the guard walked out of the guard shack, hastily zipping up his jacket.

"He won't see it," Angelino said. "Don't worry about it."

"Morning," the guard said as Levi cranked the window down. He surveyed Levi and then the inside of his truck. "What can I do for you?"

"I need to see Chuck Franklin right now," Levi said, trying to sound panicked.

The guard looked at his watch. "Do you know what time it is?"

"I do," Levi said urgently. "My name is Levi Garvey. I've known Chuck since we were kids. This is a matter of life and death, or I'd never ask you to wake him. I really need his help."

"Well, he is an early riser," the guard said. "You're that writer, aren't you?"

"That's right," Levi said.

"Let me call the house."

"Please make it fast. Like I said, time is of the essence here."

"I'll be right back," the guard said.

Chapter 70

Chuck Franklin burst into his father's office. A fire was roaring in the fireplace. His father was seated behind his desk, wearing a black silk robe and eating his breakfast off a silver tray. He was an obese man with fingers like small sausages. His thin black hair was combed back over a shining scalp. With a bored expression, he regarded his son.

"Levi Garvey is at the gate," Chuck said, running a nervous hand through his blonde hair.

Charles could hardly hide his disgust as he poured coffee out of a silver service into a china cup, which looked like part of a child's toy teaset in his huge hands.

"And?" he said as he added cream and stirred his coffee.

The bright clinking of the silver spoon against the sides of the china cup was the only sound in the library besides the occasional crackle of the fire and the steady tick-tock of an antique clock on the mantle.

"What do we do?" Chuck said. "He told Lonnie it was a matter of life and death."

"Let him in," Charles said as a smile played at the corners of his mouth.

"Let him in?" Chuck said, wide-eyed.

"Why do you think he's here?" Charles said, sipping his coffee.

"We've got his wife and his son upstairs," Chuck snapped.

"Considering what I paid for your education, you can be quite a disappointment at times," Charles said coldly.

He'd never been close to or even fond of his spoiled son. He was a dispassionate, hard man.

"Yes, you've made that abundantly clear many times," Chuck said.

"He has no idea Tori and his son are here. He's come for your help," Charles said. "Let him in. Find out what he wants. Make sure he passes through security, however. Too many have made the mistake of underestimating the Garveys, haven't they?"

Chuck nodded.

"Find out what he knows and who he has told," Charles continued. "Find out where that ledger is if he brings it up. We need to get that. I'm guessing he may have brought it with him since he's here for your help, after all. Seems like he's made this a lot easier for us. After you're done with him, we'll dispatch the Garveys and then clean up the rest of your mess in town—that uncle of his and the police chief."

Chuck sighed. "Do you still think that's necessary?"

"I didn't make this mess," Charles growled when he saw the weakness on his son's face. "You made this mess, and I'm left to clean it up. It wasn't enough that you plowed all the cheerleaders at Twin Rivers High School. Christina White wasn't hot enough for you? You had to bang all the club strippers, hookers, and porn starlets, too? Was it worth it, Chuck? Was Selena Fine that good? Or Chastity Lynn? Or Lisa Love? You never thought about your future when you were making those dirty movies, did you? But now it's a big problem, isn't it? You've got a straight shot at the United States Senate. That's because of me. And I need you there. So suck it up, Chuck! Show a little backbone while I clean up your mess. One day, when you're sitting in the White House behind the desk in the Oval Office, you'll thank me for this. Now go let Levi Garvey in so we can be done with this mess once and for all."

Chuck had turned to leave when his father added, "And Chuck, try hard not to screw this up."

Quickly, Chuck left his father's office.

* * *

"I've been waiting a long time," Levi muttered as he strummed his fingers nervously on the steering wheel.

"They're arranging your reception," Tony said in his ear. "Hard telling how this is going to go down. Just remember that they aren't planning on letting you leave, so be ready for anything. It could happen the second you walk in the door."

"I'll be ready," Levi said, glancing at Rosco.

Suddenly, the gate began to roll open. The guard waved him through.

"Chuck's expecting you," he shouted. "Just drive up to the front of the main house. He'll meet you there."

Levi waved as he drove on by the small guard shack.

"There are three guards in the guard shack, not two," he said once he was well past it. "I'm coming up on the guard house now. It sits back from the road about three hundred yards from the guard shack. There's nobody outside. No way to determine how many guards we're talking about."

"There's a guy on the road walking towards the main house," Ed said in his ear as he peered through his rifle scope. "Do you see him?"

"I do," Levi said.

"It's a cold morning," Ed said.

"Got it," Levi said.

He slowed to a stop and cranked his window down. "Morning," he said to the man.

"Hello," the man said, looking at him suspiciously. He was young and fresh-faced—maybe in his mid-twenties.

"That's the main house up there?" Levi asked, pointing.

"Yeah," he said.

"That's where I'll find Chuck Franklin?"

"Yes," the man said. "He lives in the main house."

"I thought maybe he lived in that house over there," Levi said. "I didn't realize he lived with his father."

"That's the security building back there," the man said, chuckling.

"Oh, it looks like a residence to me. You want a ride up to the main house?" Levi asked. "It sure is cold this morning."

The man looked at him questioningly, then glanced at Rosco who was panting in the seat next to Levi.

"Don't worry about Rosco," Levi said. "He looks more intimidating than he actually is."

"Okay," he said, "if you don't mind. It is cold."

"Hop in," Levi said.

The man crossed in front of the truck, opened the passenger door, and started to climb in.

"Move over, Rosco," Levi said.

"Nice dog," the man said, obviously still a little intimated by the huge German shepherd regardless of what Levi had said.

"He's harmless," Levi said. "He's just very friendly. You said that was the security building back there. Is that what you are—security?"

"Yes, I am," he said.

"You worked here very long?"

"A couple of months."

"So you live there in the security building?" Levi asked.

"Yes, except when I have days off. Then I leave. But this is onsite 24-hour armed security. Good guys to work with. All former military like me. I just got out of the Marine Corps in September." He paused, then added, "You sure ask a lot of questions."

"Sorry, I'm a writer. It's force of habit," Levi said with a smile.

"I thought you looked familiar. You're Levi Garvey, aren't you?"

"That's right. I've known Chuck since grade school. Franklins are a good family. This sounds like a good job."

"It is," the man said. "I was lucky to have a chance to join the team. Mr. Franklin calls us his 'Dirty Dozen.'"

Levi smiled. There were twelve. Those were damn good odds with surprise on their side.

"Of course, that nickname never made sense to me—there are actually eighteen of us."

Levi's smile faltered a bit. "Eighteen," he said, "that seems like a lot."

"Three shifts, six on a shift," he said as Levi rolled to a stop in front of the main house. "Thanks for the lift."

"No problem," Levi said.

Chapter 71

Tori continued to watch her captor through the slits in her eyelids. She wasn't sure how much time had passed, but she thought it'd been several hours since she'd been brought there. Convinced that she was asleep, her captor had actually gone to the window twice to peek out around the edges of the blinds. The last time he'd pulled the blind back, she'd noticed the sun was up. She'd considered rushing him but decided that wasn't a good plan. He was huge. She'd been thinking about the bathroom though. It'd been stripped the same way the room had, but she remembered something as she thought about her options. They'd forgotten about one thing she might be able to use to her advantage.

She decided it was time to wake up. Raising her arms over her head, she stretched as her eyes fluttered open.

"Now it's cold in here," she said as she picked up her shirt and pulled it back on. "And now I really have to pee."

He nodded again towards the bathroom door.

"Must you really watch me?"

He nodded.

Tori glanced over at Adam and then at him. She smiled as she twisted a coil of her kinky blonde hair around one of her fingers.

"He's asleep," Tori said, a sly smile on her face. "He'll be out for some time yet."

The man glanced at the sleeping baby, then back at her. It was the first time he'd allowed himself to take his eyes off her—at least when he knew she was awake.

"I mean if you have to watch me," Tori said suggestively, "there's no reason why we couldn't close that door for a little while."

His eyes widened a bit. Then he slowly shook his head.

She shrugged. "Just a thought. I'm bored."

She walked to the bathroom door. He followed her. For a moment, she thought he'd reconsidered her proposal. Her heart sank when he stopped at the door and motioned towards the toilet.

"Your loss," she said, annoyed, as she unbuttoned her jeans and sat down on the stool.

* * *

Chuck Franklin descended the steps to greet Levi in the driveway as the guard stepped out of the truck and quickly disappeared around the side of the house.

"Levi. What's wrong? The gate guard said it was a matter of life and death?" Chuck said as he offered Levi his hand.

As they shook hands, Chuck smiled his award-winning smile, which revealed his perfectly capped teeth and the dimples that had made him so popular with the cheerleaders back in school.

"Is there somewhere we can talk privately?" Levi said tensely as Rosco sat down beside his leg.

"Certainly," Chuck said, his smile fading. "I'm sorry about yesterday."

Levi touched the black circle under his eye and winced. Chuck made no comment about the other obvious damage to Levi's face.

"I deserved it. I hope you won't hold those things I said to Nichole against me. I could really use your help. I don't know who else to go to."

"Of course not. Come on in," Chuck said. "We'll talk in the library."

Levi followed him up the steps and through the massive door into a small room where they met a man in a dark suit.

"This is Levi Garvey," Chuck said to the man. "He's an old friend."

"I'm sorry, but Mr. Franklin is very strict about this," he said.

"I apologize, Levi," Chuck said. "I'm afraid my father requires all visitors to be screened before entering the house. No exceptions."

"No problem," Levi said. "What do you need me to do?"

"It's not that difficult. Just stand with your legs apart and your arms out straight from your sides," the guard said as he took a security wand from the cabinet. "This will take just a second."

Levi complied. The guard waved the wand up and down his front, around his ankles, and inside his legs. It buzzed at his pocket.

"Change?" the guard asked.

"Sorry," Levi said, pulling his keys and change out of his pockets and placing it all in a dish that was obviously there for that purpose.

The guard waved his wand a few more times, then nodded. "Thank you, Mr. Garvey. That's all."

The security man pulled a key out of his pocket and unlocked the second door. Levi followed Chuck into a wide foyer. They went down a side hallway to the left. Light streamed in through tall windows on one side, illuminating expensive art on the walls. Rosco's nails echoed on the tile floors.

"In here, Levi," Chuck said, opening a tall set of double doors.

"Wow, I thought I had a nice library," Levi said.

The large room had heavy-beamed high ceilings and wood-paneled columns. The grand piano in the corner looked small in the huge space. There were lots of nooks with overstuffed leather chairs. Only one wall was covered in book shelves, but they were full of thousands of volumes. Many looked like law books.

"Let's talk over here," Chuck said as a man rose from one of the chairs and walked up to them. "Levi, this is my personal assistant, Jack Reynolds."

"I'd hoped we could talk in private," Levi said,

"You can trust Jack implicitly," Chuck said. "He's one of the few people on earth I do trust."

Levi looked him over. Jack didn't look much like a personal assistant. Instead, he looked an awful lot like the kind of thug Tony O'Malley would call a Horseman. Levi quickly scanned his suit for any telltale signs of a weapon, but the man didn't appear to be armed.

Levi took off his Panama hat and tossed it onto the back of one of the leather chairs.

"Very well," Levi said. "I need your help, Chuck. Somebody has kidnapped Tori and Adam. The kidnappers made it clear no police and no tricks."

"Oh my God!" Chuck said. His reaction sounded flat. "I'll be happy to do anything I can to help."

"We were on the trail of a murderer," Levi said. "Obviously, we were closer than we thought."

"That porn business," Chuck said. "I've been hearing about that. Peter Long?"

"That's right," Levi said. "We were able to steal one of his ledgers. It details all the people he was blackmailing. But the ledger has only numbers and dates and amounts—no names. Even so, the kidnappers want it in exchange for Tori and Adam."

"Do you have the ledger?" Chuck asked.

To Levi, the question sounded a bit overeager.

"That's the problem," Levi said, hoping his face looked like that of a distraught husband and father and not that of a man ready to take down a killer. "We turned it over to the FBI. They're well on the way to figuring out who the murderer is. I don't have anything to trade."

Chuck glanced at Jack as his brow knitted. That news wasn't what he wanted to hear. After a split second, the worried look on his face melted.

"What can I do?" Chuck asked.

"I could use a drink," Levi said. "I've been up half the night."

"Absolutely," Chuck said, walking to three crystal decanters sitting on a sideboard along the wall. "Whiskey?"

"That would be fine," Levi said, sitting down on one of the overstuffed leather chairs.

Nonchalantly, Jack moved directly behind Levi—completely out of his peripheral vision. Once Chuck was done talking, Levi knew he'd never leave the library alive.

"So what are you going to do?" Chuck said as he poured the whiskey into a crystal tumbler.

"Well," Levi said. "I thought I'd just go and get them."

He stroked Rosco's head that lay in his lap. Rosco was growling low in his throat. Levi could feel it more than he could hear it. The dog was watching Jack move behind him.

"That seems like a very dangerous idea," Chuck said as he handed Levi his drink. "You could get them killed. And there's another problem. You don't know who is holding them, do you?"

Levi raised his glass, then looked at it.

"Oh, sorry, Chuck. I can't drink whiskey neat. Do you have any ice?"

Chuck sighed as Levi handed the drink back to him. He walked over to the sideboard, opened the bottom panel, and pulled a cube tray out of the mini-fridge concealed there.

"So how will you go after the kidnappers if you don't know who they are?" Chuck asked again.

"Oh, I've got a good idea who the murderer is," Levi said. "I have for some time."

Chuck glanced over his shoulder, his gaze more directed at the man behind Levi than at Levi himself. Levi sensed Jack was getting closer to the back of his chair. Rosco's muscles were tense, like a coiled spring. He sensed it, too.

"Who do you think it is?" Chuck asked as he cracked the ice cube tray and dropped several cubes into the whiskey.

"It's pretty shocking," Levi said as he stroked Rosco's head. "It's you, Chuck."

Chuck froze, his knuckles white around the crystal tumbler. Levi was surprised it didn't shatter from the force.

Chuck laughed tensely. "That's crazy," he said as his hand relaxed and he stirred the drink.

"Is it?" Levi said.

Chuck jumped when he heard the sudden crash behind him. He spun around, holding Levi's drink. Jack was rolling on the floor, moaning. Levi was standing over him with a broken table lamp in his left hand and his Webley in his right. The ice cubes rattled inside the glass that Chuck held in his shaking hand. Chuck stared at the gun.

"How in the hell—?"

"You really should have your security people screen dogs, too. Did you think Rosco was wearing that sweater because it's so pretty?"

Levi raised the Webley, cocked the hammer back, and aimed it at the center of Chuck's face. "I'm going to ask you one time and one time only. Where are Tori and Adam?"

What happened next shocked Levi. Chuck Franklin's eyes rolled up in his head, and he fainted.

"You've got to be shitting me," Levi said.

"What happened?" Tony's voice said in his ear.

"He fainted!" Levi exclaimed.

* * *

Ed's heart sank when he heard what Levi said. The plan had just unraveled. They were now on Plan B, and Plan B was a terrible plan from the beginning. Even as he settled in behind the scope of the rifle and focused in on his first targets, he knew this was going to end badly.

In his ear, he heard Carl screaming, "Go! Go! Go!"

Even from more than a mile away, in the dry cold air of winter, Ed could hear the two V-8 turbo diesel engines scream as they raced towards the gate of the Franklin Estate.

All hell was about to break loose. And they were about to lose the advantage of surprise.

Chapter 72

Tony O'Malley winced as he bounced around in the backseat of the second Humvee which was roaring down the road towards the gate. Angelino had climbed into the front seat, leaving him in the back with Ray Billings. Carl was driving. The remaining Horsemen were in the lead Humvee.

"Give me that," Tony said to Ray, pointing towards the floor.

Ray picked up Tony's ten-gauge shotgun and handed it to him. When Tony struggled to open the window in the old combat Humvee, as it bounced and rocked, Ray leaned over his lap and rolled the window down. Tony pulled the hammers back as they rounded a curve. The gate was less than 300 yards away. Two men ran out of the guard shack and took positions on either side of the road. The front Humvee was about to be hit by a monstrous barrage of gunfire from the AK-47s the men were bracing.

"Where's our secret weapon?" Tony yelled.

"I got this," Ed said calmly.

From nearly a mile away, Ed was looking through his scope at the two guards on the road. The one on the left was seating a clip in his weapon. The one of the right was pulling the lever back to load a round. Both were seconds from opening up on the lead Humvee.

Forty-five years melted away in a moment as Ed's instincts kicked in. Combat. The smell of cordite and napalm. The panic of men about to die, calling for support in terrified voices on the radio. Ed focused on the man on the right. One shot. One kill, he thought.

Slowly, his finger pulled back the trigger. The explosive report of the rifle shattered the silence of the cold winter morning. Without seeing, he knew the first gunman was down. He focused on the second, who'd paused to look at his partner. Ed squeezed off the second shot.

Tony smiled as both gunmen fell in a spray of crimson from the high-powered rounds. The first Humvee crashed through the gate and roared towards the main house. As Tony's Humvee bumped over the broken gate, the third guard ran out of the shack and leveled his automatic rifle towards them.

"Shit," Carl said.

Suddenly, an explosion sounded in the backseat. The guard jerked backwards and fell as he was hit in the chest by a double round from an old ten-gauge. Ray was stunned by the explosion of Tony's shotgun inside the vehicle. Tony grinned at him as he broke open the shotgun and pulled out the smoking shells.

"More," he said, holding his hand out.

His ears ringing, Ray looked at him blankly. Then he nodded. He grabbed the box off the floor and handed two more shells to Tony. Quickly, Tony loaded the rounds and snapped the shotgun closed.

Chapter 73

Tori hadn't stopped talking for a solid hour. Her sweating, red-faced captor was looking more and more distracted by the minute. Soon he'd get angry. That's what she needed. She needed for him to get angry because people make stupid mistakes when they're angry.

During the hour since he'd watched her in the bathroom, she'd described in explicit detail all the things he'd missed by turning her down. She'd talked about every dirty sexual act she could think of.

"You have a girlfriend, I assume," she said cheerfully. "Well, even if you have a boyfriend, and maybe you do, he'd like this one. Now you do this when she, or he, isn't expecting it. When people are in long relationships, they tend to fall into patterns in the bedroom. Sex can get kind of boring. Sometimes you just have to shake it up and do something unexpected."

Her captor glared at her.

"Anyway, what you do is you put a little lube in your hand, something like KY."

Her captor shifted uncomfortably from one foot to the other.

"I like this stuff called 'Joy Jelly' because it's flavored. I like the banana, but they make a nice kiwi flavor, too. Of course, a flavored lube is advantageous because for the first part of the surprise, you'll be using your hands, but later, when they get over that first surprise, you're going to use your tongue—"

"You need to shut up," the captor snapped.

"You can talk!" Tori laughed. "I knew it! So is it a boyfriend or a girlfriend? I don't judge. I'm heterosexual. Well, for the most part, you see I had this roommate named Karen back when I was in college—"

"No seriously," he growled. "Shut up!"

"I'm sorry," Tori said. "I tend to talk when I get bored. And I don't get turned down for sex very often. I mean I'm getting older, but I'm still in pretty good shape for middle-aged, don't you think?"

"I've about had it with you, lady," he said, reaching into his jacket and pulling out a revolver. "Now shut up!"

She put her hands up. "Sorry, I just figured any man who turns down a willing female must be gay or something."

"I'm not gay!" he shouted, his face even redder.

Suddenly, they heard a loud crack outside the window. It sounded like a rifle. He turned towards the window.

"What in the hell was that?" Tori said.

Seconds later, they heard the same explosive report again.

"I'm dying of thirst," Tori said as he peered out the blinds. "I've been here for hours, and you haven't even offered me a bottle of water."

Suddenly, she rose and walked to the bathroom.

"Hey, wait!" he said from the window.

Tori was already in the bathroom.

"I'm just getting a drink from the faucet," she called back.

He rushed to the bathroom door. When he stepped inside, Tori slugged him with the heavy porcelain lid of the toilet tank. The gun clattered to the floor as he stumbled back. Blood gushed from his shattered nose and flowed down his face.

"Damn you," he said, spitting out a spray of blood.

He glanced down at the gun that lay on the floor between them.

"Go for it," he challenged her. "Go ahead!"

"I don't think so," Tori said. "You're still stronger than I am."

"You're right," he said. "Take a couple of steps back."

Tori stepped back. When he leaned down to pick up the gun, Tori's hand suddenly whipped out from behind her back.

The point of her little strip tease earlier had been to get her belt loose. She'd rolled it up and put it on the floor. Just now, when he was distracted, she'd picked it up, rushed into the bathroom, and hidden it in her back pocket.

She swung the leather belt at his head as hard as she could. The heavy silver buckle caught the side of his head, opening up a gash in his cheek. As he stumbled back towards the window, she grabbed the wooden chair and swung it. It connected with his abdomen solidly and broke apart. He bent over double at the waist, gasping for breath. As he started to stand erect, she sprinted towards him, her head low, and rammed into his stomach. He fell back against the window. The window shattered, and in a split second, his huge body disappeared. Tori heard the heavy thud when it hit the ground below.

She leaned against the wall for a moment, trying to catch her breath. Then she moved to the window. He was lying on the concrete patio a story down, not moving.

Behind her, Adam squirmed around as if he were about to wake up. With tears running down her cheeks, she sat on the edge of the bed and rubbed his back. He stretched, then flipped over, and fell back to sleep.

She jumped when somebody tapped lightly on the door.

"Randy? Everything okay in there?"

Tori retrieved the revolver off the floor.

"You'd better come in here," she said, trying to talk like a man. "This bitch has gone crazy!"

Tori stared at the deadbolt on the door. It seemed like a long time before she heard the key in the door and saw the lock turn.

The second the lock was open, she leveled the gun at the door and fired three shots through it. She heard the man fall on the other side. Opening the door a crack, she looked out. The guy she'd shot appeared to be dead. She glanced up the hall to the top of the stairwell. She could hear footsteps going up and down those stairs.

Then she heard a shout. "Hey, the prisoner is loose!"

She leaned out further into the hall. A man was standing in fatigues, pointing at her. Quickly, Tori closed the door. She couldn't lock it since it locked from the outside, so she leaned against the door and wedged her feet against the carpet. Her heart was pounding as she struggled to breathe. Suddenly, the door moved. Somebody was pushing on it hard. When he'd apparently put his shoulder into the door, it opened a little more, and she lost her footing. Seeing a hand wrapped around the edge of the door, she lunged back as hard as she could, pinching it. He cursed loudly, and his hand disappeared.

Tori looked at her sleeping son, tears welling again in her eyes. She knew they were in trouble. She had no idea how many men were rushing towards the door at that moment, but what she knew for sure was that she had only three rounds of ammo in the revolver—likely not nearly enough.

* * *

As the two Humvees raced towards the main house, Ed watched the security office, figuring that the resistance would come from there. But nothing was happening. Ed shifted his scope to the house as the Four Horsemen in the first Humvee skidded to a stop and poured out of the vehicle. He couldn't see the front door from his vantage point. He wouldn't be of much help to them as they tried to enter the house—one of several problems with Plan B. He began scanning the house for security. The rooftop. The garage. He saw nothing. But as his scope left the rooftop, he saw motion in one of the windows from the edge of the scope and trailed back to see what it was. He could see only shadows through the blinds. But it looked like there was a fight taking place in a second story room of the Franklin Estate.

Then he saw the most remarkable thing—a man flew through a window and crashed to the ground, taking the window blinds with him.

That's got to be Tori, Ed thought as his heart beat quickened with hope.

Chapter 74

Levi couldn't wake Chuck, so he tied him up quickly with curtain cords. Jack was sitting on the floor, rubbing the side of his head, the broken the lamp nearby. Rosco was growling at him.

"Morning, buttercup," Levi said, standing over him with the Webley leveled at his head. Levi couldn't believe how naturally that phase had escaped his lips—the same phrase Tony had used in his dungeon room. "Get up!"

Jack's eyes were wide as he slowly climbed to his feet.

"Now take off your pants."

"What?"

"You heard me," Levi said, pulling the hammer back on the Webley.

Jack quickly worked the buckle on his pants and slid them off.

"Give them to me," Levi said.

"What in the hell is this about?" Jack stuttered as he tossed his pants to Levi.

"It's simple. Somebody kicked the hell out of my dog a few hours ago. You ever met my dog, Rosco, before?"

Jack began backing up as Rosco matched his steps—his growling ramped up, the fur on his back up.

"Rosco seems to know you. Maybe he believes you were the guy that kicked him in the head. Of course, because he's got a sore mouth, you can't really expect Rosco to bite all the way through your pants, can you?"

"Whoa," Jack said, his hands flying to cover himself below his waist. "Just wait. I can help you. Your wife is upstairs—I don't know in what room!"

"Thank you. Now talk to the dog," Levi said as he collected his Panama hat and strode to the library door.

Levi paused in the doorway. Jack inched slowly towards the corner of the library. When Jack could go no further, he scrambled onto the piano bench and then to the top of the grand piano.

"Levi, please," Jack pleaded.

"Rosco!" Levi commanded. "Get him!"

"No! Levi! Wait!"

Levi shut the door. As he rushed up the hall, he could hear Rosco snarling and growling and Jack's frantic cries for help.

* * *

Tori heard more feet running on the other side of the bedroom door. She took Adam off the bed, laid him on a blanket on the bathroom floor, and pulled the door closed. Then she positioned herself across from the bedroom door and knelt on one knee with the revolver. With only three rounds, she'd get the first one or two through the door. She tried not to think about what would happen after those three rounds were gone.

It'd been quiet for a couple of minutes. But they were out there—at least two of them. She could see the shadows of their feet under the door. They meant to take her by surprise. And they nearly did. The door burst open, and two men rushed in. Tori pulled the trigger. The first shot slammed into the wall over their heads. She fired twice more in rapid succession, hitting the first one in. He fell to the floor. She kept pulling the trigger, but it clicked dry.

Realizing she was out of ammo, the second gunman smiled. Tori's heart sank when a third man walked in and looked down at her.

"Sorry, darling," the gunman said as he raised his gun. "Apparently, you've outlived your usefulness."

She saw his finger tighten on the trigger. She lowered her gun and closed her eyes. Suddenly, she heard that distant crack again. Her eyes flew open as the first man fell, a gaping hole in his chest. The man behind him wavered on his feet unsteadily, his face pale. His eyes rolled up as he fell over backwards into the hall.

One shot, two victims? It was a one in a million shot. Then she understood. I'm being rescued, she thought as a shaky smile crossed her face.

She rushed over to the window. Only one person could've made that shot. She couldn't see anybody, but she knew he was out there somewhere, probably watching her through his scope.

Ed smiled from nearly a mile away as he saw Tori send him a message. Holding up two fingers, then one, she sent him a message.

Ed leaned back from his scope and wiped tears from his eyes. "I've found Tori. Second floor, back of the house, first room on the left."

Chapter 75

When Levi heard that Ed had located Tori, he ran up the hall towards the front door where he'd entered. He heard gunfire as he reached the end of the long hall.

"Levi, where are you?" Angelino said in his ear. "We can't get in the damn door. We're pinned down behind the vehicles."

Levi slipped into the foyer and peeked into the small security room where he'd been screened for weapons. The inner door was closed, but there was a window in the door. The guard was firing through a small opening beside the door, which was obviously reinforced and armored. Rounds were hitting it from the outside.

Levi tried the knob to the security room door, but it was locked The glass, however, looked like standard double-paned glass. Levi stepped back, raised the Webley, and fired at the guard through the glass. The glass shattered, and the guard slumped over. Levi knocked the rest of the glass out of the frame, reached through, and unlocked the door.

"Cease fire," Levi said. "The guard is dead, and I'm unlocking the door."

Levi walked across the small security room to a panel beside the door. It was a very simple panel with two buttons—one red and one green. The red button was illuminated. After Levi pushed the green button, he heard the heavy door bolts clunk open.

When he opened the door and stepped out onto the porch, he said to the men hunkered down behind the vehicles, "I'm guessing you're not here to sell Girl Scout cookies."

* * *

Ed had been watching the security building closely. He just couldn't understand the lack of activity there. Surely somebody had triggered an alarm in the house. If there were six on duty and twelve off duty, where was the missing dozen?

As he shifted the scope back towards the main house, he noticed something he hadn't noticed before. The main house was on top of a hill, towering over the rest of the property. The security building was on a much lower elevation. Tracking his scope slowly between the two buildings, he noticed what looked like a retaining wall—a decorative accent that stretched between the security building and the house. Oh, crap, that's no retaining wall, he thought.

"We've got a problem," Ed said. "There's a tunnel between the security building and the main house. There's a good chance the rest of the security team is already in the house. Be careful. You're walking right into a trap."

* * *

Tori picked up one of the guns the dead guards had dropped and walked to the bedroom door. She leaned out over the four dead bodies littering the doorway and glanced up the hallway. There were two guards at the top of the stairs, squatting on either side with short-barreled automatic rifles, and she knew why. They knew that, eventually, somebody was going to come up those stairs to rescue her and Adam. It was a trap. Her heart sank when she realized that she and Adam had become bait.

Tori retreated from the doorway, sat down on the bed, and looked at the gun in her hand. She pulled the clip and checked it. It was full. She snapped it back into place, pulled the slider back, and chambered a round.

Ed won't be much help this time, she thought.

* * *

"Keep your eyes open," Carl said as they all stood in the little security room. "You heard what Ed said. They've got a nasty little surprise set up for us somewhere."

"We sure could use a little something to barter with," Levi said. "Chuck is down there in the library, tied up."

"Good idea," Tony said.

"Okay," Carl said, pointing. "You two go with Angelino to get Chuck. You two come with me. We'll find Charles Sr. Levi and Ray, you go find Tori and Adam."

Suddenly, they heard running footsteps coming up the hallway accompanied by snarls and growls. Jack sprinted out into the foyer in his underwear with Rosco on his heels. He never stopped running as he raced up a hallway on the other side of the foyer.

"Rosco!" Levi yelled.

The German shepherd stopped suddenly, sliding around in a full circle on the polished tile floor. Rosco looked up the hallway at the retreating figure he'd been chasing and then back at Levi.

"Come here, Rosco," Levi said. "I need you for something else now."

"What in the hell was that about?" Tony asked, an amused expression on his face.

"Long story," Levi said. "Let's just say it's unwise to kick my dog."

"Who was that?" Carl said.

"His name is Jack," Levi said. "If I were guessing, I'd say he is to Charles Franklin what you are to Tony O'Malley."

"I'll bet I know where he is heading. Come on," Carl said to his two Horsemen. "Let's follow."

"You coming with us?" Levi said, glancing at Tony.

Tony shook his head. Shouldering his shotgun, he said, "I think I'll trail Carl."

Levi and Ray walked out into the enormous foyer with a high ceiling and railing around the top. The stairs were beyond the foyer in a small hallway. They stood at the bottom and looked up. The stairway was broken into two small flights. They could see up only as far as the landing at the top of the first flight. The second flight turned back towards them and up. The top of the stairs, somewhere directly over their heads, was blind to them.

"I don't like this," Ray whispered. "We can't see what's up there. If we climb that first flight—"

"Yeah," Levi whispered back. "Perfect place for that trap. This is where I'd set one. We could get up there and find all twelve of them looking down on us."

Ray glanced down at Rosco. Levi's heart sank. He knew exactly what Ray was thinking.

"No," Levi said.

"She's up there, and so is Adam," Ray said. "There's only one way we're going to know if there is anybody between us and them. We've got to send Rosco up there."

Levi looked down at Rosco and dropped to one knee. Rosco licked the tears off Levi's face as Levi rubbed his ears.

"Levi, we don't have a lot of time," Ray said.

"Okay, Rosco," Levi said, his voice breaking. "Go get Tori!"

Rosco's ears stood straight up. He sniffed the stairs a couple of times, then bounded up.

* * *

"Oh, no," Ed said as a knot formed in his throat.

He could hear Levi and Ray in his ear. He knew what they were going to do.

There were two boulders under the elm tree in the Garvey yard. One read "Rosco the Hunter" and the other "Rosco the Brave." It pained him to think that there might soon be a third, "Rosco the Explorer."

Chapter 76

Tori took a deep breath, then quietly climbed over the dead guards into the hallway. The two men were still stationed on either side of the top of the stairs, staring intently down the staircase. Something was about to happen. She could sense it. One of the guards looked over at the other and held his finger up to his lips. Tori realized that somebody was coming up the stairs to rescue her and Adam—somebody who would be cut down before they reached them.

Quietly, she crept along the wall, her eyes focused on the two gunmen. She didn't see the painting until her shoulder struck the frame, which canted sharply to one side. She froze, but the guards hadn't heard it move. Slowly, she backed up a step, and the painting shifted back to its original position.

Breathing a sigh of relief, she stepped out slightly and walked around the painting. She was just on the other side when it slipped off its nail and crashed to the floor. She startled. Instantly, the two guards whirled around and stared at her, stunned. Then, the one on the far side of the staircase rose and began to shift his automatic rifle around.

Tori pulled the trigger, firing as fast as she could at the two gunmen. In the blur, she couldn't remember if there were nine shots in this particular handgun or fifteen.

* * *

Rosco had bolted halfway up the first flight of stairs when Ray and Levi heard the exchange of gunshots over their heads. They didn't think. They just reacted. Both bolted up right behind the dog.

When they got to the first landing and turned to run up the second flight, Levi tripped over one guard who was rolling down the stairs. Ray kept charging up. In the hallway, Tori's pistol had just clicked empty. She'd killed the first guard, but the second was only wounded in the shoulder. As he swung the rifle around towards her, Ray raised his Glock and fired a single shot. The gunman's black cap flew off when the single round struck him in the head.

Ray climbed the last three or four steps. Tori was on one knee, her head lowered as she gasped for breath. Rosco was licking her face, his tail banging on the floor. Ray's eyes widened when he saw the four dead guards stacked up in the hall behind her.

Tori glanced up at Ray, obviously relieved to see him.

"I thought I'd let you get the last one," Tori said in a voice that didn't sound like her own.

"Yeah," Ray said, glancing back at the dead guard.

When Levi got to the top of the stairs, he froze as if afraid of what he might see. When Tori stood up shakily, he rushed to her.

"I'm fine. I'm fine," she said over and over as she sobbed in his arms.

"Adam?" he asked, his voice husky.

"He's fine, too," she said through her tears.

Ray turned his back to give them a little privacy.

* * *

Carl tried the handle. The door was locked.

"Open it," he snapped to the two Horsemen.

One pulled a shape charge out of his pack and wrapped it around the handle. Then the three of them retreated to a recessed doorway a short distance away. Carl covered his ears.

"Three, two, one," the Horseman said as he squeezed the detonator in his hand.

The explosion was tremendous. Twisted pieces of the door handle flew up the hallway. The two Horsemen rushed through the smoke and were already inside the office when Carl walked through what was left of the door. Charles Franklin was standing behind his massive antique mahogany desk, seemingly unflustered, considering that somebody had just blown up his door. Jack was standing in front of the window behind him.

"Hello, Charles," Carl said.

"Who are you?" Charles snapped.

"I'm an old friend of your brother Bruce," Carl said, "back when we all worked for the same outfit."

Charles's face blanched. "You're from the Chicago Outfit? What's your interest in this?"

When Tony O'Malley walked in with his shotgun on his shoulder, Charles sank down hard onto his desk chair. Jack raised his hands. Everybody knew the face of Tony "The Shotgun" O'Malley. Enjoying the moment, Tony walked casually up to the large desk and ran a finger across the polished top.

"What's my interest in this?" Tony said, glancing at Charles. "Did you think there wouldn't be consequences for trying to frame me with that clever little trick with the mask—for making the police believe the Four Horsemen were responsible for your sloppy work? As you can see from these two fine specimens, I have new Horsemen now. I'm sorry to tell you, Charles, that your career has now come to a bad end. That's what happens when you underestimate your opponent."

Charles's face faded from pale to ghost-white.

"You'll never get out of here alive, Tony," Charles said weakly. "We set a trap for you. You've walked right into it."

Carl and Tony both heard the boots rushing their way on polished tile.

"Then we can all go together. If I don't get out of here alive, neither will you," Tony said, pointing his shotgun at Charles's head. "You have three seconds to call them off."

Charles shook his head defiantly.

"Have it your way then," Tony said with a grin. He pulled the hammers back on the shotgun and stuck the barrel right up against Charles's chest. "You sure about this?"

Charles looked into Tony's cold blue eyes and swallowed hard. Glancing over at Jack, he nodded almost imperceptibly. With a Horseman's rifle pointed at him, Jack reached into his jacket with a shaking hand, and produced a phone.

"Stand down," he said into the phone.

The noise of the running boots in the hallway stopped abruptly.

"That's more like it," Tony said with a smile. "Very smart, Charles, but I'm going to need to hear rifles falling."

Charles nodded at Jack. "Drop all your weapons."

From the office, they heard metal weapons clattering onto the tile floors.

Carl stepped over to Jack and snatched the phone out of his hand.

"Put your hands behind your heads and drop to your knees," Carl said. "Anybody still standing when we come out of here is going to regret it."

Chapter 77

Tony watched as two of the Horsemen searched the last seven guards who were standing against the wall in the entrance foyer with Charles and Jack. Angelino returned with the other two Horsemen, shaking his head.

"There was nobody in the library," he said to Tony.

"Where's Chuck?" Tony snapped angrily at Charles.

"Gone," Charles said flatly.

"What do you mean gone?" Tony growled, raising his shotgun.

"Down the tunnel," Charles said. "You'll find that tunnel runs not only to the security building but all the way out to the gate, and we keep a security vehicle parked outside in case one or both of us need to get out of here."

"Ed?" Tony said to nobody in particular.

Ed had heard the whole exchange. He swung the rifle towards the security shack and looked through his rifle scope.

"Shit," Ed said in Tony's ear. "That security van is gone."

Tony glanced at Carl, who knew that would be a future job for the Horsemen.

"Let me explain how this is going to work," Tony said to the seven remaining guards. "This outfit is under new management. You can work for the new team or go down with the old one. That includes you, Jack. You might be useful since you no doubt know all the ins and outs of Charles's little empire here in River County and beyond."

Jack avoided looking at Charles. "I do, Tony. I'd be happy to join you."

Charles shot an angry glare at Jack.

"Anybody want to stick with Charles here?" Tony said, grinning coldly.

After quick glances among themselves, the guards slowly shook their heads.

"Excellent. Then let me be the first to welcome you to the Chicago Outfit," Carl said. "Let me introduce you to your new boss, Angelino, who will be determining if you seven men are suitable for our purposes. If I were you, I'd sure try very hard to impress him."

When Tony heard Rosco's nails on the tile, he turned around and smiled as Levi and Tori walked across the foyer towards them. Levi had his arm around Tori as if he was afraid to let her go. She was holding his sleeping great-great-nephew in her arms. Rosco and Ray weren't far behind.

"All is well?" Tony asked Tori.

Tori smiled down at her son. "It is, thanks to you."

Levi stared at Charles. He remembered him as Chuck's dad from grade school on—not a very nice man, always driving his son to do better. Chuck had grown up terrified of a B on a report card or of failing to score in a Little League game or of not completing a pass as the quarterback of the Twin Rivers Comets. Levi walked up to him.

"You planned on killing me today, didn't you? I was never supposed to leave this house alive."

Sweat popped out on Charles's forehead.

"You were going to kill my entire family," Levi said, his mouth tight and his eyes hard.

Charles looked down at the floor.

"Didn't work out, did it?" Tori said. "In fact, it is now you who won't be leaving here alive. Surely you know that Uncle Tony isn't going to let you live."

"Uncle Tony?" Charles said, his voice cracking.

"Didn't you know?" Tony said. "Levi is an O'Malley. And like Tori is so fond of saying, 'when you take on one of us, you get all of us.' It goes back to that thing I said earlier about knowing your opponent. You tried to frame us, Charles. Very stupid. All Levi had to do was call his dear Uncle Tony and ask him about it."

Levi suppressed a smile. That was a total lie, but it was a satisfying lie. He enjoyed watching Charles's eyes bulge out from his meaty face as he realized his brilliant plan to send the police investigation in the wrong direction had fooled no one—that his plan had failed miserably.

"It was too easy," Levi admitted. "We set you up with that ledger, Charles. We were the only people who knew about the ledger before I told Nichole."

"Of course, we didn't expect you to kidnap Tori," Ray said, joining in with the lie. "But we knew this all went back to your son, Chuck."

"No," Charles said. "That's just not possible. You couldn't have known."

Tony laughed—it was a terrible guttural sound that echoed through the foyer.

"Explain to me then how it is we're all here," he said, "and so well prepared."

"No," Charles said.

"You've killed your son, too," Tony said, the amusement in his eyes fading. "I know where to find him. And you know how I feel about witnesses."

When Adam stirred in Tori's arms, Tony glanced at her.

"I think the Garveys should leave now and you, too, Chief Billings," Tony said. "We have some unpleasant business to attend to."

Levi motioned Tori towards the door, and Ray followed them. Rosco remained beside Tony's leg.

"You, too, Rosco," Tony said. "I'll bring you a nice bone when we get together for Easter."

Chapter 78

As Levi, Tori, and Ray climbed into Old Blue, along with Rosco in the back, Tony appeared on the porch. He motioned to Tori. She handed Adam to Ray and walked back up to the porch.

"What is it, Tony?" she asked.

"I just wanted to tell you that I'm glad you're okay. I'm sorry about what you went through," he said. "You're one tough lady."

"Thank you," Tori said.

"I want to give you something," Tony said. "I know how much that ring Peg gave you means to Levi, so I'd like to give you something, too—something I want kept in the family."

Tony paused for a long moment. Then he took the shotgun off his shoulder and handed it to her.

"Really?" Tori said looking down at it. "Your shotgun?"

"Take it. It's old," Tony said, "almost as old as I am. This belonged to my father. He won twin shotguns in a raffle when I was a boy. Late in his life, he gave one to me and one to Lucille. Lucille never fired anything but rock salt through hers, and I never fired anything but lead through mine. I know you still have Lucille's shotgun." Tony chuckled. "I couldn't believe it when Carl told me you pulled it out a few years ago and lit up the seat of the pants of one of the Malone boys who tried to kill Levi and Ed in the carriage house. Lucille called that shotgun her Howitzer."

"We still call it Granny's Howitzer," Tori said.

"If you look, you'll find that the serial numbers are one off from each other. I look back at my father's decision to give me that shotgun. Sometimes I wish he'd given it to Peg instead."

Tori snapped the shotgun open, saw it was empty, snapped it closed, and shouldered it.

"You think this shotgun took you down the road you're on?" Tori asked.

"Probably not, but it sure helped establish my position and my reputation as Tony 'The Shotgun' O'Malley. Me and that shotgun got one last adventure together. Maybe you'll hang it up over the fireplace—let it collect dust and rust a little. It helped me do a good thing today, but if it stays with me, it'll just keep doing bad things, I'm afraid."

"Thank you, Tony," Tori said. "I don't know what would've happened to us if it weren't for your help today."

"Go home with your family," Tony said. "Return to your normal life, starting today. Act like nothing happened here. It was just a bad dream."

Tori nodded and began walking towards the truck.

"And Tori," Tony said.

She stopped and turned back.

"I sure am glad I got the chance to meet my family."

"Take care, Tony."

Tori climbed into the passenger seat of Old Blue. Levi backed up and turned around. Tony watched them as they drove away.

Neither Levi nor Ray said anything until they'd driven past the dead guards near the broken gate and had turned onto the old supply road where Ed would be waiting for them.

"What did he say?" Levi asked finally. "Why did he give you his shotgun?"

Tori sighed. "I think he's gotten to the age when he wishes he'd done things differently in life. I think he wishes he had a life more like ours."

"He's the epitome of evil," Ray said.

"Yes, he is," Tori admitted.

"But, thank God, he was there for us today," Levi said.

"You two might want to turn off your earpieces," Tony said.

Stunned, Ray and Levi glanced at each other. Then they reached up in tandem, and each quickly stuck a finger in his ear.

"What was that about?" Tori said, looking at each of them suspiciously.

"Nothing," Levi said, smiling weakly.

Chapter 79

Ed glanced at his watch as he waited for his ride. It was a warm summer day—too warm for him to be wearing a suit. Where in the hell is Levi, he thought as he stood up. He walked to the edge of the porch and looked up the long driveway, but there was no sign of him yet.

Sighing, he headed for the workshop. He stepped into the bright interior and shut the door behind him. With a smile, he looked at the old truck parked in the center of the workshop. The summer sun was shining down through the skylights and streaming in through the tall windows that looked over the river below.

After glancing at his watch again, Ed walked over to the old truck and opened the door. Getting the old motor running again had been a challenge, to say the very least. It still started only half the time. After working late the night before, he thought he had the carburetor issue worked out, but the engine still needed a lot of work.

Crossing his fingers, Ed flipped the key and smiled broadly as the engine started on the first turn. Its rumble was satisfying to Ed's ears, but then it sputtered the second time he revved it. He frowned. Not quite there yet, he thought, as he reached down to switch it off.

Ed climbed out of the truck and left the workshop. He looked at the little brown house, so cool on a hot summer day under the shade of the large trees in the yard. Nobody could believe it when Ed had sold his house in Twin Rivers. Sometimes he couldn't believe it himself since he'd lived there his entire adult life. He thought he'd miss it and regret the sale, but he realized finally that there is a big difference between a house and a home. He'd built no memories in his little house on Ash Street, even after four and a half decades. It was just the place where he slept and kept his stuff.

When Jay's house had gone up for sale, Ed knew he wanted it. It was just what he needed at his age—a little house out in the woods where he could tinker with an old truck or two and enjoy his retirement.

There had been a lot of changes since that morning at the Franklin Estate—lots of changes for all of them, especially Ed. The last big winter storm had hit the next week. With his tow truck, Ed had pulled fifty cars out of ditches during three long days. The work had exhausted him. He didn't know when, but at some point during the last few years, he'd started to get old. Towing was hard work, better suited for a younger man. Mark Dickerson had been wanting to buy his tow truck business for years. Levi and Tori couldn't believe it when he sold out to his "arch enemy," but Mark had made a generous offer, and Ed had accepted it. He kept his flatbed tow truck and the tools from his garage. But the other two tow trucks, the scrap yard, the used parts building, and all those acres of rusting cars were now the property of Dickerson Towing. And Mark had wasted no time in beginning to haul off and recycle all those old hulks—including what was left of at least two Old Blues.

When Ed heard an engine rev, he glanced up the driveway. He saw nothing there, but then he heard the engine rev again. He turned around and looked up the other driveway—the one that was impossibly steep. Old Blue was parked at the top of the sharp incline, the late morning sun winking off the chrome. Levi leaned out the window and waved.

"Don't do it!" Ed shouted. "Are you nuts?"

Levi revved the engine again and put Old Blue in gear. The hood tipped forward as the truck started down the steep driveway. Levi bounced around in the cab during the rapid descent. When he got to the bottom, he locked the brakes and cranked the wheel. Old Blue skidded to a stop sideways in a white cloud of gravel dust, sending a few rocks tinging against Ed's truck.

Grinning broadly, Levi climbed out. He fiddled with the bow tie on his tuxedo and adjusted his Panama.

"Piece of cake," Levi said with a chuckle.

There were a lot of things Ed could say about what he'd just witnessed. He could say something about the truck's old brakes or what a pain in the ass it would be to fix a bent frame on a fifty-year-old truck. But it would be pointless because he could say nothing that Levi didn't already know.

"You dumbass," Ed muttered.

"You ready?" Levi said, ignoring the remark.

Ed nodded. "You going up the way you came down?" he said as he climbed into the passenger seat.

"You don't think I could?" Levi said in a challenging tone.

"Let's try it," Ed said.

Levi glanced up the driveway, which seemed a lot steeper looking up than it had seemed looking down.

"Maybe later."

"Probably wise," Ed said with a snicker as he rolled the window down.

They both knew there was no way on earth Old Blue could climb that hill.

"Heard anything from Ray?" Levi asked as he put the truck in gear and drove down the long driveway to the road.

"Nothing."

Nobody had heard from Ray, not for three months. He'd resigned the first week of April, but the Village Board had rejected his resignation. Instead, they'd approved a leave. He'd left Twin Rivers that same week, and nobody had heard from him since. He hadn't answered his phone or responded to messages. Ben Walker had stepped up as the temporary chief, and the board hired two new officers. Most of the residents of Twin Rivers believed Ray Billings wasn't coming back. But Levi still held out some hope because Ray hadn't sold his house. Levi thought if there was anything that would bring him back, it would be the event happening today. But that hope was beginning to fade as well, especially since no one knew if the news had even reached Ray.

"He's not coming back," Levi said.

Ed shrugged as he looked away.

"I'd thought about going to look for him," Levi said.

"That would be unwise."

"Tori said the same thing."

"And how is she doing?" Ed said.

"She's finally letting Adam out of her sight," Levi said. "I was beginning to worry that kid would never learn to walk since she was carrying him all the time."

"Is she okay with what happened at the Franklin place?"

"I don't think she has any regrets," Levi said. "It's not like the first time we've ever been in a tight spot, but the part she's had trouble dealing with is the fact that our actions could've had dire consequences for Adam. It was different back when it was just her and me. She was angry with me for getting involved without thinking of those consequences. And then I sort of deserted her by starting to write another book—you know how I am when I write."

"So are you getting a divorce?"

Levi looked at Ed in shock. "A divorce? Are you crazy! It wasn't the marriage that was failing—it was the friendship. That's always been more important than the marriage."

Levi stared out through the windshield, his jaw tight.

"And?" Ed said.

"Not that it's any of your business, but let's just say that we're on the mend."

Ed looked out the side window and grinned broadly as they drove on in silence.

Finally, Levi said, "There is one thing I regret. Tori and I put Ray in a tough spot."

Ed nodded. "He's a painfully honest man. Once Tony was involved, he had few choices. He made the decision to stick with his friends through thick and thin. I doubt if he regrets having your backs, but afterwards, the moral crisis he faced was whether or not he could remain chief in good conscience."

"I think he's made his choice," Levi said, "but, in my opinion, his decision is wrong. If the truth came out about what he'd done, I doubt if there's a person in town who wouldn't still want him as chief."

"I agree," Ed said. "Speaking from years of experience, I can tell you without question that wallowing in regret is a complete and total waste of time. It's too late to worry about yesterday. Instead, learn from experience. When you wake up in the morning, look at that new day as a blessing."

Levi pulled into the drive of the First Baptist Church and started up the lane that wound through the expansive cemetery. They both looked at William Garvey's mausoleum which dominated the Garvey family plot.

With a grin, Ed pointed to the Garvey graves, and said, "Well, in case you're feeling any regrets about what we all did at the Franklins, just consider the alternatives—being over there with them or in this old truck on a beautiful summer day."

Levi chuckled. "You have such a lovely way of making a point."

When Old Blue came to a stop in the church parking lot, Levi said, "You ready to give away the bride?"

"I can't believe Amber asked me. I know I wasn't her first choice."

"I'm sure her father would've been her first choice," Levi said.

Amber's father had been a construction worker. He'd died five years earlier when he'd fallen from a scaffold.

"And Ray would've been her second choice," Ed said. "But I'll take it. It's a great honor."

"You bought a new suit," Levi remarked as he reached over and straightened the little gold square and compass pin on his lapel.

"It's a new jacket," Ed said. "Got it off the clearance rack at Target. Does it match the pants okay?"

Levi looked him over. The black pants were considerably lighter—they'd been washed many times. They didn't match very well at all.

"They look fine together," Levi said.

Even though the jacket and the pants didn't match well, the real problem was the white socks he'd worn with his black shoes.

"Let's do this," Ed said as he stepped towards the church.

Chapter 80

"It's about time," Tori said as Ed and Levi walked into the sanctuary of the church.

"We'd have been here sooner," Ed said, "but Levi decided to turn Old Blue into a World War II dive bomber."

Tori glared at Levi for a moment, blowing that errant coil of kinky blonde hair out of her face. "You didn't take Old Blue down the second drive?"

Levi shrugged with that familiar look on his face—the one that had so often prompted Tori to ask 'What did you just do?'"

A slight smile crossed her face. The last few months had been difficult. Levi hadn't done anything unpredictable in a long time. In fact, he'd done very little at all except write since that day in March. Levi doing something incredibly stupid and impulsive was a good sign that things were returning to some semblance of normality. Levi was beginning to come out from under the dark cloud that had seemed to surround him for some time—and she needed him to pull her out with him.

Levi hadn't seen that smile from Tori for some time. It was admiration.

"Levi, you have your cummerbund on upside down. Go flip it over. And Ed," she said, digging through her purse, "go put on these socks."

"Why do you have black socks in your purse?" Ed asked.

"Because I figured Levi would show up here in his tux with his brown argyle socks."

"The socks I'm wearing came with the tuxedo and shoes," Levi said, "but they are very scratchy."

"Let's have them," Tori said, holding out her hand.

Levi reached into his pants pocket and produced a pair of his favorite socks—brown argyles. She dropped them into her purse.

"Ed, you need to go down to the basement. That's where the bride and her party are preparing. Levi, the groomsmen are in the little room behind the pulpit. Reverend Millar wants to begin on time," she said, glancing at her watch. "Let's do it just like we did in rehearsal. Do you have the rings?"

Levi nodded.

Tori looked at him suspiciously.

"I've got them," Levi said, reaching into his pocket and pulling them out. He had them tied together with a ribbon.

Tori saw that look on his face as he glanced at Ed. She knew something was going on with those two. She reached over and patted his pants pocket. There was something heavy in there. Levi and Ed's faces both fell when she reached into his pocket and pulled out a pair of police-issue hand-cuffs.

"You were going to hand these to Reverend Millar when he asked for the rings," she said, her eyes narrowed.

Though Levi and Ed both shook their heads in unison, she knew that was exactly the plan.

"We're not doing that," Tori said firmly as she dropped the hand-cuffs into her purse on top of the brown argyle socks.

She tried to look annoyed with Levi but failed. For the second time, he saw that little smile on her face.

* * *

The groom's party was lined up in a short hallway on the other side of the door that led out to the front of the sanctuary. The music from the organ suddenly changed.

"Here we go," Reverend Millar said as he peeked through a crack in the door.

Ben glanced back at Levi nervously.

"It'll be fine," Levi whispered. "This is way easier than receiving the third degree."

"I'm afraid I'm going to pass out—"

"I'll catch you. I've caught you before when you've fallen," Levi said, winking at him.

Mark Walker, Ben's brother and Levi's friend since high school, said with a chuckle, "That's not the music I requested. I asked the organist to play 'Who's Sorry Now.'"

Levi laughed, but the laugh was cut short by Reverend Millar's hard glance.

"Are we ready?" Reverend Millar asked.

"I'm ready," Ben said.

"Me, too," Levi said.

"Let's get this show on the road," Mark said.

"Do I have time to pee first?" the last man in the groom's party said.

"Shut up, Floyd," Reverend Millar said as he pushed the door open and stepped out.

They followed Reverend Millar out as the congregation watched. The church was full and so was the upper balcony in the back. Levi grinned when he saw Tori and Adam sitting a few rows back on the groom's side. Adam was oblivious to the whole thing—he was in the process of demolishing a box of animal crackers. Reverend Millar took his place at the front of the church, and the groom and his groomsmen took their places—just like they'd done at the rehearsal.

Then the music changed again.

The bridesmaids entered and took their places on the right hand of Reverend Millar. Levi smiled as the two little flower girls struggled to remember how to walk in step and toss out the rose petals. Then the ring bearer, Amber's three-year-old nephew, bolted up the aisle as if running a football play and leaped to a booming stop that shook the floor. He stood grinning, very pleased with himself, as many in the audience took pictures of the ornery smile on his face.

Levi was watching the little boy when the music changed again—the bridal fanfare. The congregation rose and turned towards the door. With the floor of the church sloping towards the front and everyone standing, Levi couldn't see Amber, only a bit of white.

The congregation began murmuring, even over the music from the huge pipe organ. Levi wondered what everyone was whispering about. Then he saw Ed, walking down the side aisle alone. After taking a place beside Harv and April, he looked at Levi and winked.

Levi stood on his toes, trying to see the bride as she made her way down the aisle. When she reached the end, she stopped. As Levi stared at the man who'd accompanied her, a broad smile crossed his face and his vision clouded from the tears that had just formed in his eyes.

The man, who towered over the congregation, was wearing a police dress uniform. His shaved head gleamed in the light streaming in through the stained glass windows. He'd added a goatee to the mustache in the months since Levi had last seen him, but the corners of the mustache were perfectly waxed and curled up. What made Levi smile was that although the dress uniform was obviously not something Twin Rivers issued, the gold police badge he wore on his pocket was. It was the badge of the Twin Rivers Chief of Police.

"Who gives this woman to be married to this man?" Reverend Millar said.

"With the permission of her mother, I do," Ray Billings said.

Just as he'd done in rehearsal, Ben walked to the head of the aisle and took his bride's arm. However, unlike in rehearsal, he paused, looked at Ray, and smiled. Ray held out his hand, and Ben took it firmly.

Amber and Ben moved to the altar as Ray turned and found his seat beside Tori where Ed was supposed to sit after he'd completed the task.

"Perhaps the bride and groom would like Chief Billings to join us up here," Reverend Millar said.

"Yes, we would," Amber said as Ben nodded.

Ray walked up to the front of the church and took a place beside Floyd at the end of the groomsmen's line. The congregation applauded.

Then Reverend Millar began, "Dearly beloved, we are gathered here today, to join this man and this woman . . ."

Chapter 81

"So are you back or just visiting?" Ed said.

Ray glanced at him and then at Levi and Tori. It was well after midnight. They'd returned to the Garvey house after the reception. Levi was sitting in one of the Anirondak chairs he'd brought back from Savannah. Ray was in the other. They'd logged many hours in those two chairs in Savannah. Tori and Ed were sitting on the swing with their feet on the porch rail.

"I'm back," Ray said. "I had some things to work out."

"Let's have a beer," Levi said.

"That's an excellent idea," Ed said.

"Well, speaking for myself, I'm going to need more than one," Ray said.

"How about a Red Stripe, Ray?" Tori said, standing up and heading to the front door.

"I think that Red Stripe would've gone bad by now," Ray said with a chuckle. "I've been gone for some time."

"I bought a six pack yesterday," Tori remarked. "I just had a feeling—"

"I brought my own," Floyd said.

He was sitting on the front step, rubbing Rosco's ears. An old, beat-up 70s metal cooler was behind him.

"Good thing," Ed said. "Nobody drinks Pabst Blue Ribbon here—nobody should drink it at all."

"This coming from a man who drank Schlitz for twenty-five years," Floyd shot back.

Levi laughed. "He used to buy Blatz, too."

"I certainly did not," Ed said.

"The hell you didn't," Tori said. "Levi and I used to steal it out of your refrigerator in the carriage house. We were ever so grateful when you started buying Budweiser."

"That's true," Levi admitted. "That Blatz was hard to get down even ice cold."

"That's why I used to leave it for you dumb shits," Ed said with a cackle. "But I didn't buy it. It was left over from a fishing trip I took with a bunch of guys down to Kentucky Lake—back in '78."

"Wait a minute," Tori said, "so it wasn't only nasty to begin with, we were drinking beer that was five years old?"

Ed chuckled. "I had ten cases left over. It sat out in the garage at the scrap yard for years. It could've been worse. I could've left you Pabst Blue Ribbon."

"I've never liked you," Floyd said, glancing at Ed. "You were a pompous ass, even in 1st grade."

"And you were a clown," Ed shot back.

"And we've been friends ever since," Floyd said with a chuckle.

"I need new friends," Ed said.

Levi smiled at Tori. "Should we tell him?"

"A minute ago, I would've said no," Tori said, glaring at Ed. "But now, go ahead."

"We never drank that Blatz," Levi said.

"You didn't?" Ed said.

"Why would we," Tori said, "when Joyce would slip us a six-pack of Budweiser out the backdoor of the Beer Chaser and charge it to your tab."

"Oh, I'm going to have a little talk with her," Ed said with a grin. "And to think I finally felt so bad for you two that I started buying you good beer."

After Tori walked into the house for beer, Ray glanced at Levi and said, "Not to change the subject, but what about that Civil War journal?"

"I have it. Aunt Maggie left it as promised."

"And?" Ray asked.

"She left a letter, too. It answered all the questions I had about the two Garvey families. Then, at the end, she emphasized again that it might be a bad idea to read the journal. I took her advice."

"You haven't read it?" Ray said.

Levi shook his head.

Returning with the beer, Tori heard the last part of the conversation.

"But he didn't trust himself, either," she said. "He donated it to the History Department at the University of Illinois. It's in the archives now."

"And you're okay with that?" Ray said.

Levi nodded. "I know where it is. If I change my mind, I can read it whenever I want. For now, I have the answers I wanted."

"And what are the answers?"

"Captain William Garvey fathered a black child towards the end of the Civil War. The mother died in childbirth. He brought that child back home with him to Twin Rivers after the war—along with the child's grandmother and two uncles. The child's name was Andrew Garvey. There was no secret about it. William wasn't ashamed of the fact. Everyone knew that Andrew was William's son. They all lived together in the old Garvey house that sat back where the apple orchard is today. William married some years after he returned—in 1883—and had two girls and a boy, Abe."

Tori chimed in—she'd read the letter as well.

"The two uncles worked for William and helped him build his empire here, and they were well paid. One of them, Thomas, ran the brick yard, and the other uncle, Daniel, ran the Twin Rivers Emporium, which was part lumberyard and part apothecary. The telegraph office was there as well. That seemed to be okay for a long time, but at some point, the fact that Thomas and Daniel were in such important positions in town seemed to have something to do with what was later referred to as the River County War. That's the part that Lucille and Reverend Garvey and Aunt Maggie didn't think would be a good idea to dredge up."

"And you're not the least bit curious?" Ray asked.

Levi smiled at Tori. "I've finally learned my lesson. For now, I'm perfectly content to leave the past in the past."

"So that's it," Floyd said.

"That's it," Levi said.

"And what about Chuck Franklin?" Ray asked. "Has he ever turned up?"

"No," Ed said. "I don't imagine he ever will."

"Tony got him," Floyd said. "That's what I think."

Ray looked at Floyd and then at Ed.

Ed smiled. "Floyd knows all about our family—he always has. He knows about what happened a few months ago as well. And I agree with him. I think Tony got Chuck Franklin. And that's not a bad thing maybe, considering our part in the resolution of that conflict."

"I agree," Tori said. "I'm starting to understand Tony's aversion to witnesses. It's taken some time to get over what we did, but I wouldn't do anything different. If Chuck turned up, it wouldn't be a good thing for us."

"Nichole Larsen vanished, too," Ed said. "Humiliated, I'm sure. Tony did a fine job of destroying Chuck Franklin's reputation. He leaked all the information about Chuck's involvement in pornography to the media. The Chicago Outfit even discovered an old porn movie he was in and made sure it got out on the internet. And the feds are tearing apart Charles, Sr.'s entire organization—what's left of it after Tony cherry picked the best pieces and took them over."

"Funny thing happened the last day I was in Savannah," Ray said, leaning back and turning up the corners of his mustache. He glanced at Levi, who shifted uncomfortably.

"What's that?" Tori said.

"I went uptown to have dinner with my old boss, Captain Harper," Ray said.

"You mean Captain Hippie?" Ed said with a chuckle.

Ray smiled. "He's actually not such a bad guy. He's just young. Anyway, we went for dinner at Lady & Sons. That's Paula Deen's restaurant."

"Oh, Levi's old friend," Ed said.

"That's right," Ray said. "And you'll never guess in a million years who our waitress was."

Tori looked at Levi and smiled. Levi seemed to be concentrating very intently on the top of his beer can.

"Nichole?" Ed asked, also looking at Levi.

Levi smiled shrewdly—the smile Tori knew so well.

"What did you do?" she said.

"I gave Nichole a fresh start," Levi said. "It was the least I could do. Paula was only too happy to help, but she's a shrewd business woman. She wanted something in return."

"What?" Tori asked.

"Ask April Jenkins," Levi said with a chuckle. "Let's just say there are now two places in America where you can get the world's best chocolate pie."

"April gave her the recipe?" Ed said, wide-eyed.

"Hell no," Floyd said as he grinned at them. "She licensed the rights to her. Paula Deen isn't the only smart business woman in America. April didn't make pies at the restaurant for years—not until Levi came back and made such a fuss over them. Now she's famous for them. Thinking that someday Nichole would own Harv's Grill, April taught Nichole to make those pies, too. So Paula got not only the recipe but also the woman who knows how to make chocolate pies just like they are made at Harv's Grill. April got an upfront fee for the recipe, and every year that Paula keeps making her chocolate pie, April gets an annual renewal on the license. And Paula can never publish the recipe in one of her cookbooks. If you want a piece of that pie, you have to go to either Harv's Grill in Twin Rivers, Illinois, or Lady & Sons in Savannah, Georgia."

"You knew?" Tori said, looking at Floyd.

"Where Nichole was?" Floyd said. "I did. I helped April work out the deal with Paula."

"And what did you get out of it?" Ed said.

"Not much, but enough. April is the only person in Twin Rivers who is no longer allowed to tell me to shut up," Floyd said with a wide grin.

"I had three pieces of that pie," Ray said. "I was sitting there in one of the best restaurants in the city where I'd spent my whole life, and I had the strangest feeling as I ate that pie."

"What's that?" Floyd asked. "Indigestion?"

"No, I felt homesick," Ray said. "The minute I got back to my apartment, I packed up the few things I'd brought with me to Savannah and started back towards Twin Rivers the very next morning. I don't belong in Savannah anymore. I belong here—here in Twin Rivers with my friends."

"So how'd you know to show up at the church dressed to escort Amber down the aisle?" Tori asked.

This time Ed looked guilty. "I knew Amber wanted Ray to walk her down the aisle. I overheard a conversation she was having with Ben. I made a few calls to the Savannah Police Department and finally was able to talk to Captain Harper. He took a message, but I wasn't sure if it'd reached Ray or not."

Ray picked up the story from there. "I did get the message. At first, I didn't plan on coming back, but as the date got closer, it got harder and harder to think about not being here for the wedding. The chocolate pie pushed me right over the edge."

Ed smiled. "I had a feeling he'd show up. That's why I wasn't too concerned about those white socks."

Tori pointed at his feet. "I see you found another pair of white socks. Apparently, Levi isn't the only Garvey who's obsessive about comfortable socks."

All five of them laughed—the comfortable way friends can do.

"So are you going back to being the sheriff," Floyd said as the laughter died down.

"Chief of police," Ray said.

"Whatever."

Ray turned up the corners of his mustache and glanced at Levi.

"I've given up the idea that nothing ever happens in Twin Rivers," he said.

"Oh, I think we're done now. All the secrets are out," Levi said, glancing at Floyd.

Floyd grinned back. "I've known your dad since we were born. I always knew you were his son, even though he never came right out and told me. And I've also known for most of my life that Lucille's maiden name was O'Malley—and I knew who her brother was. I met Tony O'Malley at Ed's fifth birthday party in '44. I'll never forget him. He was still recovering from the burns he'd received three years earlier at Pearl Harbor. I've always known the Garvey family secrets, including what happened a few months ago. And let's not forget who saved all your asses a couple of years ago. If I hadn't shown up with that shotgun and evened up that little Mexican standoff you had going with Tony and the Four Horsemen, we probably wouldn't be having this conversation right now. You don't have to worry about me."

"We've definitely had a few close calls, but I'm not buying that life is going to stay quiet around here," Ray said. "It'll be quiet for a while, and then Tori will be working in some old building and find a body in the wall."

Tori sighed. "I did think about that when we were ripping up the floor in the library foyer last week."

"Or Levi will read some dusty obituary and realize the guy is still alive," Ed remarked.

"Maybe he's a Nazi war criminal that escaped justice," Levi suggested.

"Oh, that's very good, Levi," Ed said. "You should write fiction."

"I *do* write fiction," Levi snapped back.

"Or maybe we'll find out Floyd is actually Ray's father," Tori said with a chuckle.

"God forbid," Ray remarked. "I know for a fact that my father died in '80, six days after he retired."

"You feeling okay, Father?" Levi asked.

"I'm not retired," Ed said. "Haven't you told Tori yet?"

"Told Tori what?" Tori snapped.

Levi and Ed exchanged glances. Then Levi reached into the pocket of his tux, took out a card, and handed it to her.

"You know, writing isn't a full time job," Levi said.

"Garvey & Son Classic Truck Restoration," she said, reading the card. "The address seems to be our carriage house."

Levi shrugged.

"I'll get the motors running at my workshop by the river," Ed said. "God knows Levi isn't good at that. He can't even manage to change the oil on the lawn mower without starting a fire."

"One time," Levi snapped. "Thirty years ago. And that was because you bought the wrong damn filter."

"And you didn't even notice it didn't fit," Ed added.

"Anyway, we'll do the bodywork here in the carriage house," Levi said.

"Old Chevys, too?" Tori asked.

Levi and Ed looked at her sharply as Floyd's laughter rang out.

"It says 'Classic Trucks,' not 'Crappy Trucks,'" Levi said.

"Only Fords," Ed said.

"I think it's a good idea," Tori said with a smile. "So you'll find them, restore them, and then sell them."

"Yeah," Levi said. "That's basically it. You're okay with that?"

"Sure," Tori said. "Let's start with Pappy."

Ed sighed. "Sell Pappy? You helped me put Pappy together, Tori."

"We can't sell Pappy," Levi said. "That's a family truck."

"Right," Tori said. "I know how this is going to work. You two are going to spend months restoring a truck, and in the process, you'll both fall in love with it, and neither of you will ever be able to sell it once it's restored."

"It's a big carriage house," Ed remarked.

"Really big," Levi said with a grin. "You could get twenty in there easy and still have room to work."

"And three more in my workshop if we run out of room," Ed remarked.

"So let's just be clear about this," Tori said. "This isn't a business. It's a hobby, right? Your goal is to fill that carriage house with old trucks you've restored at great expense with no intention of ever selling a single one."

Ed and Levi looked at each other.

"Is that a problem?" Ed asked.

Tori laughed as she shook her head.

"I'll bring Gus out in the morning on the flatbed," Ed remarked.

"Gus?" Tori asked. "I'll bet Gus is an old beater Ford."

"It seemed like a Gus," Ed said with a smile.

"Hold on," Ray said. "I'm lost here. What workshop?"

"Oh, we've got a lot to tell you," Levi said. "You missed a few things while you were gone."

"Including the huge snow storm that convinced me to retire and sell my house," Ed said.

"You retired? And sold your house?"

"We'd better have another beer," Ed said, waving his empty at Tori.

"Go get them yourself," Tori said. "And check on your grandson while you're in there."

Ray chuckled, "I do love this town."

When Floyd saw the look on Ray's face, he grinned. "I'm sure glad you came back, Ray. Somebody has to keep these Garveys in line."

Ed stopped in the doorway. Then he, Levi, and Tori all looked at Floyd and said in unison, "Shut up, Floyd!"

Chapter 82

The man stepped into the small beach bar which sat just back of the white sands and turquoise waters of the little tropical cove. He stopped there every afternoon for a couple of shots and then returned every evening when it filled up with tourists—more often than not, leaving with one of the bikini-clad cruise ship vacationers. The bar wasn't much more than a thatched-roof hut with a sand floor and a rough plank bar along the far wall. He stood for a moment, running his hands through his shaggy blonde hair and scratching at his scruffy beard as his eyes adjusted from the bright sun of the beach. There was a TV on over the bar, but there were no patrons inside and no bartender. He rapped his knuckles on the bar as he settled onto a stool.

"Sorry, I didn't hear you come in," the young bartender said as he walked through the doorway from the back, wiping his hands on a white towel. "What can I get you?"

The man smiled, showing his perfectly capped teeth. "You're new here," he said. "I'll have a shot of tequila."

"Certainly," the bartender said.

He put a shot glass on the counter, filled it with tequila, and set out a bowl full of lime wedges and the salt shaker. As the man downed the shot, he slapped his hand on the counter a couple of times. He didn't use the lime or the salt.

"You're not from around here," the man said, looking at the bartender. "You're an American. I can actually understand what you're saying."

The bartender grinned broadly. "I haven't been here long, and this is my first day working at the bar. Judging from your tan, I'd say you've been here longer than I have."

"A few months," the man admitted as he glanced up at the television. "Are you watching baseball? Here? In this part of the world?"

"The Cubbies are about three pitches away from winning this one," the bartender said. "Damn Cardinals tied it up at the bottom of the seventh."

The man laughed. "I'm a Cub fan, too! I can't tell you how many afternoons I spent years ago as a bleacher bum at Wrigley Field, drinking Bavarian style beer out of plastic cups. It's a hell of a coincidence—running into somebody all the way down here who enjoys baseball and is a Cub fan to boot. This could be the beginning of a beautiful friendship."

"It could be, but I don't believe in coincidences," the bartender said. "All things happen for a reason."

When they heard the crack of the bat, both looked at the television.

"Oh, shit," the bartender said as the ball sailed towards the ivy-covered walls. "He just knocked that one out."

"No, he didn't," the man said as they watched the Cubs right fielder in his blue uniform race towards the wall.

The outfielder looked up into the sun. At the last minute, he adjusted his position. The ball bounced off his glove, but he managed to grab it before it hit the ground. A roar of cheers went up at Wrigley Field as the old Harry Caray clip played, "Holy Cow! Cubs win! Cubs win! Cubs win!"

"Well, they're happy at Wrigley, but that fielder damn near blew it," the bartender said.

"A win is a win, even when it's ugly. That's worth celebrating. Join me for a shot?" the man said as he fished out his wallet and laid a fifty on the bar.

"What shall we drink to?"

"What else? To the Friendly Confines of Wrigley Field," the man said with a grin.

The bartender raised his shot glass. "To the Chicago Cubs. May they win at least one World Series in my lifetime."

They clinked their glasses and drank. Then they set their glasses upside down on the bar with a clunk.

"I'd better stop. It's still early in the day," the man said, picking up his change and leaving a ten as a tip. "Maybe you're right about being destined to meet here in this remote corner of the globe. I'm sure we'll meet again. I come in here every day."

"Then I'm sure we will. Like I said, there is no such thing as a coincidence," the bartender replied. "Hey, before you leave, any chance you know anything about changing out a draft keg?"

"I might know a little something about that."

"Well, I'm new at this job, and I've never changed one. All I've managed to do is spray beer all over me and the inside of the walk-in cooler."

"Today is your lucky day, my new friend. I just happen to be an expert in the art," the man said with a chuckle. "I was the president of my fraternity back in college. Where's the keg?"

"Through here," the bartender said, pointing to the doorway behind the bar. "I'd sure appreciate it if you could show me."

"I'll be happy to. It's not that hard," the man said as he stepped behind the bar.

"I can't thank you enough," the bartender said.

"Now that I'm thinking about it, I didn't catch your name," the man said over his shoulder as he walked through the doorway behind the bar. "My name is Charles, but my friends call me Chuck."

The bartender glanced around the empty bar and then followed the man into the back room.

"Nice to meet you, Chuck," the bartender said as he screwed on the silencer. "My name is Angelino."

About the Author

Todd E. Creason lives with his wife, Valerie, and his younger daughter, Katie, near his hometown in Illinois. His elder daughter, Jackie, is grown and has recently made him a grandfather. He works full-time as a business manager at the University of Illinois. He considers writing a hobby. *Shot to Hell* is the third novel in the Twin Rivers series. The first, *One Last Shot*, was published in 2011, and the second, *A Shot After Midnight*, was published in 2012. An active Freemason and Past Master of his Masonic Lodge, he is also the author of the award-winning *Famous American Freemasons* series. He is the founder of and a regular contributor to The Midnight Freemasons blog, one of the twelve Masonic authors who write on topics of interest to Freemasons and to those interested in the topic of Freemasonry. In 2011, he received Freemasonry's highest honor, the 33rd Degree, by the Ancient and Accepted Scottish Rite of Freemasonry's Supreme Council (NMJ).

Visit the author's website at
TODDCREASON.ORG

Also visit The Midnight Freemasons at
MIDNIGHTFREEMASONS.ORG